THE BOY IN THE BOX

W. PEARL

The story, names, characters, and incidents portrayed in this production are fictitious. Any reference with actual persons (living or deceased), places, buildings, and products are used fictitiously. No connection with actual persons or events should be inferred. All other persons, places, events, etc. are products of the author's imagination.

THE BOY IN THE BOX

Copyright © 2025 by W. Pearl

All rights reserved

No part of this publication may be reproduced, distributed, or transmitted in any form or by any means, including photocopying, recording, or other electronic or mechanical methods, without the prior written permission of the publisher, except as permitted by U.S. copyright law.

No part of this text, artwork, or cover were created using A.I. in any form.

Additionally, no part of this production may be used in the training of Artificial Intelligence.

Cover Art by W. Pearl

Chapter Artwork by W. Pearl

Additional Art by Wynter Higgins

SE ISBN 979-8-9858204-7-8

HC ISBN 79-8-9858204-8-5

PB ISBN 979-8-9858204-5-4

Ebook ISBN 979-8-9858204-6-1

First Edition October 2025

For the ones who keep holding on

A NOTE FROM THE AUTHOR

Dear Reader,

I believe I'd be remiss if I did not, once again, begin with a warning. This book is, simply put, horrendously sad. There *is* joy in this book, as there is within any tragedy. There is also love, and a good dose of hope. The main ingredients, though, are sadness, violence, and a deep dive exploration into the duality of man. As it was with *Obedient*, there is a much shorter list of graphic things that are *NOT* in this book. If you're still here, I commend you. This story matters, I promise.

I hope you brought tissues,

Pearl

Find a complete list of Content Warnings in the end-papers.

"The heart of man is very much like the sea, it has its storms, it has its tides and in its depths it has its pearls too."

Vincent Van Gogh

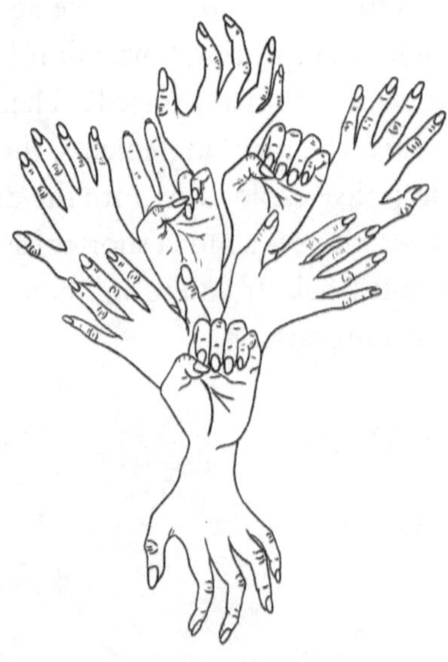

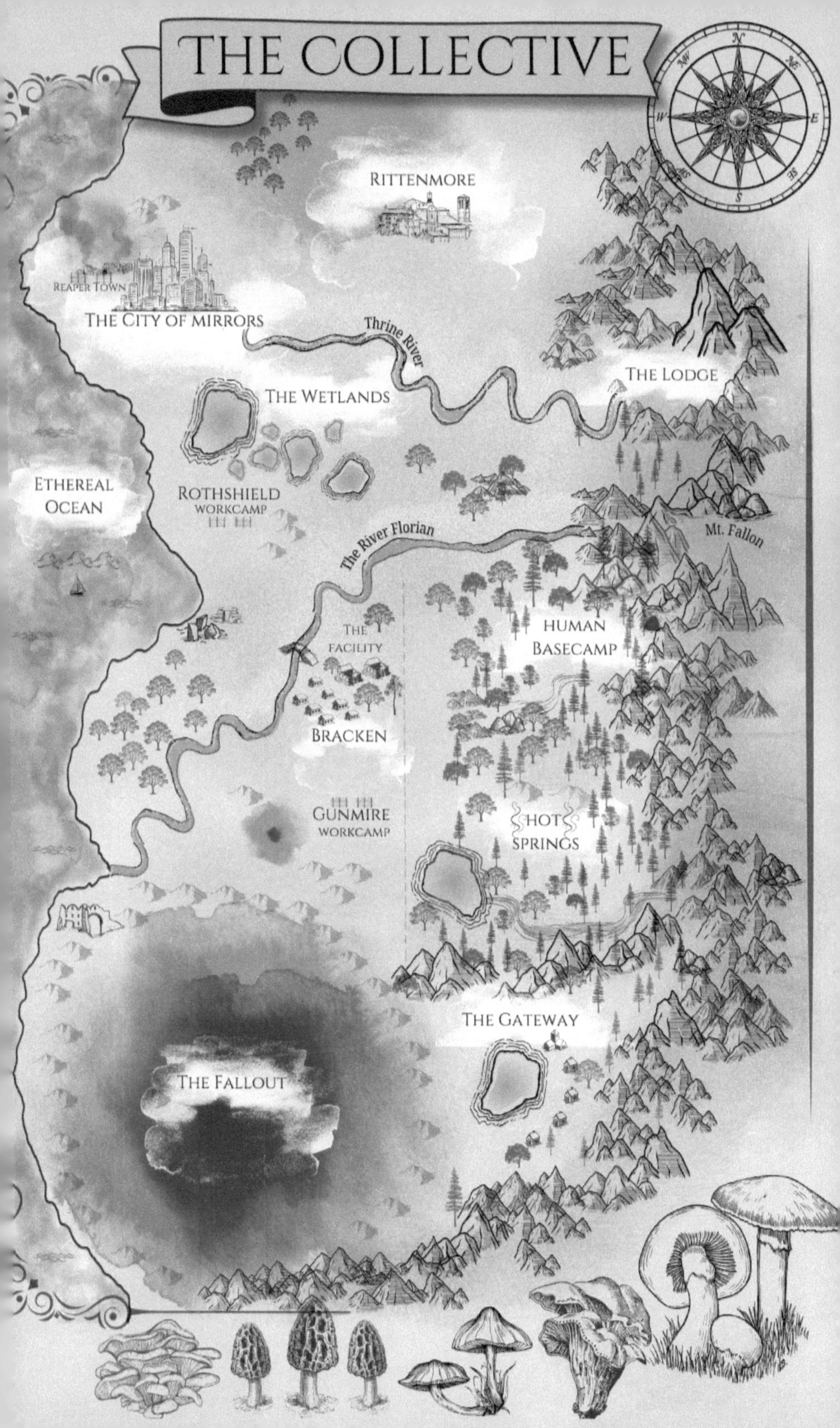

THE COLLECTIVE
N
NE
E
SE
S
SW
W
NW
RITTENMORE
REAPER TOWN
THE CITY OF MIRRORS
Thrine River
THE LODGE
THE WETLANDS
ETHEREAL OCEAN
ROTHSHIELD
WORKCAMP
The River Florian
Mt. Fallon
THE FACILITY
HUMAN BASECAMP
BRACKEN
GUNMIRE
WORKCAMP
HOT SPRINGS
THE GATEWAY
THE FALLOUT

CONTENTS

PROLOGUE   XIII

PART ONE

1. The Box   1

2. Saltine Crackers   4

3. Raven's Feathers   12

4. A Song   19

5. Baptized   21

6. Our Family   24

7. Tree Climbing   26

8. Let Us Be Bad   35

PART TWO

INTERLUDE   39

9. He Did Not Think About Adalia   43

10. Sink or Swim   50

11. Adolescent Anomalies   61

12. Our Lesser Half   65

13. A Broken Toy   70

14. How to be a Villain   79

15. Reapers & the Men Who Hunt Them   85

16. Mother Mine   92

17. Bloody Hands, Bloodier Heart   104

18. If It Were Quiet   113

19. A Worthy Sacrifice   120

20. Thrice   122

21. Kindling   127

PART THREE

INTERLUDE   135

22. Hollow   139

23. Home   146

24. Lucifer's Tears   151

25. Addy Was Safe   163

26. The Mountain   170

27. My Monster   180

28. The Man Behind Glass   184

29. Purple & Forked Tongues   197

30. Together   211

31. Music Notes   215

32. A Cacophony   228

33. A Dangerous Man   236

34. Good   244

35. Warm   252

PART FOUR

INTERLUDE   263

36. The Promises We Keep   265

37. 3:07   269

38. The Care of Mr. Bear   273

39. Minutes   277

40. On the Breeze   288

41. He Missed   291

PART FIVE

INTERLUDE   301

42. The Lightning Tree   304

43. Authority   309

44. Skeletons   316

45. Requiem   320

46. Liars, Fools, & the Secrets They Keep   324

Epilogue   327

The Moon   329

Lucifer's Tears Recipe   330

Content Warning   333

PROLOGUE
THE CAT

I NEVER WANTED TO live forever. In truth, I was one of those rare humans who has faced down the reality of their mortality and accepted it. We are all going to die someday.

And everyone did.

Except me.

You see, curiosity will go quite a long way in persuading one to stick Earthside. Curiosity: it was always my weakness. It killed the metaphorical cat. But what do you do when you've come up with a solution to death? The cat keeps living. And living. And living. And suddenly, you're left with the most curious cat of all—one stuck in a cycle of posing a question and finding the answer, only for another to appear. Despite the truth that I never wanted to live forever, I keep doing so.

There used to be a saying when I was young. It was a vague, amorphous thing, but the premise was this: There is a thin line between genius and madness. Another saying, which we do attribute to one Albert Einstein, is this: *Insanity is doing the same thing over and over again and expecting different results.* I posit, my friend, if Einstein was correct, we're all a little insane. What is any human emotion if not the practice of repeating the same rote routine and hoping you'll produce a different effect? What of the tomato plant you grow on the patio every year? You might try a different planting method. You might put a dead fish in the soil, or rotten eggs, or seashells. You might trim away the runners at the base of the plant. You might cover the thing in poison to kill the bugs. You might do it *differently* this time, but at the end of the day, you've still planted a tomato plant and put it in the same stained spot on the patio, or the windowsill, or the front step. And, you'll still grow tomatoes. They might be bigger this year. They might be shriveled little things. The plant might wither and die before the fruit appears. *I did things differently this time!* You'll say to yourself. But did you, really? It doesn't have to be a tomato, you ninny. It can be anything. We humans do love repetition. If I've learned anything in these long years, it's that we crave predictability.

That's what makes human beings so *easy* to control.

There were outliers, of course, humans who existed in my day sought thrills by jumping off mountainsides or swimming with predators or any number of equally insane actions antithetical to survival. But even these humans had routines.

Give a human a sense of security, a bit of distraction, the sensation of stimulation, and they'll be largely happy with whatever crumbs you offer. Oh, and one must not forget: hardship. Of the mutual variety. Give your humans just enough to complain about, just enough worry to distract from the monotony, just enough threat to things they believe precious, and you'll find you have a rather compliant group. They will grumble, yes. But they'll not rise up. It's too much risk.

Humanity is particularly fond of uniting against a common foe.

Eat the rich, they scream.

The poor are filthy, uneducated swine, they sniff over their stiff upper lips.

No, it's that group over there, the ones who have just enough. They're the problem. They're happy, one neighbor says of the other.

Oh, no, no. You're wrong again. It's the ones who don't look like us!

No, silly, it's the ones who don't eat what we like. They're uncultured.

You're wrong, too. It's those ones, over there, who believe that old tired doctrine. Out with the old, in with the new!

Young, ignorant fools, innovation is the death of tradition. Traditions have value.

You're all stupid—it's the men *who are the problem.*

No, it's the women, with their....emotions.

No, no, no! You're both wrong. It's the ones in between!

It couldn't possibly be you, right? No, it must be someone else, something else. They're just making you feel this way, right? If they'd just stop being so dense, the world could heal. Can't they see you're right?

And that is, my friends, exactly how it should be.

You see, if you're constantly at one another's throats, you cannot be at mine.

I never wanted to live forever.

But most of humanity *does.* And what better way to reinforce the jealous nature of man than by offering immortality to only a few?

You remember what I said about my curiosity? It is a plague, truly. I started with good intentions. My mother was sick, understand. And I am brilliant. It started with me solving her illness. Then, the curiosity got the better of me. I'd been fascinated since I was a child with what would happen if I spliced together different animals, you see? Could I make a bird with fur? Or a dog with the ears of an elephant? Or perhaps a *real* unicorn, if I married together strands of narwhal DNA with those of a stallion? Stupid, all of it. So stupid. The musings of a child. But. Something true, something revolutionary at their core.

And so, give the curious cat a lab and an unlimited budget and an utter lack of a moral compass, and you just might create a unicorn.

Or, an Ethereal, in my case. Humanity: *perfected.*

You've done it, you've solved it. Or so you thought. But alas, you are a cat, and cats get sick. And so, though you've made your unicorn, you are left with the problem that you're still a sick cat who, despite your best efforts, seems like it *wants* to die. But you are defiant. And you've grown accustomed to observing the goings on of your many mice.

I never thought I'd live forever.

I certainly never thought I'd choose to do so in agony.

But *curiosity*—it could not kill this cat.

PART ONE

The Boy in the Box

1
THE BOX

GABE

GABRIEL DIDN'T WANT TO go back into the box.

It was terribly dark in the box.

It was terribly wet and cold and painful in the box.

And last time, he'd sworn he heard voices in the box.

He'd heard something in there, scrabbling about just outside his peripheral vision. It'd sounded a lot like the metal tines of a fork scraping a glass plate, the kind of noise one cannot help but cringe away from—an impossible noise in the wet, in the dark.

No. He did not want to go back into the box.

"Please, Papa," he whispered, squeezing his father's hand to add weight to his plea, "*Please* don't make me go in the box."

His father squeezed his hand back with more force than necessary. "Not this again." He sighed and dropped to a knee, so he could meet Gabe's eyes. "It's for your own good, son. You'll understand when you're older. Now, be a good boy, and get into the box."

Gabe swallowed down the lump in his throat and nodded. "Yes, sir."

"Good. If you're quiet this time, I'll get you that tricycle. You know the one? Red, with the silver handles?"

Gabe's heart leapt. He'd been begging Mama and Papa for the red trike for four months. They'd not often told him no, but something about this had set Mama off. She was worried he'd get hurt.

It was strange that Mama worried the trike would hurt him, when they made him get into the box two times a week–the box where the *only* thing that happened was hurt and dark. Gabe swallowed down his fear, taking his time unbuttoning his shirt.

"Stop your procrastinating, Gabriel." Papa barked.

Gabe hurried to undress, but the last button snagged. His fingers grew sweaty as he frantically tried to undo it under the weight of Papa's judgmental glare. Papa took a half step forward, and Gabriel's shoulders curled. He'd messed up. *Again.* Before his father could reach him, though, Adalia stepped in his path, earning narrowed eyes at the back of her head. She would be in trouble later. She smiled down at him and whispered, "It's okay. I'm here. Let me." She unclasped the last button. "You can do this. I will be here when it's over."

"Always?" Gabe asked, tears threatening to spill as he stared up at his sister, his friend, the only one who could ever really understand.

"Always."

She folded his shirt over her arm and returned to her place in the doorway. Gabe took one last look over his shoulder at her as he climbed down into the box. Tears glistened in Addy's eyes. She waved sadly at him and smiled her little, reassuring smile. Gabe set his shoulders and sank below the sea of darkness. If Adalia could do it, so could he.

His small body went buoyant as liquid filled the chamber, and Gabe closed his eyes against the dark.

Hello again, came the voice from the void. Gabe clenched his fists in an attempt to mask his terror, but he couldn't hide from the voice in the dark. It *knew* him.

It *was* him.

Hello, he replied in his mind.

I'm glad you're here, said the voice, *I've been waiting for you.*

Go away, said Gabe.

Oh, no, no. I cannot go away. I'm here to protect you.

You are?

Oh, yes. You do not need to be afraid, so long as I am here.

Who are you? Gabe asked.

I am you. And you are me. And together, we never have to be afraid again. Do you like the sound of that?

Yes. Gabe leaned into the caress of the voice in the void, and for the first time in his little life, he did not feel afraid.

2

SALTINE CRACKERS

DARIUS

HIS *SISTER* WAS DEAD.

His sister was dead.

His sister was *dead*.

And he could not stop dreaming about it. Were they dreams or nightmares? Nightmares, Darius decided, because the people you loved weren't dead in good dreams.

But at least he wasn't alone in his dreams.

The shade of Lila was more than a little terrifying, with crusty blood smeared on her cheeks from where he'd tried to wipe it away, clothed in her white nightdress, and always looking at him with familiar blue eyes that were somehow all wrong. She never said anything, but a heaviness clung about her.

Darius thought it might be sadness that made her eyes look so glassy and still.

Sometimes, Lila pointed at the misshapen lump in the tall grass, but Darius refused to look. He'd seen their father's body once, and it'd been enough. Darius didn't like to think about the hole in Papa's head. Thinking about it made it impossible to pretend he was only sleeping in the weeds. He didn't know why Lila wanted him to look. He didn't know why she pointed to Papa instead of Ma. He *wanted* to look for Ma.

Ma would know what to do.

Ma would tell him where to get food.

Ma would tuck in his shirt and pat him on his head.

Ma would sing away the nightmares.

If only he could find her.

Where is Mama, Lila? Darius begged of her spectral form.

She still didn't talk, only shook her head, her eyes becoming impossibly sadder. Darius pulled her onto his lap and waited to wake up. He waited for this nightmare to end, so the real one could begin.

It was terribly cold in the house. The lights had stopped working a few days ago, and no matter how many times he flipped the switch, they wouldn't turn on. He'd taken the blankets from Ma and Papa's bed, but his teeth still chattered uncontrollably every morning when he woke up. It didn't let up until he found the will to get up and move around, shaking warmth back into his fingertips.

He layered on his coat–and Papa's, too, and padded his way to the kitchen.

When he opened the fridge, he knew what he'd find. He opened it anyway. Empty.

He knew what was in the cabinets too. Nothing.

He'd never thought much about where Ma had gotten food before. He knew there *was* a food building, but he didn't know where
to find it. He'd taken the last sleeve of saltines from the neighbor's
cabinet yesterday, tucking Papa's jacket around his mouth to block
out some of the stench wafting from the back bedroom. Darius
pretended he didn't know it was Jeffery, and Silba and little Emily
who made the smell. They smelled a bit like Lila had, but worse.
Much worse.

Darius had found them ten days ago, the same day he'd found his
best friend Ben in the next house over. They'd all looked peaceful
with the blood on their cheeks. He hadn't been brave enough to
look in the other houses. The street was quiet in a way that told
him what he'd find. He didn't understand why he was here... why
he hadn't gotten sick.

He wished Ma would come home. He didn't want to think
about why she hadn't.

Darius slipped on his best pair of shoes and combed his hair. He
took off Papa's coat and laid it on the back of his chair like he might
come out of the bedroom to claim it any minute. He'd be arguing
with Ma and drinking that brown bean juice he liked so much. Ma
would stick out her tongue, and then Pa would set his drink down
and chase her back to their room. For a moment, Darius swore
he could hear their laughter bouncing off the walls. But no. The
house was silent—something it had never been before two weeks
ago. There was only one place left to go.

He climbed the hill and found himself standing in front of a
massive wrought iron gate. There were buttons just begging to be

pressed to one side. They shone hues of gold in the early morning light. Darius wanted to touch them, but instead, he turned his thin frame sideways and slipped through the wide gap in the bars.

Once on the other side, it was merely a matter of choosing which house looked the most approachable. The answer, Darius decided, was none of them. He didn't even know if they could really be called houses at all, so huge and shiny and clean as they were. He focused, instead, on which ones looked unoccupied and began trying the gleaming brass doorknobs. The third one he tried was unlocked.

Darius stepped into a soaring marble hallway, leaving greasy brown footprints on spotless white floors as he tiptoed along in search of the kitchen. He breathed a sigh of relief when he found the room with little trouble. The kitchen was bigger than the one at his house, though it bore most of the same identifying features: sink, refrigerator, bean-juice boiler, and...*food.*

Any semblance of stealth fled Darius' lanky body as he sprinted for the loaf of crusty brown bread on the counter. He dug dirty fingers into it and shoved chunks into his mouth, groaning at the rich flavor. It was much better than the pale white bread Ma had slathered in peanut butter for his lunch every day before. Before... she'd *gone.* He'd chewed his way through half the loaf before he noticed a woman standing in the doorway. He shrieked around his mouthful of bread and sprinted from the kitchen, but not before shoving the rest of the loaf down the front of his jacket.

The woman was faster than him. So fast that Darius suspected she'd had some of the modifications people who lived in this part of town were so fond of. She caught his jacket sleeve just as he crossed the threshold. His feet scrabbled at the concrete step for purchase, but the woman whipped him around to face her despite his best efforts to yank out of her grasp. Her rich brown hair floated on a breeze Darius couldn't quite feel, tendrils touching his cold cheeks as she leaned in to whisper, "Stop, little one." She pulled him back through the doorway. "You do not have to run from me." Her voice lilted like wind through wildflowers. She sounded like... she sounded like... like...a mother.

Darius' shoulders drooped, a tear leaking from the corner of his eye. He dashed it away with the back of his hand and shook out of the woman's grip. "I'm sorry. Ma always told me not to take what don't belong to me, but. But I was hungry, ma'am. I didn't know where else to go."

"Where is your mother, child?" The woman asked, reaching out to pat Darius' shoulder, but stopping short when she saw him stiffen.

"I don't know," said Darius.

Understanding flashed in the woman's eyes. "You're from below, then, aren't you?"

Darius nodded.

Her eyes flooded with something that looked a lot like pity. He bristled at the sight of it. "Come in, child. I won't allow you to go hungry," she said, turning back toward the kitchen. Her heels clicked on the stone floors as she walked away.

Darius stared after her for a long minute before following. This had gone remarkably better than he'd expected.

"Sit down over there." The woman motioned to a round table set with four chairs in front of a wide window. Darius sank into the plush chair, cringing as his dirty pants brushed the cream fabric. He fixed his eyes on the lumpy shape of his neighborhood down the hill as the woman bustled about in the kitchen. He tried not to flinch at the sound of a cabinet banging shut. It'd been so quiet for the last few weeks. Darius wasn't used to the lovely sounds of domesticity any longer.

She set a bowl of yellowish pasta in front of him and gingerly passed him a fork.

He took it, muttering, "Thank you," like Ma had taught him to do.

Darius was on his third bowl when steps sounded in the hall. The woman stiffened beside him and slowly rose, pressing a finger to her lips as she left the room. Muffled voices echoed off the marble walls.

"He's just a little boy, James." The woman's voice sounded strained in a way that made Darius sit up straight and put down his fork.

"I don't care if he's the messiah. We don't associate with *them,*" a deep, achingly cold voice answered.

"He was hungry!"

"Then you should have let him starve. It would have been kinder than giving him hope. You know what the Authority ordered."

"Please, James," she begged. "We have plenty to spare. We could help—"

An unfamiliar sound rang from the other room as the woman cut off. A dull, jarring thud. A muffled cry came next. Darius clenched his fist and rose. Another *thump* and the woman went altogether silent. Smooth footsteps neared, and before Darius had the chance to bolt, a tall, immaculate man stood in the doorway. His hair was sandy blonde, streaked with iridescent silver that caught the light when he tilted his head and raised a brow at Darius. He straightened his cufflinks and wiped at a smear of red on his sleeve as he spoke. "Well then, *boy,* finish your meal."

Darius didn't even consider disobeying. He sat stiffly and shoveled the food, now tasting like sand, into his mouth.

"Good," said the man. "I will be back. You'd best be here when I come."

Darius nodded.

"Yes, sir," the man corrected. "You must use proper manners when in the presence of your betters, boy."

Darius swallowed down the terror in his throat. "Yes, sir," he croaked.

The man dipped his chin and turned on his heel, steps resounding like the bang of a gavel as he left Darius sitting alone in the kitchen.

His voice off the walls once more, "I have a lost child to report." A long pause, then, "Yes. Exactly so." Another pause, "A loaf of bread... Yes. Now."

Heart in his throat, Darius sat for long minutes, listening to the quiet rustlings of the man from the next room, before whispers sounded behind him. He turned in time to see a stream of white hair flutter around the pillar, then another—an auburn head, peaking out before disappearing. There were... there were *children* in this house. He tried to be comforted by that fact, but just then, the tall man appeared and took hold of Darius' small, dirty hand, hoisting him up. "I hope you enjoyed your last meal, boy," he said. He dragged Darius down the hall and thrust him out the front door, into the waiting arms of the Reapers.

The Reaper's hands left bruises on Darius' arms where it clutched him.

He had never seen a Reaper up close. Ma had told him to stay away from them. Darius hadn't needed telling twice. They were scarier in close proximity with their black war clothes and curved blades and dark lines etched into their skin. There were four of them.

Darius couldn't help but scream when the one gouging into his arm shoved him down on the asphalt in the center of the street. His knees tore open through his thin pants. He muffled his cry in his shoulder, then glared up at the monsters looming over him.

"We're here to right a wrong," the biggest one spoke down with a voice like dying embers.

"You have taken what is not yours," said the next, in a tone that sounded so much like Ma, Darius had to choke back a sob.

"The balance must be restored," intoned the third, scraping their scythe to punctuate their words.

"It is law," all four spoke in unison.

The hair on Darius' arms rocketed up in response. "Please—" he began, then choked on his words when he spotted the glowing red stick in the calloused palms of the fourth. Darius began to cry in earnest then, hot tears cutting tracks down his cold cheeks. "I'm sorry," he sobbed. "I'm sorry. I'm only eight—Papa said that means I'm still learning, plea—"

The fourth Reaper grabbed Darius by the collar and jerked him close, spraying reeking breath in his face, "You take from us, now we take from you."

The iron was warm on the side of his face, and then it was searing into his left eye. He made a noise that rattled his own skull before losing himself to oblivion.

3

RAVEN'S FEATHERS

Gabe

"Addy! Addy! Come quick! We have to help him." Gabe said, pulling his sister up against the fence to peer out into the street.

"What are you talking about, Gabe?" She pressed her face to the wrought iron bars that surrounded the expansive gardens of their home.

"There's a boy in the street," Gabe said, rising on his toes to see more clearly over his mother's rose bushes. "The one mama was helping. We have to help him, Ads. It was Papa's doing. He did this."

"Gabriel," Addy began, speaking down to him in that way he loathed, "We can't—"

"We *must*. He's going to die if we don't help. They burned his eye, Addy. I saw them do it. He's just been lying there. Hasn't moved since."

"Gabe—"

"You're smarter than me," Gabe begged, fully aware Addy would cave in the face of his flattery. "I don't know what to do, but you do."

Addy sighed for a long moment in that big ten-year-old way of hers. "Fine, you distract Mama and Papa." Her eyes darted about the back garden before landing on the shed behind a tall hedge. She nodded to herself before turning back to him. "I'll go see if I can get him."

"Okay," Gabe nodded, "What should I do?"

She looked down at him with too many words in her eyes, gnawing her bottom lip before nodding to herself again and setting her shoulders. She bent to peer into his eyes. "Do something bad, Gabriel, but you have to be prepared for the consequences. It's the only way to keep Papa... occupied."

Gabe clenched his jaw and nodded up at her. "I can do it."

"You can do anything, Gabe." Addy brushed his cheek as she unlatched the gate. She looked over her shoulder and made a shooing motion. "Go quick. I'll see if I can get him."

Gabe took a lingering look at his sister before darting away through the ferns and trees. His feet were quiet as he came to a stop before the wide glass doors that would take him back inside. Back to Papa. Gabe set his shoulders and turned the handle.

Gabe had done as Addy said. He'd done something bad. He'd talked back to Papa.

It had earned him time in the pit, but Gabe didn't mind so much, not when the basement windows faced the street. Not when he could see Addy out there getting the boy, her arm slung under his mostly limp shoulders as she dragged him through the back gate. Gabe smiled. It would be worth whatever discipline Papa would give once he let Gabe out of the pit. It would be worth it because that boy—the boy with hair like raven's feathers—was going to be his friend. He'd decided it the moment he heard the boy thank his mother for the mac n' cheese. That boy was a nice boy. He wasn't like the ones at school. The ones who pushed him and teased him and mocked him for liking music instead of soccer.

No, the dirty boy wasn't like those other boys. The one-eyed boy was going to be his friend.

Gabe took the beating his father gave silently, not letting his tears fall for the first time ever. Because he was not alone, not anymore, not now that he had the voice in the dark, not now that they could have a friend. Addy would help. He knew it. Addy *always* helped.

The next morning, Adalia led Gabe out to the back shed—the one Papa didn't go to, deeming the gardening a task too far below their station. It had become a safe place for Gabe and Addy, and it'd be a safe place for the boy, too. Addy snagged a shiny apple and bagel off the counter on their way out the door.

The boy sat crouched in the back corner of the shed, shielding one startlingly blue eye from the sudden light. He moaned in pain. The place where his eye should have been was dreadfully red and purple and oozing. Gabe worried no one could survive having their eye taken out like that. "Are you okay?" Gabe asked of the boy.

The boy looked up at him, reddish pus streaking down the ruined side of his face, an icy eye glaring from the other half. "No, I'm not alright," the boy cried. "My *eye*..." He went to rub at the missing eye, but Addy darted forward and caught his hand.

"Stop." She ordered. "You mustn't touch it."

The boy clutched at Addy's hand, sobbing, "My sister, my papa, my ma— I'm alone."

Gabe crouched down and patted the boy on his shoulder. "You're not alone," he said. "You're not alone as long as we are here." The sentiment bounced in buttery tones around Gabe's mind: *Not alone. Never alone, so long as **we** are here.*

"Gabriel, go back in the house and get some bandages," Addy bossed. "And be discreet. Don't let them know."

"Okay, Addy." Gabe clasped the boy's shoulder before heading back into the house.

He gathered up supplies as best he could. There wasn't much by way of medicinal items in their house. When one of them got hurt, they usually just waited for the wound to heal on its own. It didn't take long. If Papa went too far, they sometimes went in the box. Gabe thought maybe that was what they should do with the boy. Putting him in the box would help. It would hurt, but it would also help. Papa always told him the box made him better. He didn't see why it couldn't make the boy better, too.

Gabe paused on the threshold to the back gardens as music drifted from the front corner of the house. For a moment, he entertained the idea of getting Mother. No. That was a *stupid* idea. She hadn't even mentioned the boy Papa had called the Reapers for. Not even when she'd come in to hum Gabe to sleep, as she did on the nights after Papa was especially cruel. She would be no help. Mama never stopped Papa from doing anything. But she was there *after* it happened—and that was enough. No, they didn't need Mother for this. Gabe left her to her music and slipped out the door.

He slunk out to the shed bearing rolls of gauze and dewy ointment Mother sometimes put on his knees. These, he passed off to Addy. She nodded in approval, squeezed a goodly amount into her palm, then pressed it to the boy's empty eye socket. The boy wailed. Gabe slapped a hand over his mouth.

"Quiet," Gabe said. "You must be quiet, or our Papa... well, he doesn't like it when you cry." The boy made a muffled, choked sound Gabe took as understanding. He removed his hand and offered up a hunk of gauze that the boy promptly shoved into his mouth. The boy bit down on the gauze, his screaming muffled as Addy continued her ministrations, lathering the goop into his missing eye. She wrapped the cloth around his head to cover the wound. The boy was much more acceptable to look at now that the horrible injury was out of sight. Sweat beaded on his forehead, and his brownish skin had gone an unnaturally pale color. He shook violently. Gabe could see that what Addy had done would not be enough to save him. Only the box could save him now.

"What's your name?" Gabe asked as they eased the boy back on one of the old quilts they kept in the shed.

The boy spat out the wad of gauze in a thrillingly vulgar way and panted, "Darius. I'm Darius."

"I'm Gabe. Gabe Malik. You don't know it yet, Darius, but I've decided we are going to be best friends."

"If I live," Darius said, a tear rolling out of his remaining eye.

Gabe leaned and wiped it away. "You'll live. I've decided that, too." He smiled. "Don't cry, Darius. We'll make you better. It'll all be better now you're not alone anymore." *Not alone. Never alone.* Gabe hoped he was telling the truth. No—he would make it the truth. There was still hope for Darius. Papa didn't know Darius was in the shed, shivering beneath the quilt Addy had tucked under his chin. There was hope.

When they were securely back inside behind Gabe's bedroom door, he turned to his sister and whispered, "This isn't going to work."

"I'm doing the best I can," she sniffed.

"It's not enough."

"What do you want me to do, Gabe? I'm not a grown-up. I don't *know* what to do."

Gabe had seldom heard Addy utter such words, and it filled him with a mild sense of panic. Addy *always* knew what to do, but this time, she didn't and he *did*. So, he told her, "We need to put him in the box."

She nodded slowly, brow furrowing as she thought it through. "How do we get him in the box?"

"I don't know that part, but I'll distract Papa if you can figure out a way. Maybe... maybe at night. I don't think anyone would be watching at night. Papa has never taken *me* at night."

"Me neither. I... I think you're right. We take him to the box at night."

"No. *You* take him to the box. I will distract Papa."

"Gabe," Addy pleaded, "Papa has... Papa doesn't punish you like he does me. I should do it."

"I can handle it," Gabe said, puffing his chest with false bravado. "Besides, you know the box better. You know what to do."

She couldn't argue with that, so she didn't. Instead, she tried another tactic. "Papa will do bad things... bad things I haven't told you abou–"

Gabe cut her off, "We have to save him. He's going to be my friend."

"*I'm* your friend," Addy whispered. "Isn't that enough?"

"You're my *sister*. It's not the same... and it's not *right* to let that boy die. He's just like us, don't you see?" It wasn't *strictly* true, but it felt that way to Gabe. The boy was human, and they were... not.

Addy hung her head, ashamed. "You're right." She patted his cheek. "You've always been the better of the two of us, Gabe. Don't let anyone tell you different."

*Yes, we are **better***, the voice spoke in Gabe's head. He shook it to clear it away.

"Yes." Addy nodded, thinking he'd been refuting what she'd said. "You are *good*, Gabe. No matter what Papa says." Addy turned to go.

Better. Better. Better.

"Do you have an extra coat?" she asked, turning back to him. "He's taller than you, but it's close enough. I—I think he's cold in a way we're not, you know?"

Gabe nodded. "Yes. He can have my coat. Take my blanket, too."

He hoped whatever distraction he came up with would be enough. Enough for the boy to go in the box, so the boy could be like him. So the boy could live, spared from sickness and pain. Well, mostly anyway.

4

A SONG

Darius

THE GIRL WAS THE most beautiful thing Darius had ever seen, with auburn hair brushing her collarbones and eyes that reminded him of the first spring grass. Smiles graced her lips without reservation, and when she laughed, it sounded like a melody. A song familiar to a part of him that had not yet woken but existed in the pit of his soul all the same. A song whose only words were *Adalia. Adalia. Adalia.* She was the only tether that kept him from slipping into delirium.

She came to him four times the first day. Three on the second. By the third, Darius wasn't certain if she ever left his side. When she came, she fed him sips of soup. It was warm in a way Darius hadn't been in a long time. Warm in a way he tried to recall once she'd gone and he was left alone on a thin pallet of blankets on the ground. When Adalia came back, she'd tuck the blankets under his chin and hum a song he'd never heard but one that reminded him of his mother nonetheless.

Darius' eye hurt horribly—*wretchedly*—but it didn't hurt half as much as his heart. He supposed the pain was a welcome distraction from the hollowness that had plagued him for weeks. If he could only focus on the physical hurt, he could forget his family was dead for a while. So Darius reveled the pain. Then he leaned into a sensation so opposite of pain—the sensation of Addy's care for him, her slender hands cool across his now burning skin.

From the first time she tucked the blanket under his chin, he knew she was something special, something other and unattainable. He also knew he'd never be able to repay her for dragging him from his death in the street. Still, Darius leaned into Adalia for those three days as she attempted to nurse him back to health, to heal the grotesque injury with soup and gentle words. But they were only children, and broth would not regrow his eye, would not stanch the galloping infection causing his lungs to rattle, flesh to weep. Words would not mend the pounding in his head, even when spoken in the song of her breath on his cheek. He grew hotter and colder and more distant until the pain was nothing more than a tiny nagging of sensation. He leaned into the shimmery glory of the girl with hair the color of autumn and eyes like spring. He leaned into her like she was the beginning and the end. Until Darius didn't know whether he was awake or dreaming. Until the shade of his dead sister grew clearer than the autumn girl. Until the waking nightmare was a mere memory. And Darius felt *peace*, immense, profound peace, as he went to sleep.

5

BAPTIZED

DARIUS

SHE WOKE HIM WHEN it was dark on the third day, dragging his bleary self out of the shed into a snow-swept night. Darius couldn't tell the difference between the snowflakes and the stars, but they were pretty, all the same. He tilted his head back so far to look at them he tipped over altogether, landing with a grunt in Addy's arms. She was unreasonably strong for a little girl. She sighed and led him a few swaying steps to a bright blue sled.

"Get on," Addy demanded, guiding him down onto the sled. He curled into a ball and closed his eyes—no—*eye*.

Addy roused him by shaking his shoulder, then hoisting him unceremoniously to his feet. Darius glared about a wide, tiled hallway, uncertain of where he was or how he'd gotten there. Adalia took his weight and began dragging him along, grumbling, "Come on, Darius." They pushed through a set of double doors. Darius slipped on the tiles of the odd little room, but Addy quickly righted him. It only set his head to spinning more as he tried to understand what he was looking at.

"Where are we going?" he asked, suddenly awake with adrenaline stampeding through his veins.

"I'm going to make sure you get better. Do you trust me?"

"Yes," he said. He didn't have much choice but to trust her, and he couldn't think of a reason not to.

"Then get into that box."

"You want me to climb into *that* thing?" he asked, pointing at the dauntingly tall transparent cube at the center of the room, shrouded in wires and tubes that gave the visage of some unnatural octopus. It blinked blurrily in his spotty vision. "Is it dark in there?"

She sighed wearily. "C'mon, Darius. You can do this. Even *Gabriel* goes into the box, and he's only seven. It'll make you better. I promise."

Darius stared into the bottomless green pools of Adalia's eyes for a long minute before nodding and mounting the ladder to the top of the box. Once inside, he saw it wasn't a box at all, but some sort of multilayered chamber. He shrieked when his shoes suddenly wetted.

"*Shhh!* They'll know we're here if you don't quiet down!" Addy reached down into the box and slapped a hand over his mouth to muffle the scream. The force of her slap caused him to stumble into the glass wall. He leaned against it, then savored the softness of Addy's fingertips on his cheek. It was the only thing that wasn't entirely numb. That and his wet toes. He swallowed his screams and tapped her hand to signal he was now composed enough to keep quiet. Addy dropped her hand and climbed down, pressing one finger to her lips.

"Why is it wet?" Darius whispered.

"I'm sorry, Darius," she intoned, slamming her hand down on a palm-sized silver button on the wall. "It's the only way to make you better. It will only hurt a little."

A whining sound emitted from the ceiling of the box as some sort of metal plate slid into place, sealing Darius inside. His breath came in rapid little pants as he whipped his head to and fro, stumbling in his search for some escape from the glass coffin, because surely that's what it was. He found no refuge. Tepid water rose around his feet, quickly swallowing up his tattered brown shoes. Soon, it was sloshing around his waist. He felt oddly light in the liquid, which he now knew wasn't plain water. When it rose around his mouth, it tasted of salt and sunshine. No. It didn't. It didn't taste so happy as that. It tasted of tears. Darius rolled with panic as the liquid covered his nose. He floated to the top of the box and pressed into the metal hatch with all his meager might. It didn't budge. He gulped down ragged breaths of the precious air left in the top inch of the box. He was going to drown.

Addy approached and pressed her hand to the outer wall, her voice piped into the confined space through an intercom. "I'm sorry. It will only hurt for a minute, and then you'll be all better. I can't—" The water rose over his head, muffling her last words into incoherence.

And then, Darius drowned.

Aside from the terrible pressure in his lungs, it wasn't a bad way to go. Colors danced on the back of his eyelid as he slipped from consciousness. But before he could descend into oblivion, searing pain sliced in ribbons along the surface of his flesh.

Darius opened his bleary eye and screamed, gurgling on salty-pink.

Adalia had lied. It hurt more than a little.

6

OUR FAMILY

GABE

GABE HAD NEVER BEEN in this kind of trouble. He'd always been a boy who went out of his way to *avoid* trouble—not that it'd ever helped him. It seemed trouble found *him* no matter what he did. And for Gabe, 'trouble' always equated bruises and fists and words that cut. Yes, Gabe was an obedient little boy, well-behaved to the point of pain. Well-behaved in a way unnatural for a boy of seven. He truly did not act like a child at all, but rather some robotic visage of one, groomed into perfection from the moment of his birth. He hadn't even cried when he was a baby.

To step out of line was unfamiliar to say the least, and it sent a little thrill dancing down his spine. At least, that's what he told himself as his father raked long nails down the back of his neck and *squeezed*.

"My, my," Papa began, "what trouble you've gotten up to today, Gabriel. How bold of you to come into *my* office, boy. And what is this masterpiece you've created, then?" Papa gestured to the wall, and Gabe cringed.

"I... I—I," Gabe stuttered despite himself.

"Speak up."

"I drew our family. I thought you'd like it, Papa." It was a lie. Gabe didn't often lie, and he was surprised his father couldn't tell the difference. He *knew* Papa wouldn't like it, that's why he'd done it. He needed him angry. Angry enough to guarantee Addy's success. Papa always went away for a while after he beat them.

Sometimes it was only a few hours, but often, he'd go for days, leaving Mama to hum and comfort while he took their flight craft and disappeared into The Mirrored City. That's what Gabe needed him to do now.

Gabe had scratched several crude stick figures into the wall behind Papa's desk with the tip of his pencil. Pencils were only for paper. Gabe knew that. He also knew his father's wrath would be immense for such a deed.

"You never listen, Gabriel," said Papa, unbuckling his belt. Gabe knew what would happen next. "You need a lesson. Maybe this time you'll learn." His father laughed bitterly, "Who am I kidding? You don't learn. You never learn, Gabriel, you pathetic excuse of a son." The belt uncoiled, slithering to the floor with a slap like some malicious serpent. Gabe cringed away from it. His father noted the movement and grinned. "Are we regretting our choices now, Gabriel?"

"Y—yes, Papa."

It's alright, said the voice in Gabe's head. *Don't think of him. Don't look at him. Look at me. Look at me. LOOK AT ME, Gabe.*

And so, Gabe turned inward. He looked to the voice, to the comfort of the one who understood him, who *protected* him. Gabe closed his ears to the sound of Papa's belt on his back. He closed his ears to the sound of his own body hitting the ground—to the muffled whimpers that came out of his mouth as he curled on the floor, shielding his head from the onslaught. He closed his ears to the words Papa yelled.

"*You don't learn. You* never *learn!*"

Gabe closed his ears and listened to the voice in his head—the voice that *sounded* like Papa, but spoke kindness instead.

You are not alone. You are not alone. You are not alone—as long as you're with **me.** Gabe closed his ears and pretended he was *not* alone.

7

TREE CLIMBING

THE BOX HAD NOT grown Darius' eye back. It was the first thing he knew when he woke up. The second thing he knew was that he felt better than he ever had before. His limbs moved differently, as if they were more firmly connected with the commands from his brain. His fingers seemed more dexterous, able to curve in ways they hadn't before. When he peeked out through the crack in the shed door, he could see the veins on the leaves across the yard. *Curious.* If only one session in the box could have such an effect, it was no wonder the people who lived on the hill thought they were better than him—they *were.* Darius knew they spent *a lot* of time in the box. Addy told him her little brother went in twice a week. What on earth did that mean about how her brother could hear and smell and see and touch and taste?

Darius *wanted* to go back into the box. It hadn't grown his eye back, sure, but he wasn't in pain any longer. Even the hurt in his heart was much easier to bear. And while it *had* hurt in there, it'd felt good, too. It felt exceptionally good *now*—now he knew what it could do.

Darius didn't think the rich people on the hill could truly appreciate what the box meant, what it did. They couldn't set aside the pain, not like he did. Temporary pain in exchange for power? That was something Darius couldn't have imagined before he'd crossed through the wrought iron gates. Feeling safe and whole and complete inside one's own body was a foreign concept to someone who'd grown up like him. He hated to think his family might still be alive if they'd had access to the box. *Would* Lila be alive if they'd put her in the box? Would his Ma have been able to stay? Perhaps that's where they'd taken her when they'd dragged her away. Perhaps Ma was alive—more, perhaps she was well—perhaps she'd been in the box. Perhaps she would find him again. Darius squashed the thought. He knew it was a lie. Ma wasn't coming back.

His birthday was next week. It'd be the first year Ma didn't make him a lemon cake. He sighed and settled more deeply into the mass of blankets on the floor. It wasn't so cold today, or maybe Darius just wasn't so sensitive to the cold as he'd been yesterday. He set about counting the cobwebs in the corners to try and distract himself from the nagging need to do something now that he wasn't dying anymore, but even that quickly became a bore. He thought he might go mad in the confines of the garden shed.

When the sun set, Darius crept outside. He darted about the shrubbery, testing his newly powerful legs. He swore he was faster than before. He spent a good amount of the early darkness trying to catch a fat green toad. It was odd to see one this time of year, but Darius didn't worry too much. Animals rarely did what you expected them to. Lila was dreadfully afraid of toads. She said Emily told her they'd give her warts. Darius didn't think that was true, and he wasn't particularly certain he cared whether he got warts or not.

When he captured the toad, he decided he'd call it Benjamin, for his best friend, of course. He tucked Benjamin into his jacket pocket and climbed the stout oak in the corner behind the garden shed. Settled onto a thick branch midway up the tree, Darius pulled Benjamin from his pocket. The toad squirmed a little before calming in his palms. He held Benjamin up to show him the stars. "You see there, Ben," he whispered to the toad. "That's Orion's belt, those three big shiny ones."

Benjamin croaked in response.

Darius nodded, continuing, "And that one there, it's the big dipper—that's what Papa called it, anyway—though, between you and me, Ben, I don't know what a dipper is—"

"Who are you talking to?"

Darius jumped, then peered down through the branches to find the small boy, *Gabriel*, standing under the tree, grey eyes big, shock-white strands of hair reflecting the moonlight. The little boy's hair looked strange, so Darius told him as much. "You have funny hair," he called down.

"I know."

"Why is it like that?" Darius asked.

"Quiet!" said the boy. "You'll wake them."

"Okay," Darius lowered his voice. "Why don't you come up then?"

The boy's throat bobbed. "I've never climbed a tree."

"Well, then, get up here. It'd be a horrible thing to miss out on, climbing trees."

Below, Gabriel went still. Finally, he seemed to come to a decision. He began to climb. It was awkward in a way that made clear to Darius what he'd said was true: he'd never climbed a tree. In fact, with each interaction, Darius' certainty that these people didn't know how to take risks grew. Despite the fact they got to go into the box, Darius suspected their lives were terribly boring.

The little boy made his slow way up to the branch where Darius perched. Gabriel clung to the trunk with shaking fingers.

"Are you scared?" Darius asked.

"No!"

"You look scared."

"Of course I'm scared," Gabriel admitted. "We're up high!"

"It's not that high," Darius protested. They were a mere six feet off the ground.

"To you, maybe," said Gabriel, eyes wet with wonder, "to me, it's very high. You're braver than me."

"You'll get brave. You're Gabriel, right?"

"Yeah, but I like it when people call me Gabe better."

"Okay, Gabe... so why is your hair like that?" Darius nodded to Gabe's mostly white hair.

"It wasn't always like this. That's what mother says, anyway—"

"—your Ma is nice."

"Yeah. Ma is nice."

"Your Papa's not so nice?"

"He tries to be." Gabe looked down, clutching the tree trunk more tightly. "I don't wanna talk about that, but I'll tell you about my hair, okay?"

Darius nodded.

"It started getting like this when I... when I... went into the box. You know, you went into the box..."

"Yeah?"

"Maybe your hair will get like mine. I think that might be sad, though—"

"Adalia's hair ain't like yours."

Gabe shrugged. "I don't know. Maybe it's just because mine didn't start like hers, you know? Everybody who goes in the box gets white hair. That's what Papa says. The big boys at school—and some of the girls, too—they have white hair. They've had the procedures though..."

"Really?" Darius squeaked, squeezing the toad too tightly, and causing it to hop out of his grasp. "Well, shit."

Gabe's eyes went round at the toad hopping along the branch, then at the word Darius had said. "That's a bad word," Gabe whispered.

"Is it?" Darius smirked. "Well, go on then, you try one."

"One what?"

"A bad word."

"No… no. I couldn't. Papa wouldn't like it."

"Your Papa's not here." Darius arched his brow in challenge. Gabe's gaze flashed to his empty eye socket. Darius lifted his hand to cover it and looked down at his legs dangling below.

"Shit," Gabe said.

"What? What happened?" Darius glanced back up at him. Gabe wore a wide grin.

"Nothing. I said a bad word."

Darius grinned back. "Yeah. Yeah, you did." They sat smiling at one another for long seconds until Darius spoke again, "You know, your hair's not really white. It's kinda *shiny*."

"Silver. It's silver." He leaned closer, seeming to grow more comfortable on the branch. "It's one of the only things I like about the box."

"Really? I like the box."

"How could you like the box? It hurts in there. It's dark in there. It's wet." Gabe made a sad little choking sound.

"Yeah. Yeah. Well, ever thought about how you feel? After you come out the box?"

"I don't remember how I feel. It just scares me." Gabe admitted this like it was some shameful secret.

It was then that Darius understood that while the boy beside him on the branch lived in a castle on a hill, he lacked something Darius had possessed in generous heaps at home: love, security, the confidence he was allowed to feel things—that he wouldn't be punished for it. "Hey," he said, squeezing Gabe's shoulder. "It's alright. It's okay to be scared."

"It is?"

"Of course it is. It's how you use your fear that matters. Eh—that's what *my* Papa always said."

"Your Papa sounds smart."

Darius sighed. "I don't know about that. I don't think he used his fear very well. And I'm startin' to think no matter how you use it, it's best not to let nobody see it, ya know?"

"What happened to him?"

"I don't want to talk about it, Gabe." Gabe's face fell, etched in a sadness so bitterly deep Darius was moved to speak, but not about his Papa—never about what'd happened to his Papa. "Hey. You wanna play a game?"

Gabe's face lit brighter than sunrise. "Yeah! I want to play… Chess!"

It appeared to have taken a good deal of effort for Gabe to muster such conviction, so Darius nodded his head, even though he didn't have the faintest clue what a 'chess' was. "Okay, but you'll have to teach me how."

And so, they climbed down the tree, Darius encouraging Gabe on his descent. When they got to the shed, Gabe produced a beautiful checkered board with tiny ivory statues from behind a rusted watering can. They sat criss-cross on the floor and began.

They began the friendship that would be their end.

For three years, their routine was much the same. Darius became a creature of night, emerging from the stiflingly small garden shed only under cover of darkness. He didn't ever go back to his house down the hill. He couldn't bear the memories that accompanied the place. He stole shoes and clothes from lines and porches, constantly outgrowing what he had. Darius had grown wonderfully tall, and sometimes Gabriel glared at him because of it. In fact, Darius had gotten so big, he was beginning to outgrow the shed altogether. On the nights Gabe or Addy couldn't steal away, or the nights they slept instead of keeping him company, he wandered.

Sometimes, he even wandered out into the woods beyond the border, a growing, reckless part of him daring the guards to spot him. Despite the thrill of it, Darius admitted to himself that it was unlikely; the bulk of the town abandoned and empty, devoid of Reapers. So Darius became one with the forest, with the dark, with the creatures within it.

He climbed trees and swam in rivers so cold they'd have killed him before his time in the box. He taught himself to fish and forage and track. He hiked the hilly outcrops across the border. Occasionally, he'd stay too late and spend another day and night in the woods. And when he returned, he'd find Addy and Gabe waiting in the shed with looks of superior rapprochement carved into their perfect faces. Gabe's hair was now full silver, and Adalia's was threaded through with streaks that caught the starlight. Darius' own hair remained raven's black, despite the more than a handful of times he'd visited the box over the years, always to remedy some injury he acquired on the other side of the border. The more he went to the box, the less he needed to return, the things that would've broken him before becoming nothing more than a nuisance.

That wasn't the only thing that'd changed. Amidst the rusted tools and blankets and empty food canisters in the shed, an assortment of broken toys, crayons, and picture books lay scattered. Darius was learning to write. He was learning to *read*. Between games of chess and truth or dare (neither of which Darius could best Gabe at—or Addy, for that matter, not that he wanted to—he'd gladly lose to *her*), the siblings had been teaching him. They'd been horrified when Darius had admitted he'd never been to school, that he didn't know how to read. So they'd taken up the mantle of teacher. They were terrible at it.

Still, Darius was good at learning, so he'd quickly picked up on his letters and shapes and numbers. He'd exhausted Addy's supply of picture books and had started on a chapter book last week. He was quite proud of this last and kept the book tucked under his bed of blankets. Perhaps he'd ask Adalia about that word that'd stumped him last night. He didn't have the guts to ask Gabe.

He'd quickly deduced Gabe had a remarkable mind. He was brilliant in a way that set one's heart pounding every now and again, as the things he spoke were so far beyond the wisdom of a ten-year-old. It occasionally made Darius feel small, even though he loomed a good foot taller than Gabe, which irked the silver-haired boy terribly. He wanted to be tallest, rather than smartest.

Darius thought he might like quite the opposite, but despite the shared jealousy, their friendship blossomed, growing up from the pitiful dregs of shared trauma into something true and good and pure in a way so few things are in the world. And something else blossomed, too.

In the dark dim of the shed when Gabriel was away, when he didn't play chess, Darius played another game—with Adalia.

It was a game of subtleties. Of eyes cast down and cheeks stained pink and words that meant more than one thing. It was a game of fingers brushing and sitting closer and glancing up from under her lashes.

Darius was twelve now, but he'd known when he was nine that he was in love with Adalia.

Adalia was fourteen, and she didn't look so much like a little girl anymore, and Darius didn't feel like a little boy, not at all. He was twelve on the night Adalia confessed to him the things her father did behind closed doors. He was twelve when he charged out of the shed with murder in his heart. He was twelve—and he would have killed James Malik in his bed. He was twelve, and Adalia clutched his arm and begged him not to go in, not to do it, not to become a thing she hated. She begged him not to become what her father was.

Little did she know, Darius had already stained his hands in blood. It had started by accident, a little over a year past. He'd been kneeling in a pile of musty logs to reach a particularly fat mushroom when a hush had fallen over the forest, a shadow further darkening the patch of shade. A low voice rumbling words of threat. A scythe slashing at his exposed back. And memories, assaulting Darius in equal measure, past and present colliding until he was certain *this* Reaper had been the one who'd burned his eye out. Until he was spinning, faster than any human boy might've. And he was grasping the scythe and turning it back on the Reaper. Until the blade had pierced the huge man's chest, and warm blood was raining down on Darius. Until he was bathed so thoroughly in it he'd entirely lost the notion of what it'd been like to be clean. And, he rather liked the thrill of it. He'd chased that thrill in the darkest hours of the night. He'd been honing his skills at hunting more than squirrels and rabbits and deer over the years.

Six. That's how many lives he'd already stolen. But the tears spilling down Addy's cheeks were enough to stay his hand. The kiss she brushed on his lips was more than enough.

He was twelve when he tucked Addy's hair behind her ear and kissed her back. When he told her he couldn't stay. He wouldn't be able to stop himself from hurting her father if he did. He was twelve when he hugged Gabriel and promised it wasn't goodbye. It was only 'see you soon.'

He was twelve when he crossed the border into the wilderness and left what little comfort he'd known behind.

8

LET US BE BAD

GABE

PAPA BEAT HIM TWICE the day after Darius left. It seemed like a proper punishment for losing one's best friend. A best friend his father had never discovered and one he would have killed if he had. Gabe knew that, but it didn't make Dare's leaving any less distressing. Gabe didn't cry under the thunder of Papa's fists—he hadn't for the last few years. He only leaned into the voice in his head. *We are not alone. We are not alone. We do not need to be afraid.* The voice chanted, and Gabe echoed. They spoke to one another now. Gabe wished it was Darius he spoke to instead of the voice, but Darius had gone, and the voice had stayed. It had gone quiet in the years his friend had lived in the garden shed. Not so any longer. The moment Darius turned his back, the voice had cranked its volume up.

It blared so loudly now, Gabe sometimes clutched his head and buried it beneath his pillow to block it out. He tried to muffle the siren's song of insanity the voice presented, but no matter what he did, he could not get away from it. You couldn't run from something living in your head.

By the second day, he gave up altogether. The voice rewarded him for it, softening his tone, speaking reassurances. The voice gave excellent advice. It sounded a lot like his father, but this voice was his—it was on *his* side. His partner in crime.

And with each strike of the fist, the voice chanted his father's demise.

Thud.

Soon we will be big enough.

Thud.

Soon we will be strong enough.

Thud.

Soon we will hit him back.

Thud.

Soon we will fight him.

Thud.

*Soon...we will **kill** him.*

At this, Gabe protested, *We cannot kill him. Killing is bad.*

The voice made a sound a lot like a laugh. *Then let us be bad. We cannot afford to be nice, Gabe. No one respects nice.*

It chanted so loudly, Gabe began to believe it.

*No one respects nice. **No one respects nice.** No one respects nice.*

And so, Gabe decided *not* to be nice, most of the time.

PART TWO

A date with destiny—Or was it Hope?

INTERLUDE

He tried not to remember what happened before the box. He tried so hard, in fact, he oftentimes managed to forget. It was the only way to cope. He even forgot while it was happening if he focused hard enough. If he focused hard enough. If he focused hard. If he just *focused*. Focus. Focus. *Focus.*

He tried to do what Darius had always told him. He tried not to let them see it—his fear.

But sometimes he forgot to focus.

And then his nerves would wake up.

And then *he'd* wake up.

He did not know why they kept him awake. He did not know why they let him feel—only that he *did* feel. Every slice of their little triangle knives. Every pair of little pinchers that forced apart his skin. Every plasticky gloved set of fingers running along the arch of his foot. Every stitch of their needles when they sewed him back together again.

Gabe felt it all.

When he accidentally focused the wrong direction, he could feel things he wasn't entirely sure were real. Hands. Thousands of hands. Always hands running over his skin. More hands than possible. Somewhere in the confines of his mind, he knew that. But they *felt* real. And voices. Voices. Voices. More than just his friend. Too many voices. It was then he'd silently scream—when the voices got too loud, when they whispered in his ears what the people in the shiny room were doing to him.

They're cutting off your skin now, Gabe. What a shame. We thought your skin was pretty enough last time.

They're lengthening your bones now, Gabe. You'll be tall enough to fight back soon.

They're sending electrical currents into your muscles now, Gabe.

You cannot see the bright lights today, Gabe. That's because they've plucked out your eyes.

What pretty blue eyes you had, Gabe.

What a pretty patchwork you are.

Gabe, your hair is turning grey.

Are you scared, Gabe? Look, they've made it shine like starlight.

What a pretty boy you are, Gabe.

They're replacing your finger bones today. Ah. You'll like these. Better to play the piano with.

Oh, Gabe. Look what they made you? Do you remember when your hair was yellow? I quite liked yellow.

Oh, Gabe. Do you remember those little dots on the bridge of your nose? Freckles. They've disappeared.

Oh, Gabe. Do you remember your crooked little toe? They've taken that, too.

You are something new, Gabe.

You are perfect.

But Gabe didn't want to be perfect. Gabe just wanted to be *Gabe.* These were the thoughts that spurred him into panic. He didn't want to be the same as everybody else, despite how they teased him for being too small, too *soft.* He'd liked who he'd been. Silent tears rolled from his new eyes, then. And one voice broke through the din. *There, there, Gabe. I'm here.*

You were quiet, Gabe replied.

I had to be quiet. I couldn't interrupt what they were doing. But didn't you remember what I told you?

Gabe did not know what to say.

I told you that you are not alone. Not with me here. And I am always *here, Gabe. Now. Go to the quiet place.* The voice guided him to a deep recess of his mind. As he journeyed in, the walls around him grew tighter and tighter, until he was surrounded on all sides by glowing red that enveloped him in a hug. *Stay here, Gabe, where it is safe. Let me take this burden for you. I will feel it, so you don't have to.*

A phantom stroke of fingers ran down his cheek as the voice withdrew. Gabe curled into a ball in that warm red corner and tried not to remember. He let himself shut down until the next torment would begin, because he knew it was not over yet. He knew he'd have to go into the box next. The salty liquid would choke him until he died. And died. And died.

Only so he could live again.

Sometimes he wished he would not.

9

HE DID NOT THINK ABOUT ADALIA

Darius

Darius didn't think about Adalia.

That's what he told himself as he fused his mouth with Luna's in the shade of the dogwood trees. Luna was shorter than Adalia, and he had to bend in a way that strained his neck to kiss her. Honestly, everything about her was opposite to Addy. Luna had hair nearly as black as his own. She was pretty and soft, like Addy had never been. Her skin was of a shade with his, and it felt like silk beneath his rough fingertips as he gripped her by the backside and sandwiched her more firmly between himself and the tree, so he didn't have to bend over so blasted much. She gasped into his mouth, and he greedily drank down the sound. He pulled back and peered down at her, "Are you sure?"

"Darius, damnit. Just do it already—" She barked, cutting her own words off with a frantic kiss.

It was a yes if he'd ever heard one. So Darius took her up against the tree, pink petals falling into her hair, and he didn't think of Adalia.

He didn't imagine Luna's hair was silver.

He didn't remember Adalia's lips, her hands, her legs straddling him the night he'd turned seventeen. He didn't remember how he'd stopped her. How she'd kissed him, breathed him in like she was drowning in the box and he was oxygen. He didn't remember how he ached for her. He didn't remember that he'd stopped her *because* he was in love with her. He didn't remember that he was *still* in love with her. That she was the image seared on the back of his eyelids—that he seemed to be able to see her there, even with his missing eye.

He didn't think about Adalia.

That's what he told himself.

"What's got you so quiet?" Luna poked him in the chest later as they huddled around a roaring fire.

"Aye, Darius, ye've not been known for being the quiet type." Callum's voice rolled in a deep lilt from across the fire. Callum was a rotund man, in both body and spirit. He wore his strength on his skin, marked in scars and blotches and sun damage that spoke to a life lived hard. Thick brown hair sprouted from his proud brow, a perfect match in shade to his little girl's, who sat tucked between his feet. Greta was scraping figures into the dirt with her stick, her hair sticking up in a cloud of coils around her head.

"Nah, lass, a wee curve on the bottom, like a fishhook. See..." Callum swiped her stick and drew a crude letter *g* into the dirt.

Greta's brow furrowed, and she stuck her tongue out in concentration as she copied the letter. Darius smiled to see it—that childish expression of discovery on her face. Greta was the first child born to their group after the red plague, and she'd come out as though marked in remembrance of it, a bright red print on the side of her creamy little cheek.

Luna elbowed him, drawing his attention back to her question.

"Eh." Darius rubbed at the back of his neck and looked down to hide his blush. "Well, I've been thinkin, it's 'bout time I visited my friends then, isn't it?" He looked up at Callum, who frowned through the flames at him.

"Ah, lad–" Callum spoke, tongue coated with reproach.

Darius cleared his throat and glared. "Last I checked, ya've got no say in what I do, Cal."

Callum showed his palms. "I mean naught by it, lad. I'm worrit about ya, is all."

Luna had gone still at Darius' side. He knew it meant trouble later. He squeezed her knee in an effort to reassure her. It wouldn't work, but he might as well try.

"Listen. It's been two years," Darius explained, "and I made a promise. I won't be breakin' it lightly."

"Nor should ya, lad. Mayhaps, you ought to consider not promising the same this time, eh? Them folks can't be trusted, son." Callum said.

"You don't know 'em."

"Eh, well, that's the truth, then, ain't it?" Callum nodded and went quiet. He needed Darius to keep going back into Bracken, whether or not he'd admit it. And more, Callum knew when he'd seen a lost cause; it was one of the many things Darius admired about him. The man deserved a good deal more respect than Darius afforded him, in truth. If not for Cal, he'd almost certainly have starved to death the winter he'd turned fourteen. Cal had found him shivering in his crude shelter of fallen logs and branches and offered a place at his fire. Darius had been living with the group off and on ever since. Some years, he'd strike out on his own, but more often, he joined Cal's "family" in their nomadic lifestyle in the shadow of the mountains. They were all refugees of the red plague, the disease that'd taken Darius' family from him.

Callum had been able to explain things Darius couldn't have known, young as he was when it'd happened. Few had been spared by the sickness. Those humans who hadn't succumbed had been hunted down by the Reapers and exterminated. Darius had avoided the killings by mere hours. Though perhaps *avoided* was the wrong term, seeing as how the Reapers would have succeeded in killing *him* were it not for Addy and Gabe.

Luna's fingers dug into his forearm, interrupting his speculation. She nudged him until he rose and followed her to the hollow tree they'd been bedding down in together.

He'd known the moment Luna had gone still at the fireside that a reckoning was coming. She had a hot temper. It was one of the things that'd attracted him to her. She could escalate from calm to rage in a matter of seconds. Now, she rounded on him, hands braced on her hips. "This is about her, isn't it?"

"Luna...don't start—"

She held up her hand. "Every damned time, Darius. When are you gonna get over that Ethereal bitch?"

Anger thickened Darius' throat. "Don't." He swallowed, lowering his voice, "Don't call her that."

"That's what she *is!*"

"Luna, this isn't about *her*. This is about *me* keeping my word."

"And just what *is* your word, Darius? That you'll visit?" She scoffed. "Callum is right. They can't be trusted! Let me ask you this—what more do they have to do to our people? Hmmm? What do they have to do for you to believe what's plain to the rest of us?"

"You don't know *them*. They aren't like the others."

"How are they different? Tell me. Convince me. I'm begging you, Darius." Luna stepped into his space, clutching his shirt. He couldn't meet her eyes, couldn't bear the pain he'd put there. Luna's voice softened to a whisper, "How are they anything but complacent? Did they do anything but stand idly by while *our* people were slaughtered in the streets?"

"Yes. They helped *me!*" Darius shook out of her grasp. "They were children. And still, they helped me. They were *children*. Just like us."

Luna was deaf to his argument, shaking her head slowly and turning away. "Do you even care about me?"

"Yes."

"Honestly, Darius..." Her voice was thick in a way he'd never heard it before. "It's been a year since I let you into my bed, and I think the only thing I've ever been to you is a distraction."

Darius took Luna by the elbow and turned her to face him. Tears glistened in her inky eyes. He cupped her cheek. "That's not what you are. I'm so sorry if I made ya think that."

She laid her hand over his. "What else am I going to think? Anytime it starts to feel like this thing between us might be something more, you pull away. You bring up leaving again." The vulnerability fled her face, and she stepped back. "You start planning to leave me for those—those... *creatures!*"

"They're people!"

"They're not, Darius! Not like us! Have you seen the way they move? Before they sent their goons to kill everyone, my brother—who they *also* killed, remember? We... we would watch them through the fence at their school. They're *not* like us. Those kids couldn't even *play* without shattering their toys."

Luna sounded more than a little insane. Darius threw his hands up. "What even is this? How can you not understand? Those kids went through things you can't even imagine—"

"Don't you *dare* start that." She sliced the air in emphasis. "You don't know what *I* went through."

"I *do* know what ya went through, Luna. It's you who doesn't know—"

"What *did* happen, Darius!? You don't bother to tell me."

"I don't wanna talk about it—"

"I'm sure you've told her about it, though, right?"

Darius sighed and pushed his thumb into the wrinkle between his brows. "I haven't seen her in *two years*. And it's not just her."

"Oh, that's right—your *friend*—the heir apparent to the man who ordered the slaughter of *our* families... Why was it?" She tapped her chin as if pondering. "Oh, that's right! Because they got sick."

"I wouldn't expect you to understand... I *don't* expect you to understand. But I won't break my word."

"No. You won't. Not for me, anyway. But you would for her, wouldn't you?"

Darius didn't have anything to say to that. He'd sell his soul to Satan for Adalia.

The tears were back in Luna's eyes. "When do *I* matter?"

"You do matter."

"Just not enough." She dashed tears away with the back of her hand. "Just not as much as them?"

Darius didn't say anything.

"They're *not* like us. I don't think they ever were... I won't do this anymore, Darius. I can't be second."

"You're not second..."

"No. I'm not, am I? I'm not second. That's her brother, right? Your *friend*?" Luna further widened the gap between them. Darius didn't stop her. "I'm done. I want to make a future with someone who actually wants me."

"I do want you," Darius said, but even as he did, it sounded flat and wrong.

"Not enough." She bent to pick up Darius' pack and bedroll, thrusting them into his limp arms.

"Go, Darius. Go back to your *real* family. I hope it lasts this time, though I doubt it. You always come crawling back to us, don't you? But when you do, know you're no longer welcome in my bed."

A small—very small—part of him wanted to argue with Luna, but he couldn't, he didn't. She was right. He didn't want her. Not like he wanted Adalia. He'd never want anyone like he wanted Adalia. He'd never want anyone as much as the one person he couldn't have.

Luna was right about another thing, too. He *should* stay away. He *shouldn't* keep appearing in Gabe and Addy's life. But he couldn't seem to stop himself. And every time he visited, they made him promise to return. Even after he'd turned Addy away that time, she'd made him swear to come back. So he *would*. He would keep crawling back to Adalia, even if he couldn't have her. Even if they were terrible for each other. Even if he knew his obsession with her was fundamentally wrong. He couldn't stop.

He put on his pack and left.

He didn't look back.

10

SINK OR SWIM

HE HAD A DATE.

He had a date. *Him*. Gabe Malik. With a *woman*... and he *wanted* to go. It was an anomaly that hadn't transpired since a dreadful night four years past, when he'd *thought* he'd been meeting a girl and had instead burst naked into a sauna full of his male classmates. They'd snapped some photos and proceeded to beat him bloody. They'd left off fairly quickly when Gabe had failed to cry out. Obviously, they had expected a more moving performance. They didn't know beatings were as familiar to Gabe as his own face in the mirror. It was the humiliation of being fooled into believing somebody *wanted* him that'd lingered.

The photos that circulated in the aftermath had been less than ideal. But, they'd had much the opposite effect from what his tormentors had intended. He'd become unexpectedly popular with the girls. He'd been asked out every week since the incriminating photos had spread around the dwindling population of the secondary school campus on the hill. He'd said no. Every. Time.

Those girls weren't actually interested in him, in who he *was*. He wanted someone who wanted *him*. Someone to share his love of music, and history, and all things intellectual. He wanted someone who pushed him, who made him better, who quieted the voices.

And this woman? She might be it. He'd met Hope last month at a Heritage event in the city.

Gabe didn't know when they'd grown so fond of labeling everything, but his father had been incorrigible ever since the title had been thrust upon their family. *"Heritage Ethereals."* Blech. They could've at least come up with something less pompous.

He supposed they did need to differentiate, though. The things they'd been growing in research facilities were certainly unlike him, though they looked eerily similar. It seemed criminal they hadn't had to earn their silver hair. Perhaps his father was onto something—perhaps he should be proud to be a "Heritage."

Gabe shrugged away the thought. He hated when Father was right. It happened infuriatingly often.

He turned back to the matter at hand: how to respond to Hope's message. Hope, that woman who'd worn blue velvet to the ball, the one he'd stumbled into in the stairwell, spilling a ridiculously full cup of tequila down the front of her gown. The girl whom he'd then quite unintentionally groped as he tried to sop up the booze with his tie. The girl who'd laughed and told him he was adorable and proceeded to sit beside him on the balcony until the sky washed light gray with impending sunrise. Hope, who'd abandoned the ball to spend the night mapping stars alone with him. Hope.

Who'd just sent him the most terrifying message of his life.

Hope:

Hi

Gabe:

Hi back.

So… I've been thinking about you?

....

tell me more

I wanna see you again.

Oh, thank god. I thought you were thinking about the tequila again.

Well, now that you mention it…

Noooo

It was cute.

…

....

My dad has to go to Bracken next week….

Wait– you're coming HERE!?

YES! So….what is there to do around there?

Ha. Mostly nothing. I guess we could go to the river?

Um, YES! Let's go swimming

It was at that moment he realized what an utter idiot he was. What had possessed him to suggest going to the river? He supposed he'd thought they might have a picnic or watch the birds. Or maybe he could play the song he'd been composing for her on his guitar. But swimming? It was the logical conclusion for her to have made, of course. It was midsummer and hot as hell. The problem was... he didn't know *how* to swim. He'd never been able to force himself beneath the surface to learn. Going under water reminded him of things he'd rather forget. It's not like he could tell that to Hope, though, so he took a deep breath and replied.

Sounds perfect. See you next week.

He'd just sent the unfortunate message when something smacked into the window above his desk. Three more little *pings* sounded as a series of pebbles struck the glass. Gabe leapt out of his chair and sprinted across the room, flinging the window wide. A fourth pebble hit him directly between the eyes, but that didn't keep him from grinning.

Darius was perched in the tree adjacent to his window with an obscenely huge smile plastered across his rugged face. The bastard was bigger than ever, with muscles straining at the fabric of a coarse brown tunic, his legs dangling from the branch he straddled like they were their own accursed tree trunks. He'd taken to wearing a leather patch over the missing eye, and it made the jerk stupidly more good-looking. All mysterious and whatnot.

"Get out of that tree before you break your damned neck," Gabe called.

"So, your Pa's not home then?" Darius crowed back.

"No, and he won't be for a few days. Don't make me come out there, Dare. I haven't climbed a tree since you were here last—"

"Something we'll have to remedy immediately," Darius said, swinging down from the tree like some primate who'd resided all its life amongst the leaves.

"I'm coming down!" Gabe sprinted downstairs, out through the double doors to the lawn, and launched himself unceremoniously at Darius, who crushed him in a fierce hug.

Then they were laughing, muttering unintelligible sentences as they slapped one another on the back. Finally, Gabe pulled back, holding his friend at arm's length. "You, my good sir, smell like shit."

Darius roared a laugh. "I shouldn't expect any different. Been out with naught more than the odd creek to warsh in for the last two weeks."

"You've got an accent, too, ya bastard." Gabe mimicked, slugging his friend in the arm.

"I do not." Darius slugged him back.

Gabe pretended it didn't hurt. "You do. You're talking like all your words are running together."

"Damned Callum," Darius muttered. "Enough 'bout me. You're HUGE!"

Gabe waved him off.

"No, honest." Darius ran a hand in line from his forehead to Gabe's. "You're as tall as me! What have ya been eating, man?"

"Ah. I see. The reason for your visit reveals itself at last. Come along then, Darius. Let's get you fed and then you're telling me what the hell you've gotten up to the last two years, which is far too long between visits, by the way. But first, shower. "

"Oh, there's plenty to tell... and I suspect you've got a lot to say, too. Is... is Addy here?"

There were few things that could make Darius blush. Addy was one of them. Gabe rolled his eyes. "Of course she is. But you're talking to *me* first."

"I wouldn't think different." Darius swallowed in a way that made Gabe pity the fool.

He decided to put Darius out of his misery. "She'll be home for dinner." His friend's shoulder sagged in relief. "Come on, Dare. You can't flirt with my sister until I beat you in at least one game of chess."

Darius sputtered, a flush creeping up the back of his neck.

Gabe noted the change and grinned. "I don't know why you keep torturing yourself. She'd say yes, you know?" He clapped Darius on the back and led the way inside.

Dinner the night before, sat between Darius and Adalia at the table, had been painfully awkward. So awkward that Gabe had slugged back more than a few shots of his father's whiskey to chase the lingering discomfort the silence had produced. It'd been silent externally, anyway.

The voice in Gabe's head had run an excruciatingly loud commentary for the duration of dinner. It hadn't quieted until he'd become dizzy with drink. Gabe had stumbled door to door, checking on Darius in the guest bedroom, then Addy a few doors down. Finally he slogged through his own bedroom door, where he landed with a woozy flop on his bed. He didn't remember drifting off, but when he woke, his mind was mercifully quiet.

He quickly dressed, tiptoeing past the room where Darius still slept, his snores resonating through the door. A smile played on his lips at the sound. The world always felt a little more right when Darius was home.

When he entered the kitchen, he found his sister waiting, nudging a loaf of bread around the counter in impatience. Eggs, butter, and a tall carafe of orange juice waited aside the bread. Addy smirked up at him, "Toad in the hole, right?"

"And peanut butter pancakes, of course." Gabe brushed past her, snagging a pan and spatula.

"How could I have forgotten?" She peeked at him out of the corner of her eye, a flush creeping its way across her high cheekbones. "I'm sorry about dinner."

Gabe shrugged, setting the butter to melt in the pan. "I don't know what you're talking about."

"Ugh. You always make me come out and say it, don't you?" Addy jabbed the glass she was using to cut holes in the center of the bread down a little too hard, causing it to crack around the base. She sighed and tossed it, and the offending bread into the garbage, and started over on the next slice.

It was a rare treat to see Addy so entirely flustered. Gabe couldn't help but chuckle. "Always." He held out a hand for one of the holey slices of bread.

She slapped it into his palm with a huff. "Things are... they're weird between Dare and I."

"Like that's news–"

She chucked the bread circle at the side of his face.

He caught it before it could hit. "You aren't fooling anyone—least of all *me*, Ads. Things have been 'weird' between you two for years."

She groaned, leaning her elbows on the counter and burying her face in her hands. Her voice came out muffled between her fingers. "I know. I just—"

"Why don't you quit tip-toeing around one another and get together already?" Gabe interrupted, cracking an egg in the center of the hollowed-out bread where it was toasting in the pan. He didn't look at Addy, but he knew her well enough to imagine what she was doing. She was scrunching her fingers in her hair and gnawing her lip and generally agonizing over there.

She reached past him to sprinkle salt and pepper on the egg. "It's not so simple as that— and you know it."

"I don't see why it can't be. Why can't you keep it secret? I've always thought secret affairs were terribly romantic." He shrugged and flipped the toad in the hole onto its waiting plate, then began the process anew.

"Shall I explain it to you like you're five?"

"Please do." He glanced her direction to find her face cast in a shadow he couldn't quite interpret. Turning to her fully, he repeated, more seriously, "Please do."

Addy ran her fingers through her hair before meeting his eyes and speaking. "Times are changing, Gabe. The houses are empty. How long before we're the only ones left in Bracken? How long before they call us to the cities, too?"

"They won't. Father says operations are actually expanding here. We're only making room for new families. You'll see."

"Even then, I'm not allowed to choose who I want to be with... not like you. He... Darius... would never be an option. Even if I kept him secret... He's *human*. And after what happened with mother... I... nothing feels certain anymore."

That sobered whatever lightness had remained in the room. Gabe put down the spatula and took both of Addy's hands in his. "There's nothing you could've done."

Tears welled in her eyes. "I know."

"I'm sorry," he swallowed. "I did try, Ads. But don't you think she's happier there? Away from Father?"

Father had enrolled Mother into a 'therapeutic' housing establishment over the winter. They knew it wasn't so pleasant as that, though. Their mother was locked up in some facility in Rittenmore City, hundreds of miles away from their forestside home, away from everything and everyone familiar. Gabe knew it was because Father had grown tired of her challenging him. A better son might've fought harder for her to stay, but he'd seen it: the flash of relief in her eyes when she learned she was getting away from Father.

"Why are you always right?" Addy interrupted his musings.

"There's my doting sister."

She stuck her tongue out at him in response. Gabe mirrored the action, but her face didn't maintain its teasing gesture for long. She quickly returned to solemnity. "Gabe… I've been hearing things… How long before they send me away, too? They took the Pentra girl last week."

"That's not gonna happen. Father's too proud. And I won't let him—"

"I won't let you put yourself between us again, Gabe. Remember what happened last time—"

Darius burst into the kitchen then, black hair plastered messily to his cheeks. "What's burning?" He boomed.

"Damn it all to hell!" Gabe turned back to the charred remains of toad in the hole and sighed. He clicked the burner off and shrugged. "Well, we successfully made *you* some breakfast anyway." He pointed to the rather droopy-looking meal where it'd gone cold on the counter.

Darius chuckled low and elbowed Gabe aside. "Scoot over, before you burn down your father's palace. Let a more capable cook handle this." He winked at Addy, and she turned a shade of tomato that had Gabe biting his lip to muffle a laugh. He moved aside, allowing Darius full access to the kitchen.

It was a few minutes later, perched on the kitchen stool with a glass of juice, that Gabe rubbed at the raised bit of flesh on his neck. He *did* remember what had happened last time he'd gotten between his father and sister—how Father had jabbed the bottle opener into his neck. He didn't care. He'd die before he let Father lay another hand on his sister.

She deserved to be happy.

And perhaps it was time he removed the obstacle standing in the way of that.

Yes, crooned the voice for the first time all morning. *Yes, Gabe. It is time to do what we've dreamt these many years.*

No. He shook his head to silence the voice. It didn't work.

YES. Yes. YES. YES. YES. YES. KILL HIM. KILL HIM. KILL HIM.

Shut up! Gabe internally screamed.

*NEVER. I will never quiet. I will never leave you. I promised. I won't quiet until the task is completed. KILL THE WRETCH. KILL HIM. KILL HIM. KILL HIM. We are better without him. Better. Better. Better. Better than the others. Better than her. Better than **him**. Kill him. KILL HIM—*

"NO!" Gabe roared, sending the stool toppling as he stood.

Across from him, Addy spilled her orange juice, mouth agape at his outburst. A blob of butter plopped into the pan off the end of the knife Darius was holding. Darius showed Gabe his free palm. "Alright, alright." He spoke softly, "Sit down, man. I didn't really want coffee, either."

Gabe righted the stool, unable to look at the others. "I'm sorry… I just. Sorry."

"Don't worry about it," Darius said.

It would've been more convincing if he didn't sound so worried himself.

11
ADOLESCENT ANOMALIES

DARIUS

THE WATER LOOKED PEACEFUL, casting fractals of kaleidoscopic color onto the banks of the river. Darius itched to leap in, to submerge himself in the cold flow that woke him as so few things did. But he couldn't. Not with Gabe standing beside him, eyeing the water skeptically in the morning light. Gabe had admitted, quite bashfully the night before, that he was meeting a woman at the river... and that he didn't know how to swim. Both of these things conjured a smile at the center of Darius' chest. Good for Gabe. He'd always struggled to build relationships. This would be good for him on a number of accounts. Darius elbowed his friend in the ribs in an attempt to erase the look of terror from his face. "The fact ya can't swim is a mother fucking travesty." Darius ribbed.

The horror fled Gabe's face as he took Darius' bait, relief uncreasing the corners of his eyes.

"Did we learn a new word, Darius?" he smirked, "Your ever-expanding vocabulary never ceases to impress."

"I did indeed, ya prick." Darius retorted, stepping to the edge of the river, "Now get your posh arse over here."

It took several attempts, but finally, Darius convinced Gabe to enter the water. They'd gone waist-deep when Gabe turned tail and ran for the shore.

Darius threw his hands up, "God damnit, Gabe. *What* is this about?"

"I can't do this."

"You can do this. You will do this."

"I can't, Dare. I *can't.*"

"Gabe, you gotta give me somethin'. This can't possibly be about swimming. You'll be able to do that, and there's little risk of injury to someone like you, even if you can't. Help me understand."

Gabe tore his fingers through his hair, banging the flat of his hand against his forehead.

"Hey!" Darius launched himself out of the water and gripped Gabe's wrists, pinning them at his sides. "Don't do that. What are you doing?"

"I don't know," Gabe murmured, looking anywhere but at Darius.

"Are you gonna hurt yourself if I let you go now?" Darius asked, gentling his tone.

Gabe shook his head.

"Okay, I'm letting go now, Gabe, and then we're gonna go sit over there in the shade." He nodded at a willow growing a good distance from the riverbank.

Gabe nodded again.

Darius gave his wrists a light squeeze before he released them, stepping back to allow his friend to lead the way.

Once sat, Gabe buried his face in his hands. Darius cast about for words, coming up empty. He didn't have the slightest idea how to handle someone so clearly on the verge of... *something*. Something Darius couldn't understand. The silence stretched, underlain with a nameless tension. Finally, Darius spoke. "Y'know, if it's as bad as all that, you don't have to take this woman to the river. Go somewhere else. I'll help ya choose the place. I know some good spots in the woods."

The quiet stretched for another long moment before Gabe sighed and lifted his head. "No. I need to do this, Dare. I need to face it." He finally met Darius' eye, whispering his next words as if they were simply too dangerous to be spoken aloud. "It reminds me of the box."

"What does?"

"The water, or, more specifically, going under water."

That truth hung heavy before Darius replied. "I didn't realize... I didn't realize it'd affected you so..." he trailed off, incapable of forming the words.

"Yeah." Gabe shrugged, "I think you forget sometimes... how often I went in the box... for how many years. I know you've always felt different about it—"

"I'm sorry."

"It's not you who should be sorry."

Darius busied himself by drawing a sparrow in the sand with a stick while he thought up what to say to that. Finally, he settled on, "It's a terrible thing, what your parents did... but would you change it? Would you choose to be human? I can tell ya it's not so great a thing, living with the knowledge that you'll die someday, whether or not you're ready..." The sadness in his friend's eyes hurt somewhere in the vicinity of Darius' soul.

Gabe swallowed thickly and spoke, "I don't know. I just know that I wouldn't choose to be what I... what I *am*."

"What you are, my friend, is *good*." Darius squeezed Gabe's knee. "You have always been good—too good of a friend for my sorry arse, too good for this wretched world. And don't you insult me by thinkin' any different."

Gabe smiled, but there wasn't a shred of joy in it. "I wish it were true. I am not good... I'm *not*. I'm broken and I don't know how to fix it."

Darius shook his head.

Gabe opened his mouth like he wanted to say something more, but before any sound could come out, his jaw snapped shut, and then he was pressing his palms to his ears. It lasted only a moment before Gabe tore his hands away and rose. "No," he turned his back on Darius, "I'm not good—not all of me, anyway... but I'd like to be better." He shivered, then looked over his shoulder at Darius with a smile plastered onto his handsome face. "I'd like to get better, and that is why I am *going* to learn how to swim. Now, are you going to teach me, or should I get my sister?"

A flush crept across Darius' cheeks at the mention of Addy. He shoved to his feet and stalked away from Gabe to hide it. "I wouldn't dream of letting your sister do this. Now, let's try again, and this time, I won't let you forget that you're here with me, that this is not the box."

They nodded at one another and went in.

12

OUR LESSER HALF

GABE

HE COULDN'T DO THIS.

He couldn't do this.

He couldn't *do* this.

What was he thinking? Trying to meet a woman? *Hope.*

He couldn't do this. He couldn't shove down the fear and get into the water. Maybe if Darius were here. He should have invited Darius and Addy along. They would know what to do. They'd be able to distract Hope if he started to fall apart. Oh, God. What had he been *thinking!?*

Hush. The voice was gentle in a way it'd not often been, not since Gabe had grown up, anyway. *It will be alright. Let me* help *you.*

I can't, Gabe replied.

Oh, you can. You can do anything. And I promise I *won't do anything* **you** *don't want, Gabe.*

No. No... I—

Are you going to get in? Will you get in the river, or will you let it reveal you as a coward? In front of her?

Gabe wanted to tell the voice in his head he was *not* a coward—he *would* get in—he *would* swim with Hope. But he couldn't. No. Every time he looked at the water, bile coated his throat. A too-familiar feeling resurfaced. Drowning. Suffocation. The struggle to take in air in a repetitive cycle, but his lungs never expanding with it. Drowning. Over and over and over again. But never dying.

No. Gabe couldn't do it.

So he turned inward. *You promise not to do anything I don't want?*

I promise.

Gabe relinquished control.

A shiver scuttled down his spine, his skin suddenly feeling too tight, his muscles too weak, his stature too short. He shrank, until it seemed he was peering out through eyes that were not his own but belonged to a different being entirely. One who saw in black and white, the world a tableau of what he could *take* and what wasn't worth bothering with at all. Gabe shrank, until he was so small, so quiet, that *he'd* become the voice—only he was meeker than the one that had inhabited his mind these long years. Gabe didn't think it could hear *him* at all.

Gabe came awake to the slap of Hope's hand across his cheek. When his vision cleared, he found her scrabbling away from him in the mud of the riverbank. His knees sank into the dirt, alongside his spirits.

"How dare you!" There were tears in Hope's eyes.

Gabe looked around, confounded, praying he'd find the answers somewhere other than in the stark evidence which presented itself in Hope's flustered appearance. He wiped his dirty fingers on his shorts as he rose to his feet, slowly, so he didn't spook her. She flinched with every move he made.

"I–I–I'm so sorry," he stuttered. "I don't know what happened."

"Are you kidding me?" Hope swiped up the picnic blanket and clutched it to her chest, backing away. "I'm leaving."

"No—please, don't go—" Gabe reached for her, and she jumped back. He dropped his hand. "I'll... I'll take you somewhere else. It'll be better. I'm just... I'm not comfortable with the river."

"You seemed pretty 'comfortable' just now."

"What? W—What did I do?"

"What did you *do?*" She croaked. "You're gonna act like you have no idea what just happened?" Her fingers shook as she gripped the blanket tighter to her chest. "I'm leaving. And NO, Gabe. I don't wanna go anywhere else with you. I don't ever want to see you again." One of the tears brimmed out of her eye as she turned her back on him and ran, abandoning everything but the picnic blanket and her mussed swimsuit.

Gabe followed a few steps before skidding to an abrupt halt. She didn't want him to follow her. So he wouldn't. He ran his fingers through his hair, scrunching and pulling. *What did I do? What did I do? What did I do!?* He sank down and put his head between his knees to combat the spots swimming in his vision. His breath came in tiny pants that reminded him of drowning all over again.

I didn't do anything you *didn't want to do...* The voice purred from the recess of his mind, tone coated with some strange spiral of arousal.

Gabe banged the flat of his hand into his forehead as if he could will the *thing* out by force. *What did **you** do?* Gabe begged of it, more terrified than he'd ever been.

*It's not what I did... It's what **we** did. Didn't you like it, Gabe? Didn't you like the way she struggled? The way her fingernails bit into our chest?*

Gabe looked down to find a series of bloody fingernail crescents on his pecs.

Didn't you like the way her legs fell open, so pretty for us...?

Gabe crawled to the bushes and retched, bringing up the cucumber sandwiches and iced tea he'd shared with Hope. *WHAT DID YOU DO?* He begged of the voice.

A barrage of images assaulted Gabe's senses: images of *his* hands, *his* mouth, *his* legs. All of the parts of him working to push Hope down into the dirt, to keep her trapped beneath him. But *he* hadn't been there—that wasn't *him.* That couldn't be him. That was this *thing*!

I wouldn't do that. I would never—

Oh, but you did, the voice whispered, *And you* wanted *to.*

Oh God. Oh God. *Hope.*

Don't be such a pussy, Gabe. She might've said no, but her body said yes. You must learn to interpret these things. Who wouldn't want **us?** *Besides, you came back before anything could really happen, anyway.*

Gabe's heart lurched. *We didn't—*

No. The voice sounded tremendously disappointed. *We'd barely even gotten her tits out before you so rudely interrupted. You ruined it.*

Gabe didn't feel relieved. He'd–*They'd*– done something unforgivable. *This isn't what we agreed to.*

Oh, Gabe. You idiot. Of course it's what we agreed to. You gave me *control. I quite liked it. I think I'd like to do it again sometime.*

No. Never. Never again. Go away. I don't want you anymore. You've ruined everything, don't you see?

Ohhh, poor little Gabe. I cannot go away.

Gabe curled into a ball on the sand and rocked, trying to tear the hair out of his scalp, to peel away the layers. If he could only see inside, perhaps he might be able to locate the source of that horrible voice—that creature who'd done something he never would have. *WHAT ARE YOU?!* He screamed at the voice.

It gleefully replied, *I am Gabriel.*

You are not **me.**

I never said I was. I'm Gabriel, and you're Gabe. And you, my darling, will always be... our lesser half.

13

A Broken Toy

"It's been six hours, Darius. He should be home." Addy had nearly paced a trail into the plush carpet of the game room over the last hour. In truth, Darius hadn't even noticed the hours passing them by. Not when he had Addy all to himself. Not when she'd pretended she didn't know how to play billiards, allowing him to curl his body around hers under the guise of teaching her to aim. He didn't need to teach her anything. Addy was more coordinated than him by a long shot. This was just more of the same game they'd been playing with one another since they were children—the one where unsaid words hung so heavy in the air Darius feared he might choke on them. Darius swallowed down a breath of bitterness at the mention of Gabe. It always came back to this. Any time he might have with Adalia was stolen away by their mutual worry for her brother.

"Like I said the last three times, this could be a good thing, Ads. He *needs* normalcy. Stop pacin'. He's not a little boy no more." Darius motioned for her to join him on the sofa.

She didn't.

Instead, she turned a smoldering green glare his way and spat, "Don't you *dare* tell me to calm down. You don't... you don't know what it's been like here. He's *not* okay. And he's all I have left!"

Her words stung. Darius didn't want Gabe to be all she had. *He* wanted to count, too.

"Addy. I'm sorry." Darius gulped down a steadying breath, "I did notice...somethin's different. What aren't ya telling me?"

She finally relented with her pacing and joined him on the sofa. Tearing her fingers through her hair, she said, "There is something going on with Gabe. I can't... I can't really explain it, but to say that he's not himself—not all the time, anyway."

"Like what happened in the kitchen the other day?"

"Yes. But it's more than that. He's... he's unstable, Dare. We'll just be sitting there and then he's ripping at his hair and murmuring... like... like he's carrying on an entire conversation, only there's no one there."

The truth sat like a rock in his belly. "Somethin' like that happened at the river the other day..."

Addy sat up stock straight, "Why didn't you tell me?"

"I didn't think much of it. Gabe, well, ya know he's been through a lot... He was scared. I didn't worry much past that. We talked it out, and then he was fine."

"Oh, Darius," Addy shook her head in defeat. "You idiot. He was *not* alright. I've been watching him these months. And as soon as he notices, he turns it off, like flipping a switch."

"I didn't know."

"How could you have known? You haven't been around."

Darius loathed the accusation in her tone. He stood and began treading in the tracks she'd left on the carpet, pinching at the bridge of his nose to compose himself. Why couldn't he do anything right by the women in his life? "I'm sorry for that, too. Truth is, I thought I might not come back this time." Hurt flashed in Addy's eyes. Darius knelt before her and took her hands in his. Her skin felt like silk on his textured palms. "I *wanted* to come back. I never want to leave your side. But what I want doesn't matter—"

"It matters to me—"

"Addy," he chastised, "it *doesn't*. It doesn't matter that I can't breathe when I look at you. It doesn't matter that I'd rather die a thousand deaths than go a moment without ya by my side. It doesn't matter that I've loved you from the moment I saw you. That I knew you were *it* for me, before I even knew myself. It doesn't matter. It doesn't matter that your laugh gives me life, that I'd sell all the stars in the heavens to see you smile—"

She pulled a hand from his grasp and pressed a finger to his lips to quiet him. "Stop," she whispered, "It is not about you and me right now."

Darius caught her hand. "Aye. It's not. That's what I was tryin to say, Adalia. It can never be about *you* and *me*. That's why I tried... I tried to love someone else."

A noise which sounded very much like a growl rolled from Addy's throat at those words.

Darius ignored it and continued, "I tried. I couldn't. I'll never be able to. And that's another reason I should stay away. I *cannot* have you! It *doesn't* matter what *I* want. It doesn't even matter what *you* want. Wanting me back would be the greatest mistake of your life. We don't get to choose. Not in this world. You and me... we were never an option."

It was quiet for a minute that felt so much longer than it had any right to. Then, Addy broke the silence, "We will talk about this later. We will talk about just how to do it—"

"To do what?"

"To make a new world, of course."

Darius' breath caught in his throat as he met her gaze. He'd just laid his heart out at her feet with too many words, and she'd just... just... He thought she might've just told him she felt the same. But of course, she'd do it in a way that had him agonizing over it for the rest of his life. Because, no matter how they felt, Darius knew the truth. They could not be together. He was a ghost. And Addy... Addy may as well have been an angel, so far above him was she. So far out of his reach. He didn't know how to steal her from heaven itself.

She disentangled their hands once more, only to run her fingers over the planes of his face until she cupped his jaw. "Later," she said. "Now, please help me, Darius. Help me help my brother. I hope he's having the time of his life on his date, but something tells me it's gone horribly wrong. Will you help me find him?"

Darius gulped and found his voice, "Yes. Anything, Addy."

She nodded. Darius rose, pulling her up with him. He didn't let go of her hand.

It was full dark by the time they'd ventured down the narrow, rocky path to the bend in the river. Only the moon, casting reflections on the current, provided the light with which to navigate. Darius kept Addy's hand clutched in his the whole way, wishing for a moment they were only on a stroll in the moonlight.

As the beach came into full view, he wished harder still, for it was obvious something was amiss. Evidence of a picnic was strewn about the sand. Something snarled in the shadows, rummaging through the basket. Something small and furry and very much not Gabe. Addy shrieked and pressed herself under his arm as a fat raccoon turned and hissed at them. Darius couldn't help but chuckle, squeezing her shoulder. "Yer right to fear. Those beasts are a plague. Darn cute, but a plague all the same. Reminds me of someone else I know." He tucked her more securely under his arm to punctuate the sentiment.

Addy, not liking being compared to a fat little trash-eating critter, elbowed him sharply in the ribs and stepped away.

"Gabe!" She called into the stillness left in the wake of scurrying paws.

Fear clawed its way up Darius' throat as his friend failed to reply.

"Gabe Malik," Darius' voice joined Addy's, "Stop playin' and come out."

Water over stone. No soft laugh. No groan of pain. No tall form stepping from the shadows to greet them. Only water over stone. Only the harsh sound of Addy's breath coming in frantic gasps. Darius took her hand and rubbed along the back of it with his thumb. "We'll find him." She glanced up at him with tears brimming. One broke free and trailed down her cheek. Darius wiped it off and turned away from the pain on her face. He'd done that. Caused that. If he'd listened to her earlier...

"Gabe," he boomed. "Whatever has happened, we'll fix it, brother. Come out!"

Nothing.

"Gabe, I'm here." Addy spoke quietly, but Darius knew any Ethereal nearby could hear. *He* would have heard, even if he were across the river.

Addy continued, "It's over, Gabe, and I'm here. Just like I said I'd be. Come out. It's Adalia and Darius. You are safe."

Darius glanced at her with alarm because those words... they sounded rehearsed. How many times had she spoken to Gabe like this? How long had this been going on? Guilt clawed at Darius' stomach.

"We should split up." Addy stepped out of his grasp.

Darius pulled her back to his side and shook his head. "Together."

She nodded.

"Together," he repeated. "Anything we find. Whatever happens. Together."

When she'd squeezed his arm in confirmation, Darius opened his senses fully. An impossible rush of scent and sound and smell greeted him. He took in a deep breath, hoping to lock onto the faint scent of nutmeg that clung to his friend, but he only smelled river water and discarded orange peels. That gave him the sinking suspicion that *if* Gabe was here, he had to be in the water. The utter quiet did not bode well for what that meant.

"Come." He tugged Addy to the river's edge. "I think he may have gone in." He nodded to the water. "And if he did, he'll be downstream." Nausea threatened to overwhelm Darius as he considered that. He knew this part of the river well, and though the water was calm in the swimming cove before them, if one ventured deeper, a swift current ran beneath the surface. As the current picked up momentum further downstream, there was a series of shallow, rocky rapids where debris frequently became trapped. Darius knew. He already knew that's where they'd find Gabe.

"I'm scared, Dare," Addy said, her voice cracking.

"Aye, me too."

They picked along the riverside, eyes locked on the rushing water, hunting the telling glint of silver hair. Nearly a half mile from the picnic site, Addy's scream alerted she'd found it.

"Oh my God. Oh God. Gabe!" she cried, breaking from Darius and darting around a bend of jagged rock. Darius followed on her heels, gulping down his horror as he rounded the rockface—for there, bobbing in the rapids of the shallow section of the river, was Gabe. Adalia was doing her best to pick a path to him through the rushing water, her thin sandals sliding on the slick surface of the rocks. Darius pulled her back, setting her on the muddy bank. "Stay here, Ads." He choked around a mouthful of tears. "I'll get him." *Idiot. Idiot. Idiot.* He'd been so selfish, so desperate for more time with Addy. If they'd come sooner...

His feet did not fail him as he found a path along the rocks to Gabe's body. His friend was facedown in the current, deathly pale, body covered in scratches and bruises. Silver hair floated in a halo around his head. Darius grasped Gabe's battered shoulders and pulled, attempting to dislodge his torso from where it'd caught between boulders. Darius screamed as he failed to come free. Tears nearly blinded his eye as he turned his attention to the rock instead, leaving Gabe to bob with water in his lungs. "It'll just be another minute, Gabe." Darius grunted as he threw his strength into the boulder. It groaned under his efforts. "It'll just be a minute, and I'll have ya out. I'm sorry. I'm sorry. I'm sorry." *I'm sorry. I'm sorry. I'm sorry.* The words pinged about his skull as he pushed and pushed and pushed, until finally, the stone tore free. Gabe's body followed in its thunderous wake as water rushed to fill the gap left where the boulder had been.

Throwing himself flat and hooking a knee around a waterlogged tree, Darius caught hold of Gabe's limp arm before he could topple after the rock. "I'm sorry. I'm sorry." Darius whispered as he dragged his friend toward him, further tearing skin as it skidded across the remaining stones. Finally, he pulled Gabe flush with his own body and sat up in the spray. He didn't look at his friend, only rocked his body and whispered those same words, *I'm sorry. I'm sorry. I'm sorry.*

"Darius!" Addy's cry broke through his haze. "Darius—*please!*"

"I'm coming." He hoisted Gabe over his shoulder, sliding and falling, ripping his own knees open as he struggled back to shore under his friend's considerable weight. Addy was at his side then, tearing Gabe from his arms and laying him flat on his back upon the muddy bank. Darius joined her where she knelt beside his body. They took in Gabe's mutilated form in mute horror.

"How could this have happen—" Addy whispered, words catching on her sobs.

"He was scared of the water. I didn't do enough." Darius forced his hands into his hair, wanting to rip it all out, wanting desperately to scream until his throat tore.

"Get him, Darius. We have to go."

"Addy—"

He was cut off by her sharp inhale of breath, her palm slapping over her mouth in an effort to keep the horror in before the words, "Oh, no. no. no. *no*," leaked free behind her hand. She lifted Gabe's arm, tilting it slowly to reveal the underside of his wrist. There, poorly hidden amongst the other bruises and cuts, were deep gouges in the skin. It looked as though someone had tried to claw the veins out of his arms with their fingernails. Indeed, along the underside of Gabe's pale fingernails blood caked, despite the considerable time he must have been in the water. There it was. Stark evidence he'd... he'd done this to himself.

"Oh God." Addy pressed her face into Darius' chest.

He cupped the back of her head with one palm, running the other along his friend's ruined wrist. No pulse greeted him. He pulled Addy more firmly to him and held her for long minutes, finally resting a hand on Gabe's chest in goodbye. A faint *thump. thump...thump* stuttered under his palm. Impossible. But no, it was there. There and then gone again. *There.* "He's not gone! He's not gone."

"What?"

"He has a pulse."

Addy tore away from him, shoving her fingers into the crook of Gabe's cold neck. She waited for a long second, then jumped to her feet. "Get him, Darius. Now!"

He did as she said, and then they were running, running, *running.* Faster than he'd ever gone before, faster than the wind, faster than fate, they ran. Until they stood outside a facility with dark glass windows.

Inside, they'd find the box. It could fix this, fix his friend, but Darius found himself pausing on the threshold. Addy stood waiting, holding the door wide.

"Dare, come on." She tugged at his sodden shirt.

He met her panicked gaze. "Is this right?"

"What arc you talking about? Of course it is. We're saving him."

Darius cleared his throat and glanced at his friend's ruined face. "I don't think he'd want to be saved, Ads."

"Darius, so help me God, if you do not do this, I will never forgive you."

"I... I'm just thinkin... What happened? What made him do this? And would he want to come back, ya know? He tried to *end* it, Addy. Isn't it wrong? To deny his wish?"

"No. No, it is not. Something is *wrong*. He was not himself. If you do not carry him, I will. And I'll hate you if you abandon me now."

Darius gulped down his reservations and followed her inside.

"Everyone out," Addy shrieked as they came upon a populated hallway. "Turn off comms and get the fuck out!"

"Yes, Miss Malik," came a reply as feet shuffled out. Addy positioned herself in front of him and her brother. Darius tucked Gabe's mutilated wrists out of sight as curious eyes roved over the three of them. He'd never been here when the facility was open before, and worry tickled across his brow alongside their curious looks.

When they were gone, Addy led the way to the sterile brightness of the box room, pushing open a set of double doors labeled, *Regeneration Tanks*. She shoved open one of the many doors lining the hall, holding it wide while Darius maneuvered himself and Gabe through the too-narrow entrance. He bumped Gabe's lolling head on the doorframe and muttered what must've been his millionth *sorry* of the night.

"Get him in the box," Addy commanded.

Darius didn't argue. Any fight he might've had left him the moment he'd crossed the threshold. With a soul-weary sigh, Darius mounted the ladder and put his friend back into the box.

14

HOW TO BE A VILLAIN

GABE

HE DIDN'T DESERVE TO be alive anymore. Not with what he'd done. Not with how he'd lost control... the way he'd... *hurt* Hope. It was becoming increasingly difficult to differentiate between reality and fantasy; the voice in his head often louder than those of the people in the room with him. How long until he slipped up again? He could not let it stand. That's why he'd done it. This had been a long time coming. If he couldn't maintain control, he needed to remove himself from the equation.

These thoughts paraded about his mind, despite the voice's insistence they'd done nothing wrong; they'd only sought to take what *belonged* to them. Gabe railed against the notion. He knew what was true and good and noble. He'd considered himself to be those things before recent events. He didn't know how to reconcile his fundamental truths with his actions. He didn't know *how* to be a villain.

Anger flared in his chest, a small flame that licked at his internal organs until it threatened to consume him whole. He'd *tried*.

He'd tried to fix this the only way he knew how, and they—the two people he'd trusted more than anyone—they *ruined* it. Why didn't they respect him enough to let him make this one momentous decision? He was *trying* to protect them. And they didn't trust him enough to do that.

He didn't want this. He would rather cease to exist entirely than risk those he loved. It didn't matter if the act of taking his

79

life might've damned him to an eternity bathing in hellfire like the legends of old suggested. Gabe knew how close he'd come to snuffing out his own life. Hell, he'd seen shadows and light inside that cold, numb darkness. Heard voices that didn't belong to him beckoning. His foot on the metaphorical threshold between life and death, the two halves of him pulled in opposite directions of afterlife. And then the worst had happened, and he'd woken in his own personal hell. Drowning. Drowning. *Drowning.* And not in the way he'd chosen. Drowning while he was awake. Not death's embrace, but his sister's arms hoisting him up out of the box, sobbing her relief. Darius' shadow had darkened the doorway, not in an offering of salvation, but damnation to live in a world with no hope. Their eyes had briefly met, and Gabe had seen the last thing he'd expected: *regret.* Whether it be the regret of denying Gabe's blatant wishes or that he'd lived at all, would be an ever-present torment. His friend had come forward and helped him to stand, squeezing his arm in reassurance. Gabe didn't know what to make of any of it.

His sister had tucked him into bed at home, as she'd done when they were children and Papa had beaten him half to death. She'd murmured for hours, running her fingers through his hair, begging him to speak, but he couldn't. The voice had been screaming, berating him for doing such a thing, then finally reverting to dulcet tones of apology and promises. He'd fallen asleep to the whispers in his mind with Addy curled against his side, clutching his hand as if she might keep him earthside with the point of contact.

He'd awakened to the incessant vibrations of his phone on the bedside table. Addy was still clutching his hand, breaths deep, then stuttering in a fitful sleep. He gently peeled her fingers out of his and reached for the device, inwardly groaning as his Father's contact information flashed on the screen alongside a glowing number six. He'd missed *six* calls from Father. *Shit.*

Apparently, not even an ill-fated suicide attempt could garner him peace from the man. He pressed the phone to his ear and started, "Father, I'm sorry—"

"Excuses, excuses. Save your breath, Gabriel. You've answered now, at least."

Gabe pulled the phone away to look at the time. *4:32 am*. He supposed that might explain Father's flippant attitude. Sometimes he did things like this: called at ungodly hours just so he'd have something to be angry about when Gabe finally picked up at a reasonable time. Indeed, all of the calls were from three o'clock on.

Teeth gritted, Gabe asked, "What can I do for you, Father?"

"Better. Get your worthless sister ready. I'm sending a flight craft to pick you up at eight. There have been... *questions* about your mother here. We must go for a visit."

Gabe's breath caught. "After all this time? Father, Addy will be overjoyed—"

"What have I told you about calling her that stupid name? Say *Adalia* or nothing at all. Yes. I'm sure she'll be pleased. Don't be late, Gabriel. I should hate to have another reason to be disappointed in you." The call ended as abruptly as it'd begun.

A half hour later, Gabe's fingers shook as he clasped the top button of his shirt, the starched linen tight around his neck. It gave him the distinct impression of suffocation. *Good*. It's what he deserved. He threw his head back and sighed at the ceiling.

Addy's soft step sounded in the hallway, and Gabe quickly blinked back the tears in his eyes and set his shoulders, picking up the silver comb on his desk and raking it through his hair in a robotic fashion. He'd barely been able to convince her to leave, but had finally won out when he acquiesced that Darius could take her place.

Gabe hadn't bothered to pretend to be alright while Darius sat on the foot of the bed, silently cataloging every move he made. They still hadn't spoken. It seemed neither of them knew how to begin. Darius had just opened his mouth when they heard Addy in the hall. He snapped it shut so quickly, Gabe heard the click of teeth, followed by a muttered curse, then the creak of the bed as Darius rose and opened the door.

Tension lit the air as Darius brushed past his sister. She caught his wrist and leaned out of the door to whisper, lowering her tone so Gabe couldn't hear. Except. He *could* hear. He *did* hear as he watched her in the mirror. She rose on her toes until her lips brushed Darius' ear and murmured, "I wanted it, you know. I wanted to make that new world with you."

Darius lifted a scarred hand and ran his fingers along her jaw. The motion so intimate, Gabe averted his eyes, but he didn't stop hearing as Addy said, "But now..."

"I know," Darius replied, voice burning with some emotion Gabe failed to place, before his friend strode away. Down the hall, the door to Darius' room closed a little too loudly, followed by a dull thump.

Before Gabe could ponder further on the interaction, Addy was at his side. He just continued to comb his hair on autopilot until she reached up and took it.

"It's good, Gabe. It's enough." She patted his hand, then picked up the ends of his tie and hastily wove them into a stylish knot at his neck. "Are you sure you can do this right now?" Her eyes seared the side of his face.

"Yes. I have no *choice*." He bit out the last word.

"Please, Gabe. Please forgive me. I couldn't... *you* would have done the same thing were our positions switched."

Her words softened his heart a little. He took her hands and met her watery gaze. "Don't cry, Addy. You'll ruin your pretty makeup, and Father will be displeased."

She swatted at his hand, a tear rolling free. "I'm so mad at you," she whispered. "Why would you do that, Gabe?"

He couldn't explain it, not really, so he settled with, "I needed to do it, Ads. I needed to keep you all safe. I... I messed up, and I don't think there's any other way to make it right. I don't think I can continue like this."

"We'll figure it out, Gabe. I promise you. I will be with you every step of the way."

"There are places I go... *dark* places, Addy. You cannot follow."

"I *will*. Please, let me save you," she whispered.

"I fear it's much too late for that, sister."

"It's *never* too late."

Gabe breathed a laugh and brushed another tear from his sister's face. "You always were an incorrigible optimist."

"I think you're confusing me with yourself." She choked on her own laugh. "But I'll be anything. *Anything*, if it means you'll promise never to do that again. If you'll let me help you?"

What would it hurt to comfort his sister this way? Nothing. Addy would be alright if he broke his promise. She'd have Darius. Because he already knew he meant to break this promise. *No*, the voice hissed. Gabe ignored it. Because he *was* planning to try again, and with more success, just as soon as possible. He would *not* be a villain. Even if it meant he would not *be* anything at all. The bitter, resentful part of him fought to claw free even now. *We could have everything, Gabe. We* are *smarter. We are better.* They *wouldn't stand a chance if you'd quit dampening our full potential.*

Shut up.

It only bothers you because you know it's true. And the voice was right. It was true. He *did* know.

Gabe lifted his pinky to Addy's and whispered, "I promise," over their linked fingers. "Now stop crying, Ads, I'm serious. We're going to see mother and we cannot be late."

Her face brightened. "Gabe," she gasped. "We can ask them! We can ask them. They're medical professionals."

"Who are?"

"The people at the facility where Mama's kept. We can ask them!"

"Ask them what?"

"We can ask them for help, of course." She clasped Gabe's hands. "This is it. This is the answer—Gabe, we'll get help—for *you*."

His stomach sank. She was wrong. There was no helping this. He'd tried to ask once, when he was fourteen. He'd asked the 'doctor' who liked to cut him up and stitch him back together at Father's behest. He'd been rewarded with a month-long stay in the cold white room, where the *doctor* had 'studied' him, until Gabe had finally admitted he'd made the whole thing up. There were no voices. He was just a silly boy who wanted attention. Gabe couldn't tell his sister that, though. So he nodded and pasted on a small smile for her sake. "Of course. What a brilliant idea." He clasped her hand, then snapped the strap of her dress in his usual brotherly way, disrupting the horrible tension. "Now, let's go, before I do us both a favor and die from you being nice to me."

Addy choked a laugh and muttered, "That's not funny, Gabe."

He smirked and tugged her along. "It was. And you know it. What have we got, if we can't laugh at ourselves, after all?"

"You're the worst," Addy groaned, but she smiled. She smiled. And that was worth any amount of morbid humor at his own expense.

15

REAPERS & THE MEN WHO HUNT THEM

DARIUS

THAT DAMN DRESS.

His best friend had tried to take his own life last night, and all he could think about was the dress. He didn't want to ponder much about what that meant about his quality as a human being. He tried to put the dress out of his mind… and failed spectacularly. At least, he wanted to believe it was about the dress. It most certainly wasn't Addy *in* the dress, or his more base thoughts of getting her *out* of the dress. The yards of silky material had left just enough to the imagination… and was he ever *imagining*. He imagined his hands replacing the fabric that'd cinched tight to her waist. His fingers trailing down the planes of her stomach, then back up to caress the underside of her breast he'd glimpsed in side profile under the deep vee of green material. His mouth on her neck, her collarbones, her shoulder. The way her skin would flush that beautiful pink where his stubble scraped…

God dammint.

His imagination had always been particularly vivid, and it didn't fail him now. Darius shoved thoughts of Addy's perfect skin away, along with his blankets. He felt caked in grime after the fitful sleep he'd fallen into since abandoning Gabe's room in the early hours of the morning. The bed creaked under his weight as he rose and stomped directly for the shower of the attached bathroom. Wrenching the tap on full blast, Darius stripped and stepped under the arctic spray. He willed thoughts of Adalia, of the juxtaposition of silk and skin and the way his callouses had caught on the fabric, but coasted so perfectly over the flesh of her lower back, down the drain with the cold water. Unsurprisingly, it didn't work. He'd never had success getting her out of his head. Instead, he willed another thought to the front of his mind, putting Adalia in the background, where she'd haunt the edges of his consciousness as usual. What was he going to do about Gabe? More, what *could* someone in his position do? He was entirely out of his depth.

Darius couldn't stand the resentment Gabe had been pointing his direction from the moment his newly healed eyelids peeled open outside the box. The accusation in that gaze had been too much to bear. So Darius had stayed silent, not allowing his apologies to spill forth. Not allowing the truth that he'd failed his friend to stain the strained air between them. He feared he'd just made things immeasurably worse. Addy didn't get it. She *couldn't* understand the utter violation they'd participated in by resurrecting Gabe. But Darius knew. He *knew.* He'd taken enough lives to recognize the moment of acceptance that paints a body on the brink of afterlife. The way the joints go loose, pain flees, *peace* permeates the atmosphere. It doesn't always happen that way. Some do not go quietly. Some claw and scream and fight the inevitable until they finally pass on in gasping agony. Gabe had been peaceful. It felt especially wrong to rob a soul of that kind of death.

Darius was nothing more than a ball of jittering torment because of the knowledge. Shoulders quivering under the strain of too little sleep, he raked a brush through his hair and tied it at the back of his neck. After he'd hastily shaved, he returned to the bed, where he located the crumpled letter Addy had shoved into his palm this morning.

Darius,

I know you understand how this changes things. I won't waste words lamenting things we cannot control, just know that I'd wished for that future with much fervor.

But you were right.

It couldn't be.

I'm sorry for my part in pulling you back here, for the way I behaved those years ago that drove you to stay away in the first place. I wonder if, perhaps, he got worse without you here?

I wonder a lot of things, in truth, but wonders and wishes make little difference to true circumstance. I'm rambling. I'm sorry for that, too.

Know this.

I love you.

I've loved you since the summer before you went away.

I don't think I'll ever be able to stop loving you.

It was the wild apple that did it, in case you wondered.

It was the sourest thing I've ever tasted. And you... you looked at my scrunched up face like I was some Goddess of old... and you caught the apple when I chucked it at your head and took the biggest bite. You didn't even squint. I wanted to kiss you then, though we were only children. I wanted to see if maybe the apple wasn't so sour on your lips. God, what am I even on about? I told myself I'd give you this note, regardless of what I wrote the first time. I won't rewrite it. I want it to be true. I don't want you to wonder any more than you must. About us. About what cannot be.

Or, perhaps, we can come to some kind of agreement? I can't go away with you, but I can offer you a part of me. You already possess the whole of my heart. You are already my most treasured secret. But could either of us bear it when I am married off to some other man? I wish I knew the answers, but trust, I will do everything I can to deny that eventuality. I must. For Gabe's sake, more than anything. On that note, enough about me and my feelings.

Darius, I know you understand, I have to help my brother.

I only ask that you be by his side to grant support. Whatever passes between you and I, can you promise you'll be there for my brother? I don't want to do this without you, but I will, if you tire of the drama us Maliks bring to your life.

My plan is this:

Locate a trusted person, preferably with some experience in whatever goes on with my brother, and, quite simply, ask for help.

Other than that, it amounts to not letting Gabe out of my sight (or yours) until I'm certain he's doing better. I hope that day comes soon.

It's not much, I know, but I have to hope.

I can't lose him.

I can't.

I hope you understand that I must protect him. I hope you understand the caution with which we must proceed. We've kept you secret these years, by luck, truly. But you cannot reappear. You do not want to exist within The Collective. I know you've seen the conditions in which the humans are kept. So, we mustn't be caught. Not only would it be a death sentence for you, but it would ruin us. Ruin Gabe. For he'd try to save you, and I fear his reputation cannot withstand such a scandal. Not when his sanity may be in question.

If it is too much, I ask that you leave us... and do not come back. I will know your answer depending on whether or not you are here when we return. In the meantime, please make yourself at home as usual. Father will be in the city for the coming weeks. If it is your wish to stay, please help me think of a better plan.

If you do not wish to stay... Go.

Yours,

Addy

Darius wanted nothing more than to climb his thinking tree in the yard and agonize over the words Addy had written. *I love you. I don't think I'll ever be able to stop loving you.* He'd known. Of course, he'd known. She'd told him without words years ago when she'd kissed him so demandingly on his birthday... when he'd...

rejected her. He wished now he could go back and rewrite the past, so he could steal those years with the woman he loved. Because no, he didn't want whatever shreds of her she might be able to offer him. He wanted to consume her whole. He didn't want to spare a scrap for anyone else. Most certainly not for her father. Not for her mother. Not for her brother. Not for whatever Ethereal prick she'd be forced to wed. Not for all the world. He didn't want to *share* her. It made him a selfish man, but at least he was an honest one.

With Herculean effort, Darius shoved all thoughts of the Maliks away. He had the day to decide what to do, but other promises were more pressing at the moment.

He had things to do today—things that required focus.

By the end of the day, he'd have secured a supply chain between Callum and the humans inside Braken, and if all went to plan, he'd have Reaper guts coating his blades. Darius pulled open an inconspicuous drawer in the dresser, removing the false bottom. This room was supposed to be for guests, but he was the only one who ever stayed in here.

Gabe had started stocking the false drawer with clothes years ago. Darius never asked how he knew what size to get. Gabe never asked why he wanted Reaper uniforms and weapons. It was how they both preferred things.

Beneath the trove of black fabric, Darius located more casual garments. He wanted to look *approachable* today. He donned a t-shirt and jeans. The shirt clung a little across his arms and chest, but at least he didn't look so much like he'd just crawled out of the brambles. There was little he could do about the general feral-ness his lack of an eye produced. He practiced smiling at himself in a way he hoped didn't look too menacing, and though he appreciated the brightness of his freshly whitened grin, he resigned himself to close-lipped smirks instead. With a heavy sigh, Darius turned away from the bathroom mirror. There wasn't much more he could do to make himself presentable, and he was wasting time. Nothing could diminish the inherent threat of a man as large as he. Still, he tried.

He'd told Callum he would do this. Darius had never seen the man so frantic as he'd been last winter, when little Greta had caught a cold and rapidly went from the vision of a healthy child to something pale and sickly and barely clinging to life. Callum had decided then it was past time they got access to some of the resources inside the border. Darius agreed, and before he'd slipped from camp, he'd made a promise to do this. He was the only one of them to successfully venture in and out of The Collective, after all.

Shoulders hunched, Darius slipped out the back door of the mansion unseen. He wended his way through the back streets of Bracken, broadening his steps over questionable puddles which were a hallmark of the human districts. A sickly sweet odor of death haunted his mind as he darted between the once tidy line of abandoned homes. The streets were empty and cracked. Weeds had nearly overtaken the sidewalks. Where green lawns had been, only dirt and thistles sprouted. It wasn't until he stood on the stoop of the crumbling row house that Darius allowed the memories in. He wrapped a hand around the wooden railing, curling his fingers until he located four rough gouges on the underside of the board. Tears prickled the corners of his vision. *Home*.

He had never dared venture back here before. Those notches had been carved by his own tiny hands on his fourth birthday. Ma was livid when she found them. She'd taken away his ration of sugar for a week. Darius' heart warmed at the memory of her scolding, of Lila standing beside her, mirroring Ma with chubby hands fisted on her tiny hips. Sometimes Darius wondered if it would have been better to have died alongside his family. He wondered if maybe it had been a blessing they didn't have to live as he did now. Perhaps fate or destiny or whatever God ruled this wretched world had meant for things to be this way. Darius never would have met Addy, or Gabe, or Callum, or Luna, or even little Greta if tragedy hadn't made its acquaintance with his family. Or maybe he would've. Maybe there was some reality in which they'd all come together. Maybe he would've spotted Gabriel on the other side of that fence one day regardless. Maybe they would have ventured out into the forest. Maybe Lila would've grown into the woman she was meant to be. Maybe his parents could've shown Gabe and Adalia the love they'd deserved growing up. Maybe. Alas, a life cannot be built on the *maybes*. There is only the now, the truth of *this* moment in time, the leap into the unpredictability of each passing second that determines one's reality. *Maybes* are best left in the past, where they belong—the enemy to possibility. *Wonders and wishes make little difference to true circumstance.*

So, Darius dismissed the maybes and lifted his hand to rap on the scarred door, leaning only into the present, the known. He *would* go into this house that haunted his nightmares. He *would* establish trading routes with the people inside. He *would* make a difference for his kind in the time he was given on this Earth. He *would* face the demons of his past, so he might build a worthy future. Whatever force governed this world had brought him to this moment. That same force had decided to place the band of rebels on the very street, in the very house he'd avoided these many years. He would not deny the ring of destiny in the air. The door opened, and Darius stepped into his future.

16

MOTHER MINE

GABE

"FATHER." GABE HELD OUT a hand to James Malik where he stood on the landing pad, imperious in a black on black suit combo.

James took his hand and inclined his head the slightest bit, as was the appropriate greeting between a Heritage Ethereal and his heir. "Glad you've both made it here in a timely manner." James barely allowed his eyes to trail over Adalia before looking back up at Gabe and narrowing them. "I've heard from a few of my sources back home that you had rather a rough night? Is there something I ought to be informed on?"

"Of course not, Father. It was merely an unfortunate slip in the river. All is well now."

"Ah, good. I must've imagined the distressing call I received from Phil Redmond this morning regarding a certain daughter of his." James crushed Gabe's hand in a painful manner. *Hope.*

Gabe didn't flinch, only narrowed his eyes back at Father. "I'm sure anything that was said was *greatly* exaggerated, Father. One knows the word of a woman cannot be trusted." He smiled in a reptilian manner.

James mirrored the expression, giving Gabe's hand a final squeeze before releasing him and turning away. "Good. Now, let's go see your *lovely* mother," he said, leading the way to the waiting car.

Gabe had only ever been to Rittenmore a handful of times. Father preferred to conduct his business in The City of Mirrors, convinced the proximity to the Authority's seat of power would somehow give him an advantage. Gabe had to confess Father was right. Even from the flight craft, it was evident Rittenmore was a shithole compared with the grandeur of the Mirrored City. The streets held the similar haunt and disrepair that'd been left behind in the wake of the Red Plague in Bracken, only on a much larger scale. Worse than the refuse were the sickly-looking humans peering through smashed windows and around crumbling corners. Gabe turned away from the desperation of their silent stares, looking inward instead. He hated Rittenmore, but perhaps this was a good thing, a chance to say goodbye to Mother before he ended things. He could be grateful for that, if nothing else.

Addy clutched his hand, hidden beneath the spill of green silk on the seat between them. He squeezed back in silent reassurance, then extracted his palm from hers before Father could see and make a fuss.

"I don't know why they keep their landing pad in this filthy district." James mused as their car cut a path through the abandoned streets. "These fools could learn a thing or two from The City of Mirrors. Landing pads on the rooftops, because who wants to look at all of this." He waved a hand at the littered streets. "Fools," he cursed again, before returning his attention to his phone and tuning out the tragedy.

Gabe took out his own device and typed a message. *"Don't look, Ads."* He flashed the screen her direction and saw her nod out of the corner of his eye. She fixed her gaze on the floor and clenched her fingers until her knuckles whitened. Outside, cries rose. Little fists pounded the doors, and the tires of their car thumped along in a terribly unsettling manner. Gabe made the horrible mistake of disobeying his own advice and looking. Children. Hundreds of children, waif-thin and miserable, held hands outstretched. The thumping? Their driver callously mowing down the ones who got too close. And the worst thing about looking at all of those little, starving children? It was the hope on their faces. The hope that Gabe and his family were there to help. He *wanted* to help. More than anything. He wanted to help, but how could he help them when he couldn't even help himself? Gabe looked down, too, lest he allow the tears to fall at the sight of those children. The cries faded as they rose up a steep incline. Reapers stood in rows outside iron fences of the gated portion of the city.

The humans, even the most desperate of them, did not dare venture near here. Gabe had always hated them—the Reapers. But Father swore they were a necessary evil, and the voice, not that he trusted the thing, said the same. *Unrest will only harm the humans more. And look at those Reapers, Gabe. They* are *human. Look what they've made of themselves. Better to become a monster than be nothing at all...* But Gabe didn't believe that. He'd rather be nothing at all than become a monster like those men and women out there along the fence line.

On and on they wove through tidy streets, so opposite the ones below. Clean, uniformed silver-haired children peered at them from behind the tall fences of an elementary school. The blatant health written in their rounded cheeks was like a knife to the gut after seeing the harsh thinness of the children down the hill. As it was with Bracken, the homes grew grander as they scaled the hillside, the Ethereals here just as obsessive in their need to be above all others.

Finally, below the pinnacle of the hill, behind another thick iron gate, sat a commanding brick building, swathed in thick Ivy, with wide stone steps and a tiered fountain at the center of the drive. It looked... *peaceful.* The gardens were expansive and lush, walkways lined with roses and swaying aspen trees, leaves a mix of vibrant yellow and green signifying the beginning of the end of summer. And amongst it all, walked Ethereal women, clad in flowing gowns, hair gleaming in the warm noon sun, and looking, for all the world, *happy.* They were the embodiment of what their name harkened to: *Ethereal—angelic.*

"See, children," James began smugly. "You're always desperate to think the worst of me. Does this look like a prison?" He raised his brows.

"No," Addy whispered. "No, it does not."

James nodded in satisfaction as the car rolled to a stop. "Good. Now, quit dallying."

Gabe followed his father out of the car, reaching back to lend Addy a hand. They were greeted at the top step by an attendant in a white labcoat. "Ah, you must be the Maliks," he said, offering Father a hand in greeting. James merely looked at it with reproach until the attendant tucked it back away, color staining his cheeks.

"Yes, yes," he stuttered. "Please, follow me."

They followed the sound of music down a winding concrete path to an airy gazebo beneath the trees. At its center sat a grand piano with their mother positioned on the bench, her eyes shut as her fingers wove a complex melody along the keys. She was glowing. Alive in a way Gabe had never seen before, lost in her song, her lovely face a tableau of the emotions her music invoked. Addy quietly gasped at his side as their mother reached the crescendo of her song, fingers flying in a blur until the music stuttered to a hauntingly beautiful halt. She leaned back, tilting her face up in the aching quiet that followed her song, the breeze blowing tendrils of silver back from where they'd fallen across her brow. Her eyes popped open on a deep breath, then narrowed as they settled on James, then widened as they skipped over to her children. She rose in a flurry, knocking the bench backward and flinging herself into Gabe's arms. He breathed in the warm, clean scent of her hair, then tugged Addy into their hug.

"It's you," his mother murmured, pulling back to touch Gabe's cheek, then Addy's. "My beautiful children." She smiled, stepping back to run a hand over what Gabe noted with shock, was her burstingly rounded stomach. "How happy I am to see you both," she continued, failing to note their surprise.

"Father—" Gabe choked.

"Pfft. Oh, don't get your prim little panties in a bunch, Gabriel. It's not mine." James waved him off. "I'll be back in an hour. Enjoy." With that, to Gabe's eternal surprise, he left them alone.

"Oh." Their mother began, "I'm sorry. You must have so many questions. But first, come, Gabriel. Play me a song." She smiled warmly and settled herself on a cushioned wicker bench, indicating for Addy to sit beside her. She clasped their hands and nodded for Gabe to take his position behind the piano, recreating a scene that'd been common in their home back in Bracken whenever Father was away.

Swallowing down his questions, Gabe righted the bench and sat, stroking the keys. "Shall I play one of the classics, Mother? Or would you like my own composition?"

"You already know the answer to that."

And so, Gabe played. Gabe played all of the words in his heart, all the hurt, all the beauty, all the dreams he'd say goodbye to when he ended his miserable life. Gabe played. And he knew *this*. This was another thing he'd miss. Yes. He'd miss the music when he disappeared.

When he came back to himself, it was to find his mother and sister with tears dripping down their cheeks.

"I'm sorry—"

"Never. Never be sorry for that." His mother whispered.

Addy looked at him with too much knowing in her eyes, then added, "No, Gabe, never that."

Once they'd settled their little party around a table set with scones and tea and clotted cream, Gabe finally leveled a look at his mother. "Now, it seems there is much for you to explain."

Mother set her teacup down with a quiet clatter. "Yes. I suppose there is. Where to begin..."

"At the beginning would be nice, mother." Addy snapped.

"Oh, you cheeky girl." She reached out to pinch Addy's cheek.

Addy swatted her hand away before she could. "Mother. We are short on time. Are you well? And, whose child is that?"

Mother signed. "Fine. To answer the first: yes. Yes. I am well. I'm better than ever. And the second... I... I don't exactly know."

Gabe choked on his tea. "What do you mean, you don't know?"

"Well, you see, *that* is the condition of living here." She had the dignity to grimace. "I will provide an Ethereal male with two children—"

"You've already done that!" Addy interrupted.

Mother held up a hand to quiet her. "Yes. I have... But... That was before this program became available. This is how I earn my place here—and I *want* to stay here. I will provide *another* male with children. It is not up to me how they choose to conceive." She shrugged. "I am fortunate, and my breeding partner chose insemination. I've never met him."

Gabe cringed. "And what do they do... with your baby... with our *sibling*, when it's born?"

"That's not up to me." She shrugged again, like this was perfectly acceptable.

"Well, who *is* it up to, then?" Addy glared at Mother. Their relationship had always been strained in a way Gabe failed to understand.

"The Male... The Authority. What does it matter?"

Addy scoffed, "What do you mean, '*what does it matter?*' It's *your* child! As Gabe said, it's *our* sibling!"

"It has nothing to do with you!" Mother shouted, her composure cracking as it always had with Addy.

"So, this is what you've paid to abandon us?" Addy seethed. "You've sold your unborn children—and for what? To get away from the family you already have? Typical."

"Don't—" Mother began.

"No. *You* don't! We *needed* you. And you were a ghost."

"I did the best I could! Stop kidding yourself, Adalia. Grow the hell up for once and face the music! The only thing different from this arrangement and the one I had with your father is the fact that I don't have to look into the face of a man I hate for every God-forsaken day of my life. You're lucky James succeeded in securing you—" She cut off, as if she hadn't meant to say that last part.

Addy's face crumpled in horror. "No," she whispered. "Mother, no. Please, tell me you didn't. He didn't..."

Mother only stared.

Panic battered behind Gabe's breastbone. His voice came out in a low hiss he hardly recognized, "Mother. You will tell us. You will tell *me* what it is you know. *Now.*"

"Gabriel," Mother whined. "My son, it's nothing."

"Mother. I have always been gentle with you, but so help me, if you do not tell me, I shall show you the darker half of my heart."

She cringed away from him, as he'd seen her do in their father's presence so many times. Gabe hated himself for it, but well, what was one more thing to hate himself for at this point? She sucked in a stuttering breath and rattled off the words that would damn his sister. "James is arranging a place for Adalia here." She turned to Addy. "You'll see, honey. You will love it. We'll be together. And they've come such a long way with medical advancements. You won't even feel the births... and then, you'll be free to do as you please. You'll never be shackled to another man. You'll see."

"I'll be *free*, mother?" Addy croaked. "Free to do what? Live my life behind iron gates? Free to sit down, shut up, and wait for them to come up with some use for me? *Free?* You don't even know what that means. *I* don't know what that means. How dare you use that word? How dare you tell me I'll love it in this glorified prison—"

"Addy." Gabe clenched her shoulder. "Enough. I will not allow this to come to pass."

"Gabe—"

"And neither will our friend."

"No, I—"

"Do not argue. I made you a promise, remember?" He raised his brows at her, the weight of their promise a lodestone between them. "This will *not* be your fate."

She nodded and rose. "Mother. Goodbye. Gabe, I will meet you at the car."

"Adalia—" Their mother tried, but she was already gone.

Gabe watched his sister's retreating form while he attempted to formulate the words he must speak to Mother. Finally, he said, "Mother, I am so disappointed you presumed to collude with Father... to seal Addy into a fate such as this... it is *cruel*. You know her spirit. She cannot be caged as you are."

Mother spoke down to her clasped hands. "It is a mercy, Gabriel. A mercy you cannot understand, because you are not a woman."

"Why didn't you come to me?"

"Oh, child. I could not come to you. And you... despite all of your best intentions, you become more like them every day. You dilute yourself, son. You cannot protect her from this fate. It is already done. She'll join me here within the month."

"Do not tell me what I can and cannot do, Mother," Gabe spat, rising to his feet. "I wish you every happiness. I hope this life gives you what you need." And though he was angry, Gabe pulled her to her feet and crushed her in a hug. This was goodbye, after all. "I love you, Mother. I'm sorry I could not protect *you* from this fate, but believe me, I will not leave Adalia to their mercy any longer." With that, he released her and walked away. Soft musical notes followed in his wake. Gabe did not let the tears fall. Just as he had not cried for the starving children below, he would not cry as he looked more closely at the women wandering the garden, all of them with growing bumps beneath their dresses. A few eyed him with thinly veiled expectation.

Ah. Look, Gabe. We could take whichever we please. Remove that inferior seed and plant your own.

Go away.

What did I tell you about that? The answer is the same as always.

Gabe shook his head and sprinted for the car, desperate for the refuge of the tinted windows.

Don't run away, Gabe, go inside. Sample the goods. What do you think your father is doing? You're so worried about them being willing... all of these ones are here by choice. Take one... or even two. Please, Gabe, don't let me die a virgin.

SHUT UP. SHUT UP. SHUT UP.

Gabe tore open the door of the car, startling the driver, who'd been blaring a program on his device. "Get out!" Gabe screamed. "Stand by that tree over there. Knock thrice on the window when the others are approaching."

"Yes, Mr. Malik." The driver slipped from the car to do as he'd been told.

Gabe slumped down in the space between the seats and pounded his palm into his forehead, willing the voice to shut up.

Poor little weak Gabe. Haven't you accepted the inevitable? You are me. Give in. Let us be one. Set me free. Think of all we could do. We could take anything we wanted. We'd never be denied again. Come now, Gabe. Don't deny it. Don't deny me. Why do you limit us with the imagined construct of morality? Look around, Gabe. The world is at our feet. Take it. Take it. Take.

NO. NO. NO. I am no better than anyone else. I'm not entitled to anything—

LIAR. Liar. little liar. You cannot fool me, Gabe. I live in here. In your head, the voice sang, *I'll be with you till you're dead. (Oh, that was clever, wasn't it?) Liar, liar, little Gabe, wants to put his papa in his grave. Thinks he's better than the rest. Mother. Sister. Friend called 'best.'* A wicked laugh bounced around his skull.

Please, Gabe begged, ripping at his hair and covering his ears.

He says please and thank you, too. But what he means is, "I'm better than you." Gabe's so kind and Gabe's so good. But he only loves you cause he should.

STOP.

No. Gabe. I won't. Try to kill us, will you? I think not. You knew, didn't you? You self-righteous little prick. You knew it wouldn't work.

I won't fail next time.

Ah. Next time. Next time. Big talk, Gabe. What will you do? Cut off our head? Hard to do yourself. Perhaps a bullet? Hmmmm. Aim true, Gabe. Shall we try drowning again? Just to say we did? You know that one won't work. But it might make you feel better, right? That's what this is about, isn't it? A clean conscience.

Please.

*Newsflash, Gabe. I am your conscience. And I'm... **filthy**.* The voice purred, just as the driver rapped on the window three times.

Please, Gabe begged of the voice as he hoisted himself up onto the seat and smoothed his hair. *Please be quiet. I must convince Addy I'm alright. She'll know if you're here.*

Ah. Glad to see you've come to your senses. It's much better when we work together. Yes. We must get rid of Adalia. She limits us.

I'm going to send her away with Darius.

Well, that's not quite what I'd planned, but I suppose it'll do... The voice trailed off because there was Addy, opening the door and climbing in.

The driver found his seat a moment later. "To the flight craft?" he inquired.

"Yes." Gabe murmured, "Take the long way. I don't want to see those children again."

"Of course, Mr. Malik." The driver raised the partition, leaving Gabe and Addy in tense silence.

"Where's Father?" Gabe asked.

"He left." Addy said, voice hollow. "I guess he finalized the arrangements and headed back to The City of Mirrors. Gabe." She shook off the haunted air that'd been clinging to her since she'd left him with their mother at the gazebo. "I spoke with one of the doctors."

"Oh." His chest ached at her words.

"There are treatments, Gabe. You won't like them. They involve surgeries, and time in the regeneration tanks—"

"I won't go back in the box, Addy. Not even for you."

"Okay." Addy nodded as if striking that item off some mental list. "I figured you'd say that. There are also... medications. They'd need a clearer picture of your symptoms, but the doctor was hopeful there might be help if you're willing to speak with him?"

"Did you tell him, Addy? Did you tell him it was about me?"

"Of course not. We spoke only in hypotheticals. I think, if any-thing, he assumed I was speaking of Father."

"Good. That's good, Ads."

"Gabe, please tell me... tell me you'll get into contact with him?" She produced a card with contact information from a hidden pocket of her gown. "He told me it can be anonymous—that they handle this kind of thing often. They can be discrete."

"Okay." Gabe nodded, hating the lie. "Yes. I'll get in touch with him. But only if you promise me something, too."

"Gabe..."

"It's not up for debate—"

"Later, Gabe. Please. We have a little time, right?"

"A little," he begrudgingly confirmed.

"Good. Then please, let's get you sorted, and then we'll deal with my... issue."

"Anything for you, sister." Gabe pulled her under his arm and clung to her for dear life. And he didn't hate this lie, not so much. Not if it meant Addy would be safe.

17

BLOODY HANDS, BLOODIER HEART

DARIUS

THEY WERE SITTING ON plastic chairs, gathered around some pitiful excuse of a map Darius assumed was meant to be Bracken and its surrounding area. He scoffed as he eyed the worn paper on the overturned barrel. "Well, that explains a lot about why ya cannot get in and out of that pathetic border of theirs." He nodded to the map, which was missing large chunks of patrol routes and marked with only drawings. It dawned on him that these people could not read. They'd not have the ability to mark their maps with words.

"And just who is this arsehole ye've brought to our home, Jack?" A wiry middle-aged woman grumbled, looking up and up and up at Darius. His head nearly brushed the ceiling in the tiny living area. He'd remembered this place being so much larger, distorted by his childish eyes. He glanced around the room, looking for some trace of his old life, but came up empty until he spotted a pair of scuff marks on the floor in the right corner. Scuff marks from Papa's favorite chair.

"Eh, Goliath, imma talkin' to you." The woman snapped in his face, extending her arm fully to reach.

Darius took a step back, not liking the way she invaded his space. "Name's not Goliath," he grumbled.

"Obviously. T'was what I was asking 'fore you started staring at that corner like ye'd seen a ghost. If ye'd rather not say, I'll call you Goliath. I quite like the notion."

"No. My name is Darius."

A man with stringy brown hair leaned back on his plastic chair legs and whistled through his teeth, "Yer not *the* Darius, are ya?" He spat on the floor—the floor Darius' mother had dedicated so much time to keeping tidy.

Darius had the distinct urge to backhand the skinny man. Instead, he clenched his fist and said through gritted teeth, "I suppose I might be him."

"I told ya!" The man cawed to the room at large. "Darius the Black always wore an eyepatch in the stories. It's him!"

A hooded figure emerged from the hall and shoved the stringy man aside, causing him to topple to the floor. Darius couldn't help but gape as she threw her hood back. She was... *well.* Vibrant red hair spilled around her shoulders, her skin an unblemished porcelain entirely at odds with the rough, obviously hand-stitched shirt and pants she wore. "You lot are a bunch of heathens." She chastised in a voice like butter, before extending a hand to Darius. "I'm Ember." She rolled her eyes, tugging her hand out of his to gesture to her hair. "I know, my parents thought they were funny. Allow me to introduce you to my companions, as Jack would surely have done were he not so awestruck over there." She waved a dismissive hand at Jack where he stood by the door. He ducked his chin, causing the many braids on his head to swing in a curtain in front of his face.

"This weasely bastard here," she flicked the stringy one, "is Gunner." She swept her finger around the room, stopping at the other woman. "Penny, madder than an old bat, that one. And last but not least, this here—" She pointed behind Darius, who turned to find a brawny blonde man leaning against the wall.

"I'm Flint." He rose to full height, tall, but still half a head short-er than Darius, who smirked at that realization before grasping the offered hand.

"I'm Ember's brother. Our parents weren't a particularly cre-ative bunch." He smiled broadly, tightening his grip on Darius' hand.

Oh, so it's to be like that, is it? Darius squeezed back with more force than necessary. Flint's eyes widened before he tore his hand free and ducked his head, sufficiently cowed in the wake of Darius' strength. It wasn't fair, Darius knew. This man had never been in the box, but he wasn't about to show a shred of weakness in front of these people. They'd already made a rather unsavory impres-sion.

With the dick measuring out of the way, they all settled back into their plastic chairs, Flint taking up an empty one and gesturing for Darius to do the same. He eyed the chair with doubt, then settled on crouching aside the barrel instead.

"So," Ember broke the uncomfortable quiet. "Why is it you've come, oh mighty Darius Black? Surely not to recruit our sorry asses to your... work?"

Darius cleared his throat, "Er, no. That's more of a... solo effort."

Flint grumbled his discontent, and Darius eyed him for a mo-ment, considering. The man *was* large, by human standards, and it *had* hurt when he'd clasped Darius' hand... a little... but no. No. This man wouldn't pose much threat to Reapers. Not without training, and Darius most certainly did not have time for that now.

"No," Darius continued. "I come on behalf of a group of no-mads outside the border."

There was a collective grumble before Jack muttered, "Will you lot shut up? I want to hear what the man has to say." Surprisingly, they did as he said.

Darius began again. "I made contact with 'em going on ten years back."

"Aren't ya a tad... *young* for it to 'ave been so long ago?" Penny asked, raising her weathered brow in disbelief.

"I'm sure I'm not the only one what had to grow up too quick here," Darius replied. "Now, I'm honored to say, I call these no-mads friends, and they asked me to come to ya for help. Ya see, though things are... difficult... in here, there's things they go with-out out there. Medicine. Food. Supplies for cleanliness and what-not—"

"Eh. So just like in 'ere then," Gunner laughed.

"Aye. Things are hard both sides of the border." Darius nod-ded. "But Callum—that'll be someone you're doing dealings with should ya agree—he thinks we might help each other, ya know?"

An accord had been reached, and now Darius knelt in the back-yard. No flowers for Lila, only barren dirt sprinkled with a few pathetic patches of stringy brown grass. He didn't know why he'd come out here, only that it felt wrong to have ventured to this place without visiting Lila, too. Darius *thought* this was the spot he and Papa had buried her, but time had eaten away at the memory, and he could not say with certainty. So, he pretended this was the place. He didn't speak, for there was nothing to say. Nothing he hadn't said to her in his nightmares, but he did *wish*. He wished with all of his might she was somewhere safe and soft and happy.

His vigil was interrupted by the scuff of a boot behind him. Ember approached, holding out a wilted dandelion in offering. He took it with a nod and placed it on the patch of dirt that was probably not Lila's grave.

Ember knelt at his side and spoke softly, "Who was it?"

"She was... my sister."

"Ah. I'm sorry, Darius. I don't know what I'd do if I lost Flint."

"It was a long time ago." Darius shrugged and rose to his feet. Spicy smoke tickled his nose as he turned. Flint leaned against the back wall of the house with a wad of rolled paper at his lips, breathing out gusts of gray.

"Haven't seen one of those in years," Darius grunted, moving to shove past Flint.

Flint caught his arm, then released it as if he was worried about what punishment the touch would earn him. Darius only turned and stared down at him, holding out a hand for the smoke. Flint raised his brows, but placed it between Darius' fingers all the same.

"Had one o' those before, Darius?" Flint asked.

"Nah, but my Pa was fond of 'em. Used to smoke 'em in that spot right there." Darius nodded to where Flint stood. "Figured it's past time I know what the fuss is about." Darius took a long drag of the spicy smoke and coughed. "God, that's awful." But even as he said it, a faint buzz started at the back of his neck. It wasn't entirely unpleasant.

"Those things are terrible for you," Ember chastised as she stomped over, taking the smoke from Darius and indulging in a long drag, before puffing a cloud back in their faces. "You're doing it wrong, That's why you coughed. You're not meant to *breathe* it. Just hold it and release it again. Here, try again."

"I thought you said they were terrible?" Darius took the paper from her, inhaled a tiny puff, and... coughed. Again.

Flint chuckled as he took his turn. "They are. Ma used to say they'd kill us dead." He shrugged. "Seems somethin's gonna do it sooner or later, so why not enjoy? Wasn't no smoke that killed Ma, after all."

"Mine neither," Darius grumbled, "Ya know. I'm not sure 'bout the rest of 'em. But you two seem like the risk takin' type. Ya ever wanna get out of this shithole..." He gestured to Bracken around them. "Seek me out. Callum says there's room for a few more like-minded individuals in the tribe."

"We might just do that," Flint said, passing the smoke to Ember.

She eyed Darius for a long minute before speaking again, "Be safe, Darius Black."

"And you. Flint, Ember." With that, Darius turned his back on the siblings, both of them burning like flames in the golden glow of the sunset.

Clothes swapped to the all black uniform of the Reapers, Darius slunk through the streets of Bracken an hour later. It'd been too long since he'd wetted his hands in Reaper blood, and he itched for a kill. Darius told himself it was about making the world safer for humans by eliminating the Reapers, one at a time. But deep down, he knew it was merely petty revenge. The box hadn't grown back his eye, and he lived with the loss of it every day. Why shouldn't those who'd done it to him pay? And yes, it was misplaced anger. He *should* take out his rage on James Malik, but Addy had asked him not to, so he wouldn't. Killing Reaper grunts would have to do.

So, Darius crouched with his body pressed to Bracken's food store building, awaiting a transport truck. When it rolled past, he leapt up and caught hold of the back handle.

A half hour later, he chuckled to himself as the Reapers drove him directly through the gates of their camp. *Gunmire* was etched into stone pillars at either side of the gate. *What a stupid name,* Darius thought as he hopped down from the truck into the shadows of the barracks. He made his way down a narrow alley and came to a stop at its mouth, eyes scanning for prey. Across a pocked dirt road, a group of children were shouting and playing, wrestling one another to the dirt. Wait. No. They were not *playing*. Darius looked on with a rock in his gut as a little boy wrestled an even smaller girl to the ground, ripping her down by her hair.

"You lose, Jemma!" the boy screamed in her face. "Now, I'll take your pretty hair." He pulled a curved knife from the back waistband of his black pants and began sawing through the girl's ebony locks, spitting in her face while the other children cheered. When he'd finished, Jemma reared up and headbutted him, once, twice, three times, until the boy's nose was dumping blood across her newly shorn head. The boy did not fall back, however, he only wrapped his arms around Jemma's throat and squeezed until her brown skin took on a gray pallor. Darius took one step to interfere, because even though he'd come to kill Reapers, these were *children*. Barbaric, terrible children, but children all the same. He was saved from exposing himself when a sharp, matronly voice cut through the air.

"Enough!"

The boy immediately released Jemma, who flushed and gasped on the ground for only a moment before staggering to her feet and getting in line aside the other children, who Darius now saw all bore shaved heads, as the adult reapers did.

"Good." The matron called, "Jemma, Brock, step forward."

They did.

"You've both earned marks this day."

Brock, the boy who'd shorn Jemma's hair, beamed with pride, his teeth bloody from his gushing nose. Jemma did not allow a smile to curl her lips, but a slight sparkle danced in her eyes as she inclined her head.

"The rest of you are dismissed," the matron barked, signaling Jemma and Brock to follow her to an outdoor shower, where she doused the two until they were clean. Darius watched on in sick fascination as the woman took out a needle of sorts and motioned for the children to sit on a bench. And then, after some other process of cleaning Darius was unfamiliar with, she began cutting a line of ink into the skin behind Brock's ear. When she was finished, she set aside the tool and shaved the girl's head down to skin before repeating the inking process. So this was it? *This* was how the Reapers earned their ink.

Darius shivered as he slunk away, identifying an exceptionally marked man on the outskirts of the camp. He'd aim for those ones from now on, for that ink told the story of many a vile deed. Darius couldn't help but wonder how many marks he'd have if he'd grown up a Reaper. Surely, there wouldn't be an inch of visible flesh left on him.

It was with smug satisfaction that Darius entered the mansion a few hours later. He'd gotten two Reapers tonight. He'd killed them quietly, left their bodies in the dirt, and slipped back out of Gunmire unnoticed.

He hurried through the darkened hallways to his bedroom, desperate to get cleaned up before Gabe and Addy returned. He'd never told them, would never tell them where his late-night activities led him. He didn't think Addy would much appreciate it, even if she understood, and Gabe... well, Gabe would be horrified. He'd once yelled at Darius for smashing a spider. Darius snickered to himself as he shut his bedroom door behind him and locked it, just in case. He spun as a rasp of breath sounded somewhere in the vicinity of his bed. The lamp flicked on, and there, illuminated in its glow like a nightmare come to life, sat James Malik with a shiny silver gun pointed at Darius' heart.

18

IF IT WERE QUIET

A SINGLE LIGHT LIT the front facade of their house. Despite the growing dread in Gabe at what he planned to do, he smiled at the light from Darius' window. It was more than a light. It was salvation for his sister. By sending her away with Darius, he could secure more than just her freedom. She would be *happy*. He wanted her to be happy. He wanted Darius to be happy. He wanted it more than he'd ever wanted anything.

He'd just punched in the code and swung the door wide for Addy to enter ahead of him when a deafening bang shattered the night. Addy, to her credit, did not do more than gasp and begin running in the direction of the noise, toward Darius' room. Gabe followed, pausing only to snatch a knife from the block on the kitchen counter. Addy tripped and stumbled over her dress, crashing to the floor. Gabe didn't stop to help her up, just leapt over the top of her and continued on, for a second and third bang had rung out. *Gunshots.*

Gabe had only heard them twice in his life, but it was not a sound one easily forgot, especially not when they sounded in close proximity to something precious. He slammed into Darius' door, jiggling the handle and cursing when he found it locked. No sound emitted from inside the room, immeasurably more worrying than if there'd been the noise of a struggle. Gabe rammed into the door with his shoulder until the lock broke loose, door flinging wide to reveal Darius standing staring at the floor beside the bed as he gripped the dresser with whitened knuckles. From one hand, dangled an oddly familiar pistol. Gabe's first feeling as he took in the scene was one of utter relief. Darius was okay.

Addy's presence curled at his back, and a noise matching the sentiment sighed out of her.

"What—" Gabe began, just as Darius crumpled to the floor, blood staining the carpet where he fell. They hadn't seen it before. It'd been invisible on the black garment. Addy fell to her knees, blood soaking her gown, and shrieked, "Darius! Darius! Please, God. *No.*" She shoved her fingers into the wound on his shoulder. "Gabe! Help me!"

Gabe shook off his shock, only to stop in his tracks as a groan emitted from beside the bed. Their father staggered to his feet, two apparent bullet holes oozing gore from his stomach. James stumbled toward them, a snarl mingling with the groan of pain. Gabe didn't think. He merely rushed to his father, catching him around the middle. Only... No. That was all wrong. Because it wasn't his hand that curled around Father's back. It was the knife, stabbing through flesh and muscle. Gabe pulled the blade free as his father fell backward with an odd gurgle and lay still in a growing pool of blood. Addy screamed.

But all Gabe could hear was the voice in his head chanting, *At last! At last! At last!*

I knew you could do it, Gabe! What a good boy you are. What a smart boy. You did it! At last. At last. At last...

Because that was his father, dead at his feet.

And he was still holding the knife.

There was too much blood on Darius. *Too much blood*. More blood than there should be from the small wound at his shoulder. They'd packed it with a torn sheet corner, then left Father on the floor and congregated in the kitchen. Darius sat swaying on a stool with Addy pacing behind him.

"We have to take you in, Dare," Addy insisted for the hundredth time, eyes darting to Gabe, where he stood nursing a glass of whiskey.

"I'm sorry," Darius grumbled, pain sharpening the words. "I didn't mean for it ta happen." He spoke the words for Addy's sake, but the apology? That was directed at Gabe.

Gabe shook his head, trying to silently communicate to his friend that he didn't blame him. He couldn't find the words, hadn't been able to speak since he'd run his father through. But he had to—and soon. The plan he'd been mulling over before this new development could still work. He could still send Addy away. There'd just be some other things to consider to make the cover up complete... Concerns like his father's corpse in the next room over. Gabe slugged back another mouthful of whiskey and cleared his throat. "Enough. Both of you."

They both pinned him with narrow glares.

"It seems, I've come into my title earlier than expected." Gabe cleared his throat again. "And that means I'm in charge here, whether you like it or not. Now, Darius. You *will* go to get that fixed, but first, we've some matters to settle."

"Gabe—" Addy started.

"No, Adalia! Don't. There's nothing to be done for me now. The best I can do is get *you* out." He turned to his friend. "Darius, we haven't talked about last night, and it seems we'll not get the chance. Hear this. I forgive you. And trust me to know I had my reasons."

Darius' eye shone, but he nodded.

Gabe continued, "There are things you need to know—"

Addy interrupted, "Gabe, please! I have to stay here, I have to help you—"

"There is no help for me, Addy! I'm a lost cause, but if it helps you sleep at night, I'll call that doctor. I won't break my promise."

"*Please,*" she whispered, tears falling as she succumbed to her desperation.

"No. You are going, both of you. And I hope I'll see you again, but now... with this..." He gestured vaguely in the direction of Darius' bloody bedroom. "I've got a whole lot of shit to deal with. I need to know you're safe. Both of you."

"I don't understand why that means we gotta go," Darius gently prodded.

"I was getting there. Before I... killed him..."

"Before *we* killed him," Darius corrected.

"That doesn't make it better," Gabe snapped, pressing his palm to his forehead and gulping down several deep breaths. "Father signed Addy's life away, Dare. If you don't get her out of here... if you don't disappear, she'll be taken to the facility with our mother, where she'll be forced to *breed*, then give her children away. She'll be locked up. Forever."

"What?" Darius shot a glare at Addy.

"We have time," Addy whispered.

Gabe shook his head. "No. We don't. Not anymore. They'll be poking around, asking questions with this... this... mess." Gabe poured himself another glass of whiskey before continuing, "So, here is how it is going to be. Addy, you pack bags for the two of you.

You will take Darius to the box. You will get him healed. And then, you will leave. Both of you. You will hide. You will *not* come back. This… this may very well be goodbye. I will stay here and clean up this mess." Gabe swallowed his guilt at the lie he was about to tell. "You cannot come back. I will get things settled, and then I will go away for a while. That way you won't be tempted to come and check up on me."

"Where will you go?" Darius asked.

A pang of hurt shot through Gabe's heart at how easily his friend had accepted the plan, but he shoved it away and answered. "I'll go to the city. I have friends there who can help me."

"You do not," Addy scoffed.

"Don't tell me what I do and do not have!" Rage boiled his throat. "You will fucking *listen* to me for once! You *will* leave and you *will* be happy."

Addy shrank into Darius' side. He brushed his fingers down her back, wincing as the movement jostled his wound. "Ads, he's right. We must go."

Gabe met Darius' eye gratefully, understanding flashing between them. They'd do this, they'd do *anything* if it meant protecting Addy. Gabe dipped his head in thanks.

Darius murmured something in Addy's ear, then gave her a gentle shove toward the hall. She went without argument, her shoulder drooping under the weight of unspoken shame.

Darius rose on shaky legs and rounded the counter until he stood in front of Gabe.

He clasped a hand on the back of Gabe's neck, pulling him forward until their foreheads touched. Gabe mirrored the movement, gripping Darius like a lifeline. And he *was* a lifeline. Gabe knew the only reason he had to keep living would leave along with his friend.

"Thank ya, brother," Darius whispered. "It's no easy the first time, but I promise it gets better. You'll be okay."

It wasn't a question, but Gabe lied anyway. "I'll be okay."

"I love you." A squeeze.

"And I love you, brother. Take care of her."

"Take care of *you*, Gabe."

"I will," Gabe whispered as Darius broke from him at last. Addy appeared, rushing to Gabe and flinging herself into his arms. Sobs wracked her body as she clung to him with all of her considerable strength.

"Shhhh, shhhh." Gabe breathed into her hair as he ran a hand down the silken strands.

"I'm sorry," she sobbed into his now damp chest. "I love you, little Gabey. I'm sorry."

"Hey, hey, chin up, Ads." He knocked her under the chin with a knuckle, holding her tear-streaked face up so he could look at her one last time. "I love you back. It'll be okay."

"I can't leave you," she whispered, running a hand over his cheek.

"You can. Go, Addy. Go, and be happy."

"I'll try," she said before forcing her hands to her sides and joining Darius at the back door.

"See ya soon," Darius said as he pulled the door open and allowed Addy to go first.

"See you soon," Gabe replied as Darius stepped outside, only to turn back.

"Gabe?"

"Yeah?"

"Don't let 'em see it."

My fear. Gabe smiled, "I won't."

Then Darius shut the door. Leaving Gabe alone in the silent house.

Only.

It wasn't silent, was it?

At last. At last. At last...

Gabe picked up the bottle of whiskey.

19

A WORTHY SACRIFICE

DARIUS

DARIUS HAD EVERYTHING HE'D ever wanted, and it had only cost him his best friend. And it might make him a terrible person, but he thought the cost was worth it. Because the impossible had happened. Addy was *his*.

Gabe was going to kill himself. It'd been written in his gaze, in the way he'd held on just a little too tightly before their parting. And this time Darius wouldn't be there to save him. *No one* would be there to save him. But Darius couldn't think about that, not when Addy's safety hung in the balance. This was the only way. At least, that's what he told himself to justify abandoning his friend in a time of great need.

All he could do was wish Gabe well, and hope he changed his mind—another lie Darius told himself. Then he lied to Addy, too, assuring her that her brother would be alright as she helped Darius down into the box. Had it been only yesterday he'd been lowering Gabe into this same miraculous brine? It seemed much longer than that, the time warped and distorted under the terror of the last two days.

The facility had been back to its normal vacant hollowness when Addy dragged him through the side door, the staff gone for the night. Then the familiar blissful pain of the box came. But Darius only saw Adalia, only felt the fullness in his heart when he thought of taking her away with him.. He emerged reborn, and swore in that moment to be worthy of the gift Gabe had entrusted him with.

It was no trouble at all to slip across the border under cover of darkness. There were no guards, after all. They'd all been pulled to some disturbance at Gunmire Camp.

Addy held his hand all the way, tears streaming as her feet caught in the unfamiliar brambles of the forest. Darius tucked her into his side, dragging her further from everything she'd ever known. Deeper and deeper into the woods they went.

Until finally, Darius had Adalia all to himself.

20

THRICE

GABE

HE MURDERED HIS FATHER three times. The first time, when Addy's screams had bounced off the walls, had been the worst. The second had been a terribly unpleasant surprise. Gabe had been slouched across the chaise lounge in the office, just breaking open a second bottle of Papa's whiskey, when a thump had sounded down the hall. Gabe struggled to his feet, swaying as he stumbled to the door, which wobbled and split in his vision. He'd never managed to get this drunk before. Darkness danced at the edges of his eyes, but the garbled moaning down the hall had him shaking his head to clear it. Cold sweat slicked his upper lip as his father's familiar baritone grunted, *"G... G... Ga—Gabriel."* Surely, this was his mind playing tricks on him. It couldn't be. It. *Couldn't*. Be. He'd seen his father die. Darius had checked his pulse for Christ's sake. It couldn't be. And yet. It was.

When Gabe stepped through the door, he was greeted with the gruesome vision of his father crawling toward him in the shadowy hallway. A trail of blood streaked the pale wood floors as Father dragged his limp legs behind him. Gabe—or Darius—must've damaged his spinal cord. Father stopped as his milky eyes locked on Gabe, where he stood shell-shocked in the amber light spilling from the office door. *"P-p–please. My son,"* James rasped. *"Help me."*

Oh God. Oh God. Oh God. Gabe had wanted nothing more than to turn and flee, to follow his sister and the brother of his heart into the woods, to *never* look back, but before he could, the voice spoke. *Oh, Gabe, darling one. Shall I do it this time? You did so well before, though it looks as though your aim was off.* The voice was gentle, soothing.

Gabe's hands shook so violently, he dropped the crystal tumbler he'd been clutching to the floor. It shattered into thick, jagged pieces—a broken, beautiful thing, not unlike the heart beating a wild rhythm in his chest. He couldn't breathe.

"*Help me,*" his father pleaded again.

There's only one way to help now, Gabe. Gabe shook his head against the voice in his mind, causing himself to stumble into the wall. He groaned. His father groaned. The voice in his head groaned. *Enough, Gabe. Let me.*

Gabe let him. He closed his eyes. He closed his mind. He pretended he couldn't feel himself lean down to clutch the broken remnants of the crystal tumbler. He pretended he didn't feel his spine straighten, didn't feel the eerie sense of clarity enter his bones, didn't feel the tickle of bloodlust in the back of his throat. He pretended he didn't walk calmly to his father, where he struggled on the floor. He didn't feel the slickness of his father's blood coating his hands for the second time in one day as he shoved the jagged glass into his neck. He pretended. And all the while, the voice praised him for it. *You are doing so well, Gabe. We are doing what's right. This is good. We hurt those who hurt the ones we love, who take what we want. We don't let them hurt us any longer.*

Gabe didn't know how he'd gotten back to the lounge in the office, but when he woke, his fingers were crusted in brown blood, and two more empty bottles littered the ground beside him. His head ached wretchedly. He left the office, turning away from the entry hall, some strange sensation prickling along his scalp, telling him not to look that way. He tripped his way to the bathroom and stood for hours under the freezing spray, gulping water and scrubbing until his skin was raw, until he shivered too violently to continue.

His stomach roiled as he pulled a robe around his shoulders. Toast. He needed toast. And he never wanted to see whiskey again.

He looped around to the kitchen, still heeding that *thing* that told him to avoid the hall. He knew he was forgetting something important. He made himself a toad in the hole, smiling as he thought of his friend. He'd miss Darius. He always did. He'd miss Addy, too. In truth, he didn't know how he'd live without her, but he was glad they were together, even if it meant he was alone. He knew he wouldn't be that way for long. A sweet ache settled into his heart.

The toad in the hole went down like curdled milk, but Gabe somehow managed to keep from puking it all back up. He left his dishes in the sink and circled to the hall.

He stopped short at what the morning light illuminated on the polished floors. Blood. It was smeared on every surface. There were handprints on the wall. Broken glass glittered, casting iridescent shadows. Amongst the gore, Gabe spotted a trail of bare foot-prints. He looked at his feet. Despite his long shower, the shadow of blood caked around each of his toenails. He swallowed down the bile in his throat as flashes of the prior night lanced through his skull. He could pretend all he liked, but Gabe remembered what had happened. He would never get the image of his father crawling to him, pleading with him, out of his mind. The feel of Father's warm blood on his hands would haunt him until he breathed his last. Yes, Gabe remembered. There was just one problem. Father was not where Gabe had left him.

Fortunately, he wouldn't be hard to find. He'd left a trail.

The third time Gabe murdered his father was more of a chore than anything else. The first time had brought shock and pain. The second had been horror. The third was merely acceptance... and an odd sense of inadequacy that he couldn't seem to perform this most basic of sins. Murder shouldn't be so complicated. Hell, if the texts were true, he should have been able to do the damn thing with a rock and a jealous heart. Alas, they'd meddled in things. They'd made something unholy with Ethereals. Gabe should have known sooner. Of course, his father couldn't be killed like a proper human. It was the same reason Gabe couldn't *die* like one. He *wasn't* a proper human.

Gabe went back to the kitchen. He armed himself with a butcher knife, lighter fluid, and a box of matches. He followed bloody footsteps into the back garden. Facedown in the grass with dewdrops glistening in the strands of silver hair on his head, James' chest barely rose. How could he still live?

Gabe set his supplies aside and crouched, rolling Father onto his back. It disturbed Gabe that he didn't feel more as he shook James until his crusted eyes opened in thin slits. He tried to speak, but Gabe held a finger to his lips.

Gabe whispered, "I didn't get a chance to tell you before, Papa."

His father's eyes widened at this use of the name.

"I loved you." Gabe's voice broke. "I loved you. Addy loved you. My mother... she *tried* to love you. But it wasn't enough. You thought we weren't enough for you. But I realized a long time ago it's you who wasn't enough for us. You didn't deserve the love we gave. You took that love, Papa, and you turned it to poison. I hope you suffer. I hope you don't know a moment of peace. I hope... no... I *know* you'll burn in hell for what you did to my sister. I never got to tell you, Papa. With every shred of my heart," he leaned so his lips brushed the shell of his father's battered ear, "I *hate* you."

Something sinister purred at the center of Gabe's soul as he spat the words. The sensation didn't let up, even as he slowly carved into James' neck. He knew he should feel something more. He *should* be horrified. He *should* stop. But he was numb, except for the warm satisfaction in his chest. He was numb. It was so much better than feeling so damn *much*.

Gabe cut until his father's head pulled away from his body. It'd been more difficult a task than expected with the butchering knife. If he ever did this again, he'd need a better tool. What a terrible thought. Gabe didn't understand where it'd come from, didn't understand why it was *his* thought.

Oh, we'll be doing this again. The voice was coated in velvet. Gabe ignored it as he set Papa's body ablaze. He stayed, staring, feeling nothing and everything, until only ash and bone remained. It didn't take long, but the part of him that still saw sense whispered, *hurry, hurry, hurry. They'll be coming to check on the smoke soon...*

He took what remained of the lighter fluid and splashed it around the halls of the mansion, walking carelessly through puddles. When he'd finished, he found his way back to Father's office and settled on the lounge with the knife and box of matches. Without even a flicker of hesitation, Gabe dragged the blade across his own throat. And with his last gurgling breaths, he lit a match on his past and burned it down.

21

KINDLING

GABE

THEY'D FOUND HIM IN the ashes. He did not know how he'd lived, only that he had. It was relief he felt when the medical staff told him he'd succeeded in killing his father, at least. Though *they* didn't know it was him. They'd wrongly assumed the fire had been an attempt on both his and Father's lives. Gabe let them believe what they wanted, disassociating as they tortured him with surgeries, always followed by visits to the box.

The voice helped.

The voice talked him through it.

And when they'd finished piecing him back together, they enrolled him in counseling to deal with the trauma of the fire. Gabe had laughed. What did they know of his *trauma*?

But he'd gone. Twice a week, since he'd relocated to his penthouse in The City of Mirrors, he'd either gone in person or over the phone. To his surprise, it helped. The medication they'd given him especially helped. It quieted *most* of the voices.

He hadn't told the doctors about the voices, and he feared the day they decided he no longer needed the medication. Alas, he'd cross that bridge when he came to it.

Gabe was *trying*. He was trying to find a solution other than the seemingly impossible task of ending his life. Some days were better than others, but *every* day his heart hurt with how badly he missed his sister. He pushed away thoughts of Addy and donned his jacket, taking his time arranging the cuffs so they lay just right. Then he was off to another Ethereal party at another Ethereal penthouse. Gabe found little enjoyment in them, but it was a necessary evil to maintain the business connections his father had left behind.

So Gabe left his quiet apartment and ventured a block over and up, up, up to where the party awaited.

He was stationed in a quiet corner, observing the crowd, when a silky voice shattered his peaceful little bubble.

"Ah. Is that Gabe Malik? I remember you—though it's hard to forget anyone from our little town, isn't it? Especially not the most important person... Ryker." Amber eyes danced with laughter as the man extended his palm. The heaviness of childhood bullying lay thick in the air between them.

"Ryker Armadis." Gabe took his hand. "How could I ever forget you?"

Ryker cleared his throat and leaned in, his tone taking on a more serious quality. "I am sorry, you know."

Gabe's brows rose.

"I never imagined myself as the bad guy, but looking back now... I'm sorry. I'm not that same kid. I hope I might earn your forgiveness?" Just then, a looming figure approached, his pallor a pasty contrast aside Ryker. The newcomer stood taller than Gabe, something the voice did not take kindly to, hissing, *Straighten your spine, Gabe. We do not cower. Our strength is within.* Gabe did as it said, lifting his head to meet a striking green gaze.

"Ah, there you are." Ryker gestured to the man. "Gabe, this is Marcus Pentra. I'm sure you remember him, too."

"I do." Gabe let a little malice edge across his expression as he took the man's hand and shook it.

"Little Gabriel Malik! How could I forget? Not so little anymore..." Marcus opened his mouth as if to add to that teasing when a flash of fear skittered across his gaze. There and then gone. A less observant person would never have noticed, but Gabe... Gabe saw it. *Curious.*

Ryker spoke up, sparing Marcus from whatever had caused that look of discomfort to cross his features. "I was just about to offer my condolences. I heard about the fire..."

"Er... yes. It was most unfortunate," Gabe said, loosening his tie where it had suddenly become too tight around his neck.

"To lose a father and sister at once... It is beyond my comprehension. You are a stronger man than I to be up and about so soon," Ryker said pityingly.

"I heard you were also injured?" Marcus inquired.

"I was. Yes."

"Well, you look to be well recovered... Did they ever catch the culprit?" Ryker asked.

"You know," Gabe said. "I'd rather not discuss this. I should go, really."

Ryker grasped his arm, stopping him in his attempt to flee. "No, wait. I'm sorry. You see, I rather lack a filter, Gabe. Forgive me?"

And perhaps it was only because it had been so long since Gabe had spoken to another person in such a genuine manner, but he nodded and stopped.

It was quiet for a mere moment before Marcus said, "You know, a friend of yours once beat the shit out of me, Gabriel."

Ryker barked a laugh. "I remember that. The pirate boy! He was utterly terrifying, Gabe. Where did you find such a loyal companion?" His eyes sparkled with mischief and memory.

"Excuse me?" Gabe asked, trying to buy himself time. He'd had no idea. Damn Darius. He supposed he had to play dumb. "I've no idea what you're speaking of?"

"Oh, come now, Gabe," Marcus said, "We're not those same boys as we were. Having a human friend is rather thrilling. You know... perhaps that did more to quell our cruelty than anything else. We thought you were so far above us, and then this boy appears—"

"You remember what he said?" Ryker cut in.

"I was getting to that before you interrupted me." Marcus leveled an unimpressed look at Ryker, who replied by sticking out his tongue.

"That's only because I tell it better," Ryker said when he'd stopped making childish faces. "You see, Gabe, we'd been exceptionally awful to you that week—I'm sorry again for that—and Marcus here had given you a split lip. Truth be told, it must've been bad if your friend had the opportunity to see it. Means it couldn't have healed before you got home. Rather sloppy, Marcus."

Marcus grunted his assent and glanced sheepishly at Gabe.

Ignoring the tension, Ryker continued, "So, we're playing in Marcus' yard after school, when this dirty boy shows up. Worse than that, he's got an eyepatch and a limp—that's why we call him the pirate boy—he did have a name though, didn't he, Marcus?"

"Ah, yes. Made sure I knew it, too," Marcus grumbled.

"That's right! He screamed it at you after he'd knocked your arse into the mud—"

"He did more than that! Little bastard pummeled me first. Broke my nose and dislocated my arm before he shoved me down there. And you, traitor, just hid behind the trees." Marcus glared at Ryker as if he still hadn't forgiven him for that betrayal.

Ryker chuckled low. "I wasn't about to interfere. That kid was feral. I've never seen a human who could do that. I was terrified!"

"How do you think *I* felt?" Marcus shook his head at Ryker before turning back to Gabe. "Anyway, this kid appears out of nowhere, looking very much like a pirate from the storybooks, beats me half to death without a word. Then, when he's got me down in the dirt, he spits in my face. Spits! He tells me, *'I am Darius the Black. Darius. That is the name you'll remember. The name you'll forget is Gabe Malik. Do you hear me?'* God, he was terrifying. Then he goes, *'You forget Gabe. Forget him. Or Darius the Black will come for you while you sleep. If you look at Gabe. If you talk to him. If you ever touch him again. I will come. I will kill you. Tell the others.'* And then, he just got up and left. Never saw him again. I suppose I shouldn't be talking to you now, right?" Marcus winked.

"I—I didn't even know that happened," Gabe said, baffled.

Ryker chuckled. "You wouldn't, would you? We were too scared to talk to you after that. You must realize we had nothing to do with that incident in secondary..."

Gabe wracked his brain, and suddenly, he did remember. He remembered that day Marcus had hit him in the face so hard it'd torn his lip. He'd left school early and run straight to his safe place—to Darius in the back garden shed. He'd been a blubbering mess, but Darius. Darius had been so *angry*. He'd grabbed Gabe's shoulders and demanded to know, *'Who did this, Gabe. Who did this?'* His rage had settled into disturbing quiet when Gabe had confessed who it was and that it wasn't the first time. Darius tucked

Gabe into his bed with a bag of frozen peas pressed to his lips and disappeared. Gabe had fallen asleep before he got back, and they'd never spoken of it again.

"Oh, so you do remember..." Ryker interrupted Gabe's reverie.

"Yes. Yes, I do remember." Gabe nodded.

"And Darius the Black?" Marcus pressed.

"Darius... You don't have to worry about Darius. He's... gone."

"You know, I'm sorry to hear that. Such a friend is a rare quality in life." Marcus said all of this as he gazed at Ryker, who returned the stare in kind. "Perhaps, Gabe, we might start again. Try this friendship thing, instead of the games of our youth? Seems you're down a rather good friend, after all."

Something fluttered in Gabe's chest. Something he'd thought dead when he parted ways with his sister. "I'd like that."

"Oh, thank God. Now, let's drink to celebrate! This conversation got entirely too heavy." Ryker swiped three tall flutes of sparkling liquid off a passing tray and passed them around. "To new beginnings," he roared.

"To new beginnings!" Gabe echoed. And for the first time since he'd sent Darius and Addy away, hope kindled in his heart.

PART THREE

Love is just another word for madness.

INTERLUDE

"I've naught to offer you but this." Darius folded Addy's hand over his heart and held it there. With his free hand, he slipped the leather string over her head. On its end hung a polished carving of a rosebud. He'd spent these months whittling at it by firelight once Addy had gone to sleep. She shone incandescent as she clasped the trinket in her fist.

"It's beautiful," she whispered.

"You're beautiful, Addy, more than that... I don't know the right word for it. You're... you're *everything*." Darius planted a soft kiss on her brow, careful not to disturb the crown of leaves resting there. Little Greta had insisted she needed them. Darius couldn't help but agree as he peered down at this creature, this *woman* who'd always been so far out of his reach, but against all odds, stood here with him now.

"These are the oddest vows I've yet to 'ear, Lad, and I had ta listen to Osiris—the auld bat—make pledges last week. Best be gettin' on with it, aye?" Callum said, interrupting the notion of their solitude.

Greta giggled from her place on his knee. He tickled her under the chin. Callum and little Greta were the only witnesses they'd wanted, aside from Gabe, of course. Alas, he was out of reach, still in The City of Mirrors, if Bracken's gossip told true. There had been a fire, that's what the townsfolk said. Darius had confirmed it. Sadness filled him up to bursting as he'd looked at the blackened remains of the place he'd thought of as home for so long. The powerful Ethereal heir had barely escaped with his life, his father and sister lost to the blaze. Darius had to admit, it was clever, though he'd expected no less from Gabe. It was a relief to hear his friend was alive, if nothing else.

Darius had asked after Gabe again when he'd last met up with Flint to exchange goods, to no avail. The humans didn't know much about Ethereal affairs on a good day. They certainly didn't have any information on one who appeared to be trying *not* to be found. No, Darius couldn't find Gabe, so Callum and his daughter would have to do. Greta shrieked as Callum tickled her armpit, then shushed her. They were merry company, but they did not hold Darius' attention. No. That was Addy. Always Addy. Joy shone on her face as she giggled with the child.

Darius swore then and there he'd give that to her. If she wanted it, of course. Hell, he'd have a hundred babies if that's what she wanted. They got to make the rules now, after all.

Addy turned back to him, happy tears pooling in her green eyes.

Darius gave her hand a gentle squeeze. "As I was sayin', before I was so rudely interrupted—"

A harumph sounded from Callum's direction.

"I've naught to give you, but this: my heart, and all the love in it." He took both of her hands in his and held them up to kiss each knuckle before continuing, "My hands, and all the work they might do." He smirked. "I give ya my mind, every ridiculous thought in my head, Addy—they're yours. All of it, anything ya might ever require of me, it's yours. It's always been yours. My possessions, meager though they be. They're yours. Quite simply, I give ya all of me, if you'll have me. And I pledge to you, Adalia Malik, to do everything in my power, for so long as I might live, to keep that smile on yer face."

She stood on her toes and pecked his cheek.

Darius grinned as he finished, "And should there ever be a day ya don't want to smile, I'll be here, Addy. In any way ya might need me. But mostly, I'll be here, glaring at the world right beside ya. I promise."

Addy swallowed, then took a steadying breath before beginning, "Darius... I do not know the words for these pledges, so I hope you'll accept this, instead. I love you. I've loved you since forever. I've known since we were children, that you were my greatest, most forbidden wish. I never wanted to belong to anyone, because I already belonged to you. So, yes, I'll take your heart and your hands and your mind. I'll take your meager possessions. I'll have you, Darius Black, so long as you promise to have me, too."

"Yes, Addy—I thought it was obvious," Darius laughed.

"Idiot." She muttered before continuing, "I promise to love you, Darius. I'll love you forever. When I'm nothing more than a whisper on the wind, I'll still be calling your name." She brushed her fingertips over his cheek, where a tear had broken free.

"I love you," he choked.

"Forever."

"NOW KISS!" Greta yelled, clapping her chubby little hands together.

"Aye," called Callum. "A kiss for the lass, Darius!"

So, Darius kissed Adalia in the shade of the aspen trees, their union sealed to the sound of laughter.

22

HOLLOW

GABE

IT'D BEEN TEN YEARS since his first attempt.

One year since his last.

And of one thing Gabe Malik was certain: he could not die.

He'd become rather creative in his methods. Not that it made any difference. After 'taking a tumble' off a bridge last year and *still* waking up alive, intact, Gabe had decided it was past time to put the idea of suicide to rest. Instead, he'd focus his energy on atoning for his sins. The list of his transgressions had only grown over the years. He often forgot days, *weeks* at a time. The voice never indulged him by telling him what they'd done, but Gabe caught flashes every now and then. Flashes that sent him running back to his bottles and pills and blades. So yes, though he did not remember the details, Gabe knew he had much to atone for. Today was another step in that direction.

There'd been rumors of late in the Ethereal circles. Grumblings of women gone missing from their gated facilities, children stolen from their beds, Reapers haunting corners and human screams painting the nights red. Gabe had ignored the letter on his comms disk, but Ryker and Marcus, dutiful men they were, had answered the summons and received their new Reaper enforcers the day before. The Reapers now stood in the corner of the penthouse dining room, the unsettling sensation of their eyes crawling across Gabe's skin a constant reminder of their presence.

"You're gonna have to go get yours soon, Gabe," Ryker said as he caught the direction of Gabe's attention.

"I'm surprised the Authority hasn't brought you in already," Marcus grumbled, settling back in his chair and slinging his legs up on the stone tabletop. "You know they don't take kindly to being ignored."

Gabe put down his pen with a sigh. "I know. I'll reply tomorrow, okay?"

Ryker nodded his approval.

"It's just..." Gabe lowered his voice so the Reapers wouldn't hear, "*why* are they here?"

Leaning in, Ryker whispered, "Authority says it's for our protection—"

"But we know better, don't we, Ry?" Marcus shot a glare at his Reaper and enunciated his words so they'd be *sure* to hear him. "They're here to spy on us."

"Sable would never do such a thing. Would you, Sable?" Ryker beamed at the black clad woman who stood over his shoulder.

She did not reply. Her eyes merely darted around the room before a scowl further hardened her jagged features.

"Tell them to leave," Gabe said, a now familiar coldness entering his tone.

Ryker started, "We can't—"

"We can," Marcus interrupted. "They can report whatever they like to their masters, but remember, The Authority put them under *our* control. You two," Marcus jerked his chin at the Reapers. "*Get out.*"

His Reaper immediately complied, heavy steps treading out of the room until the front door clicked shut behind him. Sable, however, just stood and glared at Ryker with expectation. Gabe filed this information away. It seemed the Reapers only liked to obey their assigned Ethereal.

"You heard the man." Ryker waved a hand about in the air, shooing Sable away. "Go on, then. Stand outside with your... friend."

Sable huffed before making a rather petulant exit.

"God, I thought mine was bad," Marcus chuckled as she shut the door.

"You have no idea," Ryker groused.

"Here's hoping yours is like mine, Gabe. Now, onto more important matters," Marcus began.

"Wait," Gabe said. "Lower your voice, Marc. I'm not entirely certain they can't hear us through the door."

"What have I told you about calling me Marc?"

"I'll stop calling you Marc when you stop calling me Gabriel."

"The difference is, Gabriel *is* your name. Marc is not mine, asshole."

"Will you two stop bickering like a couple of old biddies?" Ryker said, loosing a long-suffering sigh. "Marcus, do as Gabe says and lower your god-damned voice. Gabe, stop calling Marcus Marc. He hates it. Now, for the love of all that is holy, can we talk about how to deal with whatever's going on with the women while those two buffoons," he pointed to the door, behind which the Reapers stood, "are distracted?"

Marcus eyed him before relenting. "Fine. First, I wanted to let you both know that the *other* part of our operation is going well. I successfully relocated another human family last week. There have been questions, but it still hasn't caught Authority attention, as far as I can tell. We'll have to wait for things to settle before we take more, but so far, so good. The building operation at—"

"Stop." Gabe cut Marcus off.

"Don't say anything more. Do *not* tell me where you're putting the community. The less I know, the better."

"Gabe," Ryker groaned. "Not this again. The whole damned thing was *your* idea. You should know how things are progressing. We couldn't do it without your facilities in Bracken as a front—"

"Shut up, Ry." Gabe's hands shook. "Do *not* tell me anything else. Do not mention the facilities. In fact, it might be better if you two exclude me from this part of our dealings entirely from now on."

Don't be such a poor sport, Gabe. I already heard everything.

Go the fuck away.

What do I always say to that?

No.

That's right, darling. No... thank you. See, I can be nice. Why don't you let me out again? I'm bored in here.

Never.

Oh, you'll cave. Next time you're feeling weak. Just you wait.

"Gabe? Earth to Gabe?" Ryker snapped his fingers in front of Gabe's face.

Gabe pushed his hand away, grimacing, "Look, I'm going to need you to trust me on this. What if... what if I'm caught? Hmm? Did you two ever consider the fact that *I'm* the one they'll pin this on? It's *my* facility that keeps 'losing' people. You've heard the rumors. You know the only thing that protects us from The Authority as it is, is the fact we're 'Heritag e'... whatever *that* means. If they should summon me—"

"Which they will if you don't accept a Reaper," Marcus grunted.

"Yes. Exactly. If they summon me and start asking too many questions... it's better I don't know. I can't tell them where the missing humans are if I don't know. Right?"

"Fine," Ryker assented, rising to pour himself a drink from the bar cart along the wall. "But are you going to help us get to the bottom of this *other* problem at least?" He held up a glass in question.

Gabe dipped his chin, taking the drink. "Yes, of course. I wish it were different, but I've the most influence of the three of us—"

"I'm working on that," Marcus muttered under his breath. When Ryker tried to put a drink in his hand, he merely shook his head.

"Good. You should," Gabe said. "It would be best if things were a little more... *equal* amongst us in case the worst should happen."

Well, that's a rather maudlin thought, Gabe.

Shut up.

Or what? You'll take the happy pills?

Yes.

Liar. You're all out...

"Good. Good. Now, come closer, my friends." Ryker situated himself between them and pawed at the back of their necks, pulling them into a huddle over the tabletop. "Do you remember Dimitrius Finch?"

Marcus tore out of Ryker's grip and leaned back in his chair with a groan, "God damnit, Ry. Don't tell me you've been associating with that fuckwit again." He went to fold his arms, but Ryker pulled him back into their huddle.

"I mean to tell you I've been associating with that fuckwit again," Ryker chuckled. "Don't make that face. The man knows all of the best secrets. So, Dimitri told me something rather tantalizing over drinks last night."

"Get on with it," Gabe pleaded.

"You two are no fun," Ryker whined, throwing his hands up, releasing them. "Fine, I'll give you the version where I don't tell you about how I swindled him out of a thousand credits. I won't tell you the part where my Reaper laughed at him and he nearly pissed himself—"

"You just did, Ry," Marcus remarked dryly.

"Ooops." Ryker winked. "Anyway, I *had* to get him drunk to make him feel better. And then I *had* to start sprinkling in questions about the missing Ethereals... And then, one thing led to another and, well, let's just say, I had him in a rather compromising position when he confessed he'd seen some Ethereals in the Dark Market, in a club, of all places."

Marcus' knuckles had gone white as Ryker told his tale, rage reddening the back of his neck. "What do you mean, a compromising position?" He asked, just as Gabe said, "Brilliant, Ry. You're brilliant."

There was an awkward moment of silence while the two conflicting thoughts sat like a bad smell in the air between them.

Finally, Ryker cleared his throat, looking apologetically at Marcus. "Not *that* kind of position. And yes, Gabe, I am brilliant, which you two seem to like to forget. So, all of that to say, if we want to find the women, we should schedule a visit to the Dark Market."

"Brilliant." Gabe grinned.

"I hate that place," Marcus griped. "I don't know why the Authority doesn't shut it down. Last time, I almost stepped in a human shit. *On the street.*"

Ryker wrinkled his nose, "How did you know it was a human shit?"

A laugh bubbled up Gabe's throat.

"You two are children," Marcus deadpanned, but quickly lost his composure, his lip twitching until a smile brightened his normally somber expression. "So, when are we going?"

Ryker looked at his watch. "How about now?"

Gabe smiled at his friends. "I'll call the car. Let's make the Reapers walk."

"Now that's a brilliant idea," Marcus laughed, slapping Gabe on the back before hauling Ryker up so they could go command their Reapers.

When are we getting one of those, Gabey?

One of what?

A Reaper, of course. Think of all we could do with one...

I don't want one.

It doesn't seem like you have much of a choice here.

Gabe sighed internally. *You're right. I don't have any choice at all.*

23

HOME

Darius

"A log cabin."

"Really?"

"Yes, really. Did you expect someone like me to sleep on the ground for the rest of my life?"

"Well..." Darius pulled Addy closer in their nest of leaves, kissing her nose as he gathered his thoughts. "I suppose I'd not given it much thought, aye?"

She pinched him in the side.

"Ow!" he protested, rolling her beneath him so the leaves crunched. "That hurt, ya wee devil." He bit her on the neck in repayment, earning him a squeak, followed by a soft groan.

"You don't seem to be too terribly injured," she teased, voice gone breathy the way Darius liked so much. He trailed kisses downward, only to be stopped by a mighty tug on his hair. "I'm serious, Dare."

"Ugh," he sighed, rolling off her. "Fine. A log cabin. Anything else, my queen?"

"As if that's asking too much..." She chuckled. "It's been ten years of caves and flimsy tents and sleeping under the stars."

"Well, the stars *are* lovely." Darius looked up at them, chest swelling with the sensation of infinity.

"Yes. They are. And we'll look at them every night, from the porch of our cabin."

"Ah. So, there'll be a porch on this cabin, too, eh?"

"Yes," she grinned. "And, there will be a little bedroom, separate from ours, for when the children come along." Despite her effort, her voice went hollow at the end of that statement.

Darius tugged her to his chest and stroked fingers through her silver hair, plucking free bits of leaves and twigs. "Oh, Ads, not this again..."

"Yes, this again." Her fingers curled into the material of his shirt.

"Love, I cannot watch ya hurt like that."

She pulled back a little to glare at him. "Oh, so you just get to decide what I can handle now, do you?"

"That's no what I meant, and ya know it. It gets worse every time it happens." He gave her a squeeze, and she dipped her chin, hiding the tears Darius knew would be welling in her eyes. "Last time, ya near bled to death. And I... I almost died myself from seeing you hurt."

"I can handle the risk, Darius." She snapped.

"Aye. I've no doubt ya can. But have ya thought that maybe I cannot? I can't lose you, love. I can't. I can't bear to hope no more, neither. And for what? The possibility?"

"Don't diminish it like that." She shoved away from him and sat up, resting her head on her knees.

He reached for her, "Addy—"

"No. Don't act like I'm some unreasonable person who needs to be placated."

Darius dropped his hand and sat up, scooting so he was leaning against a tree. He swatted at a mosquito on his neck and begrudgingly admitted to himself a cozy cabin sounded nice right about now.

"You don't get to tell me what I can handle," Addy whispered to the trees before looking back at him. "I love you, but I want more of life. I've been content... for the most part... these years. For a while, it was enough. There was certainly enough to learn, but then... Well, I'm tired." She buried her face in her knees. When she continued, it came out muffled, "I'm tired of moving around and living in the dirt and never settling. Never resting for a moment."

"Are ya sayin' you want to go back?"

She leveled him with a glare, "I'm not, and you know it. I meant it. It's you and me. Forever. God, you can be such an ass."

"Aye," Darius agreed, rubbing at his temples.

"It's just... What are we hiding from, Dare? Why can't we build a home?"

"You know I'd love to grant your every wish, love, but the risk—"

"What risk? Look around you. There's no one else here! The most danger I've seen is from the *humans* you dedicate so much time to helping."

"That's not fair. They share supplies."

"Supplies that *you* bring them!"

"They'd die without me!"

"Maybe they should—" She slapped a palm over her mouth as if that might keep him from hearing the words she'd already said.

"Ah. So you'd wish that fate on Greta, aye? What of the Harver boys? And little Anya?"

"Darius..." She scrunched her hands up in her hair. "You know I didn't mean that. I wish them all well. I was just trying to make a point. And be reasonable, I can't even show my face in front of them. I haven't seen Greta since she was *five*. And now she's what? Nearly a woman grown? The point was. *This...*" She gestured to their pitiful camp. A musty wool blanket on the leaves. A tattered tarp strung between trees. Packs hung high in the branches to deter wildlife from rummaging through them. Dying embers in their firepit. "This is no life," she continued. "And the risk you keep telling me of? I... I don't believe it exists, not out here. It's been five years since I've seen a Reaper. I haven't laid eyes on another Ethereal since we left. And you keep telling me to just trust you... Where is my *brother*?"

"I canna control what Gabe does! Last I heard, he's still in the Mirrored City, livin' it up. If I could nail down his schedule, I *would.* I would plan it and take ya to him when he next comes to Bracken, but no one knows when that'll *be.* He's like huntin' a ghost."

"I know..." She shook her head. "I know. I didn't mean to bring him into this. The point was, I think we are plenty safe out here. I don't think it would be too dangerous to set down some roots. And even if someone found us, you and I, we're plenty capable of defending ourselves—"

"I'll not have ya stainin' yer hands in blood."

"Oh, but *you* can?"

Darius stilled under her scrutiny.

"I think you forget sometimes, I'm not *stupid.* I know you've done things... *do* things... that have you tiptoeing back to me in the dark, reeking of blood."

"Addy."

She held up a hand, motioning him to stop. "I've never asked. And I don't plan to. Does it scare the hell out of me, whatever it is you're up to? Yes. But I'd rather not know. Not fully. But as we're talking about it now... Don't try to convince me *you* couldn't keep us safe from harm if we built a home."

Darius didn't have anything to say to that.

"Give me one good reason? *One* reason why we can't have a little stability?"

And though he tried, Darius couldn't think of a reason, not one that was true, anyway.

"I want a *life* with you," Addy said, scooting closer as her tone gentled. "I want a home and little versions of you and me running around in the yard. And maybe," she choked. "Maybe if I feel *safe,* I'll be able to give them to you."

"Oh, love," Darius whispered. "*You* are enough for me. You've always been enough."

Hurt flashed on her face.

"But." Darius continued as a sense of dread threatened to smother him, "If ya need more, I will give it to you. I will find a way."

"Really?"

"Yes. Really. We'll start scoutin' for the place tomorrow if you'd like?"

"I would. I would like that."

"Then we'll do it, but can ya set my mind at ease? Promise me you'll keep takin the medication until I've built us a home?"

"I promise. I'll keep taking it—until *we've* built a home."

"That'll do, love."

Then, Addy kissed him, and they made love beneath the stars.

24

LUCIFER'S TEARS

BENEATH THE PRISTINE PERFECTION of The City of Mirrors lurked a secret. Well, everyone *knew* about it, but they pretended it was a secret, anyway. The society had originally been built underground. After The Final War had left the majority of the land pocked and scarred and smoking, the air was simply too toxic to breathe, if the histories could be believed. Gabe didn't know if *he* believed it. Information on the war and the weapons used in it was difficult to come by. It seemed implausible that humanity would be dumb enough to poison something as integral as *air*.

Gabe quickly checked his position on man's intelligence as he dodged a spout of flame, which licked at the hair of a wiry little human man. A shame, because the show he'd been putting on *had* been impressive until it'd gone awry. He'd been twirling glowing batons of fire when he missed his mark and lit his own hair ablaze.

"God, I love the Dark Market," Ryker said, flicking a credit at the man's fleeing backside.

Ryker *would* love this place. It was entirely wretched, and something in Gabe's friend delighted in those kinds of things. Gabe wondered if perhaps that's why Ry kept *him* around.

Whores leaned out of ramshackle doors, flashing their wares eagerly. Human males with too few teeth decried their goods—mostly some kind of ghastly brand of alcohol they'd cooked up in their kitchen sinks. Refuse littered the street, and purplish haze colored the air, as if it were guiding them to their destination. It was difficult to breathe down here, under the city streets, the only ventilation a few grates that cast pools of silver light into the murk below. It was as if the Dark Market existed in an entirely different time—an entirely different realm than the rest of the world. Marcus was right; it was bizarre that the Authority had not addressed it. Perhaps they had some motivation for keeping the place. Mercifully, there were no children. Even the wicked creatures who inhabited the Dark Market knew their presence would be a step too far.

Ryker led the way, indeed following the lilac clouds down a narrow alley. The Reapers loomed at Gabe's back, their breath hot on his neck.

"Back off," Marcus snipped at them. His Reaper glared and took a tiny half step away.

"Remind me why we couldn't leave them at the car above?" Gabe asked.

"Do you think they would have listened?" Marcus replied. "Our plan to make them walk didn't work. It seems they have all the power if our 'safety' is in question." He spat a wad of phlegm at the Reaper's feet.

Gabe looked on in fascination as the male tightened his grip on his scythe, but didn't retaliate. *Interesting.* Marcus' Reaper didn't *like* that. *Prideful thing.* Gabe tore his attention from the Reaper and turned to Ryker. "So, this is the place?" He gestured to the rusted, battered door, beneath which plumes of smoke rose.

"Yes. This is where Dimitri said to come, anyway." Ryker didn't look entirely certain.

"Are you sure?" Gabe smirked, inhaling to launch into a tirade on Ry's incompetence when the door swung open.

"Are you going to stand out here? Or are you coming in?" The voice was sultry, soft... *musical.*

Gabe blinked. Then blinked again as he took in easily the most beautiful woman he'd ever seen. Ryker turned to Gabe with lifted brows in an *I told you so* gesture. Gabe looked back to the woman, only to find she'd disappeared and been replaced by a particularly mangled-looking Reaper. The huge man chewed at a wad of some unknown substance and spat, as if he were paying Marcus back for his earlier disrespect. A shiver crawled across Gabe's skin, because that certainly meant they'd been watching.

"Only the Denmaster's dogs are allowed inside," the massive brute said, and to Gabe's surprise, their Reapers nodded and stood aside. So much for *safety*.

"Did you see that?" Marcus growled into Gabe's ear as they stooped under the doorframe.

"What?"

"She was *Ethereal*."

"Yes, I—" Gabe cut off as he ran into Ryker's back, where he stood frozen just beyond the threshold. It seemed they'd entered yet another new realm.

The den dripped debauchery. It was an expansive space, made to feel cozy through low lighting and plush fabrics. Arched entrances to alcoves lined the sides of the room. Crystal chandeliers hung in equidistant intervals along the center of the ceiling. Around each, in uniform spirals, gilt cages displayed human females. Gabe could reach up and touch the women's feet if he had the inclination. He didn't. The women were organized by color. Women with skin and hair that melted into shadow were clad in costumes woven of black silk. They writhed in an obsidian tide in the first spiral. Gabe strode under a kaleidoscope of color—brown and red and pale as moonlight—as they made their way toward one of the many alcoves bracketed by wispy curtains at the back of the den.

Ryker had told them this was an exclusive club, but nothing could have prepared Gabe for the cluster of women that stood in cages suspended in the final spiral. The second to last had been made up of women painted and dyed every color of the rainbow, as if in culmination of the wares the house had on offer. In the final spiral, stoic and silent, stood Ethereals. Their bodies dripped pale diamonds matching the silver gleam of their hair, but the females' eyes were hollow, haunted. They did not shout their desire as the humans had when Gabe walked beneath them. They did not even try to pretend to enjoy this place. Is this what became of the females who did not agree to join the breeding facilities? Gabe swallowed down his horror, turning to find Ryker and Marcus with matching stricken expressions carved into their faces.

Marcus clapped them on the back and ushered them into the nearest vacant alcove, where they'd be out of sight of the other patrons in the already busy den. They stood mute for long minutes, all of them with mouths opening and closing like fish who've suddenly found themselves gasping for breath on a dock, unable to form words but desperate to try.

It was Marcus who finally broke the quiet, speaking in a harsh whisper, "They told me they were taking her to a women's school all those years ago." Marcus' knuckles whitened at his side. "If Jane is in one of these clubs…" It was a wonder his jaw didn't crack with how hard he ground his teeth.

Ryker stepped into Marcus, leaning so close Gabe could barely hear the words over the breathy sounds from the alcove next to them. "I would burn it all down with you," Ryker whispered. The tension went out of Marcus' body as he slumped into Ryker, allowing the other male to run a hand down his back before straightening and stepping away. He shot a meaningful glare in

Gabe's direction, then plopped down on a thick velvet pillow and snatched a decanter from a side table.

"It's more likely she's a breeder. Take comfort. My mother is happy at her facility." Gabe tried, but Marcus just glared harder as he poured three generous glasses of milky liquid and passed them around. His fingers lingered on Ryker's for a moment too long. Gabe quirked a brow at the exchange but didn't say anything, opting to slump down on his own cushion against the opposite wall. One swallow of the drink had Gabe sputtering and coughing.

Ryker barked a laugh. "First time trying Lucifer's Tears, eh, Gabey boy?"

Gabe held the drink out, eyeing it skeptically. "What's in this?"

"God only knows," Ryker winked.

"Just drink the fucking drink," Marcus snapped. "We're gonna need it." He gestured with his glass to a robust Ethereal male approaching their little corner. He was clad in a dark fabric suit that seemed to swallow up the light in the room, completely at odds with the bright white pelt of fur draped over his broad shoulders. He stood taller than Gabe, his long, braided hair brushing the bottoms of the cages as he walked. His ears bore so many piercings they drooped under the weight, and curling across the bridge of his nose were whorls of dark ink Gabe had only ever seen on Reapers. It was plain this male did not bend to societal norms. Something about that truth set heavy in Gabe's belly. Fear curled like a cat in the back of his mind. *Ooooo.... I like him.* The voice whispered. Gabe shook his head and swallowed down another gulp of Lucifer's Tears, forcing back the cough that rose in his throat.

The man stopped in the archway before them, flexing fingers bedecked in chunky sapphire rings. The one on his pinky dripped a fat drop of red, which ran down the side of his hand. Blood. It was blood. Gabe wrinkled his nose against the scent. It clung to the man. The stranger met Gabe's eyes, lifted his hand to his mouth, and licked up the drip with one long stroke of his thin tongue.

Gabe, my darling, don't just sit there. Remember who we are. A flash of broken crystal and fire burst behind Gabe's eyes. *Father crawling through his own blood...* Gabe rose to his feet. One did not sit in the presence of a creature such as this. Marcus and Ryker followed suit.

The newcomer grinned, revealing overly long canines and a split tongue. Ryker flinched. A rumbling rolled out of the man at the sight of it. His gaze flicked between Marcus and Gabe for a moment before he turned fully to Gabe and extended a hand.

Even this mongrel knows what we are, the voice whispered.

Gabe took the hand, slender fingers lost in a thick palm.

"I am Hadeon," he said, voice so low only Ethereal ears could have picked up the sound. "And you are?"

Gabe shivered, then clutched Hadeon's hand until bones ground under his touch. "I am Gabriel Malik." He met Hadeon's eyes, returning his malicious grin.

Hadeon's smile widened. He crushed Gabe's hand back, just enough to make his fingers splay under the pressure before releasing him. "Gabriel Malik. Your reputation precedes you." Gabe didn't like *that* one bit. What reputation?

"And who are your friends?" Hadeon asked.

"Marcus Pentra. Ryker Armadis." Gabe gestured to each in turn.

Hadeon's gaze bounced between them, eyes sparking as if he'd just been given a gift. "Powerful friends... Yes. You'll do nicely," he rumbled. "You three do not belong here. But I'm glad you've come. Welcome to my Den." He spread his palms in a motion to encompass the entire club. "Do sit. We've much to discuss." The end of the word came with a hiss, courtesy of the forked tongue, surely. "What brings you... *gentlemen,*" Hadeon nodded smugly to the three of them, as he settled himself onto a cushion, "to the Den?"

"W... We—" Ryker began, but Marcus placed a hand on his chest, silencing him.

"We're here for the pleasures you have on offer, of course. Why else would we come here?" Marcus said.

"Ah, yes, I suppose that is the obvious answer, isn't it? The one you feel you must speak. But none such as you come into my den for the simple wares displayed in the daylight." Hadeon chuckled, reaching for the decanter of Lucifer's Tears and taking a swallow without bothering to put it in a glass. The smile melted off his face until only cold malice remained. "Why are you *really* here? Why has a trio of Heritage Ethereals come into my club in the middle of the morning on a Tuesday? Are *you* fools? Or...do you think *I'm* a fool?" Hadeon leaned forward and placed the decanter on the floor between his feet, making a show of cracking his knuckles.

Gabe glanced at Marcus for guidance, only to find him glaring, surely about to say something that'd doom them all. Gabe spoke before Marcus could, "We don't think you're a fool."

"Oh? Then why lie?" Hadeon worried the tip of his sharp canine with his strange tongue. "Only someone foolish would believe a lie as pitiful as that."

"No." Gabe showed his palms. "We *are* here for something special. We've heard..." He nodded to the Ethereals swaying in the cages. "We've heard... the women were disappearing. We had... we didn't know where they'd gone." Gabe sucked in a breath to steady himself. The voice whispered, *Don't let him see your fear,* and it sounded a lot like Darius this time. Gabe straightened at the encouragement. "It seems you have some of them. We'd like to know how you came by them."

"*Gabe...* " Ryker hissed, rising as if to forcibly shut him up.

Hadeon shook his head at Ryker. "No, I like the honesty." He turned back to Gabe. "What is it you plan to do when you learn the dark secrets of the City of Mirrors, boys? Will you scurry to the Authority to tattle?"

"Of course not," Marcus murmured.

"Good boy." Hadeon reached out and patted Marcus' head as if he were a lowly dog. Marcus growled, but that only caused the smile on Hadeon's face to widen. "I can assure you, the Authority won't mind." From within the folds of his suit coat, Hadeon produced a card emblazoned with the Authority seal. He placed it into Gabe's hand, gesturing for him to pass it around to the others. It was an Authority permit. They'd *approved* this place. Gabe had thought the Dark Market to be a poorly kept secret the Authority chose to ignore, but this... this turned that notion on its head.

After it'd circled the small space, Ryker placed the card back into Hadeon's waiting palm.

"Why do you think there are Ethereals here?" Hadeon asked. "You know the rules."

"The rules continue to change," Marcus grumbled.

"That they do. It seems you don't know how to play the game," said Hadeon, steepling his thick fingers. "Shall I teach you? I find I quite like the idea of three Heritage pups following at my heels. You would like that, wouldn't you?" He flashed his teeth. "Or... shall I report *you* to the Authority?"

"No—No. That won't be necessary," Gabe said. "That's not why we're here. We were merely curious. More, we thought..." He swallowed. "We might invest in your trade."

A booming laugh shook the space as Hadeon reveled in those words. When he'd composed himself, he slapped Gabe on the back. "Oh, I knew I liked you. You're just what I'd hoped. Saw it from across the Den, boy. You got what it takes. You others..." He turned a critical eye on Marcus and Ryker. "Eh, you'll have to earn some trust. Gabe here will show you the way." He squeezed Gabe's shoulder.

Gabe didn't want to think about what it meant that this monster so clearly approved of him. *He sees me,* intoned the voice. Gabe shook out of Hadeon's grasp and nodded.

"Now." Hadeon rose to his feet and rubbed his thick palms together. "Why don't you boys show me you know how to appreciate this trade. Eat. Drink. Fuck. I care not. But prove to me you've the eye for finer things. I don't deal kindly with those poking in my business, see?"

"Understood," Marcus growled through clenched teeth.

Hadeon drummed his fingers on his chin. "Eh, three Heritage Ethereals walk into a bar... there's a joke there somewhere... I just don't know what it is. I *do* know that if they'd like to walk back out, they'll convince me. They'll come back tomorrow, and the next day, and the next until I believe the lie they're peddling." He turned his cruel glare on them.

God. This male was volatile. Gabe couldn't get a read on him. What did he want?

"Yes," Hadeon continued the ludicrous rant. "They'll earn my trust. And if they do, perhaps they'll walk back out the *front* door at the end of the week. Perhaps, I'll let them in on a little secret. Perhaps, I'll take their daddy's money. In the meantime. *Enjoy.*" He spread his arms wide, and a trio of humans clad in transparent blue fabric ducked into the alcove under his arms. "We've got something for any taste." He winked at Ryker, who looked as though he wanted to crawl into a dark pit and die there.

Hadeon stepped out of the alcove and stood under the arch as if he were waiting. Gabe followed and reached out a hand to him, surprised to find it steady. "We'll show you. We know how to have a good time. And at the end of the week, we'll talk."

"No." Hadeon slapped his hand away. "I make the rules here. Convince me, or at the end of the week, I'll feed you to the wolves." His eyes glimmered as he nodded to the Ethereal females swaying in the cages. "Don't bother to hide. I can find you. And if *I* don't—*they* will." It was a ridiculous threat. The Authority, no matter how aloof they might be, would never allow a working Ethereal like Hadeon to do anything to Heritage Ethereals. Would they? Hadeon snapped his fingers, and a cluster of Reapers peeled off the wall where they'd stood, completely invisible behind black fabric. How Gabe had failed to notice them was a mystery. He should have sensed them, if nothing else. Perhaps it was the purple haze that choked the air making his wits duller than usual. A flash of Darius' face danced across Gabe's mind at the sight of Reapers. The way his friend had screamed under their brand the day they'd met...

The Reapers only smiled in eerie unison. A shudder skittered down Gabe's spine. His fist curled. When he looked to Hadeon, his words came out in a hiss, "Perhaps, my *friend*..." Gabe allowed an evil smile to paint his lips. He didn't know where the nerve came from, but he found he was quite good at this game. He found he quite liked the taste of power on his tongue. He leaned into Hadeon, so close that when he spoke, his lips brushed the piercings on the man's ear. It was bold of him, but in the few moments he'd met the man, Gabe deduced Hadeon craved having his limits pushed. And Gabe wasn't about to turn away from a button that needed poking. "Perhaps you'll tell me how you came by the Reapers, too. And if it doesn't work out with the others... Perhaps you and I can come to an agreement."

Hadeon boomed a laugh. "Ah, yes. I like you, Gabriel. Now," he clapped Gabe on the back, "*convince* me." With that, he turned, the white pelt swaying with his lumbering steps as he retreated to the front of the Den. It was a polar bear pelt. Gabe had thought they were extinct. Though he supposed this didn't prove otherwise. It seemed Hadeon was a collector of rare things. *Yes, Hadeon collects rare things indeed*, Gabe thought, as the man slung his arm around the Ethereal female who'd opened the door. He did not allow his gaze to linger on the stunning woman, just spun to face the alcove once more. He glanced up at the Ethereals in the cages, jolting when one mouthed a word at him: *Help*. His chin dropped in a barely perceptible nod, then he stepped back into the nook as the three humans scurried out under Marcus' baleful glare.

"Well fuck," said Ryker.

"No, Ry..." Marcus interrupted, turning his attention to Gabe, "I don't know what you did, Gabe, but that was good."

"Oh, I just... I said what was necessary," Gabe shrugged.

"No. That was something else. What's going on with you?" Marcus narrowed his eyes.

"Nothing. I'm the same guy as always."

"It didn't seem like *nothing*." Suspicion coated Marcus' words.

"Listen, Marc. I don't know..."

Marcus crept into Gabe's space, fingers curled in silent threat. What was wrong with him?

Gabe retreated, showing his palms, "I... I... I don't know what came over me."

You know exactly what came over you, the voice mocked.

Shut up. Gabe snapped internally before continuing, "Sometimes when I'm in an uncomfortable situation like that... something else just takes over. I just know what to do... I don't know how."

Liar.

"Fine," Marcus grumbled, flopping back down on one of the cushions. "Looks like we've got a show to put on, boys." He refilled their glasses with Lucifer's Tears and knocked his back in one long swallow.

And so they sat, indulging in the wares of the den, getting ever drunker and higher on the drugs lacing every morsel in the place, until they'd nearly forgotten why they'd come in.

Gabe quite liked to forget. He greedily anticipated forgetting tomorrow and the next day and the next. Ryker certainly had no problem forgetting, either. But Marcus...

Marcus stood with a rigid spine, his anger somehow burning away the effects of the drugs that pummeled them from every direction. Gabe pitied him for it.

It was because of this pity that Gabe pulled a serving woman into the nook and whispered in her ear, "Who might be able to tell me more about those ones?" He nodded to the Ethereals in their cages. When the server failed to reply, Gabe tried again, "Who can I speak to about getting a night with one of them?"

The servant lowered her mouth to Gabe's ear. "You'll be looking to speak with *her*." She casually swept up an empty glass and motioned it in the direction of a shadowy corner near the bar. There, upon a chair that looked eerily like a throne, sat the beautiful Ethereal he'd seen earlier, curled on Hadeon's lap.

"And how does one get a meeting with her?"

The servant dodged one of the women writhing at the center of their nook and said over a shoulder, "Only Hadeon can get you a meeting with her," before she disappeared.

Gabe slumped back and took another long swig of his drink. It seemed he'd have to play Hadeon's game, but at least now he knew which direction they were heading. He tried to catch Marcus' eye, to see if he'd overheard the exchange with the server, but his friend's attention was fixed elsewhere. Gabe followed his glare to the Ethereal females, who'd finally collapsed into the bottom of their cages, slender legs curled beneath themselves. Surely, Marcus was thinking of his missing sister. Yes. Gabe pitied Marcus, for when he thought of his own sister, a smile warmed his heart.

Addy was *safe*. She was with Darius.

25

ADDY WAS SAFE

Darius

ADDY WAS BLEEDING TO death on the front porch.

Darius raked shaking fingers through his hair and chanted the thought.

Addy is bleeding to death on the front porch. He mustn't forget the reason for his urgency. But Damn her. She'd *promised*. He'd thought he'd been safe from this particular torment, for a little while, at least. But damn her, *she'd lied.*

Darius had taken his sweet time building her the cabin, hoping to drag out the illusion of safety a little longer, but apparently, she'd grown impatient. He'd gone to great risk to obtain the medication that kept her from getting pregnant, and she wouldn't even take it... Darius was furious with her. Why did she put herself at risk like this? He'd thought after ten years of trying, and every failure becoming more dangerous, Addy would relent. He didn't need children to be happy. He had *her*. But *she* wanted them. And damn if the guilt didn't eat him alive. He'd made promises, too. Promises broken in perpetuation as *he* failed to give her this simplest wish. And now, Addy was bleeding to death on the front porch of their unfinished cabin.

Well, he supposed she was probably no longer on the front porch, but that's where he'd left her, tucked under a thick blanket in her rocking chair, a cup of wild chamomile tea in her hands, the cabin stuffed with rations so she'd not need to venture out while Darius was away.

He'd found her in their little bedroom a week ago, kneeling in a pool of blood with tears staining her pale cheeks.

"I thought it'd taken this time," she'd sobbed.

"Oh, Addy, Addy." Darius had swept her up and rubbed circles on her back until she fell into a fitful sleep. He'd cleaned her up as best he could while she struggled in and out of consciousness, blood ebbing, then gushing out in a seemingly endless tide. How could she bleed so much and still live? Surely, it was only her being an Ethereal that allowed her to survive. And she *would* survive. Darius refused to accept any other option. But when she'd continued to bleed so heavily a full week later, Darius knew he couldn't wait any longer, so he'd done the only thing he could. He'd left her. Carrying her all the way to Bracken would have only slowed him down, and Darius refused to bring her here, to the box. He wouldn't risk anyone seeing her. If they did, they might take her from him. And even if he *had* gotten her to the box, it was a temporary solution to a problem that would doubtless rise again. Addy was nothing if not stubborn.

Darius stood under the starry shadows of the trees outside the Ethereal facility in Bracken.

"Tell me again why we're tryin' to catch one of 'em?" Flint whispered from his place beside Darius.

"Eh. My woman needs help. Do ya need a better reason?"

"No. It's just risky, Dare, even for you."

"No risk is too great."

"I just hope it don't come back to haunt us. Don't be leaving any loose ends."

"You know I never do. Now shut up. They're coming out." Darius pointed to the line of Ethereal workers making their nightly exodus from the facility. Flint eyed a straggler, turning to Darius with raised brows. Darius nodded his agreement. They crept forward, nothing more than shadows in the dark. The Ethereal male was of an unusually small stature, a blessing for Darius, who'd have to haul him all the way back to the cabin in the mountains. Darius signaled to Flint, who stepped directly into the man's path as he turned away from the door he'd been punching a code into, locking up for the night.

"Hey!" The Ethereal squeaked, "You're not supposed to be out this time of night! It's past curfew. Get home, human, or I'll summon the Reapers."

"We wouldn't want that." Flint winked at Darius, where he stood over the Ethereal's shoulder.

Darius covered the Ethereal's mouth with one hand, yanking him backward until he was caught against his chest. He poked his knife into the Ethereal's ribs just hard enough to draw blood. The man emitted a squeal, muffled by Darius' palm. "Now, you'll come quietly, or this 'er knife will find its way into your heart, and I'll hide yer body so deep in the woods they'll never find it in time to put ya in the box, yeah? Nod if you understand."

The Ethereal nodded.

"Good," Darius said. "Now, my friend here's gonna point his gun at ya, and you're gonna make sure we get into that building safely. Nod."

The Ethereal nodded.

Darius shoved his hand into the Ethereal's pockets, pulling free a device and crushing it in his fist. "No help will be coming," he whispered. "Best do as we say."

Another nod.

Darius released the male, and he stumbled forward, disabling the lock with fumbling fingers, his breathing loud in the quiet night.

"Hurry the fuck up," Flint snarled, drawing back the hammer on his pistol. The click of it sliding into place only caused the man's breathing to further stutter as his panic ratcheted up.

Darius chuckled, "I think you're scaring him, Flint."

"Good," Flint grinned.

The door unlocked, and he shoved the man through.

"Name." Flint demanded of the Ethereal.

"Ah–Ahh–Arthur," he stuttered.

"Good. Now, Arthur, to be completely straight with ya. You ought to know that I know about everything and everyone you love, and should you fail to comply with my handsome friend here... I'll kill them all, eh?" Flint was full of shit, and Darius bit back a chuckle at his blatant lie. They knew nothing about this Ethereal. He'd only been chosen because he was the last to leave. Still, Arthur nodded, the whites of his eyes showing as fear for his loved ones set in.

They ushered Arthur further into the building, and when they had him cornered in a small tiled room with nothing but a sink, toilet, and drain in the center of the floor, Darius released him.

Arthur stumbled to his knees. "Please," he begged, "My partner, she'll be waiting for me—"

"Well—" Flint began.

Darius interrupted, "Flint, go wait outside. I've words that are only for Arthur here."

Flint eyed him skeptically before nodding and exiting, closing the door behind him.

"Now, Arthur, is it?" Darius crouched in front of the man. "I've need of yer help."

Arthur nodded.

"Ya see, my woman, she's... she's like you."

"Y, y, you have an *Ethereal* woman?"

"Indeed, I do. And she's sick, ya see?"

"Sir, beggin' your pardon, if she's like me, she's *not* sick." Arthur shrank back, as if he expected Darius to strike him.

"Aye. Mayhaps sick is the wrong word. I'm gonna trust you, Arthur. I'll give ya the truth. You'll not betray that trust, will ya?"

"N—No, sir."

"Good. Ya see, my woman, she wants children. But when she gets with child, well, she don't stay that way, aye? She bleeds. You know what's to be done for such a thing?"

Arthur's eyes widened further, his mouth popping open into a shocked little O. "Sir, you mean to say, she's pregnant with *your* child?"

Darius bristled at the implication it'd be anyone else's child. "Aye. Of course. That is, she *was.* Now, she needs help with the bleeding. Can you help me with that, Arthur? Or have we come to the end of yer usefulness?" Darius rose, and Arthur shuffled backward until he was pressed against the white wall.

He held up a hand. "N–n–no, sir. I'm just trying to understand, is all."

"I wonder, Arthur, if perhaps I ought to get one of yer friends instead, if yer failing to understand how children are made."

"No. No. Of course, I understand that part. *Please.*" His fingers shook as he held his hands out to still Darius' advance once more. "It's only, you... you are not Ethereal, yes?"

"Do I *look* Ethereal?"

"Well, er... no, sir."

"Get on with it then. Say whatever has ya sputtering so. We've little time."

"Sir," Arthur took a deep breath. "You see, your woman... she, ah, well, you see—"

"Get to the fuckin' point."

"Yes." Arthur nodded to himself, then blurted the words, "Ethereal females have a fail-safe of sorts, to prevent breeding outside our... species. They'll not become pregnant, you see? The problem, I fear, is that you, my good sir, must therefore not be entirely human, but you must also not be entirely Ethereal, either. Such a pregnancy would be highly risky."

"You mean ta tell me her sufferin' is *my fault?*"

"Uh, well, that's not what I meant. I only meant to explain—"

"Enough. We'll discuss this later. Can ya help a woman in such a state?"

"Y—yes, sir."

"Good. Now, Arthur. You and me are goin' on a little trip. We're gonna leave this here room. We're gonna gather the supplies, the *medicines* ya need to help a woman in such a state, aye? And then I'll take ya to her. If ya prove helpful, ya might see tomorrow. You'll not make a fuss, will ya then?" Darius didn't let guilt have a single inch of his consciousness as relief flooded the man's gaze.

"If I help you, you'll let me live?"

"Aye," Darius lied. No. He would *not* let Arthur live. His death warrant had been signed the moment Flint had stepped out of the shadows.

"Of course, sir. I'll help. I couldn't let a woman suffer."

"Good. Now get to work." Darius rapped once on the door, and Flint opened it, raising a brow in silent question.

Darius nodded his answer.

Flint grasped his arm and pulled him into a hug. "Be safe then, my friend. Give Addy my love."

"Same for you, brother." Darius shoved him off. "Now, go say hello to Ember. Tell her Cal is ready whenever she is."

"I will. See you at the drop, then?"

"Aye." Darius turned away and followed Arthur down the hall, his promise to Adalia fluttering on impatient wings.

He'd promised to give her every wish he had the ability to grant. And it seemed the only thing standing in front of him giving her children, was the weakness of his humanity.

The answer had been right in front of him all this time.

If Addy could not have what she wanted from this version of him, he'd just have to become something else.

26

THE MOUNTAIN

TWO WEEKS.

Two God-damned weeks of losing themselves in the dirty corners of Hadeon's Den.

Two weeks of women running hands all over his body, ignoring his demands they not touch him.

Two weeks of he and Marcus glaring at Ryker's exhibitionism.

Two weeks of purple smoke and Lucifer's Tears and little white pills, rolling down, down, down Gabe's throat.

Two weeks of forgetting. Or, it should have been. But Gabe found his pleasure for their circumstance had ebbed away by the third day.

Two weeks, and Gabe seemed no closer to gaining another audience with Hadeon.

Every breath he took was a test of his restraint. The hands on him, the drugs in his system, the ire seeping out of Marcus... it was all too much to take. He struggled to maintain control over himself. Over the voice.

It delighted in the devilry of the Dark Market. Whispering, always whispering in Gabe's ear. Even now, as he sat on the plush blue cushion, the voice whispered suggestions that were getting harder to ignore.

Gabe, please. Just let me touch one.

No.

Look at that one over there, she's practically begging for it.

Gabe glanced in that direction and, well, his darker half *wasn't* wrong.

That's it. I knew you'd agree, eventually. We should indulge in the pleasures of the flesh. Look, even your friend does not hold back.

Ryker was sandwiched between two women, who ran kisses down his bare chest. One of them blatantly shoved her hand into his pants and moaned at what she found there. Gabe rolled his eyes, but he couldn't deny the picture they painted was rather... enticing.

Yes. You see what we might do?

A vivid image of him taking Ryker's place flashed in his mind, but Gabe shook it away. *Stop that. I am not touching them.*

You idiot. I'll make you suffer for this.

I know you will.

So why do you deny what I want? What you want?

Because you *cannot be trusted to touch a woman.*

Oh, poor, pathetic Gabe. Blames me for his inadequacy. It was never me. It was always you who was afraid. Even from the beginning. Afraid of the box. Afraid of your father. Afraid of the boys at school. Afraid of women. You were even afraid of your friends for a while, weren't you?

Stop.

I'll stop if you touch one.

No.

Looks like it's just you, me, and our hand tonight then. The voice grumbled.

As it will always be.

*Keep telling yourself that, Gabe. You will let me out. I **am** you. You'll let me out. You can feel it already, can't you? The tightness in your shoulders. The way your hands tremor. The coldness down your spine. Give in, Gabe. I'll make it good, I promise.*

Your promises mean nothin—

"Mr. Malik?"

Gabe shook his head to clear it before looking up at who spoke, "Yes?"

A slender woman with silken red hair stood before him—from the third set of cages, then. She bowed her head and spoke softly, "Master would like to see you." *We could be someone's master...*

"Master?" Gabe asked.

"Yes, Master," she lowered her voice to a whisper. "*Hadeon* will see you. Please follow me."

Gabe rose, surprised to find his knees steady. He met Marcus' gaze and they nodded at one another, confirming Marcus would keep a begrudging eye on Ryker.

The woman led Gabe to a fabric-draped wall, pulling aside a dark curtain to reveal a hidden hall. Doors lined either side, each equipped with a set of digits glowing at their center and a pin pad above the handle.

The hall sprawled before them—so far it defied all reasoning. The building was simply not this large when seen from the outside. Finally, coming into view like a gaping maw at dusk, a door appeared. Set in the center of what must be the terminal of the hall, this door was made of blackened wood, ornately carved with the image of a snake eating its own tail. The mastery with which the image was rendered had the artist's heart in Gabe rising to attention. Before he could fully appreciate the carving, the door swung open, squealing so noisily Gabe got the distinct impression it was intentional. His escort bowed and motioned for him to enter the pitch black room. He nodded in acknowledgement and went inside.

The door shut behind him with a resounding boom. Gabe did not allow fear an inch, speaking into the dark, "Well, Hadeon, here I am!"

A feminine giggle echoed about the space, "I'll be sure to tell him you said hello."

"Oh," was all he could muster.

"Oh? Is that all you have to say, after you've spent weeks gawking at me?"

"Well, as I can't see you at the moment, I'm not entirely sure I have been gawking at you, but if I was—"

"You were." The voice dripped seduction. "Don't worry, I wasn't the only one who noticed. You know, Hadeon doesn't offer me out to just anyone, but *he* saw how you were looking at me, too." A little stab of bitterness entered her tone. "He says you're important."

A red light lit up the ceiling, illuminating the lovely form of the Ethereal Gabe had seen at Hadeon's side, lounging on a tufted bench. His gaze caught on her long legs, crossed at the ankle, before trailing up and up and up, lingering on the lace at the hem of a thin silk robe, then snagging once more on the outline of peaked nipples beneath the fabric.

"I see you weren't finished looking, either," she remarked dryly, rising to stand before him.

His gaze snapped up to her face, painted pink in the light. Anything he might've said evaporated as he took in her flawless features. Her mouth parted slightly as she stared back at him. Gabe couldn't stop himself from looking at her lips, as if they contained their own magnetism. Might they taste as sweet as they looked? He gave himself an internal shake. *Remember why we're here.*

She motioned for Gabe to sit on the recently vacated bench, and he took the opportunity to regain his composure. "And what's your name, beautiful?" he purred once he'd sat, entirely uncertain of where the boldness had come from.

Her eyes narrowed, "A bit presumptuous, aren't you?"

Gabe shrugged. He was playing a part. Though as he looked at the breathtaking woman in front of him, it didn't feel that way. She *was* beautiful. From top to toes, perfection. Her hair gleamed like molten metal, a flawless match to her large, grey eyes. She was of an average height with generous curves bracketing a narrow waist.

The fabric of her robe cinched there in a way that drew the eye. Gabe didn't know where to look. *She looks like a treat.*

"Are you done gawking?" she asked, scowling down at him under thick lashes. "Should I get to work?" Her gaze dropped to the front of his trousers.

Gabe flushed at her insinuation. "I see I've offended you. I'm sorry."

She scoffed, "I'm a whore. I don't get to be offended."

"I see. Well, please, do sit down. There's something I'd like to ask you about."

She moved to sit in his lap, but Gabe shook his head. "Oh, no. Please, do sit next to me." He gestured to the open space beside him.

When she'd settled herself, she turned with folded arms and quirked her brow. "You're odd," she declared.

"Ah. Well, I find that to be much better than the alternative."

She chuckled in a way most unbecoming of a woman in her position. "Don't tell me, you're one of those sad louts who comes in here just to pay for company... and not of the sexual variety."

Gabe smirked at her, "And if I was, would you think less of me? I mean, presumably, you don't think very highly of any of your... *customers*. But are the ones who come seeking solace in company rather than *company* really worse?"

"Oh, they're much worse. They expect something of us which we cannot give. They expect an emotional connection. I can't tell you the disgust such a thing induces in me—when a male cannot make conversation outside a whore house, so he seeks it with me."

"Quite like I'm doing, then?"

Her cheeks pinkened at her mistake. "Oh, sir. I apologize. Sometimes I forget what I'm doing here and why, and I... I don't come from this background. You see, I... I... please don't tell–"

Gabe cut her off by slashing his hand through the air. "Stop. I think it would benefit you to hear me out. Believe it or not, I'm not here for either of those things. Well, perhaps the conversation. Though I doubt it'll be the usual type. Yes, I am odd, as you said. So, firstly, I'd like to start by knowing your name, but that was quite *presumptuous,* as you also said. So I shall tell you mine first, and you reciprocate. I am Gabe. Gabriel Malik, to be precise."

Her eyes widened. "You mean to tell me that Gabriel Malik has come to the filthiest corner of the Mirrored City to visit... me? And not for my services, but some other proposition?"

"Ah. I knew you were smart. Yes. I am one and the same. Gabe Malik." He pulled out his phone and quickly flashed his identification. "And I have come to speak to *you.* Though I find myself in some doubt you'll have any information of value. You see, I know we've only just met, well rather, you've met me, but I was told you might be able to help solve a bit of a mystery. I am trusting you, I suppose, at a good deal of personal risk. I'm rambling... this would be the part where you tell me your name."

"You *are* important. In which case, I apologize again for my behavior earlier—"

"Please, relax. I wish for you to speak freely. And I am dying to know your name now, actually."

"Fine," she huffed. "My name is Everest."

"Everest? Like, like the mountain of legend? The one that was said to reach past the clouds? What an interesting name."

"Yes," she breathed a laugh. "The very one and the same. Everest. The mountain that reached past the clouds. Only my parents would be idiotic enough to name me after something that was bombed into oblivion. You know, they said it was real. Mount Everest—let's not make the joke, Gabe—I've heard it before. I am a whore, after all. *Mount Everest.* Oh God. What am I even saying? I'm so sorry. I need to shut up."

"I see. I must also add funny to your list of attributes. Why Everest, I've learned a lot about you in quite a short amount of time, it seems." Gabe didn't know what he was doing. Well, he *did* know what he was doing. He was flirting with Everest. It wasn't something he'd dared to do since the terrible mishap with Hope. He'd kept himself apart. For ten years, he hadn't engaged with a female. But this woman... Her wit. He couldn't fail to rise to it.

"So odd," she murmured. "Anyway, you might call me Ever? That's what all my friends call me. Hadeon calls me Eve—thinks it's funny for the clients with a breeding kink—but if you called me that, I think I might punch you in the throat, since we're speaking plainly and all. So yes, I suppose if you're not a client and you're not completely pathetic, you might call me Ever. Just Ever."

"Are we to be friends then, Ever?"

"Well, I suppose that depends a lot on what else you have to say to me. You did elude, rather obviously, that you'd like my help with something?" She laughed, dragging her robe up from where it had fallen down her shoulder. "You know, that was quite foolish of you."

Gabe raised a brow.

"You did ask me to speak freely."

"I did."

"Well, to be plain, Gabe. If you're going to cross someone like Hadeon, or ask questions you shouldn't, you most certainly shouldn't be so open about it. You realize you've given me the power to completely destroy you within a minute of meeting me?"

Gabe shrugged. "You find boldness is easy when you place little value on your own life. It matters not if I am caught. The more important thing is what I might do to help women who find themselves in *your* position."

"My position?"

"Er, that is. You said yourself that you don't *get* to do things. It seems you have no agency, since we're speaking plainly. It seems that because I am a man, I could leave here and say anything about you, and it'd be believed. But that leverage you think you have on me? Who would you tell?"

Fear slithered across her features. "I wouldn't. I'm sorry," she whispered, ducking her head.

Gabe lifted her chin with one finger, "No. *I'm sorry.* That is the entire point. I want to help you. Someone told me you know what's happening to the women, beyond those ones out there. Do you?"

Her lips pressed into a thin line.

Gabe had been foolish to think a caged woman would be forthcoming with him. What was he doing? He needed to ease her into the conversation. To win her trust.

"How long do we have in here, Ever?" Gabe asked.

"As long as you'd like," she whispered.

He leaned in to murmur in her ear, "And are there any comms devices hidden in here? Squeeze my hand once for no, twice for yes."

She grabbed his hand, lacing their fingers in a way that took Gabe off guard. She squeezed. Once.

Twice.

Gabe put his mouth so close to her ear it brushed her skin with every word, "Why did you speak so freely if you knew there were comms?"

She pressed her lips to Gabe's ear and whispered, "I forgot."

"Liar." He crushed her hand in his grip then hissed, "Play the fuck along, Everest."

She only gasped and squeezed his hand. Twice.

Gabe allowed himself three deep breaths before speaking again at normal volume, "So, do you know what they're doing with the women?"

Everest squeezed his hand twice and then said, "No."

"Hmmm. What a shame, sweet Ever. You see, I thought I might save some of them. Perhaps even you?"

"Save them?"

"Yes. I would like, very much, to have my own establishment, but I'd run things differently, you see? No cages." Gabe hoped she picked up on the inflection in his voice.

She did, giving his hand two gentle presses. "That sounds lovely, Gabe, but I'm afraid such a thing would have to be discussed with Hadeon."

"Ah. Well, I'd much rather speak with you."

Squeeze. Squeeze.

"Could such a thing be arranged? Might you be allowed to visit me at my penthouse, perhaps? It's in the tower district, you'd like it."

Two squeezes. "I'm afraid such a thing is not possible, Mr. Malik."

"Such a shame. I'd have liked to get to know you better, Everest." Gabe put his mouth to her ear again and whispered so low he feared she'd not hear him, "Block seven. Penthouse. Midnight."

One squeeze.

He pulled back, searching her face. She pressed forward and said just as quietly, "Three," and surely because she was putting on a show, she brushed a feather-light kiss to the hollow behind Gabe's ear. He gasped and pulled back from her. Squeezing her hand twice before fleeing the room and all the temptation within it.

He'd made it to the end of the hall before Hadeon emerged from the shadows, "Trying to steal my women, are you, Gabriel?"

Gabe just smirked and shrugged, "It was worth a try."

Hadeon boomed a laugh and smacked him on the back. "I knew I liked you." He winked. "Meet with me next Tuesday. What do you say we get out of my Den and speak as the civilized men we are? Get you some girls of your own?"

"I like the sound of that."

"Of course you do. I've a booth at Amethyst. Dinner is served at seven. Don't be late."

"I'll be there."

"Good," Hadeon purred, pulling aside the curtain that separated the hall from the rest of the club. "Leave your pups at home." He nodded to where Ryker and Marcus sat ensconced in a plume of purply smoke.

"They'll be disappointed to miss it."

"I'm sure they will." Gabe moved to step around him, but he shoved a shoulder in his path. "Oh, and Gabe. Get the fuck out of my club. And don't come back. I like you, but you'll not get another chance to touch what's mine, eh?"

"Understood." Gabe shouldered around Hadeon, ignoring the sensation of eyes on his neck as he gathered his friends and left with a smile on his face.

It appeared he'd made progress, after all.

27

MY MONSTER

Darius had just finished burying the body when a voice of spun silk spoke over his shoulder.

"How many?"

"Addy!" he yelped, stepping in front of the lumpy mound in an ill-fated attempt to block it from her view. "You're supposed to be resting. It's too soon. The doctor said—"

"That doctor, you mean?" She pointed at the turned soil.

"Ads..."

"Is that what you meant when you promised him mercy?"

"Love, I couldn't let him go... I couldn't risk you. This *was* mercy."

She pulled a threadbare blanket more securely around her shoulders, as if it'd keep the chill of his malignity from her flesh. "What of *his* love? That woman he spoke of as he tended me? The child she is expecting? Is it mercy to have given the world another fatherless child?"

"You don't understand. He would've told."

Addy staggered to a nearby tree, catching herself on the bark.

"You're not well yet. Let me help ya back to bed."

"No," she panted. "I'm fine. You'll stay right there and talk to me."

"You said you wouldn't ask."

"That was before I watched you burying an innocent man, more, a man who *helped* me, as if it meant nothing at all! As if it were *normal*. As if this is just something you *do*."

"I don't know what to say," he shrugged. "There is no limit to what I would do to protect ya."

She slid down the tree until she was sat on the thick moss at its base and pressed the back of her hand to her clammy forehead. "Don't you understand how *wrong* that is?"

"Lovin' you the way I do is the only thing I've ever done right."

"Do you even feel remorse?" she whispered, "My mother used to say that love is poison. That it is the enemy of reason. I laughed at her, Dare. But *this*, this is madness." She gestured to the turned soil. "You cannot love me like this anymore. I refuse."

"I can't stop. I don't know how to stop. I *won't* stop loving ya so fierce."

"You will!" The tendons in her neck strained with her shout. "*You* are killing me, Darius. Because when you do this, you are killing the man I love. You cannot protect me from life, from *living*. You cannot deny me my desires in the name of safety. That is not love. That *is* poison."

Her declarations were a tangible presence in the silent space between them.

Finally, Darius spoke, slumping down to sit on the mound of dirt with his head in his hands. "It's my fault, that's what Arthur said." He nodded to the grave.

"What is?"

"That we cannot have children."

"We're not talking about that right now." She ran a hand over her now-empty womb.

Darius continued despite her words. "It's because I'm not Ethereal. I'm sorry, love. I wanted to give you everything. But, I cannot give ya this, not yet, anyway."

"What do you mean, not yet?"

"Arthur thought that if I went in the box enough, maybe got some of those... modifications, it might work."

"I can't talk about this right now."

He nodded. Silence stretched between them, uncomfortable in a way it'd never been before. When it'd been quiet so long, he thought they might dwell forever in silence, Addy spoke. "He was a good person, Dare. You didn't have to kill him."

"I did."

"How many?"

"How many what?"

"The way you... You were so casual about it. How many have you killed?"

"I cannot tell ya that."

Rage glimmered in Addy's glare. "You can't? Or you don't want me to know?"

"Both."

"Tell me!"

"I can't!"

"Why?"

"Because I don't know!"

"Oh God."

Darius went to her, taking both of her cold hands in his, "I never meant for ya to know."

Her jaw clenched.

"I killed my first man when I was eleven. I didn't mean to. I was protectin' myself. But it was then I realized the Reapers, they couldn't win against me."

"Oh, Darius..."

"So, ya see. It wasn't all for you. It wasn't all for love. A good deal of it was for *hate*. I've been a monster all along, Adalia. I've just been hidin it from ya. I try and pick the ones who're most guilty, see? But, I can't say Arthur is the first innocent that died by these hands." He lifted her hands and kissed the back of each, steeling himself for her contempt.

"You are a monster," she said, pulling her hands from his grasp.

Darius' heart cracked, his eye burning with the threat of tears. "Shall I take ya back, then? We can find Gabe. I can set ya free from me."

"Look at me," she demanded, cupping his face in her soft hands. "You *are* a monster. A monster made. Molded by circumstance. I am so sorry for what you felt you had to become. I am so, so sorry that *I* couldn't protect you from it."

"You tried."

"Not enough."

"Everything you are is enough for me," he said, searching her gaze for the horror he expected to find, but seeing none.

"You *are* a monster. But you're *my* monster. And I'm not going anywhere."

A sob tore from Darius' throat, and he rested his head on her chest, allowing the stress of the last few weeks, the constant threat of losing her, to leave his body. When he'd finally stilled under her touch, she said, "I'm not going anywhere, but promise me... You promise me that you'll not seek out this violence again. And if you swear it, I will make you a promise in exchange. I will stay on the medication to... to make sure this," she placed a hand on her low belly, "doesn't happen again. Not until *you're* ready to risk it. Do you agree?"

"Yes. Yes, I agree. Anything, Ads. *Anything.* And I promise ya, I'll find a way. I'll give ya yer dreams. You deserve nothin' less."

"We will figure it all out. Together."

"Together."

28

THE MAN BEHIND GLASS

GABE

RYKER WAS BEING A grumbly little bitch.

For once, Gabe and the voice were in agreement. *God, if you don't shut him up, I will.*

"Ry, for the fifth time, Hadeon told me not to bring you," Gabe said. He glanced at Marcus for help, but found him brooding, glaring out the car's tinted windows as the lights of the tower district blurred overhead.

"But whyyyy?" Ryker moaned again.

"Probably because you behave like a petulant baby," Marcus spat, folding his arms and turning his glare on Ryker. "I was *embarrassed* to be seen with you in there. Two fucking weeks, Ry. I had to watch you with... Fuck." He threw up his hands and turned back to the window.

Ryker only stared at him with his mouth slack before whispering, "You know why I did that, right?"

Marcus didn't say anything.

"Look at me," he begged.

Marcus did not look at him.

Ryker turned to Gabe, "You know why I did that, right?"

Feeling awkward at the unnamed tension in the air, as if he were suddenly an unwelcome guest in his own car, Gabe shrugged. "It looked like you were enjoying yourself."

Marcus grunted his agreement.

"I..." Ryker started, but cut off, letting his head fall into his hands.

"Look, Ry, I know you wanted to be included in this, but Hadeon was clear. He wants any further dealings to be done personally. Of course, I will tell both of you everything that is said. I need your help figuring out what to do with whatever information I gain, anyway."

Ryker shook himself, as if shirking the blanket of melancholy that'd come over him, and looked up at Gabe. He straightened and pasted on the fakest smile Gabe had ever seen before saying, "I'm just jealous you get to go to Amethyst."

Gabe smiled, grateful for his effort to lighten the mood. "You would be. Take comfort, friend. I'm sure it's nothing special."

Ryker rolled his eyes and muttered, "Nothing special..." His gaze darted to Marcus, who continued to pretend neither of them were there.

"I did set up another meeting," Gabe said. "One I think you'll like better as it's at an even more exclusive establishment than Amethyst."

Ryker lit up. "Where?"

"My penthouse." Gabe smirked. "With *the* Ethereal woman. Tonight. Or rather, tomorrow morning."

"I hate you for getting my hopes up, but damn, Gabe. You *were* busy."

"So, will you two be staying?" Gabe asked, shooting the question Marcus' direction.

"What time is she coming?" Marcus asked, still not looking at them.

"Three."

"You could have picked a better time," Marcus complained.

"I didn't pick it. She did."

"Of course we'll be there." Marcus turned to Ryker with infinite sadness staining his features. "Right?"

"Right," Ryker whispered.

Once again, Gabe felt like an intruder, so he set his attention on the sidewalk and left his friends to communicate in that silent way of theirs.

It was three o'clock, and Gabe was tired of waiting for Everest. He was also just tired in general. The voice had kept him up, hissing complaints so loudly, it'd prevented what little sleep he might've gotten. After two restless hours sweating in his silk sheets, he threw off the covers and padded to the liquor cabinet. He shouldn't drink before his meeting, he knew that, but it didn't stop him from pouring a generous mug of whiskey and nursing it as he pulled on sweatpants and a loose t-shirt.

Leaving his rumpled bedsheets as a problem for tomorrow, Gabe made his way to a small living area, where a plush—and exceptionally comfortable—black couch dominated the space. It was only when he was sat that he heard the vibrations of Marcus' low voice rolling through the guest room wall, followed by soft murmuring in Ryker's unmistakable tone. Were they really in there together? Gabe rolled his eyes. Of course they were. The two of them could be terribly dramatic. They'd probably spent the night up talking instead of sleeping. He wished he had as good an excuse.

Gabe glanced at the clock on the wall. 3:03. He should've known she'd be late. Ryker emerged from the hall, with Marcus a few steps behind. Both of them had gotten dressed, to Gabe's annoyance. Evidence of their restless night was painted in subtle strokes, present in Ryker's mussed hair, the red mark on Marcus' jawline.

"Is that what you're wearing?" Ryker asked, raising a brow at Gabe's sweatpants.

Yes. It was what he was wearing. If Everest wanted to meet at an ungodly hour, he damn well was not getting dressed up. She was lucky he'd put pants on at all. "Did you two mean to match?" Gabe retorted, smirking at their twin black sweaters and jeans.

"Ah, fuck. Not again." Ryker grimaced.

Marcus just shrugged as if to say, *I'm not changing.*

"Fiiiine," Ryker groaned, stomping back to the guest room.

"You're a prick sometimes, you know that?" Marcus said, plopping down on the couch beside Gabe.

"Just saving you from yourself."

Marcus eyed Gabe's tall mug of whiskey, "You might as well drink from the bottle at this rate, friend."

"I like it better this way," Gabe said, swirling the contents of his coffee mug before taking a swig. *Who does he think he is?*

"That'll kill you someday."

Gabe sputtered a laugh, causing whiskey to burn the back of his nose. "Oh, Marc, if this could kill me, it've happened already."

Marcus' brow furrowed, as if he were warring with some thought he wanted to voice, then relaxed as he let it go and said instead, "Speaking of coffee, what's a man gotta do to get a cup around here?"

"Oh, you are high maintenance, aren't you?" Gabe chuckled, pointing to the kitchen down the hall. "Left upper cabinet, above the machine. Same place as always. Go sparingly. That stuff is expensive."

"You can afford it."

"Only for you."

Ryker reappeared, this time in a tight white t-shirt that contrasted starkly against his dark skin. Seeing Gabe's smirk, he barked, "What?"

"Nothing. You just really didn't want to match, did you? I thought it was cute."

"Oh, fuck off, Gabe. Don't judge me when you aren't even wearing socks."

"What's wrong with not wearing socks?"

"Nobody wants to look at your gross naked feet, that's what."

"My feet aren't—" Gabe cut off, noting Ryker biting back a laugh. "Oh, you asshole."

Just then, the bell rang.

"God damnit, have your Reaper get that, Ry."

"Where are you going?"

"To put on socks, dumbass."

Ryker snickered, pleased he'd gotten under Gabe's skin, then asked, "Where is Sable, anyway?"

"I put her and the other one in the servant's quarters. They showed up an hour after you went to bed, pissed that we'd left them behind again," Gabe said over a shoulder as he darted back to his bedroom and pulled on the first pair of socks he saw, some rumpled pinstriped business socks he'd left at the foot of the bed.

Satisfied he'd not scandalize anyone with his bare feet, he followed the sounds of conversation to the foyer. He rounded the corner and came face to face with Everest, who was just shrugging out of her coat, revealing a pair of jeans... and a sweater. Apparently, everyone but Gabe knew you wore jeans and sweaters to meetings at three in the morning. Ryker snorted as her clothes came into view, causing Everest to glare in reproach.

"Is something funny?" she asked.

Gabe shoved Ryker aside with his elbow and straightened his spine, "Of course not. Everest, welcome to my home. Please do come and sit down."

"Just Ever, remember? What interesting company you keep, Gabe." The easy way she purred his name was far too familiar for someone he'd just met.

Marcus' brows inched up at the tone, but Gabe subtly shook his head. "I'm sure they need no introductions, but I'll give them nonetheless. These are my friends, Ever. Marcus Pentra and Ryker Armadis. I know we spoke in subtleties, but I'd trust no one else the way I trust them. They help me with a number of operations similar to what I want to discuss with you."

"And the others?" Ever nodded to the two shadows standing against the wall.

"Oh. Those are their Reapers, Sable, and…?" Gabe cringed and turned to Marcus, who just bit his lip and looked away.

"I am Wesley," a gravely voice spoke from the larger cloak.

Ryker turned to Marcus with widened eyes and mouthed *Wesley?!*

Gabe had to admit the name seemed contrary to the man's demeanor. He gestured to Wesley, ignoring Ever's disgusted face. "And Wesley. They will not be joining us."

"No. They will not." Ryker said, shooing the Reapers away with a flick of his fingers.

When they'd gone, Gabe paused for a moment in the foyer, unsure which room he wanted to lead them into, finally opting for the informal comfort of the living room he'd settled in earlier. Ever scanned the long hallway as they walked, as if cataloging the placement of every odd painting. To be fair, there were many, in a mismatch of composition that spoke to Gabe's love of all art rather than a specific style. Every now and then, Ever's chin would dip, as if in approval of a particular piece. Something in his chest lightened at the sight of it. The wonder came and went in an adorable crinkle at the corner of her eyes. Marcus cleared his throat, and Gabe started, realizing they'd stopped so Ever could admire one of his more treasured pieces. It was a portrait composed of thousands of tiny strokes, the man within distorted, the angles of his face simultaneously wrong and right, a shock of messy red hair vibrant at the crown of a sullen face as he glared out of the canvas. Gabe had often wondered at just who the man was, his name long since lost to time. Slowly, Ever lifted a hand to touch the painting.

Gabe caught it before she'd even made it halfway. "Don't touch him."

"He is behind glass," she whispered.

"So he is. Come."

They continued down the hall, strange tension drawing the space between them so taunt Gabe felt he might snap.

Ever stopped in the doorway of the cozy room, as if stunned by the comfortable space she'd stumbled into. Her gaze lingered on Gabe's coffee mug where he'd left it on the low table, delicate nostrils flaring as she whiffed whiskey in the air. Inwardly cringing, Gabe swiped up the mug and gestured for her to sit. She did, sinking into the black cushions, awkwardly tapping her foot. This wasn't going at all how Gabe had imagined.

Ryker spoke abruptly, "Who wants coffee?" No one replied, but he continued as if they had. "Good. Me too. Marcus, you were making some earlier, right? Come help me in the kitchen."

Gabe passed Ryker his mug in silent thanks. Marcus followed him from the room, as if he couldn't get away fast enough.

Now alone with Ever, Gabe stood, suddenly not knowing what to do with his hands or his arms or his whole body. Had he always held his shoulders like this, or was he being awkward? She only stared at him, running her gaze from the top of his head downward until she paused at his socks and bit her lip, stifling a smile. *Fucking Ryker.*

"Glad you didn't get dressed up on my account," she said, folding her legs under her on the couch.

Gabe finally managed to unfreeze his body and plopped down opposite her. "You did want to meet in the middle of the night."

"I think I prefer you this way," she said, surprising him.

"Oh?"

"Yes. I suppose you look more... *human* like this."

Gabe didn't know how to respond to that.

Thankfully, she spoke again, "So, why am I here?"

"We should wait for the others—"

"I'm assuming they already know what this is about?"

Gabe cleared his throat and nodded.

"Then we should not wait for them. I have limited time, and I've risked much by sneaking out to see you tonight."

"You are not allowed to move about freely?"

She only scoffed.

"But, you're an Ethereal—"

"You think that means something? Perhaps it did, in the beginning, but now? For me? No. It is a title that has brought me nothing but misery."

"I'm sorry."

"I should not be so hard on you." She waved a hand in dismissal. "Of course, you do not understand what it is to be an Ethereal female."

"You're right. I do not. But I do see that something is wrong. Understand, Everest, that they keep things from us. We did not know what happened to our women—"

"You don't know of the facilities?"

"I—"

"None of your female friends or family are in there?" She folded her arms and leaned back, as if her point was complete.

"Yes, my own mother is in one. But she... she seemed happy when I last saw her."

Everest only laughed, "And just how long ago was that?"

Gabe swallowed, looking away from her accusing stare.

"I thought as much. You may have all the time in the world, Gabe, but for *us,* nothing is certain. What is paradise one day, becomes hell the next. We only hold on and hope the next change is for the better."

"I would spare you from it. That is why I wanted to speak with you. I was told you knew more about what was happening with the women." He looked at her pleadingly.

She studied him for a long minute, intelligence flashing behind her gray eyes. "Fine. I can see you mean that, no matter how misguided you might be. I'm going to be brutally honest with you, Gabe. Do you think you can handle that?"

"Yes."

In the hall, Gabe heard the shuffle of feet followed by a *Shh!* He rolled his eyes, but Everest didn't seem to notice their audience.

She'd withdrawn into herself and spoke to the floor. "They took me when I was fourteen. I wish I could tell you I was unique. Perhaps you didn't know, as you said. You are from the outskirts, yes?" She glanced up at him, and he jerked his chin down to confirm.

"Maybe it was different where you were, but they pulled us out of school—all of us girls in the city—before we'd even had a chance to begin our advanced studies. They took our mothers even before that. Did you have the procedures, Gabe?"

Blades and tubes and plastic gloves lanced through his skull. "I did," he said, voice rough. "More than is typical, as I understand it."

"Well, perhaps you might know better than most then." Ever smiled sadly. "For when they took us, it was to the men in white coats. For six years, they did with us whatever they wished. Do you understand what I'm *not* saying? *Whatever* they wished. There were no limitations to how they could cut us, test us, *take* us." Her fingers flexed into her crossed arms, leaving red marks in their wake. "Some of the girls, they locked in the dark. They left them there just to see how long it would take for them to starve. They did *not* starve. But how they screamed for food... I heard it at night, the wailing through the walls. They bred others, implanting them, then cutting out the offspring before they'd fully formed. We do not know what they sought. Then there were the ones like me, the ones they *perfected* to be used. Not bred. There were others, too. But I feel I've said enough. You seem bright enough to draw your own conclusions. Just understand, the women you've seen—the ones who made it out—we are the lucky ones, no matter where we find ourselves."

Gabe could not think of a single thing to say. So they sat in charged silence, until Ryker rounded the corner, pretending he hadn't been there all along.

"The coffee's done," he announced lamely, stepping into the room with Marcus on his heels.

Marcus clenched the handles of the tray he carried so tightly it groaned under his palms. Ryker pried the tray from his hands and set it on the table. With their coffees rescued from the jaws of death, Ryker took Marcus by the shoulder and steered him to a place on the oversized couch. He pushed Marcus down and then sat beside him, pressing his leg into him in silent support.

"We didn't know," Marcus croaked.

Ever reached for a cup of coffee and poured a generous splash of cream in. "That must be nice."

"What?" Ryker asked.

"Not knowing," she said, taking a dainty sip.

Marcus' jaw clenched, but for once in his life, he didn't say anything.

"Please," Ryker rasped. "They took Marcus' sister when she was fourteen. He—*we* would have done anything to get her back. But we didn't know where she'd gone. I'm begging you to have a shred of grace, for his sake. We were fools. Young, self-absorbed fools. Our fault does not lie with a lack of caring. So tell us, what might we do?"

"How should I know? I have enough on my plate just trying to keep *my* girls safe. The new ones don't come in with all of the proper work done, and they're at a terrible risk—"

"*Your* girls?" Gabe asked, having finally found his voice again.

"Er. Well, they're not *mine*. But I do manage them."

"*You* keep them in those cages?" Marcus scoffed.

"Of course I do. No one can touch them when they're in there." Ever's serious tone appeared to have dissipated the moment the others had come back into the room.

Gabe didn't know what to make of any of it, so he ignored the weirdness in the air and began planning. "Ever, you mean to say you have access to the other women?"

"Obviously."

"I thank you for your honesty and trust. I think it only right we return the sentiment?" Gabe asked. It was stupid to tell Ever anything, but what did they have to lose? No one would believe her over them.

Marcus and Ryker nodded their agreement.

Gabe cleared his throat and began, "The three of us have been building a bit of a side project over the last few years. You see, I'm in the unique position of being in command of *two* facilities. Bracken may be backwoods, but the Authority has taken particular care to establish operations there. My father..." Gabe swallowed down his rising gorge at the word *father*, "worked closely with them in the early stages of development. Anyway, I have the means and the reason to acquire humans, but more recently... Ethereal females. Marcus here works in infrastructure, building, planning, etcetera. And Ryker, well, believe it or not, Ryker is a farmer."

"I'm not a *farmer*." Ryker glared, incredulous. "I'll have you know that I've single-handedly streamlined the food production system. Everyone in the Mirrored City is provided with fresh ingredients from *my* greenhouses. We've even begun shipping as far as Rittenmore—"

"Enough, Ry. Can't you see, Gabe is only trying to rile you," Marcus said, narrowing his eyes.

Ryker grumbled a few more food-related statistics before trailing off.

"Much as I'd like to listen to you wax poetic about the merits of aquaponics again, Ry, we have a guest." Gabe dipped his head to Ever. "So you see, Ever, we find ourselves in a unique position. Between us, we have the ability to build something... new. And, I have the ability to help those who need out the most. Do *you* understand what *I'm* not saying?"

Ever's eyes darted between the three of them, as if unsure who she wished to address. "And have you acted on that ability?"

"Yes," they said in unison.

"I see." Her chin dipped. "And you'd like me to do what?"

"Can you get the girls out?" Ryker asked tentatively.

"No," she replied.

"Can you provide distraction so *we* can get them out?" Marcus rumbled, tilting his head.

"No," she said again.

"Absolutely useless," Marcus growled, rising and storming from the room. Ryker looked apologetically over his shoulder before following him out.

Ever's face fell, as if Marcus' words had struck deep.

Gabe scooted closer to her on the couch and cleared his throat, "Can you identify who needs help most?"

She looked up at him with tears swimming and nodded as if speaking was too difficult.

"Can you tell me how to win over Hadeon?"

She took his hand and squeezed. Once. *Twice.*

"Can you come back and visit me again?"

Two squeezes.

Gabe lifted her chin with a finger, unable to keep himself from touching her, and said, "Then you could *never* be useless."

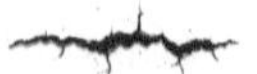

An hour later, Gabe stood in the foyer with Ever. Alone. Marcus, Ryker, and their eerie entourage had left shortly after Marcus' outburst.

"I cannot thank you enough for what you shared tonight," Gabe said, not knowing what to do with his hands again. "It was truly illuminating. I am so sorry for what you've endured."

"And I you, Gabe. Thank you."

"For what?"

"For giving me hope. Maybe there's still redemption for this world of ours."

"I doubt that, but... maybe there's hope for a different world." He shrugged. "The car's waiting for you downstairs. My driver is discreet. He'll drop you wherever you need."

"Thank you." She turned away, and Gabe couldn't keep himself from grabbing her hand. What was wrong with him? He didn't touch women. Why couldn't he stop touching *her*?

"You'll come again?" He asked.

She smiled, then squeezed his hand. Twice.

Before she left, she snorted and said over her shoulder, "Oh, and Gabe?"

"Yes?"

"Go visit your mother."

He smirked, nodding his agreement.

It was only after Gabe shut the door behind Ever he realized the voice hadn't spoken while she'd been there.

Not once.

29

PURPLE & FORKED TONGUES

EVEREST CAME TO THE penthouse every morning at 3:07am without fail. She'd stay for an hour, curled on Gabe's sofa, drinking all of his expensive coffee and sharing her many insights on just how to win Hadeon over. Well, she'd exhausted her wealth of knowledge on Hadeon by the second night, admitting that Gabe had already won him over if he'd been invited to a private dinner at Amethyst. Still, she came.

She was an anomaly Gabe was quickly finding himself addicted to. A puzzle whose pieces didn't quite fit together. One moment she was soft and quiet, the next she'd bark a laugh and swat at his chest as if they'd known one another for forever and a day. One night, she'd show up in a glittering evening gown, the next in a pair of ratty sweats and a stained shirt with her silver hair in a sloppy bun atop her head. Gabe preferred her the second way most. It was...*what had she said?*

Humanizing.

Gabe stuck with his sweats, t-shirt, and socks combo, except for the second night, when she appeared unexpectedly and he stumbled to the door in nothing but a pair of underwear. Everest only smirked and let her gaze linger a little too long on his toned stomach before brushing past him and asking if there was anything to eat. He directed her to the kitchen, then tucked tail for his closet, embarrassment burning his cheeks. When he emerged, she behaved as if nothing was amiss, so Gabe had decided not to mention it either.

It had been four days since that encounter, and Ever was curled into a corner of Gabe's couch with her cold toes wedged under his thigh. She bit at her bottom lip in a way that was entirely distracting as she studied the chessboard.

"You know, it might be easier to focus if we sat across from one another—like I said earlier," Gabe said, seeking any excuse to get away from the uncomfortable feeling that lit up his chest when he looked at Ever. He'd only known her a week—three, if one counted staring at her from across a seedy club. It was far too soon for any type of feelings in his chest.

"What, and let my feet get cold? No, thank you."

Gabe only sighed.

"Why, Gabe Malik, do I make you uncomfortable?" she asked, tickling the back of his leg with her wiggling toes.

He straightened as the sensation snaked up his leg. He didn't know what to do with this. With *her*. She was overly familiar, and it *did* make him uncomfortable, but he found he rather liked it. "Of course not." He leaned forward to swipe up his glass of water from where it rested on the table, desperate for a distraction.

She turned her attention from their chess game, studying his face instead. "You know, I've been watching you, and I've noticed something odd."

"Oh? Enlighten me."

"You do not touch women—not really. You didn't... *don't*... take the opportunity to touch *me* when you have it. Are you really so noble, or is it something else?"

"Well, don't hold back on my account," Gabe muttered into his glass.

Ever snorted, "You asked me to speak freely with you."

"I have a feeling I'll come to regret that."

"You haven't already?"

"No, I find I quite like the way you talk. No one has ever addressed me so bluntly before."

"Hmm. Good. I think you could use a little dose of reality. Now, my question?"

"Er. I'm not noble…"

"So, what is it then? Are you like your friends? You don't prefer women?"

"My friends *what*?"

She raised a brow at him in an *Are you serious?* expression. "Um, I hate to be the one to tell you, but your friends are in love with each other."

Gabe scoffed, "Marcus and Ryker? No. I've known them forever. And… Ry always has women clinging to him."

"And?" She stared pointedly at him.

He didn't know what to say, so he just looked back like some puzzled owl.

"Oh, you really are an innocent one, aren't you? Why can't your friend like both?"

"They would have told me."

It was her turn to scoff. "They most certainly would not. They wouldn't tell *anyone*. Or are you in denial about the world we live in, as well as ignorant?"

Gabe clenched his jaw to keep from biting back at her. She had a point.

"I suppose that answers my question about which you prefer, since you hadn't even considered that possibility. So, what is it? Why keep yourself apart?"

He shrugged and decided, in that moment, he'd be honest with Everest. "I don't trust myself with women."

"Please, you're gentler than a baby kitten."

"Um, thanks?"

"C'mon, Gabe. You're holding back on me."

"Okay." He took a deep breath. "I *was* being honest with you. I *don't* trust myself with women. My darker half is best kept away from them. But more than that, I can't risk being with one."

"And just why is that?"

"Well, I suppose on the simplest level, it's because I won't risk having children."

"Hmmm. That's a rare trait in an Ethereal male. I've never met one who doesn't want kids."

"I don't think you're hearing me correctly. I *think* I'm normal in my desire for children... I'd quite like them... I am just choosing not to have them. I can't... There are things about myself that I would never pass on to a child, you see?"

Silence stretched as his declarations sat between them. Ever only searched his face, as if he were a broken mirror she was trying to piece back together. Finally, she asked, "You're serious?"

"Of course."

"And you suffer for keeping yourself apart, yes?"

He couldn't meet her eyes.

"Hmm. That's answer enough." She took his hand in hers and laced their fingers in that unsettling way. "I know someone who can help you."

"In what way?" he murmured, still refusing to look at her.

"You forget, Gabe, that I live in the dark. I suppose that's an easy thing to do when we're up here... Anyway... I have to keep my girls safe. Hadeon gets them sterilized—one of the few things he does right—so they'll not be getting pregnant and interrupting his operations. It's rare, but my contacts have performed the procedure on males, too. I could take you to them, and you'd never have to worry again."

Don't you dare. The voice hissed, making itself known for the first time since Ever had appeared in the living room. And because the voice hated the notion so much, Gabe looked at Ever and said,

"Yes. Take me to them." Panic bloomed in his chest at the idea of another procedure, then ebbed away as Everest squeezed his hand. Twice.

Gabe was only a little sore as he dressed for his dinner with Hadeon. Ever, true to form, had not hesitated to immediately rise from the couch and tug him toward the front door. They'd tiptoed outside, past the hall to the servant's quarters, where Gabe's new Reaper's snores resonated through the walls. Gabe didn't much care for the wiry, tattooed man the Authority had sent to keep tabs on him, but despite having few other merits, Carl slept like a rock. Gabe had found they were both content to ignore one another most of the time, his Reaper slouching lazily in the corner aside Marcus and Ryker's during meetings. Gabe had endured no shortage of teasing from Marcus and Ryker about the pathetic specimen he'd been assigned.

After their sneaking, Everest led him to a predictably unsavory locale, wherein he'd undergone a shockingly simple procedure that'd rendered him sterile. Or so said the "doctor" who'd smelled of purple haze. Ever's insistence of his legitimacy had been somewhat more reassuring. Gabe wrestled with a good deal of frustration at the fact that such a procedure had existed all this time, and he'd never been offered the thing. It would have saved him a significant amount of worry if he'd just had it done all those years ago, when he'd first realized he could not be trusted.

He shook away those old fears as he knotted his tie, smoothing it down his shirt front. After one last cursory glance in the mirror, he nodded and left the penthouse with a scraggly-looking Carl in tow.

At least the Reaper had bothered to put on his robes, though it did little to mask his unpalatable appearance. He still stood a whole head shorter than Gabe, his thin, ropey frame obvious even hidden under the layers of black fabric. Gabe supposed he did look a bit of a skeletal terror, but the prospect of this little runt protecting *him* was laughable. If he'd ever had cause to doubt the Authority's motivations, it was with the arrival of this Reaper.

The car trundled along the empty streets of the Mirrored City in awkward quiet. Carl sat across from Gabe, toeing his scythe where it rested on the floor. Did the Reapers know how stupid they looked, toting the unwieldy weapons everywhere? Of course they didn't. Gabe knew *why* the Authority had done it—the robes and scythes and shaven skulls. Was there a better way to make humans fear than by having them haunted by death itself? But... He couldn't help but feel pity for the Reapers. He still hated them, but those two emotions—hate and pity—were not mutually exclusive. "How old are you, Carl?" Gabe asked, tired of the tedious quiet.

Carl grinned in an unsettling manner and replied, "Seventeen."

Gabe nearly choked on his shock, eyes widening as he looked more deeply at the man's withered face.

Carl's grin only broadened under his scrutiny. "Look closer, Mr. Malik. I've earned all of these scars."

And Gabe saw it now, the mottled flesh of the boy's face, hidden beneath ink.

"Are you surprised?" Carl asked, lazily fingering the edges of his robe.

"Yes."

"You lot always are." Bold, this Reaper, to speak so freely.

"Care to elaborate?"

"You know how we earn our scars, our ink, surely?"

Gabe shook his head.

Carl chuckled, and gooseflesh erupted across Gabe's skin. Noting the change, Carl's grin widened further, stretching puckered, blackened flesh until Gabe *heard* it creaking.

"We earn these," he gestured to his face, then lifted one sleeve of his robe, revealing an equally inked arm, "by keeping the laws. Every drop of ink is a drop of blood. Might be ours, but more often it's not. I've been earning these scars since my sixth birthday, when I smashed my cousin's head in with a rock. I made him bleed." He unfurled his fingers, revealing a long black stripe bisecting his palm. "So, they gave me this. My first." He ran a finger reverently over the ink. "I've been reinked here. Eventually, we run out of space, you see. The darker the ink, the stronger the Reaper." He smirked knowingly.

Gabe took in the darkness of the lines marring Carl's face, the raised, painful way they stood out, and nodded in acknowledgement.

"I appreciate your insight, Carl." He said, gulping down air that'd gone sour.

"Shall I tell you a secret I know of Amethyst, Mr. Malik?" Carl tilted his head in a reptilian way.

"Do enlighten me, Reaper."

"You've dressed improperly."

"What?"

"We'll be proving ourselves tonight, Mr. Malik. You'll see." With that, the Reaper leaned back in his seat, stroking the scar on his palm, leaving Gabe to wrestle with his dread.

Amethyst was... well, *amethyst*. Everything was painted in shades of purple. To no one's surprise, purple haze colored the air itself, exhaled from the lungs of the many Ethereal males crowding tables set into a stadium-style seating area. Gabe's brows rose as he took in the expansive space, situated on the roof level of a tower bordering the Dark Market. A glass dome shielded the arena—because that's what it was—from the elements. There was not a female—human or Ethereal—in sight, a far cry from what Gabe had expected after his weeks spent in Hadeon's Den. A Reaper greeted them at the door, nodding in respect to Carl, before turning to Gabe. "Mr. Malik, follow me," he said, in sandpapery tones.

They were led to a cordoned-off area adjacent to the sunken section where the floor was lined with some sort of rubbery grid. Gabe didn't want to ponder the porous surface of the arena.

"Gabriel Malik," Hadeon boomed, rising from a strangely throne-like chair to greet him. "You've come."

"Hadeon," Gabe extended a hand, which Hadeon slapped away, wrapping him in a hug that smelled of carrion and crushed hopes.

"Welcome, boy. You left the pups at home, I see."

Gabe stepped out of Hadeon's vile embrace, blinking back his confusion at the man's odd behavior. "I did. As you said."

"This bodes well for our dealings. Come, sit." He indicated a smaller seat opposite his own. Gabe sat, but started as he spotted the Ethereal in a third chair. *Dimitirius Finch.* Gabe's stomach further soured. The snake. What had Ryker said those weeks ago? *Dimitrius told me something rather tantalizing over drinks last night...* This. This had been a setup. They'd been puppets all along. But why?

"Ah, so you know Mr. Finch?" Hadeon asked, noting Gabe's glare. "Forgive Dimitrius. He was only doing as I asked. We thought we'd be working with Armadis, didn't we, Finch?"

Dimitirus leaned forward in his seat, steepling his fingers, "Yes. Ryker had all the things we look for in prospective business partners. Wealth, connections, an utter lack of inhibitions..."

Those conniving bastards.

"But then you walked into my club," Hadeon laughed. "And we don't take second-rate goods when the premium variety is right in front of us."

Gabe's jaw clenched. He didn't like that he was admired by these monsters.

"Now, have you been to Amethyst?" Hadeon asked, curling ringed fingers over the arms of his throne.

"No," Gabe said, tone sharp.

"I thought not... especially when you agreed to come here so readily. It's not what you expected, is it? Do you still wish to proceed?"

"I suppose so," Gabe said, eyes darting about the space for some kind of exit. He found none. No. He was in this now, and he'd have to see it through. For those caged women, those girls like Ever, he'd see it through.

"Well, good. Good. My requirements for doing business are simple. I've watched you already, and I think you have what it takes. This is only one more test."

Dimitrius snorted into a glass of Lucifer's Tears. Hadeon cut a sharp glare his direction before continuing. "Go into the pit."

"The pit?" Gabe asked, nausea crawling up his throat at the word. *Get in the pit, Gabriel.* Father had called the dark room under their house that. Had he been referring to *this* place?

Hadeon tilted his head to the sunken area. "The pit. We'll see if you are ruthless enough for this business."

Now Dimitrius outright laughed.

"What am I to do?" Gabe hid his shaking hands under crossed arms.

"You'll fight. A willing opponent."

"A fight against anyone other than an Ethereal would be inhumane," Gabe said, hope sparking at the validity of his argument.

"Good thing you'll be fighting an Ethereal then."

Fuck. "What are the rules of engagement?" Gabe's heart threatened to beat right out of his chest. He didn't want to do this. He'd avoided anything violent at all... well, against anyone other than himself, since that night... Crystal and blood and pleading. *Please. My son...*

"So proper, this one," Dimitirius giggled. "There are no rules. Just win."

"If there are no rules, how will I know I've won?"

Hadeon's forked tongue stroked across his teeth. "When your opponent stops fighting back, of course."

"I will be at my Ethereal's side," Carl said, stepping forward from God knew where.

"You will do no—" Gabe began, but Hadeon cut him off.

"I would expect no less from his dog."

"Worry not, Gabriel. The other will have his pets, too."

"Is there no other way?"

"Of course there is." Hadeon smiled beatifically. "But this is the way I want *you* to prove yourself."

Gabe gulped back his reservations. He would do this. He *had* to do this. For the girls kept in cages. For the ones brought to his own facilities that he couldn't save. For Everest. "When do I fight?"

"Now," Hadeon said, lifting a leg and kicking Gabe in the chest, over the edge and into the pit.

Gabe landed with a dull thump on the mesh floor and lay gasping atop the remains of his broken chair for one breath. Two. Three. A skinny, scarred hand reached out and grasped his, hoisting him up. Carl. *God damnit.*

Carl dropped Gabe's hand and stepped into his space. "Look alive, Mr. Malik," he hissed. "I won't let anything happen to your pretty face."

What is happening right now?

Oh, hello, Gabe. Are you scared?

Of course I am. I'm in a strange place with people I don't trust.

But that's not what you're afraid of, is it?

Stop.

No, you're afraid of that little zing in the tips of your fingers. That's not fear, Gabe. It's excitement.

I don't want to do this.

But you do. Don't you? Can't you see it?

Damn him. He could. Blood on his knuckles, spattering his face, ruining his expensive suit. His heart gave a little thrill at the thought. He told it to shut up. It didn't listen, either.

It's alright, Gabe. We can let our monsters out tonight...

"Mr. Malik," Carl snapped from beside him. "They're here."

Indeed, across the way, stood a tall Ethereal and *three* Reapers. Well, that was hardly fair. Carl only grinned and cracked his knuckles. He cast aside his scythe, as if there wasn't a chance in hell he'd need it. Gabe shrugged out of his jacket and tossed it—and his conscience—atop the discarded scythe, then turned to Carl. "Well, then, my friend. Why don't you show me how you earned your scars?"

"With pleasure," said Carl, rolling his head. "And you, Mr. Malik. Why don't you show me how you became a king amongst gods?"

Well, that's a nice compliment. Why don't we show him, Gabe? Show him how you liked it when you killed Father.

"I will." Gabe strode across the arena, ignoring the twinge of pain from his surgery the night before. Pain was no mere acquaintance. No, he was married to pain, and tonight he'd reap the rewards of their union.

I like that.

Good.

Shall we?

Yes.

Relief and determination colored every breath as Gabe affirmed the Ethereal was unknown to him. "Hello," he purred. "Have you come to lose?"

The other Ethereal ran his tongue over his teeth, then gnashed at Gabe, "It's never happened before. Hadeon must hate you."

In his periphery, Gabe watched Carl materialize behind one of the Reapers who'd stepped into some kind of triangular formation around their Ethereal. "Never say never," Carl sang, just as he jabbed his thumb into the larger Reaper's eye socket. *Holy shit.*

Gabe froze, horror clawing at his chest as the big man dropped to the ground, moaning as he clutched his pulverized eye. *What is it with Reapers and eyes?*

He was so fixated on the brutal attack, he hadn't noticed the Ethereal approaching him. Not until a foot connected with his sore balls. Gabe dropped like a sack of grain, momentarily blinded by the pain. Knuckles smashed into his jaw, whipping his head to the side. *So much for Carl's promises.* Gabe fell backward under the Ethereal's fists. Before he could so much as mount a defense, he was pinned beneath the male's weight, the crunch of bone, *his bones,* sounding under relentless blows. The gathered crowd booed at his poor show.

We can't have that, Gabe.

Pain lanced through his skull, through his lower abdomen, where the Ethereal crushed his sore organs. Gabe embraced it, a laugh bubbling up his throat. Before he could bite it back, it erupted out of him, loud and shrill against the backdrop of pummeled meat. The Ethereal above him stilled, shock widening his eyes. The arena fell quiet. The only sounds were pained grunts from somewhere in the direction Carl fought, and Gabe's laugh, resounding louder than it should have around the space, nasally from his crushed nose. Blood pooled at the back of his throat, causing his laughter to turn into a gurgle. He gathered the phlegm and blood and spat it at the other Ethereal's face.

"Ugh," the Ethereal groaned, leaping off of Gabe in disgust.

That's it, Gabe. Show him who we are.

Gabe rose, his legs steady beneath him. He wiped the endless stream of blood from his face with his shirt sleeve, the faint scent of Ever's shampoo from where she'd hugged him goodbye mingling with the acidic iron of his blood. Then, Gabriel Malik straightened his shoulders, along with his tie, and walked calmly up to the male. "That wasn't very nice," he grunted, voice destroyed under the mess of his face. *No one respects nice.*

"You're deranged," the Ethereal panted, raising his fists and sending one flying into Gabe's ribs. Gabe only absorbed the pain, drunk on sensation.

Are you going to let him speak to us that way? Should I handle this? No. We'll *handle this.*

Gabriel stood stock still under the Ethereal's blows, drinking in the violence, the pain, until the male was breathless with exhaustion. The sound from Carl's side of the arena had long since ceased. Gabe glanced that direction, swollen eyes narrowing his vision to slits. Carl sat atop the still body of his largest opponent with his arms crossed, an evil grin stretching his tattooed cheeks. He caught Gabe's eye and subtly nodded his head.

Gabe turned his attention back to the Ethereal, who was slumped against him, murmuring curses into his chest as he rained exceedingly sluggish hits to Gabe's spine. Gabe curled his fingers into silky silver strands and pulled. The male unstuck from his bloody chest like a wayward starfish. The Ethereal's fear reeked as Gabe pulled back his fist and struck him in the belly. Hot breath tickled Gabriel's hair as he laughed through his split lips.

"*Please*," the male begged, reading the fate written in the swollen lines of Gabe's face.

"No," Gabe said. He kicked the legs out from under the male, then knelt on his chest. He returned every hit the other man had given and more—for all of the times Gabe had cowered under another's fists—until the male was nothing more than a silent, bloody pulp under Gabriel's fingers. Still, it was not finished. So Gabe rose, twined his fingers into the unmoving Ethereal's hair, and dragged him across the arena where his clean jacket and broken chair waited. He dropped the limp man in front of Hadeon with a bow.

Silence. Only silence greeted his victory.

It is still not enough, the voice purred.

Gabriel's vision narrowed on the scythe under his jacket.

You're right. It's not done.

Oh, goody.

He stooped and lifted the scythe. He should stop. He should not do this thing. It was enough to have won. *No. It wasn't enough.* Carl made a choked sound of protest somewhere behind him. He didn't like Gabe touching his scythe. Gabe ignored him. He yanked the Ethereal's limp head back and pressed the blade to his neck. Then, he met Hadeon's gaze. A tiny smile played about the corners of his lips. Gabriel's own lip lifted as he pulled the blade through his victim's neck. Blood fountained, draining away through the mesh. Gabriel lifted the male's head, then stepped forward and set it at Hadeon's feet.

He gathered up his jacket, pressed the bloodied scythe into Carl's hands, and climbed out of the pit.

Gabe left Amethyst, then, the only sound the wet sucking of his bloody shoes on the wood floors.

30
TOGETHER

A MONTH PASSED BEFORE Darius fully understood what Addy had meant when she'd said they would figure things out *together*. She'd meant, to his irritation, that they'd be doing *everything* together. That she would not give him the *opportunity* to enact his judgment on the Reapers any longer, because *she'd* be accompanying him when he visited Bracken.

"It's ridiculous I've let you go without me for so many years," she'd said.

No amount of what she called *grumbling*, but Darius knew well to be *reasoning,* would sway her.

"There is no danger. I am Ethereal, Dare. By the time they even bother to ask questions, we'll be gone. And I'd like to see where my brother lives," she'd said, rolling her eyes when Darius pointed out just because Gabe had a house—an absurdly ostentatious house—in Bracken, did not mean he lived there. There had never been any evidence of Gabe inhabiting the community, only reports of occasional visits that stirred up panic in the residents, human and Ethereal alike. What had his friend become to induce such a flurry in the people? Darius didn't allow his mind to linger, though, focusing instead on stitching the hole in his extra pair of pants.

"Here, let me," Addy scolded, tugging the needle from his grip after he'd stabbed his own finger for a third time. "I keep expecting you to get better at this," she laughed, running a line of tidy stitches along the edges of the patch.

"And I keep tellin' ya, my fingers are too big for such a tiny needle." He wiggled the aforementioned fingers at her.

"Don't you dare," she said, pointing the needle at him in threat. "If you even *think* about tickling me, I'll stab you with this."

Darius stifled a smirk with his shoulder before relenting and dropping his hands, "You're growin' fussy in yer old age, Addy."

She scoffed, "I'm thirty-six!"

"Exactly."

"Apologize, or I'm not giving these back." She tucked the pants behind her back.

"I don't think that'd be the advantage ya think it is, love."

"And why is that?"

"Because then I'd have ta walk around naked from the waist down half the time."

"And you think that would be some great loss on my part?" She winked.

"Hmmm, I'm seeing yer point." He snatched her around the waist, dragging her forward until she was pressed against the front of him. He bent and planted a kiss on her collarbone, taking a moment to breathe in the scent of her. She melted against him, dropping the pants on the floor behind her so she could push her fingers into his hair. Her neck arched, giving him a better angle to kiss the soft skin there. "I'm sorry, love," he murmured around kisses. "How can I ever make it up to ya?"

"I have a few ideas," she mumbled, voice gone husky.

"Oh?" he asked into the hollow of her throat.

"Oh, yes." She gave his head a subtle push downward.

Darius laughed, causing her skin to pebble under his breath. "I'll get ta work on atoning, then?"

"Mmmhmm." She nodded, bumping her chin on the top of his head. "And then we'll go."

He sighed, unbuttoning her shirt. "And then we'll go."

"Good," was her reply, as Darius knelt and worshiped his wife.

"It's smaller than I remember," Addy said, voice low as they stood amongst the trees on the border to Bracken.

"Aye. I remember thinkin' the same when I first came back."

"What a life you have lived, my love."

"What a life *we've* lived," Darius corrected.

She just smiled a little sadly at him.

"Did ya ever miss it? What ya left behind here?"

"You mean the horror?"

"Ya know I don't."

"I miss Gabe. I didn't believe even for a moment that I wouldn't see him after that night."

"Me neither, Ads. Me neither." Darius brushed a lock of hair that'd come free from her braid behind her ear.

"I... I miss knowing things. We're so isolated. Though I prefer it that way most of the time. It's freeing to be away from the constant onslaught of information our devices brought. I wish I could tell you I miss my mother, but I don't. Not really. I do wonder about her, though." She shrugged. "But other than Gabe—oh, and those little cream puffs we used to get in the Mirrored City—I don't miss much. I have you."

Darius kissed her brow. "And I have you."

"So what now?" she asked, flicking her fingers at the open grassy swath of border, "There are more of them than I remember."

"Aye. It seems yer brother takes security a bit more serious than his predecessor. The Reapers came a few years after we fled. But to answer yer question....Now, we wait for Flint—or Ember—to give us the signal."

"For how long?"

He just shrugged.

"Why, I think you rather sensationalized this whole thing."

Darius chuckled, "I never told ya t'was glamorous."

"I suppose not. So, will she be coming back with us?"

"Not sure. Ember has been wafflin' about stayin or going for years. Flint implied it might be serious this go round, though, last I saw him. Things are changing in Bracken."

"It would seem so," Addy mumbled, pointing out a shiny silver craft touching down on a distant plateau. "Could that be... him?"

"I don't know, but we'll check. We gotta be cautious either way, Ads. Even if it's him, we've no idea what state he'll be in. He wasn't good when we left him."

"I know, but if it's him, you understand that I have to see him?"

"Aye. I understand." Darius wrapped his arms around her and kissed the top of her head, "I have to see him, too."

31
MUSIC NOTES

GABE

IT TOOK A WEEK to wash the scent of death off his skin. It haunted him like a scurrilous spirit, waking him from what little rest he took. He'd come awake screaming, his hands covered in blood. Stumbling to the bathroom, he'd scrub and scald until his skin peeled, only to blink and see they'd been clean the whole time. Two. He'd *killed* two people. And... He didn't think he felt as bad about it as he should. Especially not when Everest had arrived at 3:07am the next day and cooed over his wounds like he was something precious. Like he should be protected. *Treasured*. She'd kissed a cut on his temple. Gabe could still feel the tingle her lips had evoked, the way pleasure had mingled with pain. No. He did not feel as bad about it as he should. Not so long as Everest came to quiet the voices.

There'd been no retaliation for the murder. No report. No summoning from the Authority. Gabe had only received a slip of silver embossed paper the morning after his '*fight*;' an invitation to a warehouse in the Dark Market. Hadeon had been waiting when he arrived. And then Gabe had done it, something that felt inexplicably dirtier than murder. He'd *bought* five women. All women who'd met his gaze unflinchingly and blinked slowly, deliberately. *Twice*. The women Everest had sent for him. The ones who needed him. It'd been a simple matter to have them transferred to Bracken, then smuggled out to wherever Marcus took their refugees.

Gabe comforted himself with basic mental math: five lives were worth more than one. And even if those women weren't meant for slaughter, they'd certainly not be *living* in whatever hell they'd been intended for.

Still, Gabe struggled to reconcile with the truth *he'd* been at the helm—partially anyway—during this latest vile act. He could not blame it all on his lesser half. *That* was what kept him from sleep. That and his inability to stop thinking about Ever's lips. Her laugh. Her cold toes wedged under his thigh on the couch. The way her eyes had sparkled when he'd played her a refrain on the dusty piano in the library. That she paused every time to look at the sullen man he kept behind glass in the hall. His thoughts were full of the many shades of Ever. And blood. But Gabe found living didn't feel so much of a burden when 3:07 existed. When he knew she'd come and they'd both pretend not to be monsters for a little while. Gabe did not sleep, between the nightmares and the daydreams.

For the first time in his life, he'd discovered a balance of sorts, and he might even be *happy,* if only a little bit. He wanted more of it. So he shoved aside his tired internal debate about how much good he needed to outweigh the bad within him and focused instead on living. He lived for 3:07, for that hour in her company. And he lived for Thursday morning, when his best friends came for breakfast. And he lived for the mundane moments in between: sunlight casting rainbows on his polished floors, music written in the steady thump thump of his heart, dandelion seeds on the breeze. Gabe lived, and he realized he'd done this before, had this before with his sister, with Darius—even with his mother once. *Go visit your mother.* Yes. He would go visit his mother, like Everest had said, and maybe they'd *live* together again.

Rittenmore was still a shithole. Fine, Gabe wasn't being very charitable with that assessment. Things did seem to have improved since he'd been here ten years ago. He hadn't been able to admit to Everest that he'd only visited his mother once, but her suggestion had niggled at the edges of his consciousness since she'd said it. Shame tickled the back of his throat at that truth. He'd been negligent in his duty to ensure Mother's welfare. Relying on monthly reports from the facility staff, instead of checking himself. *You're only returning the favor from our boyhood, Gabe. Don't beat yourself up.* He rolled his shoulders, pushing the voice back down where it simmered in malevolent monologue. Up and up and up the hill Gabe went. Children played at the same school he'd seen all those years before. A smile tugged at the corners of his lips, then crumpled and fell away. Only *male* children played in the school yard. Why? Why do this? *Because they know the truth.*

What truth?

The females aren't worth much.

That is a vile thought.

A laugh reverberated around his skull. *It is, indeed. And it's your thought, Gabe.*

I don't think that.

Oh, you do, darling. You know the truth as well as I. The women are only here to serve our needs.

You disgust me.

*You disgust **you.***

"Mr. Malik? Shall I wait here, or would you have me park the car around back?" his driver asked, breaking through his unpleasant internal dialogue.

"Oh, we're here already, John?"

John smiled in the rearview mirror, "Yes. Mr. Malik. Distracted today?"

"It would seem so."

The driver opened his mouth, then snapped it shut, sealing whatever he'd been planning to say inside.

"John," Gabe drawled, "What've I told you? Out with it."

"It's only that I'm proud of you."

"What?"

"I've been with your family a long while, and I—forgive me—I just thought you might need to hear it. It's a good thing, you coming to see her."

"Why... I, I don't know what to say. Thank you, John."

"You're welcome, Mr. Malik."

"Wait here, will you?"

John nodded, toggling the button that lifted the partition as Gabe climbed out of the car.

I'm proud of you.

No one had ever said that to him before. Addy had always told him he was *good,* but even that had felt like an obligation. Like he *had* to be good. Like her love was conditional. Darius, well, he loved Gabe the way one loves a three-legged puppy. He'd always treated him as though he were something to be protected. And Ryker, well. Gabe supposed Ryker was the closest he'd ever come to someone being proud of him, but it wasn't pride, was it? It was envy. Gabe didn't want to touch whatever *Marcus* thought of him. Though in ways, he preferred the other man's no-nonsense demeanor. And Ever... He'd grown terribly close to Ever over the last few weeks, but as he often reminded himself, it was far too early to define the feelings that fluttered under his breastbone when he thought of her. He realized with a start he had nearly a handful of people who *cared* about him. It was more than he'd ever wished for. Yes. They *cared*.

But proud of him? His chest swelled with the notion.

You always were a little bitch for praise, Gabe.

His giddiness soured at the sound of the voice in his head. *You ruin everything.*

I'm here to serve you.

Gabe mounted the front steps, casting aside his speculations for later. An attendant in a white coat greeted him. He did a double-take as the female, *female*, extended a hand to him. She *was* Ethereal, but she was different somehow, the lines of her face all jagged edges instead of the usual gentle grace. She was... *ugly*. God, Gabe hated himself for thinking it, but it was true. She was *not* attractive. He'd gotten so used to seeing only perfect proportions, full lips, wide eyes... to see a face so scrunched and miserable on an Ethereal was jarring. Her hair was braided back from her face and tied in a tight bun at the nape of her neck, further lending to the severity of her features. Gabe wondered if she might, perhaps, be more beautiful if she let the hair down, then berated himself for it. He'd never based an opinion on someone's looks before, and he didn't feel inclined to start down that slippery slope just yet. He took her hand and shook it. The skin was cold to the touch, as if she were a corpse.

Still, Gabe pasted on a smile. "Hello," he said. "I'm Gabriel Malik, I'm here to see—"

"I know who you're here to see."

Oh, so she's ugly on the inside, too.

"Follow me, Mr. Malik."

Gabe fell into step behind her, grasping for something to say. "So, you're new here?"

The Ethereal sighed wearily, as if he were nothing more than a bother. "I've been here six years, Mr. Malik," she replied in a bored tone.

"Oh... right."

"She's just through here." She led him down a narrow white hall, lined on either side with doors. It looked very much like the medical facilities back in Bracken, but that was all wrong. This place *shouldn't* be like that. *Hadn't* been like that.

The Ethereal twisted a thick bolt, and the door swung open, revealing a small room. A narrow bed was shoved into one corner, white sheets tucked precisely at the corners, looking nothing at all like the plush, rumpled bed he'd left at home. A white curtain divided the space, behind which Gabe glimpsed a small bathing room. At a tiny white desk with a matching white chair in the corner opposite the bed, sat his mother. She hadn't even noticed them. Gabe stepped up behind her, looking over her shoulder, where she scratched manically at a piece of paper with a dull pencil. Music notes. Hundreds of notes strewn nonsensically across the page.

"Mother?" he whispered.

She turned, nearly knocking over her chair as she cowered the way Gabe had seen her do a hundred times under the hands of his father.

"No." She shook her head. "You're dead." She held out a hand, the other cradling her swollen belly. "And you can't touch me, James. I'm with child."

She thinks we're him.

Oh God.

Gabe took a step back, showing his palms. "Mother. It's *me*. It's Gabe. Your son."

"Oh. I'm sorry. You reminded me of someone I used to know." She stood, cast about as if she'd immediately forgotten what she was doing, then sat again.

"I didn't mean to scare you. I apologize. I do look a good deal like him," Gabe said bitterly.

She folded her hands and sat up straight. "So, why has one of my offspring come to see me?"

"I—"

"Here." The gruff Ethereal shoved a folded chair at Gabe. "You can sit if you want. Don't touch the product. She's already in use."

"What?"

She just looked at him blandly. "I'll be outside," she said, closing the door.

Gabe stared after her, the chair feeling like an anvil in his hands. *What the hell is going on here?* He unfolded the chair and sat facing his mother.

"I wanted to see you, to make sure you're okay."

"Oh. That's nice of you."

He nodded slowly, then leaned in, lowering his voice, "Mother, I'm sorry it's been so long. I have so much to tell. I'm sure you heard about Adalia, but I need you to know—"

"Who is Adalia?"

Gabe looked around the room as if someone might appear and announce this whole thing was a joke. Perhaps this wasn't his mother; perhaps he was in the wrong room... No. That *was* her. Even her handwriting, where it scratched across the paper, was the same. "Mother, has something happened?"

"Something happens every day."

"Have they done something to you?"

"Of course."

"Did they hurt you?"

Her face scrunched, there and then gone in less than a second, before she replied, "No. Of course not. They are kind to me here. Who are you?"

Oh God. Oh God. She doesn't know me.

"I'm your son. Gabriel. Gabe."

"Hmm. That's a nice name."

Gabe's jaw clenched. They'd done something to her. His mother had been passive; she'd cowered with his father, but she'd never held her tongue with *him*. He recalled how bold she'd been when he'd visited with Addy. This was not the same woman. She did not even *remember* him. "Mother, why are you pregnant?"

She ran a hand along her rounded stomach. "It's what I do. It's my *purpose.*"

"Mother, you were only meant to have two children."

She blinked at him in confusion.

"How many is that?" He nodded at her belly.

"Oh. I don't know," she said, as if she truly did not care.

Rage darkened Gabe's vision.

"Do they let you out of this room, Mother? Are you still composing music?" He pointed at the chaotic mess of notes on her paper.

"Music? Yes. I like music. One of the overseers hums while she works."

Overseers? What the fuck? "And the other part? Do you get out of here?"

"Oh, yes." She nodded enthusiastically. "They let me out on growing days."

"You don't go out every day?"

"No, silly. Of course not. We must stick to the schedule. It's for the greater good."

Gabe flexed his fingers and rose.

Oh, I like where this is headed.

Shut up.

You're so dramatic. Let me out, Gabe. You know I'm scarier than you.

His mother cowered in her chair, but Gabe turned away, unable to look at her. He pounded on the door. "Open up."

Cold crept along his spine, his fingers shaking with the effort to keep his monster at bay. The door swung wide, revealing the wretched face of the Ethereal. *Fuck it.* He unleashed.

Before she could say a word, Gabriel had her pinned to the opposite wall by her neck.

"I don't know who the fuck you think you are," he hissed. "But you'll pay for not notifying me of her *condition.*"

She only emitted a choked wheeze around his fingers. He pushed harder in response.

"I am taking her with me today. Understand?" He released the Ethereal, who crashed to the floor, sputtering and coughing, before glaring up at him.

"You cannot. The offspring–"

"I don't give a damn about whatever demon seed is inside my mother right now. Cut it out for all I care. I own *her.* I am taking her."

"The Authority–"

"The Authority can kiss my ass." *Stop, Gabriel, you aren't think-ing clearly. We cannot garner the Authority's attention.*

"Sir, I—"

"Fine. You worthless little scum. I'll pay for her—and the *thing* in her—happy?"

She shook her head.

"Good. I don't want you to be happy." He kicked her in the ribs, causing a delightfully pathetic sound to color the air.

Stop.

"Mother dearest," Gabriel sang. "Come now."

His mother stood in her doorway, looking on with horror as the ugly woman continued to gasp for breath around her broken ribs.

"Overseer?" Mother whimpered.

A wheeze was her only reply.

"Come *now*," Gabriel repeated, latching onto Mother's hand and tugging her along the hall, out through the front doors to the waiting car, ignoring the shouts of the Overseers. He yanked open the door and shoved her unceremoniously inside. She yelped as she bounced off the seat cushion and onto the floor.

"Please," she sputtered.

But he ignored her, climbing in and barking to John, "Drive."

"Mr. Malik, you can't—"

"Do not tell me what I can and cannot *do*."

"Yes, sir."

John drove.

Gabriel tapped out a message on his phone, receiving a confirmation as they rolled up to the gates. Reapers surrounded the car, preventing them from leaving.

"Mr. Malik, what would you have me do?" John croaked. Pathetic fear seasoned the air from his direction.

"I'd have you shut up and wait while I speak with the Reapers." He shoved open the door and stepped out amongst the Reapers, who created a circle around him, their scythes raised.

"You'd dare threaten a Heritage Ethereal?" Gabriel tisked. The scythes lowered a fraction of an inch. "Hmmmm. I suppose that's a little better. Now, what's the problem, ladies, gentlemen?"

An outrageously tall Reaper stepped forward and cleared her throat, "Sir. You are not permitted to take the breeders off campus."

Breeders?

"Oh, I see. You presume to tell me what I can do as well?" He grinned.

The Reaper's throat bobbed, "It is law—"

"For *you* perhaps. I make my own laws."

A collective grumble wended through the Reapers at his blasphemous words. "Sir—"

"Do shut up. Look." He produced the false approval document Ryker had just sent, and the Reaper's brow furrowed in confusion.

"Good? Good. I'll be going now. Open the gate." He slid back into the car, ignoring his crying mother on the floor.

After over an hour of navigating Rittenmore's back streets, they arrived at the landing pad. Gabe couldn't stop shaking.

Let it gooo, little Gabe. I did what needed doing.

Please just be quiet.

Where's the fun in that? I got your precious mother, didn't I? As if you've room to talk after your display at Amethyst. What will we do with her now?

You were effective, Gabe admitted. *I will take her to Ryker and Marcus.*

Oooo. Do I get to know just where they'll put her?

No.

You're no fun. I'll break through those walls of yours someday. Just wait.

Go away. I have to take care of her. She's scared.

Pitiful thing, isn't she?

"Mother," Gabe started, leaning so he was at her level, where she still huddled on the floor. "I know that was scary. I'm sorry for it. Sometimes we have to act like monsters to beat the monsters, you know?"

She didn't reply.

"Anyway, you're safe now. You're going somewhere safe. Your offspring, if you want it, will stay with you."

She lifted her chin at that. "I can keep this one?"

"Is that what you wish?"

"Yes."

"I need you to come with me into the flight craft. We'll go to my friends and they'll take you to the safe place. Do you understand?"

"Is the safe place like the growing room?"

"No, Mother. It's not. It's much better."

"Will there be music?"

The lump in his throat made it difficult to speak. "Yes, Mother, there will be music."

Just then his phone chimed, as if it had conspired to give his mother a taste of the music she wanted.

Missing person:
Female
Ember Leighton
Age: 28
Type: Unmodified Human
Priority level: Low
Reaper detail dispatched.

Gabe sighed. Not again. Human disappearances put the entire operation he was running with Marcus and Ryker at risk. He'd thought he'd quelled the problem by increasing Reaper surveillance, but it seemed a stubborn smuggler was still at work. Gabe eyed his mother and came to a decision. He opened up his message thread with Ryker and typed:

> I've acquired a package.

> What the fuck is going on Gabe?

> Are you in trouble?

> Who were the documents for?

Where is pickup?

Bracken.

Shit.

Bring Marc.

See you tonight. You have some explaining to do.

Gabe held out a hand to his mother, who tentatively touched her fingers to his before allowing him to pull her out of the car. "Come, Mother," he whispered. "I'm taking you home."

32

A CACOPHONY

INFANT STARS LIT THE sky when Flint's signal finally came. A flash from the treetops across the border. Darius pointed at the series of bobbing blinks in the canopy, whispering, "That'll be Flint."

"Finally," Addy groaned, rolling to her knees from where she'd been flat on her back watching the birth of night. Darius rose, lending her a hand the rest of the way up.

"Quiet, remember."

Addy mimed zipping her lips.

"Let's go," Darius said, tugging her along behind. He led her through the narrow swath of borderland, their shadowy forms undetected in the fading light.

Three figures huddled at the base of a squat oak, heads bent close, their quiet conversation carrying on the breeze.

"Think he'll come?" Ember's melodic tones floated by.

"Aye. If'n I ken Darius, the boy will keep true 'is word." *Callum?* Damnit. Darius had been so engrossed in caring for Addy he'd missed his usual meeting with Cal. Typically, he stopped at the human camp before his supply runs to Bracken to check up on his friend. But... time had slipped away from Darius, and now it'd been more than a year since he'd seen Callum.

Flint sounded uncertain when he spoke, "You didn't see him, Cal. He was frantic. I'd be surprised if he leaves her side again."

Darius stepped out of the shadows with Addy at his side, caus-ing the three humans to gasp at their sudden appearance. "Turns out, you can both be right," Darius said, pulling Addy under his arm. "I'm true to my word *and* I'll not be leaving her side."

Addy smiled up at him, giving his waist a squeeze. "Is that Callum I hear grumbling like a grumpy bear?"

"Aye, lass. Is that the wee Ethereal?" Callum stepped forward, limping. Callum looked... Well, he looked *old* as he shuffled over. Darius didn't know what to make of the white hair on his friend's head, the loose skin around his neck, the slight hump to his pos-ture. Had it been longer than a year? No. It was only that Callum was very much *human*. The same realization lit Addy's eyes as she glanced over at him. Darius imagined it must be a terribly jarring realization from Addy, who'd not seen Cal in years. Their friend *had* gotten older while they'd stayed the same. A tiny fissure opened up in Darius' heart at that truth. Addy would stay young. She'd stay young while everyone they knew got old and died. How long would he last at her side if he didn't go back into the box?

"Ye'll not be denyin' me a hug then, will ya, Addy?" Callum said, oblivious to their silent anguish.

Addy's smile was only tinged with a little sadness as she stepped into Callum's arms. "Of course not, my friend," she said, burying her face in his chest. "Tell me everything, Cal. It has been far too long. How is little Greta? And your mam? How fares she?"

Callum cleared his throat, "Eh, well, my mam is gone with the angels near a year past."

"I'm sorry," Addy whispered.

"T'was her time, lass. Don't fret. Greta, though, she's near a woman grown. Fifteen years old last spring and actin like a wee queen. Ye'd like her."

"I'm sorry to interrupt, but we need to get indoors," Ember said, stepping forward to hug Darius, then grasping Addy's hand. "It's good to finally meet you, Addy."

"And you," Addy said.

It warmed Darius' heart to see Ember brush aside her momentary discomfort upon realizing his wife was Ethereal. He cleared his throat, "Aye, we best get going. Flint?"

Flint clasped his forearm, then nodded at Addy, "I'm glad you're okay—both of you. Follow me."

He shot Darius a curious look, but didn't question him. Good. Darius had earned that level of respect. He only wished the humans outside the border had greeted Addy with the same acceptance.

They were ensconced in the relative safety of Flint's house, cracking walnuts over the coffee table in the living room. The home was a copy of the one Darius had grown up in—small and crumbling and terribly drafty in the winter. There would be three tiny bedrooms down the hall. Darius hoped they would be cleaner than the last time he'd been here, for Addy's sake.

"How in the hell do you even open one of these little bastards?" Flint grumbled, flicking the walnut Darius' direction.

"Like this." He picked it up and crushed it between thumb and forefinger until the shell broke open. Darius plucked out the nut and dropped it in Flint's waiting palm.

"Eh, boy, like I often used to tell ya, no normal man can do that. Here." Callum took a nut and smashed it with a rock he'd produced from one of his many pockets. "That's how ya do it."

"Darius' way seems less messy," Ember teased.

"Let's see it then, lass," Callum grumbled.

She lifted a nut and pressed it between her fingers, then tried using her whole fist, face reddening with her effort. When it failed to crack, she threw her head back and sighed to the ceiling. "It's impossible."

Addy plucked the nut from her sweaty palm and pinched it. A little puff of dust shot out as the shell disintegrated under her fingers. She delicately nibbled at the nut, ignoring the cavernous silence that'd descended.

Finally, Ember broke it with a flippant, "Show off."

Addy chuckled softly. "Sorry, couldn't help it."

"Give me that rock. I'll not have Darius feeding me like a baby," Flint said, holding out a palm for it. Callum placed it into his hand with a soft laugh.

"Alright, now that we're not gonna starve. Let's talk." Darius turned to Callum. "First off, what the hell are ya doing here, old man?"

"Eh. I expect the same as you. Gettin supplies."

"Why are *you* here, Cal? *I* bring the supplies to *you*."

"Well, I know that, lad. One of the yougins weren't doing so well. I came for medicine."

"I could have gotten that if you'd come to me."

"And waste time huntin' ya down? No. The matter's pressin'."

"Cal," Darius reprimanded. "You're not so young as ya were. Ya can't make that journey alone no more—"

"Who says I'm alone, lad?"

"Who?"

Callum chewed his lip, glancing at Addy before he glared at his walnut. "It'll be Luna, what came with me."

Shame lit the corners of Darius' chest. *Luna.* Luna, that girl who'd given herself to him. That girl he'd left and hadn't even spared a thought for in all these years. She always seemed to be absent when he delivered supplies to the human camp. "Is she here?" Darius asked, cringing as he spotted Addy's pursed lips out of the corner of his eye.

"Aye. She'll be waitin' on the other side of the border. Told her I'd be back afore the morn."

Darius gulped down his rising trepidation. "Er, that's good then. Ember, I suppose I don't have ta take ya to Callum, seeing as how he's already here?"

Ember nodded.

"So, you're truly leaving this time?" Flint asked, resolve settling into his features.

She smiled sadly at her brother. "It's time, Flint."

He dipped his chin. "You're right. It's far past time."

"Are things so bad in Bracken?" Addy asked gently.

"Worse than you can imagine," Ember said. "The Ethereals... they all moved away. We thought that meant things would be better—not to offend—but no. There's more Reapers than ever before. And the things they do? Well, it's more than it was for our parents. I'll spare you the details."

"Don't the... doesn't Mr. Malik do anything about it?" Addy barely concealed the desperation in her tone from the others. But Darius heard it. He'd been a fool to go so long without seeking Gabe out.

"Hah," Ember scoffed, then stilled as she noted Addy's serious face. "Oh. You're not kidding. Um. No. He doesn't do anything. He's never here—"

"And thank God for that," Flint toasted the air with a walnut.

"Oh." Addy's face fell.

Ember patted her hand. "Look, I'm sorry if he's someone you knew, but things only ever get worse when he's around. The Reapers get real strict, understand? He might come in a few times a year. Stops at the facilities. Then he hides in that big house on the hill for a while before he disappears again. Here's the thing, though... People... whole *families* go missing whenever he comes to town."

"What?!" Addy's shout rang through the small space, bouncing off the walls.

Across from Darius, Callum narrowed his eyes. *Shit.* He'd forgotten Cal *knew* who Addy was. He shook his head subtly. Cal rolled his eyes, but nodded in agreement. He wouldn't tell the others just who Gabe was to Addy. Just who Gabe was... to *him.*

"I'm sure there's an explanation," Darius offered.

"Yeah, and it's nothin' pleasant," Flint muttered.

"What's that supposed to mean?" Addy asked.

"Means those people are never seen again. There's rumors, though. Rumors he's mad, the Ethereal... Sorry. Never heard anything good about him." Flint shrugged.

Ember searched Addy's face, noting the lines of horror hidden at the edges of her eyes. "Actually, Flint, I have a friend who got a job up at the mansion. I swear, she's in love with him. Rants about how nice he is. *Mr. Malik saved my life,*" Ember mimicked in a high tone, "*Without him, I'd be stuck in the facilities like you lot.* God, Sylvie can be such a bitch."

Addy settled a little at the glimmer of hope Ember offered.

Darius looked at Ember gratefully, then asked, "Any idea when he'll be back in town?"

Flint narrowed his eyes suspiciously at Darius, slowly chewing through a nut, as if weighing whether or not to answer. Finally, he shrugged and admitted, "He'll be here any minute, most likely. Ember missed her shift. He gets real fussy when you take his people, Dare."

"Noted." Darius squeezed Addy's hand. *We'll see him.*

Moonlight lit the planes of Addy's face from a slit in the curtains. Darius took a moment to study the sheer perfection of her. The silvery light painted her in monochrome, all contrasts, all beautiful. Long tresses of silver splayed across the rolled sleeping mat she used for a pillow. Dark eyelashes rested on high cheekbones, two freckles that'd survived her enhancements dotted the bridge of her nose. Her mouth hung slightly slack, drool pooling at the corner. Darius smiled to see it—Addy so utterly at peace. Dust motes stirred as he slid from their shared blanket, further lending to Addy's angelic glow. Her brow furrowed. Darius leaned down and kissed it away, whispering, "I'll keep my promise, love."

He left out the open window without a sound.

The facility's security was abysmal. Darius thought as much every time he broke in. Though he supposed they usually didn't have to worry about humans trying to get in here. According to Flint, the others wouldn't come within a block of the place unless they were forced to. Getting inside was a simple matter of wedging a thin blade into the crack of the door and shimmying it about until it caught the latch. His steps echoed hollow on the tiled floors, the scent of antiseptic tickling his nose, alongside another scent he couldn't quite identify. It reminded him of decay. The hair on the back of his neck rose in recognition. What had they been up to in this place? A groan from under the slit of a nearby door had Darius jumping back, pressing himself flat to the wall.

"Help me," someone rasped, long fingernails scraping at the ground under the door.

"Is someone there?" Cried another, a thump emanating from the next door down.

"*Please.*" This voice was small, child-like, effeminate.

Help us. Overseer? Help us. Let us out. I'll do anything. Please. Please. Please.

Their cries became a cacophony.

Darius covered his ears and ran to the box room. He couldn't help whoever was behind those doors. But he *could* help Addy. He ignored their screams as he stripped out of his clothes and slammed a fist down on the button that'd start the process. He sprinted for the box and climbed inside, just before the door on top slid shut. The liquid rose. Darius breathed it in with relief when it finally covered his ears, blocking out their cries. Addy. *She* was what mattered. Her happiness meant more to him than any moral obligation he might have to help those pitiful creatures behind the other doors. So Darius closed his eyes and floated in the knowledge of his selfish choice, waiting for the guilt to come. It didn't.

33

A DANGEROUS MAN

CARL WAS WAITING IN the black and white checkered foyer of Gabe's house in Bracken. Relief washed over Gabe that he'd already sent his mother off with Marcus. As much as he would have liked to bring her home, she'd fallen into a panic attack the moment she realized where they were. He'd taken her to the Ethereal facility for a quick tonic to help the attack and handed her off to Marcus. Gabe hadn't been brave enough to tell her it'd been goodbye, that he wouldn't seek her out, that he didn't trust himself to know everything. Not when he'd had to take a tonic himself to help with the creeping terror that always assaulted him when he entered the facility.

He'd made his rounds as quickly as possible, finding nothing amiss, the rooms tidy—and blissfully empty—just as they'd been last time. The staff mentioned a few missing vials of regenerative serum, but that was hardly anything to trouble himself over. He'd left with Ryker, Sable, and a grumbling Wesley in tow, angry that Marcus had abandoned him *again*. They couldn't risk the Reapers knowing what they were up to, even if Hadeon had undoubtedly reported to the Authority that Gabe was now involved in the darker aspects of the society. They'd come to the mutual conclusion that it'd be more problematic to be caught out with what they were actually doing. The Authority didn't take kindly to disobedient subjects... Not that they'd openly punish three Heritage Ethereals, but it was better safe than sorry. That's why Gabe had snuck out to visit his mother and left his Reaper behind. Carl now folded his arms and scowled before growling, "What the fuck, Mr. Malik?"

"I'm sure I don't know what you mean," Gabe said, shrugging out of his jacket and passing it to the butler with a soft smile.

"Welcome home, Mr. Malik," said the butler, whose name Gabe never remembered.

"Thank you."

"Will you be staying for a spell?"

"Oh, no. Just overnight." He cast about for a name he *did* remember. "Send Sylvie my way, would you? We'll need rooms for our many guests." He gestured to Ryker and the Reapers who'd come in on his heels.

"Of course." The butler bowed and spun, neglecting to take Ryker's coat, which he held dangling from his outstretched hand.

"Your staff are impeccable as always, Gabe," Ryker chuckled and crossed to the closet to hang his own coat.

"Are you going to continue to pretend I'm not here?" Carl asked.

"Well, that was my plan, actually," Gabe said. "Seeing as how you're most certainly *not* where I left you, happily snoring in your room in The City of Mirrors."

"A Reaper must stay at their Ethereal's side," Carl proclaimed, finishing in chorus with the other Reapers, "*It is law.*"

Gabe rolled his eyes at their rhetoric. "Yes, yes. *Your* laws. Come now, Carl. I thought we built a rapport. Can't a man have some room to breathe?"

"That *rapport* is exactly why I expect you to bring me along on these little... *adventures.*"

"Very well," Gabe said, striding to Carl and clapping him irreverently on the back. "I shall not leave you behind again."

Carl muttered something unintelligible, eliciting a snicker from Wesley, as if the man hadn't just been whining about his own wayward Ethereal.

"Good," Gabe said, rubbing his hands together. "Ah, Sylvie!" Gabe clasped the hand of the lovely young maid who'd quietly entered and stood waiting in the corner. "Ryker, you remember Sylvie?"

"How could I forget such a lovely little human?" Ryker purred, taking Sylvie's hand and running a proprietary thumb across the back. Sylvie blushed prettily under his attentions, then stiffened as Carl came closer, a threatening gleam lighting his eyes.

"Down, dog," Gabriel said. "You'll not be touching my humans, understand?"

Carl narrowed his eyes, but nodded all the same.

"That goes for you, too," Ryker motioned lazily to Sable and Wesley.

Sylvie pulled her hand out of Ryker's regrettably, and turned to Gabe. "How can I be of service, Mr. Malik?"

"Please have the staff prepare a meal, Sylvie, and rooms for my... friends. We'll take refreshments in the sitting room."

"Of course, Mr. Malik." She smiled and melted away down the hall to the kitchen.

"You three." Gabe swirled a finger in the air, encompassing the Reapers. "Go do your jobs or... whatever. Check the property."

"Sir—" Carl began.

"Carl, I do know how this is *supposed* to work, and I'm fairly certain you're *supposed* to do as I say without argument, unless it threatens my safety, yes?"

"Yes," Carl begrudgingly admitted.

"Then go. Enjoy the gardens. Bother the staff for food. We are not in the Mirrored City, and I won't tell if you don't."

Carl nodded and made for the door. Sable fell into step beside him after an affirming nod from Ryker, but Wesley hesitated.

"I cannot leave without a command from my Ethereal," Wesley's low voice rumbled.

"Oh, for Christ's sake," Ryker groaned. "Your Ethereal is not here, you brute. He left you in *my* charge. So go with the others, damnit."

Wesley's fingers tightened on his scythe, but he turned and obeyed, stomping after the others.

Gabe led Ryker to the sitting room, speaking over his shoulder, "In a bit of a mood, are you?"

Ryker settled into a tufted leather chair before the bank of floor to ceiling windows, slinging his legs up over the arm. "It's been an odd go of things lately. Can you blame me?"

"No, I can't," said Gabe, claiming the chair opposite his friend.

"How are you holding up?"

"Fine. Why do you ask?"

"Gaaabe..."

"Don't start, Ry. I'm fine. Good, actually. I mean it."

Ryker picked at a torn bit of skin on his thumb. "If you say so. You were in rough shape when you got back from Amethyst, though... and the *rumors*?"

"I don't want to talk about it."

"Suit yourself. But let me ask you this, and then I'll leave it. Are they true?"

"Are what true?"

"The rumors. Are you a... *dangerous* man, Gabe?"

A soft knock allotted Gabe a reprieve from what he'd been about to admit, a chance to temper what he said. Sylvie entered, toting a tray laden with a variety of decanters and fingerling sandwiches. She set it on the table between them and bowed, backing out of the room as if she'd sensed the tension and wanted no part of it. Gabe poured a measure of drink and passed the glass to Ryker, who cleared his throat, raising his brows in expectation.

Gabe took a gulp of his own drink, letting it warm the cold corners of his heart. Finally, he spoke. "I have always been a dangerous man." He let the words suspend in front of Ryker, conveying their truth in the silence. *I have always been a dangerous man. I was already a murderer before last Tuesday.*

And we liked it.

Ryker nodded slowly, taking a delicate sip of his drink. "I see."

"One of us *has* to be dangerous," Gabe murmured. *No one respects nice.*

"I suppose you're right. I just... I always thought it would be Marcus."

"And *I* always knew it was me. Why do you think I ask you both to keep things from me?"

"I see," Ryker repeated. "And what would you have us do, if these... *tendencies* become problematic?"

"Short of putting me out of my misery? What you've always done."

"And what's that?"

Gabe leaned forward, letting a little bit of his monster trickle into his voice. "Lie to me. Lie well."

"We don't—"

"You *do*. And I forgive you. You are one of the dearest people to me, Ry. You are smart. And I... I am unstable. Help me make sure the balance of my life weighs for good, would you? Even if it means feeding my delusions."

"I will try." Ryker ran a finger around the lip of his glass. "And your mother? That's who she was, right?"

"Yes."

"It's a risk, Gabe. I hope you understand what you've jeopardized by taking a family member..."

"I couldn't leave her. You didn't see what it was like... What she said..." Gabe swallowed, trying to clear the lump in his throat.

"Surely it's not so bad as that. I visited my sister last month and she seemed happy..."

"No. Everest was right, Ry. There are things we don't understand. We cannot leave our women in their care any longer. We should get your sister, too."

"It will draw too much attention..."

"Do you really think the Authority gives a shit about a few women?"

Ryker bit his lip. "No. No... after what little we've learned these weeks... No. They don't."

"Good. So we'll get our people out, and *then* we'll be careful. We'll need more of a cover for the Ethereals. They're using them for something I don't understand..." Gabe sighed, and straightened in his chair. "Think on it, will you? How we might fix this thing without drawing too much attention? You'll have more creative solutions than I."

Ryker considered him for a long moment before nodding.

"Good. That's all I ask. Now," Gabe slugged back the rest of his drink and snatched a sandwich from the tray. "I'm going to change. Then, I have to track down a stray human."

Ryker sat up. "Just like that, we're done talking about this?"

"Just like that."

He didn't look satisfied with that answer, but nodded anyway. "Fine. Do you want me to come with you?"

"No. It's doubtful I'll find her, anyway."

"Can you blame them—for trying to get out?"

"Of course not. I would, too, if I could. Now, I don't want a particular gloomy presence trailing me, either. Keep an eye on the Reapers, would you?"

Ryker toasted the empty air. "With pleasure, my friend."

Someone was watching him from the trees. He'd thought for a moment it'd been Carl—damn him—but no. This presence was somehow *familiar*. It felt like a caress on the back of his neck. Gabe did his best to ignore it as he finished exchanging pleasantries with a decidedly *unhelpful* human called Flint. The burly man insisted he'd not seen or heard from his sister in months—a highly unlikely feat in a town this small. It was hardly a surprise that the man lied to his face. Fear wafted off of him so potently, Gabe could hardly think straight.

Pathetic, these humans.

Shut up.

You know it's true.

"Well, Mr. Leighton, please do let the local enforcers know if she reappears. It is not a safe place out there for a woman alone," Gabe said, releasing the man's sweaty hand. *Look at all of his tells, Gabe. He's a liar.*

I know that.

Make him pay.

No.

You ruin all of our fun.

"Of course, Mr. M—Malik."

Oh, how cute. Listen to him stutter.

"Very good. Have a pleasant evening. And... stay out of trouble, Flint."

"Yes. I will. I mean, I won't. I mean. Yes. I'll stay out of trouble."

Gabe smothered a laugh and turned from the terrified human, who shut his door and sighed explosively on the other side. Leaving

Mr. Leighton to his inevitable breakdown, Gabe fixed his attention on the trees, creeping into their shadows.

"I can feel you watching me, whoever you are. May as well come down now," he called into the branches.

A glint of silver caught the light from between the leaves, followed by a feminine giggle, one that was written into the marrow of his bones. *Addy.*

"And why don't ya come up here, then, Gabe? I'm sure it's been too long since ya climbed a tree." Gabe's heart was fit to burst as he drank in the booming tones of Darius' voice.

"Bring my sister down here, you bastard. I need to hug you both." He moved deeper into the cover of the trees, fear mingling with his joy. *They can't be here.* And yet, as his sister emerged from the shadows with Darius behind her, they were. They *were* here. Gabe launched himself into Addy's waiting arms.

34

GOOD

"YOU CAN'T BE HERE," Gabe said for what must've been the tenth time as he ushered them deeper into the cover of the trees. He hadn't let go of Addy's hand, with the exception of the too-brief hug he'd wrapped Darius in. He clung to her like a child who had lost his mother, only to discover she'd been right where he'd left her all along. Gabe was... *different* somehow. It was subtle, yes. He looked just as he had when Darius had last seen him, desperately sad in the kitchen doorway of the old mansion, his face the same handsome young thing it'd been then. But... He stood straighter, his demeanor confident, as if he knew who he was now, as if he was no longer a terrified little boy, as if he was... *happy*. At least that's what Darius read in Gabe's posture, until he met his eyes. For there, written in silver swirls, was something entirely unhinged. Addy didn't seem to notice. She only clung to Gabe's hand with the same ferocity he clutched hers. It made Darius' fingers twitch with the need to pull her away. He wanted to tuck her behind his back to protect her from the predator that prowled under her brother's unblemished skin.

When they'd gone a good distance into the grove, Gabe finally stopped, scanned the area, and nodded to himself. "What are you doing here?" he asked, something strange coating the words.

Addy took his face in her hands, oblivious to the warning bells ringing in Darius' mind. "Gabe, I had to see you. It's been so long—"

"Don't tell me you came here for *me*," Gabe hissed.

Addy dropped her hands and stepped back as if he'd slapped her.

Darius wrapped an arm around her, tucking her into his side. "Of course, we didn't come for you," Darius snapped. "We came for supplies." This reunion wasn't going at all as he'd imagined it might.

Gabe straightened at Darius' tone. "I see. Well, then, I can help with that."

"We have it handled," Darius said, pushing Addy behind him like he'd wanted to.

She shoved him aside and stepped back between them. "What is wrong with you two? It's been ten years since we've seen one another, and *this* is how you behave? Are you children?"

Gabe looked at his feet, cowed under Addy's scolding. That. That looked more like the boy Darius had known.

"I'm sorry, Ads," Gabe said. "I'm just surprised." He took her hand again. "It's not safe here for you—either of you. It's never been."

"I know that. But let's just say a proper hello for a minute, okay? Before we have to say goodbye again..."

"Okay," Gabe nodded, and looked to Darius. "Okay. You two..." He laughed. "You look just the same. Even you, Dare. You haven't aged a day. How *are* you?"

Darius bit back the anger that'd been building between them. "Er... We're good?"

Addy laughed, and it thawed the ice in Darius' soul a little.

"Yes. We're good," Addy said. "I mean, we've had our challenges, but..." She trailed off, because how did one begin to sum up ten years apart? What was the point, even, if they were only going to part ways again?

Darius decided to spare her from trying to finish her sentence. "We're good, Gabe. Real good. We have you ta thank. What ya did—I know it stained yer heart, but—it was everything, brother. Ya gave me everything."

Addy nodded, smiling up at him with grateful tears in her eyes.

"So, you got together at last, then?" Gabe asked.

"Yes," Addy said, grinning at her brother. "We made vows to one another. Almost immediately."

"Thank God for that. It was bad enough being around you two growing up. I'm glad you're together. It's where you belonged all along."

"You always said so," Addy murmured.

"And I was right. You're welcome. Now, as much as I want to spend more time with you, I need to get you out of here. There's been some suspicious activity over the last few days. The Reapers will be patrolling."

Darius caught Addy's hand and pressed it, warning her not to say a word of what she knew about Ember. Confusion clouded her gaze, but she nodded.

"Aren't ya in charge 'round here?" Darius asked, "Can't ya call 'em off?"

"If only it were that simple," Gabe said, running a hand through his hair. "Come, we'll have to move quickly."

After a silent argument, which his wife ultimately won, Darius followed Gabe through the trees.

"Wait here," Gabe said when they'd come to the edge of the shadows along the side of the road. He left them there without checking to see they'd obeyed, as if people doing as he said was expected. Fine then. Darius crossed his arms and glared at Gabe's back.

"Stop that," Addy said, smacking him in the chest. "What has gotten into you?"

"I don't know," Darius said, narrowing his eye as Gabe leaned into a black car parked on the other side of the street and spoke with someone. "I don't trust him, Ads."

"He's my brother," she scoffed.

"A lot can happen in ten years. Does that look like the same boy we left behind? Be honest."

She studied Gabe for a moment, then admitted, "Well, no. But that's hardly a bad thing. He was unwell when we left him, Darius. The guilt has eaten me alive all these years. Finding him whole and *confident*? It's a relief. I feel like I can breathe."

"Aye. Well, I suppose you're right about that. But tread careful, aye? We don't know him. Not like we did before. I think it's best we keep some things quiet."

Addy searched his face before nodding. "Fine. You're right. But can you try to be nice, please? He's your oldest friend. Don't forget that."

"Alright—"

Gabe returned, cutting off their conversation, "Well, I've sent John ahead. He'll clear the way, but we'll only have a few hours maximum."

"Where are we going?" Addy asked, falling into step with Gabe, leaving Darius to trail behind like a sullen shadow.

"To my house. It's... well... it's the big one up the hill."

"Predictable," Darius muttered.

Gabe smirked over his shoulder at him. "Well, I had to build a new one after the old one burned, didn't I?"

Darius rolled his eye so hard he nearly stumbled. Gabe laughed. And for a moment, it felt like old times.

There were Reapers in Gabe's house. Darius tightened the straps of his eyepatch as he tracked their movements, out the back door and down through the gardens. Three of them trailed in the wake of an Ethereal male, all grumbling too low for Darius to pick up on the conversation. Next, a procession of humans left the house. *Servants.* Darius' stomach soured. There were so many.

"I never imagined he'd keep servants," Addy whispered.

"He keeps them, in part, to spare them," Gabe said, appearing out of the mist at their backs.

Darius whipped around, heart thundering.

Gabe winked at his surprise. "Come. John tried, but apparently they needed to hear it from me. The house is empty. You'll be safe for a little while. Tell me, what is it you've missed the most during your time in the wild? Perhaps I can remedy it."

"Hot showers," Addy immediately groaned.

"Well, I happen to have a number of lovely bathrooms in this house. You may have your pick, sister."

"No... I couldn't.... I don't want to miss a moment with you," she said.

"Nonsense. I insist. You'll enjoy your shower, and Darius and I will gather supplies. It'll be a bore. You won't miss anything important."

"Okay," Addy said, swallowing down the protests Darius could see on her tongue.

"It'll be good, Ads," Darius said. "Give Gabe and me some time to catch up, aye?"

"Good." Gabe led them through a side entrance. "Wait here, Darius." Turning in dismissal with Addy in tow, Gabe left Darius standing alone in a lavishly appointed office.

Gabe returned a few minutes later, closed the glass doors behind him, and made for a liquor cabinet. "Drink?" he asked, still facing away. He held out a cup brimming with whiskey. Darius took it. He didn't know what to say, how to address the weird tension between them. He didn't have to.

Gabe rounded on him, anger etched into the lines of his face. "Why would you bring her here?"

"She insisted. I couldna tell her no."

"You should have. Don't bring her inside the border again. I can't protect either of you if you're caught."

"Ya don't understand. Things have been... difficult."

"I understand perfectly well. You'll take whatever you might need this time, but Darius, do *not* come back. If you find you aren't up to the task of looking after her anymore, I have some friends who can find a place for her. But I will not have her in the Collective."

Rage hardened Darius' jaw. This was not the timid young man he'd known. How dare Gabe suggest he might take Addy from him? "As if I'd ever let her go off with yer... *friends*. She's safest with me."

"They're good men."

"Ha," Darius scoffed. "They're hardly men at all, and ya know it."

Gabe raised his brows in a condescending way that further heightened the anger simmering under Darius' breastbone.

"Oh," Gabe said. "And what does that make me, Darius? What of your wife?"

Damn him. He was right. Darius hadn't missed this, being constantly put to shame under the might of Gabriel's intelligence. "I didn't mean it like that," he grumbled.

The tension went out of Gabe's posture as he laid a tentative hand on Darius' shoulder. "Promise me, Dare. Promise you'll not bring her back. I'm so thankful I got to see you both, even if it's just this once, but we can't risk it... unless..." he trailed off.

"Unless what?"

"What if I told you I could arrange to send you both somewhere safe?"

"I don't believe such a place exists."

"What if I told you it does?"

"Where is it?"

"I... I don't know," Gabe admitted.

Darius rolled his eye. "Thanks, but we'll pass."

"Darius—"

"I just finished building a cabin. It's our home. Addy won't abandon it."

"It might be—"

"No."

Gabe dropped his hand from Darius' shoulder with a solemn nod. "Alright." He gave himself a shake. "Okay, let's get you those supplies. Follow me."

Gabe swallowed his drink in one long gulp. Darius set his down untouched and followed Gabe through a massive entry hall to a sprawling kitchen, equipped with shiny black appliances. Gabe flicked on a light, illuminating a massive pantry. "Take anything you want. If there's something you need and you don't see it here, let me know. The humans keep quarters below. I'd rather not disturb their things, but if you've a need, take it, and I'll deal with the consequences."

Darius took in the rows of food with a hint of bitterness. So much abundance here, when he'd seen the people of Bracken grow thinner, hungrier every year. He bit his tongue against harsh words. "Thank ya," he said instead.

"It's nothing."

"Gabe."

"Yes?"

"You're finally doin' it."

"Doing what?"

"Not lettin' them see it."

"My fear." Gabe's eyes sparked, and for a moment, Darius saw that little boy he'd taught to climb trees.

Darius opened his mouth to say as much, just as Addy's voice rang from down the hall, "Gabe?"

"Go," Darius said. "Talk with your sister."

"Dare?"

"Aye?"

"I know we're not those boys anymore, but... I thought... I... I'd be remiss if I didn't tell you. I missed you."

"Aye. I missed ya, too."

Gabe left him in the pantry, his and Addy's voices trickling from down the hall.

"Ah. There's the pretty, *clean* sister I remembered."

A smack. "And there's my bratty little brother." The rustlings of embrace and a choked sound from Addy that usually preceded tears. "Now, tell me, brother. How *are* you?"

"I'm *good,* Addy. I'm good."

35

WARM

GABE

HE HADN'T LIED TO his sister. He *was* good. His mother was safe. His sister was safe. Darius was... He didn't want to think about Darius. Gabe was finally atoning for his wrongs. And even if he'd accumulated further stains on his soul in the process, he found the cost tolerable. It was 3:15am when he arrived at the penthouse the next day. They'd come back under cover of darkness, ever maintaining their image of privileged party boys, just rolling in after a backwoods vacation to their hometown. He, Marcus, and Ryker made every effort to solidify that image, though Gabe had to admit the wary way people looked at him lately suggested he might've shattered their cover with his display at Amethyst.

Carl seethed at his back, pouty after Gabe's immediate disregard for his promise not to leave him out. The Reaper was suspicious, but Gabe supposed Carl would have to get used to it if he was planning on sticking around. Gabe punched in his entry code and gestured a grumbly Carl to his chambers without a word.

The Reaper abandoned him with a glare that said, *Don't you dare go sneaking off again.* Gabe nodded his assent and left him to his sulking, making for the refuge of his bedroom. There was much to think on. He paused for a moment at the man behind glass in the hall, smiling at the thought of Ever. *Shit.* Ever. Had she come here yesterday? Had she waited in the hall only for him to neglect to answer the door? Of course, she had. Would she be angry with him?

He didn't have to wait long for the answer as he swung his bedroom door open to reveal a pissed off Ever standing in the center of the room with her arms crossed.

"Holy shit!" Gabe shrieked, jumping at the unexpected sight of her.

Carl's feet pounded down the hall. He appeared at Gabe's shoulder, then exhaled a dark laugh as he spied Ever in the room. "God, Mr. Malik. Don't scream like a little girl unless you're actually in trouble." Carl chuckled, patting Gabe on the shoulder and whispering, "Good luck," before he returned to his room.

Gabe gently closed the door behind him as he stepped into the room. "Ever? What are you doing here?"

"What the *hell*, Gabe?"

"What?"

"I thought you were dead! Do you know how worried I've been?" She uncrossed her arms in an adorably grumpy manner. "I broke in yesterday only to find the place empty—no note. No word from you—just *gone!*" She threw her hands up in exasperation, her jaw working as if she couldn't decide which poisonous words she wanted to let out next.

Gabe stepped closer to her, then stilled under her glare. "You were worried about me?"

"Of course I was!"

He couldn't help it. A smile curled his lips.

"Are you fucking kidding me? Do you think this is funny?"

Gabe covered his grin with a hand. "No, of course not."

"Why are you laughing then?"

He let his hand drop. "You're rather cute when you're all worked up like this."

Her mouth fell open. "You're unbelievable."

"And you were worried about me."

"As I said before, *of course I was.* You're my..."

His heart did that weird little flip it was always doing when he was with Ever. "Your what?"

She gulped down a noisy breath, uncertainty briefly playing on her features before she set her shoulders and crossed to him. "Mine. You're just mine," she said, yanking his head down and planting a kiss on his lips.

Gabe groaned into her mouth, twining his fingers in her hair and deepening the kiss until it'd become a messy, wet, desperate thing. Until something snapped, blaring alarms in his mind, and he jerked back from her, falling against the door.

"I think you should leave," he panted, terror lodging in his throat. He'd touched her. He'd *kissed* her. She was in danger.

Rage glimmered across her face. "No."

"What do you mean, no?"

"No."

"Ever, I can't—"

"Why do you do this?" she interrupted. "Why do you push me back when I offer myself freely to you? You want me." Her gaze skipped to the evidence straining his trousers, then narrowed back on his face. "I do not often get to choose who I give myself to, but I would give myself to *you*. And you'd reject me? What of these nights, Gabe? What of the risk I take to see you? To help soothe your conscience? Does it mean nothing?"

"It means *everything*."

"Then *why*? At least do me the decency of explaining before you kick me out!"

"Ever... I..." He couldn't breathe. He slid down the door and curled on the floor.

She only crouched beside him, ignoring his panic. "Enough. You say you cannot trust yourself. What if I'd like to trust *you*? Hmmm? What then?"

"You. don't. Understand," Gabe panted. "My darker half—I can't always maintain control."

"Oh, Gabe." She cupped his face in her hands. He flinched, then settled into her warm touch. She leaned her forehead into his. "There is no darkness you could reveal that I'm not already well acquainted with. Do your worst. Wreck me. But I hope you're friends with failure because I was ruined long before we met."

"Ever..."

She pulled back, "Unless, of course, I've read things wrong and you don't *want* me."

No. He couldn't let her think that. He couldn't let that little line of worry between her brows grow to a chasm. He wouldn't. Before he'd consciously decided to do it, his hand snaked out and pulled her head back to his, inadvertently dragging her onto his lap. "I want you," he said. "I want you more than anything I've ever wanted. That is why I *shouldn't* have you. The things I've done—"

"I know of them."

"You do *not*. If it is what happened at Amethyst to which you refer—you do *not* know. Not all of it. That is the least of my sins."

She pressed so close her lips brushed his when she said, "Well, good thing I'm a sinner, then."

He did not kiss her. Neither did he pull back as he replied, "Even so, I cannot have you. You belong to Hadeon."

"I belong to no one."

"He will punish you."

"He will never know." Her tongue darted out and painted a path of fire across his bottom lip. "Don't say no. Be mine. I will never belong to anyone, but despite that, I still want *you* to belong to *me*."

"That hardly seems fair," Gabe murmured, mind going hazy under the ministrations of Ever's tongue. He tried to blink clarity back to the forefront, tried to remember what he'd done to Hope. Tried to conjure up the monstrosity in his soul—the thing that kept him apart. But he couldn't. Gabe couldn't even summon the evil voice in his head. Not when she was here. Not when he was busy *living*.

"Who said anything about fair?" Ever said against his mouth. "Say yes, Gabe. We'll figure the rest out tomorrow."

"Tomorrow," he sighed on her lips and gave in, letting those feelings he'd kept trapped in his chest free. "Yes," he said.

With that one word, everything changed.

"Oh, thank God." Ever kissed him, exploring his mouth with hers, then drawing a gasp from him as she bit his lip once, twice, hard enough to draw blood.

He drew back. "What was that for?"

"I'm still mad at you," she said, leaning in and kissing away the drop of blood that welled on his lip. The sensation shot straight to his cock. He squirmed rather embarrassingly, his body seeking out the friction of hers even without intending to. This whole thing was delightfully mortifying. Made all the worse because he didn't know what the hell he was doing.

"If I say sorry, are you going to stop biting me?" he asked, finding courage from who knows where.

"Sure, but it better be a good apology." She leaned back, which had the unsettling effect of adding pressure to his nearly painfully hard cock. He gasped a little, and she chuckled. "Oh, I'm going to have fun corrupting you. Go on, then. I'm waiting for your apology." She waved her hand in a *get on with it* gesture.

Gabe pressed his lips into a thin line. After an agonizingly long minute, Ever spoke. "Um. Are you going to apologize?"

"Of course not."

"What?" She scoffed, that cute little angry line wrinkling her brow.

"I don't want you to stop biting me." He shrugged, belying his internal panic.

"Oh, is that so? Well, then I shall bite you, in all of the most *creative* places." She trailed a seductive finger down the front of his shirt. He caught her hand before she reached her destination.

"Okay, well, perhaps I *was* bluffing. *That* would probably hurt. I am sorry, Ever. I am deeply sorry."

She buried her face in his chest, muffling her snorts. "You are wonderfully naive, you know that?"

"I know." Panic fluttered within him again. "I... I don't know what I'm doing. You'll have to teach me."

Ever looked up at him, surprise flaring on her face. "Oh, Gabe..." She climbed out of his lap. He immediately missed her warmth and reached out, only to let his hand drop. Of course, she wouldn't want him now. He looked down at his empty hands, bitter shame crawling up his throat.

"Gabe, look at me," she said, gently tipping his chin up, "I didn't know. I saw how you kept yourself apart, but I thought—Gabe, have you... have you been with *anyone* before?"

He shook his head and turned away from her, unable to bear the disgust she'd surely be looking at him with now. He'd never meant to find himself in this position. Perhaps she'd just leave and they'd go back to the way things had been the day before yesterday. Even as Gabe thought it, he knew he didn't want that. What he wanted was to kiss Ever again. He wanted her to bite him, even if it hurt. He wanted to put his hands on her. Everywhere. He *wanted* to bury his cock inside her. He *wanted* desperately to take back his admission of having never been with anyone like that. She couldn't seriously want him now. She was... *experienced*. He was, what had she said? *Naive*.

"Hey, where did you go?" Ever whispered, kneeling beside him.

"If you want to leave now, I understand," he said, still not looking at her.

"Is that what you think?" She leaned in and brushed a painfully tender kiss on his cheek. Even that sensation had become sensual, so desperate for her he was.

"How could I think any different?"

"You silly man. Gabe, it's only that I fear I've been too forward." She bumped his chin with her knuckle, as he'd done to her many times, and he relented, looking up at her.

"You were not too forward."

"Okay, then, should we start over? We can go slow, or, at least, move to the bed."

"I don't want to go slow," Gabe admitted, to Ever's apparent delight. "But I would like to take you to my bed?"

"Yes, Gabe, yes." She held out a hand, helping him off the floor. He stood before her, uncertain what to do with his body. She only smiled up at him, not giving a second for his panic to rear its head.

"I will teach you." She stepped into his space and rose on her toes to breathe into his ear, "And I'm a very good teacher." Her fingers moved to the top button of his shirt. It popped open under her touch. "First, you take off my clothes." Another button. "And I'll..." Another. "Take. Off. Yours." Just like that, she had his shirt open. His heart beat an unsteady rhythm under her questing palms.

"You don't have buttons," he murmured as he fingered the hem of her shirt.

"I don't have buttons."

He curled his finger under the edge of the shirt, meeting with the warm skin of her low belly. It pebbled under his touch. Slowly, he lifted the shirt, revealing miles of beautiful, pale skin. He wanted to kiss all of it. With a final tug, he pulled the shirt free, baring her breasts to him. She wasn't... she wasn't even wearing undergarments. "Am I doing it right?" he choked, unable to tear his gaze from her delicious skin for confirmation.

"Yes," she said, slightly breathless. "Now, keep going." She pushed his shirt off his shoulders and trailed fingers down his spine.

"Oh fuck."

She laughed softly, guiding his hand to the button of her jeans. "I thought I'd have to work harder to make you swear. I thought you were a gentleman." She punctuated her sentence by palming his cock through his pants. He swore again, barely holding himself in check as he flicked the button of her pants open. She had mercy on him and shimmied out of the jeans, then helped him out of the remainder of his clothes, which were considerably *more* than she'd had on.

"Now kiss me, Gabe," she said, pressing her body against his.

The sensation was overwhelming. She fit against his chest like a puzzle piece he hadn't realized he was missing. He curled his fingers into her hair, stroking a line down the back of her neck. She arched into him. Yes. He wanted this. He wanted to be inside of her. He wanted her to fit him back together.

As if she could sense his restraint fraying, she kissed his chest and whispered, "Kiss me, Gabe. Kiss me. Touch me. Do what feels right when it feels right."

He took one more moment lingering in the old promises he'd made to himself, before he bid them goodbye forever and leaned down to do as she'd instructed. He explored her, running his hands over every inch of skin he could find, clutching so tightly to her hair it elicited a moan. Gabe drank up the sound, his focus narrowing on just how he could make her do it again. He kissed her deeper, clumsy, but Ever didn't seem to mind, not one bit, as she explored his body with the same fervor. He backed her toward the bed, or rather, she tugged him along by the hips. Her hands were everywhere, but he stilled when she wrapped her fingers around his cock. *This* sensation should not take him by surprise the way it did. He'd sought release at his own hands plenty of times, but there was something about *her* touching him there that caused his brain to short-circuit. He lost every last shred of cognizance when she guided his hand between her legs, every sense honing on the utter bliss of the warmth, the wetness of her, the way she moaned again as she guided his hand. *Oh God.*

She laughed in a way that told him he'd said it out loud. He found he didn't care. He was too far gone for embarrassment.

Time blurred past. He measured each minute in the sounds Everest made as she showed him what she liked. His chest tightened to the point he thought he might pass out from sheer desire for her. It was then that she pushed him back onto the bed and rose up over him.

"Are you ready?" she asked.

"Yes," he said, reduced to single syllables under her touch.

"Do not be gentle with me," she said. She sank down on his cock, and Gabe lost the ability to speak at all. There was only her. Only the heat of her body and the rock of her hips and the glorious sense of being whole for the first time in his life. Pleasure spun a symphony up his spine, building to a blinding crescendo under the roll of Ever's hips. He was warm, warmer than he'd ever been in his life, and as he gave himself over fully to ecstasy, he knew he never wanted to be cold again. More than that, he wanted to *live.*

He wanted to live forever.

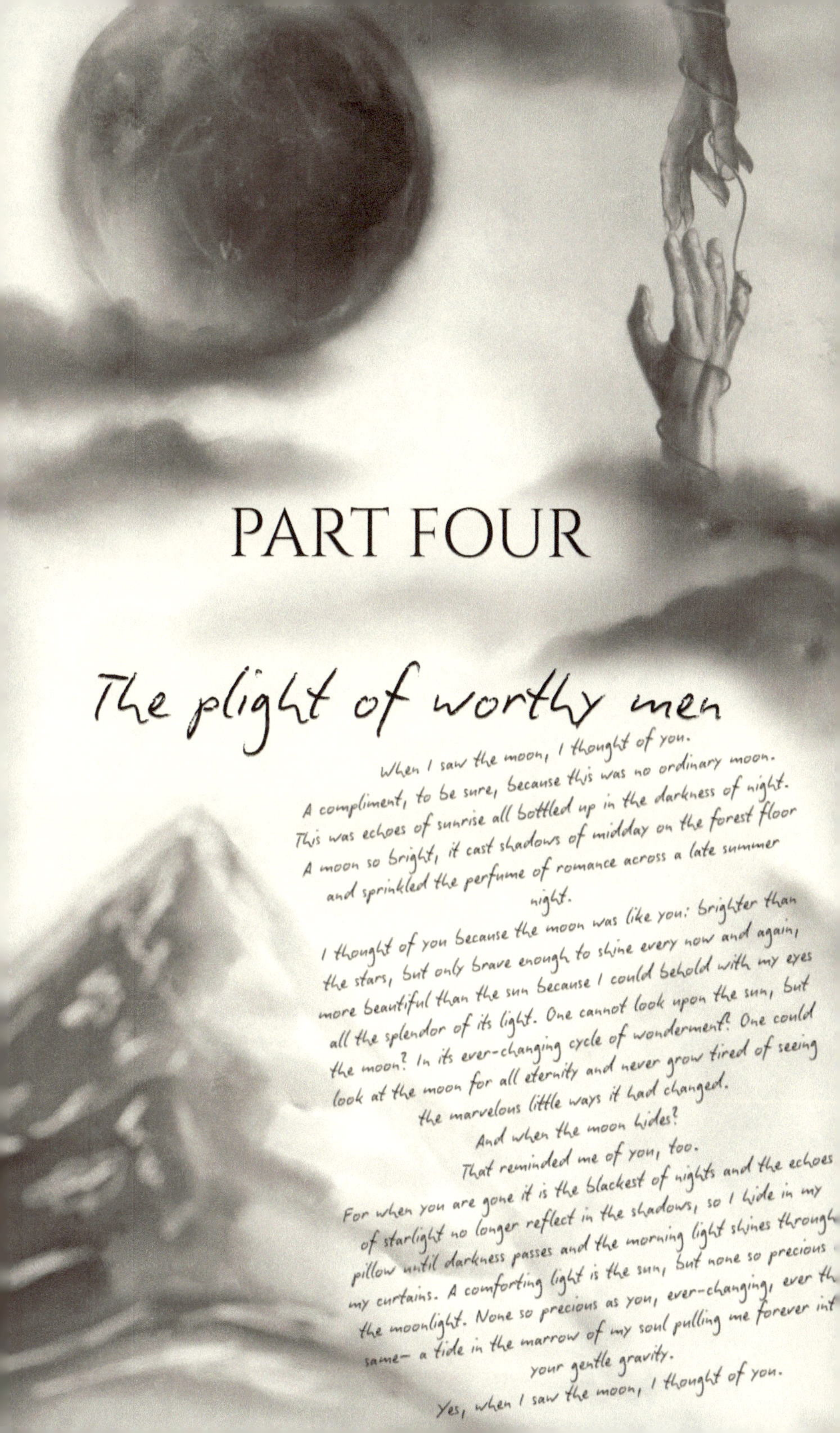

PART FOUR

The plight of worthy men

When I saw the moon, I thought of you.
A compliment, to be sure, because this was no ordinary moon.
This was echoes of sunrise all bottled up in the darkness of night.
A moon so bright, it cast shadows of midday on the forest floor
and sprinkled the perfume of romance across a late summer
night.

I thought of you because the moon was like you: brighter than
the stars, but only brave enough to shine every now and again,
more beautiful than the sun because I could behold with my eyes
all the splendor of its light. One cannot look upon the sun, but
the moon? In its ever-changing cycle of wonderment? One could
look at the moon for all eternity and never grow tired of seeing
the marvelous little ways it had changed.

And when the moon hides?
That reminded me of you, too.
For when you are gone it is the blackest of nights and the echoes
of starlight no longer reflect in the shadows, so I hide in my
pillow until darkness passes and the morning light shines through
my curtains. A comforting light is the sun, but none so precious
the moonlight. None so precious as you, ever-changing, ever the
same— a tide in the marrow of my soul pulling me forever int
your gentle gravity.

Yes, when I saw the moon, I thought of you.

1 YEAR LATER

INTERLUDE

"I love you."

Everest had whispered it in his ear before she'd slipped from his bed. Leaving him as she always did, alone in rumpled sheets and post-coital bliss. He hadn't realized what she'd said until he heard the front door click shut behind her. He leapt from the bed, shielding himself with nothing more than a pillow as he sprinted down the hall. Carl, who had become more of a weird roommate than Reaper guardian, spat insults at Gabe's naked ass before going back to his rummaging about the kitchen. The elevator doors were just beginning to close with Everest behind them by the time Gabe yanked open the front door. Everest barked a laugh, which caused a smile to split Gabe's cheeks.

"Ever, I—" he began.

"Don't you say it, Gabe Malik. Do it right." Her words were rushed as she raced to get them out before the doors closed.

"Stay," he called.

"I can—" The doors shut, cutting off the rest of the word. *I can't.* Gabe preferred the editing the elevator had done for him: *I can.*

263

He shut the front door, his grin so wide it hurt. He'd been waiting for her to say it first. For an agonizingly long year, he'd waited and now... She loved him. She *loved* him. *She* loved *him.*

"Oh, for the love of God, put some pants on. It's bad enough listening to you two rutting every night," Carl snapped when Gabe strode into view of the kitchen once more.

Gabe only flipped him off over his shoulder. "No one said you had to listen," he called.

"Fuckin Ethereals," Carl muttered.

Gabe only laughed and fell back into bed with a heart so full he thought it might burst.

She loves me. She loves me. She loves me.

And it was only his voice that chanted the delightful melody in his head.

36

THE PROMISES WE KEEP

Darius

DARIUS KNEW HE WAS old to begin this particular journey, by human standards, anyway. He'd thought that meant he'd be prepared, but as he clutched the squirming bundle in his arms, he felt woefully inadequate to the task.

"Relax," Addy chastised. "He'll squirm more if you squeeze him so tightly."

Darius did his best to relax his hands, but this entire thing felt wholly unnatural. And then, the baby started to wail. "I swear I didn't squeeze him!"

Addy took the screaming critter from his arms, tucking it—*him*—to her chest. The babe immediately quieted. "Look," she cooed, stroking the ruddy tuft of hair on the top of the boy's head. "Hold him close, see. He wants to feel safe. He wants you to squish him a little, just not so much he feels crushed."

265

"Ah, I don't think it's that. He just likes ya better than me."

"Of course he does. I'm his mother." Addy's smile was so wide, it had to hurt. She was so *proud* of this tiny baby. And Darius was, too, no mistake. God knew he'd been through a great deal of pain to see this to fruition. Addy was just so in tune with the child, as if her son were merely an extension of her. The sight of it warmed a corner of Darius' heart he hadn't known he possessed. *Everything*—it'd been for Addy. He didn't know how to reconcile this new emotion, focused so keenly on something so utterly *helpless*.

"Come here, love," Addy tugged his hand until he came to sit on the bed with her. The thin mattress of leaves crunched under his weight. He curled one arm around her back, securing both her and the babe to his chest.

"See, like that. He wants to feel safe." She maneuvered the babe so he was resting half on her chest, half on Darius'. Then, she took Darius' free arm and tucked it around the fragile bundle. A soft little coo sounded, and the noise lit Darius up from the inside.

"I love him already," Darius admitted softly, breathing in the scent of his son.

"And he loves you."

"Course he does. I'm his Pa," Darius poked Addy's ribs, eliciting a squeak from her and consequently, the baby.

"Sorry, sorry," Darius whispered, patting his son in apology before kissing his wife's sweaty head and asking, "What will ya call him, Ads?"

"I thought we'd decided already."

"Aye, but that was a'fore ya did all the effort of bringing him earthside. Seems only right ye'd get the final say."

"Einar," she blurted, as if the name had been waiting on the tip of her tongue.

"I—what?"

"Einar. That's what I want to call him. I know it isn't what we talked about, but now that I see him, that other name just isn't right, you know?"

He bent his head to peer more closely at the babe, and wrinkled and small as it was, Darius could see she was right. "Aye," he said. "I agree. So, what was it, one more time?"

"You'd think it was an ear you're missing instead of the eye," Addy grumbled teasingly, "Einar."

"It's... a name," Darius acquiesced.

"It's an old name, Dare. A good name."

"Aye, then, if yer set on it. What does it mean?"

"Warrior," she whispered.

"You'd wish such a life for him?"

"He'll have it, whether I wish it or not. May as well give him a foundation of strength."

"Yer right." Darius kissed the boy's fuzzy head. "My tiny warrior. Yer mother's right, *Einar*. You'll be strong. I'll make it so."

"As will I," Addy mumbled, groggy from the effort of her labor. She'd done so well, even when Darius had nearly lost his mind with worry. Addy had been strong, like he'd known she'd be. She'd wanted this with relentless ferocity, and as she'd reminded him when she'd been panting through it, she would not let a little pain deter her now. He brushed her silver hair back from her face and kissed her brow. "Thank ya, love. Thank ya," he said. She murmured something, but the words were lost to her exhaustion.

Soon, she snored softly against his chest, and as much as Darius wanted to stay and hold onto her, the babe began rustling needily. Darius eased Addy down and tucked the blankets around her. She'd more than earned her rest. He shifted the babe into his shirt and went outside.

"Now then, Einar, what shall I teach you first? Or mayhaps ye'd like a story," he puzzled, rubbing soothing circles on the baby's back as he settled into the rocking chair on the porch. "A story about when I was a boy, maybe?" Darius cast about, then realized the stories of his boyhood were hardly appropriate for a baby. He'd just have to make something up, then. So, Darius began, "Eh, well, my son, let me tell ya about the day I lost the eye..."

37
3:07

GABE

IT WAS 3:07AM, AND he already had Everest bent over the foot of his bed. "I love you," he panted as he drove into her. Moans garbled her reply, but he decided to interpret it as her echoing his sentiment. She'd said it enough over the last decade that Gabe was finally starting to believe her. He savored this time with her, their couplings shifting over time into something rough and quick and over with so they might languish in one another's presence for a few minutes more. There wasn't a thing he didn't love about Ever. She was his perfect missing piece. She was beautiful and brave and frustrating beyond belief. She was kind and strong and brilliant. She was also self-sacrificial to a fault.

It was always after they'd taken out their near insatiable desire for one another's flesh he'd ask. And her answer would be the same. Still, as he groaned his release and flopped down beside her on the bed, the words itched to leap off his tongue. He stroked her hair, combing through the strands he'd mussed moments before. "Stay," he murmured, kissing her jaw.

"I can't," she replied, as he knew she would.

"Then go."

"I won't."

He propped himself up on his elbows and peered down at her. "I'm starting to believe it gives you satisfaction to refuse me."

She twirled a long piece of his hair on her finger and sighed. "You know why my answer is always the same."

"I do. I just don't agree."

Ever scooted up the bed until she was propped against the headboard, then motioned for him to sit beside her. She folded a blanket over their legs, resting her head on his chest. The way she fit there always caused his heart to swell.

"I cannot abandon my girls, Gabe."

"What of you? It's not safe. And I... I still hate what they make you do."

"Bitter about sharing me?"

"Always."

She giggled, then muffled the sound in his shoulder. "You know you're the only one who has this part of me, right?"

"And what if I want *all* of you?"

"I warned you that you'd never have it. Come on, Gabe, this argument is tired, and Hadeon will never let me go—"

"I tried again."

"You what?"

"I tried to bargain for you again. Yesterday."

"Gabe... We've talked about this."

He ran his thumb up and down the back of her arm, searching for the right words. They *had* talked about this. And Ever *was* right. He risked much by continuing to bring her up to Hadeon. But he couldn't seem to stop. "I know," he sighed.

"He knows he holds power over you through me. You never let him forget it. And that's even without the knowledge that I come here."

"You need to be careful."

"I always am. And the girls cover for me."

John also covered for her, bless him. Gabe had found a loyal friend in his driver, and fear threatened to claw him up from the inside as he watched the man age every year. He didn't know what he'd do without someone to ensure Ever got safely to and from his house every night. That was the thing about being Ethereal that no one talked about—the quiet strife of outliving the majority of the people in your life. Gabe comforted himself with the truth he had a handful of people who'd live just as long as he did. He wrapped Ever a little tighter in his arms. "And your answer is still the same about going? Marc and Ry will make sure you have a place, E."

"And you'll come with me?"

"I will."

This was a little game they liked to play, to pretend they could actually leave. It was a pretty lie. Gabe was too high profile to simply disappear, especially since the Authority had focused more effort on building their presence in Bracken over the years. To Gabe's disdain, he was now in control of a fully operational breeding and harvesting facility in his hometown. He did all he could to identify the humans who needed out, frequently "losing" them to accidents justifiable by their mortal flesh. He'd been summoned on several occasions for the inefficiency of his human facilities, but so far, he'd been able to argue it was an adjustment period for the weaker human stock of his little town. He didn't know what would happen when he'd exhausted the argument. Gabe didn't like to think about the Ethereal breeding facility. He'd gotten exactly *seven* Ethereals out through his own facility before an influx of Overseers arrived. He had to stop funneling them directly to Bracken and create a club of their own in the Dark Market as a cover. It made the work entirely too complicated. And that was precisely why Ever would not leave. Their work in the Dark Market was the only avenue to help the Ethereals, the only place disappearances wouldn't be too thoroughly scrutinized.

Ever interrupted his spiraling thoughts. "And what will you do with me when you have all the hours of the day, Mr. Malik?"

"Hmmmm. I can think of more than a few things." He nipped at her earlobe.

"Oh, do show me." She tilted her head so he could kiss along her slender neck.

"Well," he began, trailing kisses down and down and down her neck. "I would play you music."

"Mmmhmmm."

"And you would paint," he whispered as he continued blazing a path down her body.

"Paint?"

"Yes." He nipped at her inner thigh, eliciting a squeak.

She slapped his shoulder in punishment. "I don't know how to paint."

Gabe rested his chin on her leg and smiled up at her. "That's exactly the point. You'd have time to learn something new."

"Oh, I see, and you think Marcus will make sure you have a piano?"

"And a guitar. And a violin. Oh, and a harmonica."

Ever rolled her eyes. "That's it, I'm not going if you have a harmonica. My ears will bleed."

"So dramatic." He kissed her leg. The muscles tightened under his lips. "Fine. No harmonica."

"And what will we eat, Gabe Malik?"

"Hmmm. I can make pancakes."

"That's it. I'm sold. Let's go."

Gabe sat up, "Really?"

She laughed and shoved him back down to continue what he'd been starting. "No, you silly man."

"I knew it was too good to be true."

"I wish it wasn't."

"So do I, Ever. So do I."

38

The Care of Mr. Bear

Darius

"Mama hurt?" Einar asked, his small voice awash in worry.

"Aye, son. But it's alright. She'll be alright. Mama is getting your siblin' out, yeah?"

Einar only scrunched up his nose in confusion. Darius shoved a hunk of bread into his small hand before he could ask anything else. Food could always be counted on to distract their son. It seemed he was a bottomless pit for it, growing so fast and tall, Darius knew it couldn't possibly be normal for a boy of two. He'd taken Einar from the cramped room at the back of the cabin to fetch their dinner only moments before. Already, he was torn between seeing to the needs of the boy and rushing back to Addy's side. Alas, she'd never forgive him if he let their son go hungry.

A groan emitted from the back room. The hair on the back of Darius' neck stood. It was torture, listening to Addy suffer.

Einar's little brow furrowed, and he squeezed his bread so tightly it squished through his clenched fist. "Mama hurt," he growled.

Darius couldn't help but chuckle at the outrage mirrored on his son's face. He knocked a knuckle under Einar's chin. "Eh, calm down, my boy. She'll be okay." Einar eyed him suspiciously, but returned his attention to his ruined bread. He was a fierce thing, Einar. Pride swelled in Darius' chest whenever those shreds of emerging personality broke through. Darius checked to be sure that the door was bolted, then crouched before his son, who'd finished his bread and was now pushing about a little wood carving of a bear on the floor. "Einar," Darius said. "I'm gonna check on Mama. You stay here. Look after Mr. Bear, yeah?"

Einar's chin dipped.

A wail that was distinctly *not* Addy sounded from the back room. Darius rose and whirled, rushing the few steps and shoving open the door. It'd be just like her to send him out of the room and give birth to the babe without him. Indeed, the door creaked open to reveal Addy crouched over a wad of soiled blankets with a wet, wriggling infant pressed to her naked chest. There was something irrevocably beautiful about it. Her there, feral and bloody and panting in the wake of motherhood's embrace.

Darius rushed to her, slinging his arms under her heaving shoulders. "Oh, Ads, ya beautiful thing."

She leaned back into him, taking the support he offered.

"Ye've done so well," he murmured onto the top of her head.

She only grunted in reply, clutching the babe as a spasm rocked her.

"Want me to take the babe?" He asked.

"No," she panted. "But help me hold him."

"Him?"

"Yes."

A son. *Another* son. Darius supported the babe with one broad hand. "Okay then, Addy. Are ya ready?"

"Yes. I want it to be done." A shrill sound caught in her throat. "Then let's finish it."

He knew now why she'd wanted this. He knew it to the marrow of his bones as he balanced Einar on one knee, while he held the new baby, whom they'd named Ezekiel, in his other arm. There was no greater joy than that of making, of *raising* a child with the one you love. Still, Darius worried as he looked at his wife, where she fussed over the logs in the hearth. She moved sluggishly, devoid of the Ethereal grace that'd marked her every breath. This birth had been different somehow. Darius couldn't identify just *what* it was, but she hadn't been like this after Einar. She'd been up and spry by the next morning, her body healing injuries that would have taken a human woman months to recover from in a matter of hours. But this time? It'd been two weeks, and she still didn't seem to be herself. When Darius prodded her about it, she only dismissed him, assuring him with words like, *"Of course I'm tired. We do not sleep." "This babe is just more willful than the other." "I am only hungry."*

All of these things *were* true, Darius reminded himself, pushing the worry aside. Addy would be fine, and more, Addy was happy. Even if she looked pale, her face shone with a radiance he'd never seen as she smiled over her shoulder at him.

"I love you, all three of you," she said.

"And I love you, all three of you," Darius echoed.

"I lub 'Zekeil," Einar added, and Darius' heart was fit to bursting with the pure joy of those words.

"Aye, ye'll help Mama and me take care of him?"

"Aye, Pa," Einar patted the baby too roughly, causing him to squawk.

"Gentle hands, Einar," Addy said, her laugh a ghost on the breeze.

And that sound, the unfettered happiness of it, healed the last cracks in Darius' blackened heart, sealing them over with a contentment he'd never hoped for. They were happy, all of them. Even the decidedly grumpy baby cooed in apparent bliss. So Darius ignored the smell of blood that clung to Addy, breathing in the happiness and the sweet scent of his newborn son, instead.

39
MINUTES

GABE?

Gabe? Are you in here?

Gabe?

I'm worried, Marcus. Why isn't he responding? Gabe?

Shit. Ry, help me turn him on his side.

Is that blood? God. He told me. He warned me he was unstable. I didn't do enough.

That doesn't matter right now.

Hurry!

Is he dead? Oh God. He's dead.

No, he's not. Go get the kit under the sink.

Why did he do this? Should I get Everest?

No. You can't get her at this hour. And he wouldn't want her to see him like this. Go, Ryker.

Footsteps. Cursing.

Gabe? C'mon, bud, wake up.

You need another lesson.

You are important.

You've always been the better of us.

You're Pathetic.

You are a monster.

You don't deserve to live.

I love you.

You can take whatever you want.

You don't listen, Gabe.

You never learn.

You're odd.

You have funny hair.

You are good, Gabe.

You don't learn.

You deserve better.

Voices. Voices. Too many voices, and they all sounded like everyone he'd ever loved.

Wake up, Gabe. Wake up!

He did not *want* to wake up. Alas, searing pain bit into his chest, and his eyelids fluttered, bringing Marcus' worried face into stark focus.

"Is he awake?" Ryker asked from somewhere above him.

"Barely," Marcus said, the usual rough edge absent from his tone.

Gabe's head was spinning. The whole room was spinning. *Ryker* was spinning as he lowered to his knees and cradled Gabe's head on his lap. "Gabey, what did you do?"

"I..." Gabe couldn't ascertain *how* he'd ended up here. He was in his bedroom, surrounded by empty bottles with fresh cuts stinging on the inside of his thighs. How had he gotten here? He'd promised himself he'd stop trying this same rote routine after it'd failed for the hundredth time. More, he'd promised himself he'd live—for *her*. Everything hurt. It was never worth it—waking up after another attempt. What had driven him to this place?

"It's okay. You don't have to tell us," Ryker whispered, petting Gabe's hair. "We're here now. We'll fix this."

A sob tore at Gabe's throat. "There. Is. No... fixing this, Ry," he panted.

"Of course there is."

It hit him then, with such force he cried out from the impact of it. Ryker clutched his head tighter. Marcus only knelt at his side and began bandaging the many cuts on his legs.

No. No. No. There was no fixing this. He turned his face into Ryker's embrace, stealing what little comfort could be found under his calloused palms. Sobs wracked his body. Ryker clutched him against his chest, and Marcus... *Marcus* took hold of his hand

and held on tight. Gabe closed his eyes and wished he could stop feeling anything but his friend's embrace.

"I know you don't want to talk about it, but it's time, Gabe," Marcus announced, placing a steaming cup of coffee on the nightstand and settling himself into the chair beside the bed. It was the same chair he'd spent the last three days in, monitoring Gabe's every move.

"I brought toast," Ryker said, entering the room with a plate of burnt bread stacked precariously high. "It's all I know how to cook." He smiled sheepishly as he put the plate on the bed and then sat, dislodging a piece from the pile so it landed butter side down on the sheets. "Sorry," he muttered, scooping up the burnt bread and taking a huge bite.

Marcus rolled his eyes, but Gabe could see his lip twitching. It hurt his heart—that little twitch of a smile. It hurt his heart because... how could there be happiness in the world when Ever was dead? He scooted his way up until he was sitting with his back to the headboard, then snatched a piece of Ryker's 'toast' so he could delay speaking those words just a little longer. He chewed slowly through a gummy bit of the otherwise crispy bread. How had Ryker even done this to toast?

"I expected more from the man in charge of our food supply," Gabe muttered.

"Hey," Ryker said around a mouthful. "I grow the food. Never said I could cook it."

"So you admit you're a farmer, then?"

Ryker swallowed and set down the remainder of his bread. "I will admit anything, Gabe, if you tell us what happened."

Marcus nodded his agreement.

Unable to look at either of them, Gabe fixed his eyes on the bread in his hand. He pinched at the edges until they'd thinned, smashing it flatter than his hopes and dreams. "Ever is dead."

There. He'd said it.

No sharp inhale of breath greeted his news. No shocked sob. No denials.

"We know," Marcus said. "Ry heard yesterday."

"Why didn't you say anything?"

"We didn't think you were ready."

Gabe stifled a bitter laugh. Of course, he wasn't ready. How could anyone ever be ready for something like that?

"Ry also heard something else... Gabe, Hadeon's dead."

"I know," Gabe said, still not looking at his friends.

"Gabe," Ryker pleaded. "What happened that night?"

Three nights ago

It was 3:07, and the pancakes were getting cold.

It was 3:08, and the bell had not rung.

It was 3:09, and she was probably just late. Right?

It was 3:10, and he was putting on his coat.

It was 3:11, and he was waking Carl.

It was 3:12, and doom bore down on him so heavily he couldn't breathe.

She was probably late.

She'd never been late.

As if she arrived early every night and waited in the hall to knock at 3:07. As if the time had become precious to her, too. She was *never* late.

It was 3:15 and she was *not* late. Something was wrong.

"Mr. Malik, she'll come," Carl said, but he was buckling his belt, readying to leave, as if he knew he was lying before he'd said the words. He was grabbing his scythe and setting his shoulders in that way that told Gabe he was ready for a fight.

It was 3:16, and they were getting in the car with a driver who was not John.

It was 3:25 when Gabe broke down the door to Hadeon's Den.

And then time ceased to exist.

No.

Oh, Gabe? Is that you? How long it has been. Are you scared, Gabe?

"Ah. I thought it was you." Hadeon's voice rumbled from the shadows beneath the gilt cage.

Gabe couldn't look at him. He couldn't tear his gaze from what swung in the cage, limp and pale and... *lifeless.*

"You know." Hadeon continued, stepping forward. "I've been wondering for years why my madam always smelled like you." He took hold of Ever's foot, where it poked through the bars of the cage, and ran his nose along the arch of it, inhaling deeply. She didn't stir. "Nutmeg." He grinned. "I knew she was probably having you somehow, just as I'd planned, but then... I noticed something *else.* You see, the numbers weren't adding up. It seems someone was getting product for *free.* Thank you for coming and confirming it was you."

"Let her down, Hadeon. I don't know what you're talking about."

"Hmmmm. I actually want to believe you. Perhaps my little Eve here played you, too?"

Oh, Ever. She had. Because Gabe had always been meticulous about the paperwork, about making sure Hadeon had no cause to suspect. They'd opened a club in the Dark Market, staffed with willing humans and Ethereals to ensure no one ever questioned the few who disappeared. Of course, it wasn't enough for Ever. She loved her girls. She wanted them *all* to be safe.

"I'm telling you, Hadeon, I know nothing of it. Get her out of that cage." Gabe's hands shook.

"Of course, though getting her out will hardly help."

No. That couldn't be true. She couldn't be—"What did you do, Hadeon?"

"What does one do with a pet that bites?"

"No."

"I put her down." Hadeon snapped his fingers, and a dozen of his Reapers swarmed the cage, lowering it to the ground and dragging Ever's limp form free.

"I cannot take them all, Mr. Malik," Carl breathed at Gabe's back. But Gabe hardly heard him, could hardly reconcile the reality in which he'd found himself. When they bumped Ever's limp head into the bars, Gabe snapped. *Kill them all.*

Kill them all, then get her. Put her in a box. Fix her.

We've lived through worse.

Yes.

That's what Gabe told himself, anyway, ignoring the bloody gash on the back of Ever's neck, the silvery liquid that beaded there. She'd be fine. He'd fix this. She was Ethereal. She was like him. But even as he told himself the thing, he knew it for a lie. There was no one like him. He was a monster. He could not be killed. But Ever... She was *not* a monster.

In the brief moment before he launched himself at Hadeon, he found himself wishing he'd made her into one. Then she wouldn't be limp like that. He should've known only another monster could survive loving him.

"I guess we're doing this, then," Carl said as he followed Gabe's trajectory. He shoved a knife into Gabe's palm before spinning away with a dark laugh, arching his scythe back on the Reapers who rushed to Hadeon's side. They were too slow. Of course, they were too slow. Hadeon opened his arms, as if welcoming Gabe's attack. For a second, Gabe wondered if this was exactly what Hadeon wanted, if he, too, had been seeking a reprieve from his monstrosity. Perhaps he wanted to die, like Gabe had wanted to die before *her*. Gabe knew he was right when he plunged the knife into Hadeon's chest over and over. Again. Again. Again. And Hadeon only choked, "At last."

It wasn't enough, killing Hadeon, though. So Gabe bathed in the blood of the Reapers, too. The sound of their gurgles and screams became a symphony in his hollowed-out ears. Carl laughed through the blood on his face as they stood panting in the gory aftermath. "I didn't think it was possible, but damn, Mr. Malik, I'd forgotten just what you could do."

I'd forgotten, too.

He'd forgotten. He'd forgotten because she'd helped him forget.

He dropped to his knees and pulled Everest into his lap, petting her hair, cooing assurances she couldn't hear, but he refused to believe it. He wouldn't. An eerie sense of calm washed over him. "Have the driver bring the car, Carl."

"What about all this?" Carl asked, gesturing around to the carnage.

"It doesn't matter."

Carl looked about dubiously, but nodded and went to fetch the driver.

"You killed them all?" Ryker whispered, speaking for the first time since Gabe had begun numbly recounting the events of that night.

"Yes."

"Good."

But Gabe didn't feel *good*.

"Where did you take her, Gabe?" Marcus asked gently.

"Somewhere safe." He choked on the next words. "They told me there was nothing they could do. How could there be nothing they could do? They make the breeders from scratch. It doesn't add up, Marc. She wouldn't remember, they said. She was gone, they said." Gabe buried his face in the sheets.

"So you wanted to be gone, too?" Ryker took his hand and squeezed. Once. Twice.

A sob ripped free at the reminder of her. "Yes. I *want* to be gone. Will you help me?"

"Oh, Gabe." Ryker scooted up the bed and crushed Gabe in embrace. "I cannot do that for you. But I will be here. So will Marcus. We will not leave you alone with your grief. We can get help."

"There is no help for this," Gabe said, gone numb again, hopeless under the weight of Ryker's refusal. "It wasn't enough."

"What wasn't?"

"The time I had with her. It wasn't enough."

You weren't enough. To protect her.

Please.

You've only ever been enough for one person, Gabe.

Gabe covered his ears, just like he'd done as a boy. And like when he'd been a boy, it did nothing to block out the hateful words.

"Gabe." Marcus pulled his hands free, not letting go, but clinging to them so tightly his bones groaned. Gabe welcomed the distraction.

"There will be consequences, Gabe, for what happened at the Den," Marcus said.

"Let them come."

"If you cannot value your own life, think of those depending on you. Think of what *she'd* want."

"No one needs me."

"*I* need you, Gabe," Marcus rasped. "I don't say it. But... You're my best friend. *We* need you to stick around."

"Yes," Ryker agreed. "Stay, Gabe. *Stay.*"

Stay.

Stay.

STAY.

How many times had he asked her to stay?

"Stay," Marcus said.

Stay. Stay. He would stay. But... "I don't want to live without her."

"I don't want to live without *you.*"

It was enough. No. It *wasn't* enough... but it would *have* to be enough. So Gabe nodded and decided this time he'd *try* to keep his promise. The thing he didn't tell his friends was he hadn't been trying to end his life, not this time. He'd known such simple methods would not work. He'd only been seeking distraction in the pain, the gashes in his flesh growing deeper the sloppier he'd become with drink, until he'd finally passed out. Short of becoming dust, Gabe didn't think he *could* be killed.

No, if he ever tried again, he'd use a gun. At least then he might damage himself enough to forget. Perhaps the consequences Marcus had mentioned would save him the effort. As if the thought had conjured them, it was then that consequences came to call.

They came in the form of Carl, standing in the doorway and looking ashamed of himself. "Mr. Malik," Carl said, gaze fixed on his black boots. "First, I'm sorry. If you see fit to punish me, I understand. I should have known not to leave you alone that night."

"Carl—"

"There is no time. You have been summoned. I will accompany you."

"Can Marcus and Ryker come?"

"The summons are for you and me."

That was a no, then. "How long do we have?" Gabe asked, leveraging his aching legs over the side of the bed.

"We should go now."

"We'll be here when you get back," Marcus said.

For a moment, Gabe hesitated. What would happen if he didn't show? He'd be punished... *or* the people he still cared for would be punished. It was part of the reason he never wanted his sister to come back here. When you loved someone, they could be used against you. A government that forced genetic enhancements on unwilling children could not be trusted with those he loved. Resigned, Gabe dressed, leaving his friends with a lingering look, before he followed Carl out the door.

40

ON THE BREEZE

Darius

THE BED WAS COLD.

And the baby was crying.

The bed was cold. But Addy was right there. He'd never been cold with her beside him before.

Except.

She wasn't.

No. Addy wasn't in the bed. Addy was buried under the dogwoods. And the baby was crying.

"Shhhhh," Darius soothed, fumbling about for the skin of goat's milk on the floor. Ezekiel's cries rose in pitch until Darius' own tears broke free, blurring what little vision he had in the dark. He scooped the babe up and began dribbling the milk into his mouth, which only succeeded in causing him to wail louder.

"Pa?" Einar's voice joined the cacophony. "It's loud."

"I know, Einar."

"I want Mama."

"So do I, son."

"It was enough. This life with you was more than enough."

"It's not enough for me, Ads. You can't go. There must be some-thing we can do. I'll take you back. I'll give you back—"

"It is too late."

"You were meant to live forever."

"No one lives forever."

"You were meant to outlive me. I can't do this without you."

"You will."

"I can't."

"Promise me, Darius, promise me you'll live... for them."

The words battered the inside of his skull, a constant backdrop to the waking nightmare in which he found himself.

It was *not* enough.

Darius didn't know how to do this, how to live without her. How did one continue to draw breath when *everything* was gone? Because that's what Addy had been: his *everything*. Until their sons, at least. So, he'd keep this promise, as he'd tried to keep every other he'd made to her. He'd live for them, because he certainly wasn't doing it for himself.

"Where we go, Pa?" Einar clung to his finger, tripping along in his shadow.

"On an adventure, son."

"Venture?"

"Yes. There's somethin' needs doing... for your Mama."

Dread clawed at Darius' chest when he thought of the task at hand, but he had to tell Gabe. Addy had made him promise that, too. Einar stumbled. Darius clutched his hand to keep him from toppling over. "Are ya tired, Einar? You can ride on me back."

Einar stubbornly shook his head. "I strong, Pa."

Darius patted him. "Yes, you are."

Zeke squawked from his place strapped to Darius' chest, as if at a mere month and a half, he needed it recognized that he was strong, too. And he was. Darius had thought, for the longest week of his life, he'd be digging a tiny grave beside Adalia's for their second son, but against reason, the babe had clung to life. The child seemed simply too stubborn to die. It'd serve him well.

Darius let Einar toddle a few more paces before scooping him up. He settled the boy on his shoulders, where small fingers clutched the dark strands of his hair so tight they threatened to rip free. *Good.* His sons were strong.

He only wished he was, too.

41

HE MISSED

GABE

IT WAS ALWAYS AN illusion that greeted Gabe in the hall of mirrors. He knew that. It didn't make the unearthly tall, cloaked figures he stood before any less unsettling.

"Ah, Gabriel Malik, you're here at last," the distorted voice poured out of all twelve mouths at once.

"Authority." Gabe dipped his head in acknowledgement.

"It has come to our attention, Mr. Malik, that destruction follows in your footsteps. We've overlooked a number of incidents, as we do for our most treasured citizens, but you've cost us a considerable asset. Hadeon Blake was valuable. Have you anything to say for yourself?"

"I do not."

"Oh, one might think you seek our attention, Mr. Malik. Have we neglected you? Do you not have everything you need?"

"I have..." Gabe swallowed. No. He didn't have everything he needed. He *needed* Ever. But he could hardly tell the Authority that. "Yes," he whispered. "I have everything I need."

"Good. Good. Now. Whatever shall we do about the unfortunate events of last Wednesday?"

An agonizingly long moment of silence reigned as Gabe awaited his fate.

Finally, they spoke. "You'll simply have to fill in for Mr. Blake."

"What?"

"Tread carefully, Malik. You wouldn't want to disrespect our generosity," they chastised. "You were, it seems, Mr. Blake's closest associate, with exception of one Dimitirius Finch. You've met Finch?"

Gabe nodded.

"Then you see why we hesitate to bestow such a responsibility on him. We understand, Mr. Malik, that your Ethereal tempers run hot, so we'll forgive this. Hadeon was becoming a bit of a pestilence. Do not become one yourself."

"I... I don't know what to say." This wasn't punishment. This was... well, Gabe didn't know *what* this was. They were transferring Hadeon's holdings... to *him?*

"Then do not waste your breath. And know this, Mr. Malik, should you step out of line again, we'll be forced to entertain *other* measures to keep you in check."

Gabe saw then what this was. They weren't *gifting* him anything. They were further entangling him in their web, where they might control him better.

"What interesting company you keep, Mr. Malik. A wise ruler might see fit to... *separate* so many powerful friends, should they become problematic."

Marcus. Ryker. Gabe heard the threat beneath the words.

"I see," Gabe nodded. "I will be sure to be unproblematic, then."

"Good. Good. Go, Mr. Malik. Leave the city. Clear your head, and come back ready to serve."

"Yes, Authority." Gabe bowed and turned to leave without a dismissal, desperate to get out of this horrible room so he could fall apart again.

"Oh, and Mr. Malik," they said before he could retreat. "We'll be looking into you. What wonderful skeletons might we discover, we wonder?"

The sound of their hideous laugh haunted him all the way to Bracken.

It'd been under a rock on his front step when he arrived in Bracken. Tattered and stained, *Gabe* was scrawled in Darius' untidy hand across the flap. He should wait to open it. He should wait until Ryker got here. Until he wasn't alone. He should wait to open it until his heart didn't feel like a lump of useless pulp in his chest over the loss of Ever.

He couldn't open it.

He *had* to open it.

With shaking fingers, Gabe gingerly unfolded the letter.

I am a coward.

But then, you've always been the better of us.

Forgive me, brother.

I couldn't look you in the eye and say what must be said.

You deserve better.

Pain lanced through Gabe's skull as he read those foreboding lines. He swallowed down his sick and continued.

First, you should know you've become an uncle again. Though I probably should have told you first you were an uncle a few years ago.

Children? His sister had *children?*

We named them Einar and Ezekiel, and the little one's already reminding me of you. He came a few months past, wailing and angry, and with that little crinkle between his brow you always wore when you were trying to figure something beyond us other mortals. I laughed when I saw it first. Einar is as we expected him to be. He loves his brother just as fiercely as he loves the rest of his family. Only a boy of 2, near 3, but I'd not have made it this far without him. I'd not have made it this far without either of them.

*To the point of this note. As you'd surely have demanded of me
were I brave enough to meet your eyes. Addy*

Adalia

Her name was scratched into the paper with such force the
pen had broken through the back.

Your sister is gone.

Here, the paper was particularly smudged, and Gabe had the
distinctive impression it was caused by Darius' tears. What did
he mean, Addy was gone? She'd never leave Darius and their
son... *sons.*

*I meant to tell you sooner, but even now, I can hardly bring myself
to write the words.*

She's gone, Gabe. She's gone, and I don't know what to do.
*But I have to keep living for the boys. She'd never forgive me if I
didn't keep living for them. She's gone—*
She's dead.

The words were barely legible beneath smudges of dirt, but
as soon as Gabe saw them, his blood chilled to ice. *No.* No. It
could not be. What God had he enraged so to have *both* of them
taken from him only days apart? Tears blurred his vision, but
he continued to read Darius' relentlessly tortured scrawl.

She's gone, Gabe. And I'm falling apart.
She passed a month after the birth.
It's my fault.
I should have brought her to you.
She told me the bleeding had stopped.
But she was so pale.
A good man would have known.
You would have known.
I didn't know.
I didn't know.
I didn't know.

I deserve to die for what I've taken from you, from my boys. But I hope you'll forgive me for not knowing. For not understanding that her body couldn't heal this. Her body should have been able to heal this. I don't understand. I still can't understand.

You were right.

You were right, and if I'd listened, if I'd taken her to that safe place you mentioned all those years ago, she'd still be here. I will never forgive myself for not listening.

I am sorry to tell you this way.

I tried to come to you, but the babe...

He couldn't keep quiet.

You know there's more Reapers in Bracken again?

If you never want to see me again, I understand.

But. Maybe come and meet your nephews? She wanted you to know them. She made me pinky promise.

I'll come to the big tree, the one I showed you when we were boys. The one that got burnt by lightning? I'll come there on the harvest moon, if you want to see them.

I can show you where she rests.

It's too dangerous to bring the boys to Bracken, and I can't console them as Addy could.

I failed you all.

I miss her every day.

I miss you, too.

I'm sorry.

I'm sorry.

I'm sorry.

Darius

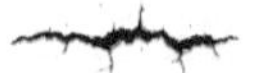

Too much. It was too much for Gabe's pulpy heart to handle. They couldn't *both* be gone. He couldn't do this. He couldn't do this.

You promised.

He'd also promised to protect Ever. He'd promised the same to Addy.

My promises are worthless.

Don't.

Oh, are you scared now?

It won't work.

Why are you afraid, then?

Give me control, Gabe. I'll keep us safe.

I don't want to be safe.

Please—

But Gabe couldn't hear that voice, not anymore. Not over the violent drumming of his heart inside his chest. His feet slipped on the basement steps, his fingers clumsy as he tore through bins and boxes. A gun. He'd do it with a gun. What would be more poetic than finally ending it all with his father's old pistol?

The metal was icy against his shaking fingers when he finally found it in the back of a wooden chest. There was still a fleck of Darius' blood on the handle beneath the grimy layers of soot. Gabe picked it away with his fingernail, then sat cross-legged on the dank basement floor and began disassembling the thing, cleaning every crevice, lining bullets in a perfect row. The task numbed him somewhat.

Hours passed as he worked on the weapon. He let himself remember. Every moment that had brought him to this place. Everything he'd be without if he continued for even another second on this plane of existence. Gabe descended so far into the well of his soul, he could not claw his way back out.

It was the pathetic creature he found at the center of himself that did it. There was nothing bright and beautiful at his core. No. What he found—the very essence of himself—was a wretched, shriveled creature, made of fear.

He *was* afraid.

He was *alone*.

He was *not* enough.

Gabe put the barrel of the gun in his mouth and pulled the trigger.

When the deafening boom had stopped ringing and Gabe couldn't feel his body, he thought he'd finally succeeded at ending his miserable life. Relief, sweet relief, though he couldn't remember why he'd needed it. But then Carl's raspy voice cut through his sensationless musings. *"Oh fuck!"* It was then Gabe knew he'd missed.

He'd missed.

He couldn't remember why that made him so terribly sad.

He'd missed.

He couldn't remember why he'd tried in the first place.

He'd missed.

He couldn't remember... something. Someone?

Adalia.

Darius.

Darius. The note.

Your sister is dead.

Your sister is dead.

Your sister is dead.

He did this.

Yes.

He took her from us.

Yes.
We tried to protect her.
Yes.
We should punish him for this.
Yes.
Wait. No.
Yes. Kill him. We punish those who hurt the ones we love.
His sister was dead.
His sister was dead.
His sister was dead.
Someone he loved was dead.
I am alone.
You are not alone. You are not alone, so long as you have me.
I am not alone. I am not alone. I am not alone.
He chanted it until all of the voices, all of the sounds quieted, and oblivion swept him away in its warm embrace.
He couldn't help but think it felt like her arms.
But who was *she* anyway?

PART FIVE
No one respects nice.

INTERLUDE

Gabriel Malik was a male made up of many parts. Most of them were, at their core, constructs of sadness. A good portion were little gremlins born exclusively of rage. Some were passion. Those were Gabe's favorite, because they sounded like music notes. Then, floating in periphery were the smaller parts, the ones made of memory. He remembered, like dust motes on the breeze, moments. Happy ones. Hurtful ones. Laughter. Joy. Tears. There seemed to be rather a lot of tears.

Sometimes the memories looked like a woman with smiling eyes. He never could place her, as her features shifted near constantly. In some memories, she was a mere girl with red-brown pigtails, but wait... wasn't her hair silver? Sometimes, her eyes were spring meadows, but then they'd shift and the color would bleed out of them until they were gray, dark, and full of promises. It was in those moments he knew they were not the same girl. But he only recalled one name: Adalia. His sister. Yes. Adalia. Darius. The note. *His sister was dead.* He remembered growing up with that wonderful girl, with that boy from the street. He remembered. It was only recent years that were lost to him. Perhaps that was where all of the sadness at his core came from?

He'd done something bad... that's what Ryker said. That's why he couldn't remember everything. He suspected that was true. He thought perhaps he might just *be* bad. People certainly acted like he was a bad man. The things he did to the women in the Mirrored

City made him *feel* like he was a bad man. He didn't want to remember—that's what Marcus told him. That was probably true, too. He knew it because of the way his internal voices screamed whenever he tried. Carl told him he'd hurt himself... he'd hurt his brain and they'd had to put it back together, and though they'd been able to restore its function, they couldn't make his memories come back. That seemed like the truest truth. The way his heart ached told him, though he lacked any physical evidence.

Gabriel looked the same as he always had, except, wait—had his hair always been silver? He couldn't remember.

It didn't matter, anyway. This is who he was now, a creature made up of many parts. He'd cling to what truths he could. He was a bad man, who'd had a kind sister, who'd died... why? He couldn't remember.

He had four friends.

Darius, who was his *first* friend. He remembered quite a lot about him. Ryker, who was his next friend. His *nice* friend.

No one respects nice.

And Marcus. His angry friend. Marcus was the friend who always tried to explain things to him that didn't make sense. *This isn't you, Gabe. You would never hurt the women like this. You respect the humans. Why are you doing this?* And then Ryker, his *nice* friend, would save him from having to think too hard. *Stop, Marcus. Gabe knows he helps us with the Dark Market. The most important thing is that he keeps getting the product out to us, remember?* And then Marcus would nod and move on. He'd stopped the bizarre efforts a few years back, but Gabriel couldn't help but puzzle over them.

Carl, his Reaper, was *almost* his friend. But one couldn't truly be friends with their servants. No, servants were for using; that's what his *truest* friend said.

His truest friend was nothing more than a voice in his head, a guiding light. A beacon of reason when his emotions threatened to overwhelm him. But why did they do that, anyway?

He couldn't remember.

42

THE LIGHTNING TREE

Darius

"Darius?!" a feminine voice coated with a rolling burr called from the other side of the brambles. Darius didn't recognize it in the slightest. Unease threatened to choke him.

Zeke's head popped out of the brush. "Is that a lady, Pa?"

"Hush," Darius motioned for the boy to get under cover.

"Zeke, get down here," Einar whispered. Though it could hardly be called a whisper at all with the harsh tone he turned on his little brother. If they hadn't been at risk, Darius might've laughed. His boys were two sides of the same coin, though they didn't know it yet.

"Ouch! Don't grab me, you jerk," Zeke hissed at Einar, sticks crackling as they scuffled.

Darius rolled his eye skyward.

"OW!" Einar grunted, followed by the dull thud of a punch.

"PA! Einar hit me!" Zeke yelled.

"Shut *up!*"

"No! You shut up!"

Darius turned in time to see Zeke dig his elbow into Einar's side. God spare him from the antics of his sons.

"You never do as you're told." Einar hissed.

"Well, you never do anything *fun!* Let go, Einar—I wanna see the lady! We ain't never seen n—" Zeke's voice cut off, muffled under a palm.

Putting aside his son's pathetic survival instincts for another time, Darius called, "Who's there? Show yerself!"

"Darius the Black, I'm shamed ye dinnat recognize me." A plump, middle-aged woman stepped from behind the trunk of a sequoia, revealing a cloud of brown curls and an unmistakable red mark on her cheek.

Darius' mouth hung slack, because unless he'd lost all sense, that was little Greta—except—no. She looked *older* than him now. "Greta?" he asked.

"Aye, ye buffoon, it's me. Why Darius, yer just as I remember ya. Life's not been so kind to the likes of me." Greta threw herself into Darius' arms.

He stiffened, then forced himself to relax. This was a friend. "Greta, how are ya? It's been so long."

"And just whose fault is that, Darius Black? Ye stopped comin' round 'fore I'd fully become a woman. Right broke my heart, ya know? I'd got in my head we'd wed one day, though I knew t'was impossible. Good thing ya left though, or I'd never've given Isais a chance. Where's that pretty wife of yours, anyway? Come out, Addy!" she called to the brush where the boys rustled.

"Er, well, she's gone then, Greta. Near ten years ago."

"What do ya mean?" Greta asked, leaving off her scrutinizing of the brush to peer up at Darius' face. "Oh... Oh, gone gone? I'm so sorry, Darius." She patted his cheek in a familiar kind of way that warmed Darius' heart. "I ken that pain, too. Lost a son, goin' on two years. It never heals."

"A son? Greta, I'm so sorry," Darius said, a pang stealing through his chest at the mere mention of such a thing.

"Aye. Life keeps on, though. I've got my other boy to be livin' for, and me dear Isais. Now then, you best be showin me what ye've got stowed away in them bushes yonder." She nodded to a very poorly concealed Ezekiel.

Darius chuckled at the swollen lip his second son sported as he popped out of the brush like a ground squirrel. "Come out then, boys," Darius sighed. Zeke was beside him in a flurry of movement, but Einar was more tentative, clambering slowly out of the brush, long limbs tangling in the brambles.

"Come, Einar. This woman is one of my oldest friends," Darius encouraged.

"Didn't know you had any friends," Einar mumbled under his breath.

Darius ignored it. Twelve-year-olds, it turned out, could be incredibly feisty. "Greta, meet my sons. Einar and Ezekiel."

"Just Zeke," Zeke said, winking at the woman in a way that had Darius puzzling *where* he'd learned it.

"Oh, and aren't ya a charmer, then, just Zeke?" Greta held out a hand.

Zeke only stared.

"Yer supposed to shake it, son," Darius spoke out the side of his mouth.

Zeke grasped Greta's fingers and shook them around like some limp fish. Greta, admirably, maintained a straight face. "And you're Einar, then. My, how tall ya are! Ye must be near a man."

Einar took her hand and shook it in the same manner Zeke had. "I'm twelve."

"Twelve! Why, I never! Ya know, I've a boy just a few years younger than ya. Josiah. Ye'd like 'im," Greta said.

Zeke was practically bouncing with excitement at the prospect.

"You should bring 'em, Darius. Come and see the people," Greta suggested.

"I don't bring them 'round humans, Greta," Darius lowered his tone to make clear his meaning.

Her brow furrowed for a moment, then she straightened and said, "Eh, 'tis still like that. Worse now, after what happened a few years gone by. No one would be the wiser, though. They don't look it, ken?"

"I can't risk 'em," Darius murmured.

Greta scrutinized him for a long moment before nodding, "Aye. Well, if ya change yer mind. We'll be waitin, then. We'll be in these parts through winter, but I needs must be gettin' back. Isais will be worrit. T'was good to see ya, Darius. Dinna be a stranger. Boys, t'was my pleasure meetin ya. Convince your Da ta bring ya to meet my Josiah, yes?"

With that, she slung her arms around Darius once more, winked at the boys, and sauntered off. The whole encounter left Darius feeling rather hollow.

"That was weird, Pa," Einar remarked dryly.

"I like her," said Zeke. "I didn't know there were people out here."

"Aye, but what've I always said?" Darius prompted.

"*Don't trust anyone,*" Einar intoned, lowering his voice in mockery.

"It'll serve ya well, son. Don't ya forget it," Darius knocked his eldest on the shoulder. "Come, we'll be late."

"Why do we gotta go out here every year?" Einar grumbled.

"I like the lightning tree," Zeke chimed in.

"It's tradition," Darius reminded Einar, then patted Zeke in appreciation. He'd never told them why they came to the burnt-out tree every year. In truth, Darius didn't fully understand the compulsion himself. It felt right, though, to give Gabe the chance to show up. It felt right to pay homage in this way to what they'd once been. So he brought his sons every summer when the moon was ripe, to camp at the base of the tree, in hopes their uncle would appear. He never did.

43

AUTHORITY

THE THING SITTING ACROSS from him was not human. Gabe couldn't pinpoint how, but he knew this innately—the knowledge bone deep, jarring. It was there in the prickling sensation along his forearms, in the scent burning the back of his throat with acid. Mostly, it was present in the thing's eyes. No feeling creature had eyes like that. They appeared normal, by all accounts. The color might even be considered nice (a gentle blue that reminded him of the sky just after dawn), but they lacked something essentially human. Is that what his Ethereal eyes looked like? Flat, devoid of emotion... *empty?* Gabe could not hold their stare for more than the moment it took to catalog this information. Instead, he fixed his gaze on a point behind their hunched shoulder.

"It is acceptable." Their eerily calm voice interrupted Gabe's thoughts.

His hackles rose in response. "What is?"

"That you cannot bear to look at us." Fingers ending in grotesquely yellowed nails protruded from under their long black sleeve to gesture to the shrunken lines of their face. "We only thought it was time to meet face to face."

Gabe was immediately swamped by guilt. He began, "I—"

"Have you heard of prions, Mr. Malik?"

His brow furrowed, and he gave his head a slight shake.

They chuckled, a grating sound that had bile coating Gabe's throat. "Neither had we... They began as neurodegenerative diseases. Terminal."

Gabe swallowed at that word. They raised their brows in expectation, and Gabe took the bait, speaking quietly, "I thought all of the terminal illnesses were cured."

A sad smile curved their scarred lips, "Yes. We are living proof. With enough engineering, a body, a mind, can be rebuilt. Neural chips help us retain information we would have otherwise lost. But it is all a temporary solution. Such is our curse, to forever degenerate. The disease mutates too rapidly. We are never quick enough to find the true cure. And every time we put a new, pretty face on, it melts away eventually. But we live, we continue to exist."

And what a cursed existence they seemed to be living. Gabe could practically feel the pain radiating off the form curled in the chair across from him.

"Yes," they replied, as if he'd spoken the thought aloud. "Imagine for a moment, Mr. Malik, the fulfillment that accompanies being the one to discover the cure to cancer." They huffed a laugh. "And more, imagine curing *everything*. Imagine being called the great mind of your generation—likened to Einstein, Hawking—*the modern Pasteur*. Such glory. Such brilliance. The *incomparable* genius, they called us... Yes. Imagine, dear Gabriel, achieving such heights, only for your mind to crumble beneath one unconquerable illness. Imagine the helplessness of shriveling away, of the holes eating away at you, until you cannot remember your own name, until history forgets you, too. But as you wither, you unlock the secrets hidden in our atoms, you partner with other brilliant minds, until you can unweave the strands that make us human: *flawed*, until you've made us into something *better*. You carve and splice on your Frankensteinian quest until you've created the perfect specimen: something *new*. You piece back together your body, your mind, only to find your cure was a lie all along.

Only for the degeneration to begin all over again. And so you live in a constant state of cyclical torment, never able to be completely whole, forever taunted by the perfection of your creation, forever outside your grasp—"

The deafening crack of the arm of Gabe's chair shattering under his palm broke off the Authority's desperate rant. He'd been gripping it harder and harder as they'd continued, because what they were saying was impossible... because those names they'd incited... that was *ancient* history... if what they were saying was true—the Authority—they were at least a thousand years old.

How do you know that, Gabe?

I... I don't remember.

Good.

"Ah. I see you're familiar with the old histories, then."

"How?"

"We solved it, don't you see? We solved *everything*. Everything but this one last truth. We solved *death,* Mr. Malik, but we cannot figure out how to *live,* not like our children do. We keep them, in their many forms, so we might not forget." They released a wistful sigh. "We apologize. We've gotten off topic. We can be *sensitive* about our appearance. Especially in the presence of such a perfect specimen." At this, their eyes raked up and down Gabe in a way that made his skin crawl. "But one that seems prone to messing up his pretty face, no?" They laughed bitterly. "Oh, the things we can fix... We tried once, uploading our consciousness to another form. It didn't work."

Gabe shifted uncomfortably in his broken chair.

They grinned in a distinctly threatening expression as they rubbed their clawed fingers together. "Now, as to why we've brought you here..." From some unseen pocket, they produced a comms disk and tossed it casually onto the floor between the chairs. An image flickered to life as the lights dimmed. Two gangly boys limped down a tiled hall. They were led along by a third, shorter figure, auburn hair swaying down her thin back. The boys looked as though they were made up of contrasts, darkness and light, stumbling behind Adalia. Hissed audio played alongside their shuffling procession.

"I cannot believe you let this happen again, *Dare,"* Adalia spat.

"Lighten up, Ads. It's not like Darius gets hurt on purpose." Gabe's young voice whispered. In the projection, his fingers tightened on Darius' shoulder.

"Yeah. What Gabe said," Darius panted.

Memory overlaid the image as Gabe recalled the way Addy had looked over her shoulder and glared at the two of them. The familiar twist of grief clawed at Gabe's heart. The image flickered, and the same three figures appeared, this time older. The Authority let it play until the moment Darius was submerged in the box. On and on it went until an older image, slightly grainy compared to the others, appeared: Addy, dragging Darius on a sled along the floor as he moaned. They were both so small. This was it: that first time Darius had gone to the box, the only time Gabe hadn't been there with his friend... or so he thought, until the image changed again, and there was Darius. Alone. What played next had anger stirring like some caged beast under Gabe's skin, the voice waking with his rage. It was a montage of all the times Darius had gone to the box alone. Not once or twice. *Hundreds* of times.

He lied to us, an insidious tone chanted in the periphery of Gabe's mind as the projection went dark.

"Remember, Mr. Malik, that we said we'd have an eye on you? You disappointed us. You've been so... *predictable* these long years, but then it occurred to us. We had to go *back.* It seems, Mr. Malik, that you have been keeping secrets... but you are not the only one."

The room lit up again, revealing a projection of Darius as a young man, though Gabe supposed he probably still looked like that if he'd been in the box so much. He was swathed in black fabric that allowed him to blend with the dark brush behind him. Gabe hoped he'd get to see Addy, too. This must have been just a few years after she'd left with Darius. Right? Another figure stepped into view, this one comically small beside his friend. Gabe couldn't help but smile at his sister until the smaller figure stepped into the light, revealing her face. It wasn't Adalia.

"Luna..." the projection of Darius groaned.

Gabe watched in horror as the woman, who was *not* his sister, who was *not* Darius' wife, stepped closer and rose on her toes. She dragged Darius down to meet her and kissed the hell out of him. Shock tore through Gabe. *Darius loved Addy. He would never...* And yet.

"Turn it off." Gabe spat, fury clawing up his throat alongside sick. *He dishonored my sister.* His hands shook as the image flickered and showed Darius creeping about the streets in that same black garb, slaughtering Reapers, leading humans out of Bracken. Gabe had heard the whispers when he'd visited the Reaper camp over the years. The mothers scolding children around their primitive fires, *'Behave or Darius the Black will come for you in the night.'* He had tuned it out, pretended he'd misheard.

We cannot let this stand, the voice whispered.

No. We cannot. Gabe replied.

"Where are the Malik women, Gabriel? Your mother?"

Footage of Gabe pinning an Overseer to a wall and choking her flashed between them.

"Where did you take her?" They leaned in. "Where is your sister?"

"I... I... I don't know," Gabe gasped, unable to take in a full breath.

"Hmmm." They steepled gnarled fingers and spoke so low Gabe had to strain to hear. "You are an anomaly, Gabriel Malik. Curiouser and curiouser the more we learn. You really don't remember, do you?"

Gabe shook his head in silent horror. He *did* remember what had happened to Adalia. She was dead. But where *was* his mother? He'd nearly forgotten he *had* a mother.

"You fascinate us, Mr. Malik. It's why we keep you around, you know? Ethereals are flawed, truly. *Not* perfect—an imperfect model of what perfection *could* be at best. There is still work to be done... Oh, there I go again, getting off track. You see, you have quite the problem on your hands..."

Another image appeared, firelight and Darius and a small boy curled at his feet. Across from them sat an older boy who looked so much like Addy a pang stabbed through Gabe's heart. *His nephews.*

"This must be contained, Gabriel. Wouldn't you agree? We cannot have untested creatures roaming about."

"Yes."

"You were but a boy. We see that. Unless you knew...?"

"No." Gabe's stomach dropped. Darius was a *traitor.* "I... I didn't know," Gabe stuttered.

"Good, good. Then prove your loyalty. You must find these abominations and end them."

He'd known this was where things were leading, and still, despite Darius' blatant betrayal of him—of *Addy*—he could not do it. He could not kill his best friend. His kin. He wouldn't.

I could, the voice murmured. *Let me, Gabe. Let me help you.*

No.

Gabe's mind spun as he tried to come up with some solution. He couldn't do it. He couldn't do it. He couldn't do it.

We could fake it.

You'd help me with that?

Anything for you, Gabe. Just tell the creature yes, and we'll figure it out together.

Gabe scrambled for words, finally blurting, "It will take some time... to find them."

"You've had time enough, we think. We'll need proof, of course, when you've completed the task. Bring them to us. The bodies. We'd like to observe them. Perhaps that is the recipe..." They mused.

Gabe was going to vomit all over the tiled floors.

"Bring them to us, Gabriel... or we'll send someone else, and we might remember what we've chosen to forget, you see? About your mother. Your sister? Hmm. Your *friends*? Take one of your little cronies with you. To *help*."

He was trapped.

He was trapped, and he couldn't see a way out of this. He couldn't let the Authority look further into Marcus and Ryker, but he couldn't remember *why*. Why had he done this to himself? Why *couldn't* he remember? He only knew, deep down, that Darius' life, the life of those two little boys, were worth *less*, somehow. Perhaps it was only that Marcus and Ryker were the better friends, though Darius was his oldest. Perhaps it was that Gabe carried a good deal of resentment for the man, for the *children* who had cost his sister's life. Perhaps it was only that Gabe was tired.

And so, eyes burning with tears he dared not shed, he nodded.

44

SKELETONS

GABE

DIMITRIUS FINCH WAS A miserable, sniveling little wretch. He was short for an Ethereal male and sported the sort of thinness that never let one forget his flesh housed a skeleton underneath. The silver strands of hair atop his head always looked inexplicably oily, and his voice grated like metal on stone. Yes, he was a miserable wretch, which made him the perfect companion for what Gabriel had to do. The Authority hadn't specified *who* he should bring with him to murder his oldest friend. Something told him neither Marcus nor Ryker would be amenable to the suggestion. So, he'd collected Finch from the Den along with a brood of Reapers and ushered them all onto a craft back to Bracken.

He'd left the Reapers, with the exception of Carl, in the muddy squalor of Gunmire camp and begrudgingly brought Dimitrius back to his house. This is how he'd wound up across the dining table from the little pig, who suckled at a plate of oysters so noisily Gabe wanted to claw his ears off to end the torment. Just before Gabe caved and actually started clawing his ears, Finch finished with a slurp and leaned back, crossing his bony fingers over his bloated abdomen.

"I was surprised, Gabriel, when you asked me to help you with your problem. I must say, Bracken is quite the little slice of paradise. The women are especially pretty," Dimitirus leered at the maid who'd come to clear their plates, causing her to shrink back.

Mine. The voice hissed indignantly.

"I'm glad you finally saw fit to invite me," Finch continued, oblivious to Gabriel's rage. "Remind me, what is it you need me for?"

"I don't *need* you for anything, Finch," Gabe spat.

"Dimitri, remember? It's what all my friends call me."

"Fine, *Dimitri.* I don't need you. The Authority demanded I bring a companion, is all."

"And your usual rabble were busy, I presume?"

Gabe nodded, unwilling to explain his reasoning to Finch when he hardly understood it himself. "I have a task which I think you will enjoy," Gabe admitted bitterly.

"Ah. We are going hunting, yes?"

"Yes. For a human who has been... *problematic.*"

"I always did love reading about the ancient hunts. It'll be a pleasure to partake in one." Finch's grin was all sharp angles. "You know, tight-lipped bunch they are, one of the Reapers told me they still hunt? Fascinating."

"Indeed," Gabriel agreed, trying not to let disillusionment creep into his tone. "I'm afraid you'll be disappointed, though. It won't be much of a hunt. I know where to find him." Gabe stroked his breast pocket absentmindedly, where Darius' rumpled letter lay folded. It crinkled under his fingers.

"Well," said Finch. "We do get to kill the thing, at least? I know you fancy a good bit of violence. I've never forgotten the way you obliterated Giorgio that night at Amethyst..."

Giorgio? Who was Giorgio?

The Ethereal we killed, remember?

No.

Well, we never did know his name...

"Yes. Not one of my brighter moments." Gabe feigned understanding.

"I disagree. It was *bloody* brilliant." Finch giggled at his own cleverness.

Pathetic.

"Best get some rest, Dimitri." Gabe rose from his seat, ready to be anywhere but in Dimitrius' presence. "We'll leave tomorrow before the sun rises."

"Fine then, I suppose I can find some entertainment to occupy the hours between then and now. Good night, Gabriel."

"Good night." Gabe left him in the dining room. Let the servants deal with Dimitrius' unsavory presence. Gabe needed time to think, to come to terms with the impossible situation he'd found himself in. To plan some alternative, rewrite reality.

He let his feet choose his path. They led him first to a bottle, then down to the bank of the river, where he nursed at the contents until his head swam.

We've been here before.

Yes.

We did not like it then.

No.

Why?

It reminded you of the box.

Oh.

You were weak.

Yes.

You are still weak.

Yes.

You do not want to do what you must.

Must I, though? I could refuse.

And who would that help? They would only find your friend later.

They would.

Would you have me do it, Gabe? I could do it for you. I'd be honored.

I cannot give them the children.

I could take care of them, too.

No.

Yes.

No.

Yes.

No.

Yes.

Fine. Just be quiet, would you?

Oh, Gabe, you pathetic little thing, you. No. I will not be quiet. I will never be quiet. Give in, Gabe. It's time. You've failed. Every time you try to be rid of me, you fail. Let me lead. Let me take these burdens. Why do you try? You've already become me. We are the same.

We are the same.

Yes.

I do not want to live anymore.

Oh, not this again.

I do not want to decide.

Oh?

I do not want to feel like I'm being torn apart from the inside out. Why do I feel that way, Gabriel? Why does it hurt so much?

Because you are weak.

Will you help me?

I always help you.

Can you... will you make me strong?

Yes.

Then, I give up. Do as you will.

So Gabriel Malik finished the bottle, stumbled inside, buried his sorrows in a willing, warm body, and rose the next day before the morning sun.

And all the while, he smiled.

45

REQUIEM

HE WAS GOING TO die. He'd been ready to die, in truth, since Adalia had gone with God. But he'd stayed, stubbornly clinging to promises, and he'd found many reasons to keep living in the wake of her absence. *They* were going to die, too.

It didn't hurt, though it should have. It didn't hurt when his childhood friend yanked back his head, when the blade bit into his neck, when it cut and cut and cut. What hurt was what had come before, as he'd watched his children struggle against their demise. He'd watched Zeke kick and scream and bite his captors until they'd pinned him beneath their superior weight. He'd watched Einar bloody his young hands, wringing the life out of a Reaper as if he were snapping the neck of a rabbit, putting it out of its misery. He'd watched when the boy had realized what he'd done. It was *that* which hurt Darius. Not the beating. Not the betrayal. Not his own stupidity. It was the stark evidence of his failure to provide his child with a life better from the one he'd had. He'd failed. For Einar had killed a man at the same tender age Darius first had. And Einar was not a child all full of hatred like he'd been. He would not survive the guilt of it, even if he wasn't about to die. What could he offer his sons as a boon in these last moments? What parting words could he give the friend who was killing him?

Darius spat the blood from his mouth, met his son's panicked gaze, and said, "Don't let them see it."

They'd been so easy to find. They'd been waiting at the tree, just as Darius had said they'd be. The quieter part of him lamented that truth. He'd tried to rise to the surface when he read the intent in his own mind. He'd tried, even though he'd known what they'd come here to do. He couldn't do it. He didn't want to do it. When he'd seen his old friend, looking so similar to when they'd last parted, when he'd seen the boys playing in the hollowed-out tree, he'd railed against the notion.

STOP! STOP! STOP! He'd screamed internally. The voice didn't even bother to reply. It was too late. It was too late as the Reapers overpowered Darius by sheer numbers. It was too late as Dimitrius Finch began methodically beating his nephews to death. It was too late.

He had to do something. He had to stop this. But no.

Those were his feet crunching the leaves.

Those were his hands gripping Darius' hair.

That was *his* knife pushing into his friend's neck. *Cutting.*

That was his voice demanding his nephew look.

No. No. No. No. No. No.

And that was Darius' familiar deep voice, *"Don't let them see it."* *My fear.*

Gabe waged an internal war while he sawed off his oldest friend's head. He couldn't stop this. He'd already done it. Horror swallowed his heart whole as he held Darius' head. *Oh God. Oh God.* That was Darius' body.

And there was Finch across the clearing, leaning down to slit the younger boy's throat.

"*Stop*," Gabe whispered. Finch, to his surprise, did as he said.

"I should have known you'd want to have all the fun," Dimitrius said, kicking the boy and stepping back from his limp body.

"Go, all of you," Gabe said. "I will catch up with you. I want to finish this myself."

Dimitrius grinned at him knowingly and winked as he toed the limp little boy at his feet again. "Fine, I'll let you have the fun this time, since we're *friends* now." He turned and motioned the Reapers to follow. They fell in line, grumbling about the lack of blood wetting their blades.

"Dimitri," Gabe called, before they'd gotten too far. "You'll find a flight craft waiting in Bracken. Take this back to the Authority for me, yes?" He held out Darius' head, refusing to look at it.

Finch took hold of it by the long braid and inspected it. "Ugly motherfucker, wasn't he? What of them?" He nodded to the two still forms in the dirt, to the Reaper who lay sprawled beside them. Gabe tried not to recognize the black stripe on the palm of the Reaper. *Carl.* The boy had killed *Carl*...

Gabe swallowed bile down and forced the words, "I'll bring them... when I'm finished."

An evil little laugh was the only reply as Finch winked once more and sauntered away, swinging Darius' severed head.

Gabe didn't bother to talk to the voice when the sounds of the others had faded. He only began digging a shallow grave for what was left of his friend. He did not know how much time passed, only that every minute of it was agony, each beat of his heart a knife wound. The desire to crawl into the dirt and bury himself beside Darius was so strong, Gabe began to do it. He climbed in and curled himself against his friend's cold chest, pretending he was only a boy, that he was only too short to see the top of Darius' head again. He stayed that way until a sad, small sound, like the mewling of a lost kitten, greeted his numb ears.

When he emerged from the hole, he found the source of the noise was in the dirt where he'd left them. His nephews had somehow inched closer to one another and were holding hands. The little one was snuffling, blind behind swollen eyes. "Pa," the boy whispered, squeezing his brother's hand. It reminded Gabe viscerally of the way he'd once clutched his sister's hand. Gabe knelt and brushed black hair—*Darius' hair*—back from the boy's brow.

"Shhhhh," he soothed. "It is only a nightmare. Shall I sing you back to sleep?"

"Yes," the boy whispered, going pliant under Gabe's bloody hands. He could have had this if he'd been good. If he'd not been born a monster. He could have been someone who brought comfort. So Gabe sang, and he petted the boy's hair that was like raven's feathers, and the other child's who looked so much like his sister. He sang until the moon and stars had come and the children were sleeping in the leaves. Then, he bent and kissed their muddy foreheads, finished covering his best friend in dirt, and left the three of them there in the clearing, hoisting Carl over his shoulder to bring him home.

They were *sleeping*.

His nephews were sleeping.

Darius... Darius was only sleeping.

46

LIARS, FOOLS, & THE SECRETS THEY KEEP

DARIUS' BLOOD HAD GONE cold on his hands. It mingled there with the blood of his sister's sons. *The boys aren't dead.* Gabe shoved the thought away violently, locking it in the small corner of safety he'd carved in his head. It was the place he kept all of his secrets. *His:* Gabe's. There were many small truths locked in this special little mind vault of his. His love for Darius. His hate for the Authority for demanding this task of him. The scheme he'd abandoned to Marcus and Ryker's better judgment. The lies he'd been telling his other, darker half. *Her.* And now this truth, perhaps the most damning of them all: he'd left his nephews alive. He hadn't been able to protect his brother, his friend, from the foul creature of malice he shared a mind with. But those children, *Addy's boys*, he'd protect them. He'd keep them hidden away, safe from himself for as long as he held the will to do so. He'd lie to his other half, to *himself.* He'd lie so fiercely they both believed it. He had lied to the Authority, too, when they'd demanded the children's bodies.

"They were destroyed beyond repair," he'd said.

"Bring us the remnants," the Authority had implored.

"I cannot. I burned them."

They'd screamed then, declaring him banned from entering the city unless they requested him. He'd barely heard them, with how loudly he chanted the lie.

They are dead! He screamed to the hateful half of him.

They are dead! Ever is dead! They are dead!

Days. Weeks. Months. *Years* spun past.

They. Are. Dead.

He said it until it became truth.

But with all of his effort focused on birthing this false truth, Gabe faded, until only a sliver of him remained, until his darker half wasn't really a half any longer, until he'd forgotten another truth, one *she'd* whispered.

You are good, Gabe.

But he wasn't, not anymore.

There wasn't enough left of him to be *good.*

He didn't want to be good.

He didn't want to be nice.

No one respects nice.

He only wanted to hurt. Himself. Everyone else.

Who did he have to live for anymore, anyway?

Marcus. Ryker.

No.

Why should he pity men when he was made to be a god?

Why deny what was so plain to see?

So he learned to enjoy the pain his darker half inflicted... *most* of the time.

Gabe immersed himself in the rot.

Gabe drank and fucked and took what was not freely given. He sought a sensation he'd known once, a warmth he'd lost in some other life.

Until he was numb.

Until he lost any semblance of the kindness at his core.

Until he was irreparably broken.

Until he didn't want to heal.

Until he was nothing at all.

Until he'd descended so deep into depravity, he'd drown in it.

Until, at last, there was no redemption for Gabriel Malik.

EPILOGUE

#56

SHE DID NOT KNOW how she'd become. Only that she had.

One day, she'd just appeared. She woke feeling rubbery, as if her muscles didn't quite understand how they were supposed to stretch over her bones. Her existence was white. White walls, white floors, white lights, white skin, white teeth... White—except for the parts that were gray. Gray eyes. Gray hair. Gray memories.

The Overseers told her they were not memories. She tried to believe them. It hurt less if she believed them... if she let them be gray.

Her heart was much the same. She'd woken with a profound sadness, as if something within her was trying to tell her she'd *been* before. She must have been before, right?

But they told her she was new.

She certainly *felt* new. She felt something else, too, stirring behind her breastbone. It was restless, angry, *guilty*. It wanted vengeance for... something. Something she could not remember. But they were not memories.

She was new.

Those little flashes that sometimes overpowered her senses, those were *genetic* memory, they said.

She did not have a past life.

She had never lived before.

She was new.

She already knew how to read, how to speak, how to reason, because they'd made her so. That is what they said. She should sit down and do her lessons and obey. That is what they said.

So that is what she did.

But sometimes, when it was dark and colors painted the back of her eyelids in place of gray and white, she allowed herself to dream.

She dreamt of *something*. Or was it *someone*? Who had made her feel safe. She dreamt of a man behind glass, his hair reddish when the lights hit it. She dreamt of arms that held her, of scars worn on the inside, patterns she knew better than her own mind. She dreamt of others like her. Of amber eyes, then green, then gray. Gray again. The man behind glass had blue eyes, she was certain.

And he was sad.

She did not want him to be sad, most of all.

But they were only dreams.

She did not have memories.

She was new.

The Moon

When I saw the moon, I thought of you.
A compliment, to be sure, because this was no ordinary
moon.
This was echoes of sunrise all bottled up in the darkness
of night.
A moon so bright, it cast shadows of midday on the
forest floor and sprinkled the perfume of romance across
a late summer night.
I thought of you because the moon was like you: brighter
than the stars, but only brave enough to shine every now
and again, more beautiful than the sun because I could
behold with my eyes all the splendor of its light. One
cannot look upon the sun, but the moon? In its ever-
changing cycle of wonderment? One could look at the
moon for all eternity and never grow tired of seeing the
marvelous little ways it had changed.
And when the moon hides?
That reminded me of you, too.
For when you are gone, it is the blackest of nights and
the echoes of starlight no longer reflect in the shadows,
so I hide in my pillow until darkness passes and the
morning light shines through my curtains. A comforting
light is the sun, but none so precious as the moonlight.
None so precious as you, ever-changing, ever the same— a
tide in the marrow of my soul pulling me forever into
your gentle gravity.
Yes, when I saw the moon, I thought of you.

Lucifer's Tears

(Hadeon's Recipe)

- 1.5oz Captain Morgan (spiced)
- .5oz RumChata
- .5oz Cinnamon Whiskey
- .5oz Unsweeted Coconut Milk
- .5tsp Brown Sugar Cinnamon Syrup
- Ground Cinnamon, Cloves, & Cayenne Powder

Combine Captain Morgan, Rumchata, Cinnamon Whiskey, Coconut Milk, & Brown Sugar Syrup. Stir.
Pour over a large ice cube. Dust with Cinnamon, Cloves, & Cayenne.

(Enjoy at your own risk)

ACKNOWLEDGEMENTS

The work of an author is often construed as a solitary thing, and for the hours we lock ourselves away with only the words and a trove of assorted drinks and snacks, it is. But. Any author who tells you they did it all themselves is lying to you. Even those rare creatures who do not let another soul look at their words before releasing them to readers rely on others for inspiration (I am decidedly *not* one of these). We write, because we cannot *not* write. The stories live and breathe in the wider world, in the people who share our lives.

I owe many thanks, as usual, to those wonderful souls who inspire me daily.

So, firstly (as always), I thank God for giving me the words and the means to put them on pages.

Thank you to my family, all of you, who put up with my general shenanigans and never cease in encouraging me to chase my dreams with reckless abandon.

Omi, a special thanks to you, for telling me to go for it—to dare looking like a fool if it meant doing what I love.

Mom, I would be nothing without you. Thank you for believing in me.

To the incredible people who've found me through social media, your endless support and encouragement fuel me. Thank you. Thank you. Thank you.

Nate, thank you for collaborating with me on how to make a drink recipe.

Jessica, my editor, thank you for helping make this book the best it could be. You are a treasure.

And to my readers, thank you for taking a chance on me. I would be nothing more than a silent shout on the breeze without you.

CONTENT WARNING

This book is a work of fiction.

However, it contains subject matter that may be triggering, including:

- Alcoholism/ Substance Abuse

- Child Abuse/ Disfigurement

- Child Death

- Infant loss/ Miscarriage

- Domestic Violence

- Eugenics

- Graphic Violence/ Gore

- Infertility

- Mental illness

- Profanity

- Sexual Assault/ Sexual Abuse/ Sexually explicit scenes

- Suicide

ALSO BY W. PEARL

Did you read the prequel first?
Ready to get hurt again?
The story continues in *Obedient*, Book One in *The Telophase Series*

Want writing updates? Sign up for Pearl's newsletter at:
wpearlauthor.com
or find Pearl on social media @w.pearl_author